GOOD NEIGHBORS

"Connor's ability to richly develop each character and plot thread is fascinating even when the horror is reserved... the constricting pressure as the dread piles on makes this book hard to put down and even harder to go to sleep after reading. This is a great novel..."

-David J. Sharp, *Horror Underground*

SECOND UNIT

"Intricately plotted and vividly layered with suspense, emotional intensity and strategic violence."

-Michael Price, *Fort Worth Business Press*

"Drips with eeriness...an enjoyable book by a promising author."

-Kyle White, *The Harrow Fantasy and Horror Journal*

FINDING MISERY

"Major-league action, car chases, subterfuge, plot twists, with a smear of rough sex on top. Sublime."

-Arianne "Tex" Thompson, author of *Medicine for the Dead* and *One Night in Sixes*

THE JACKAL MAN

"Connor delivers a brisk, action-packed tale that explores the dark forests of the human--and inhuman--heart. Sure to thrill creature fans everywhere."

-Scott Nicholson, author of *They Hunger* and *The Red Church*

Also by Russell C. Connor

GOOD NEIGHBORS

RUSSELL C. CONNOR

DARKFILAMENT.COM

Visit us online at
www.darkfilament.com

Contact the author at
www.facebook.com/russellcconnor
Or follow on Twitter @russellcconnor

Cover Art by SaberCore23 Artwork Studio
For commissions, visit sabercore23art.com

ISBN:
978-1-7331133-3-5

Second Edition: 2015

For Falen,
My little sweetheart booty butt.
Remember that even when the world doesn't
believe in you,
I always do.

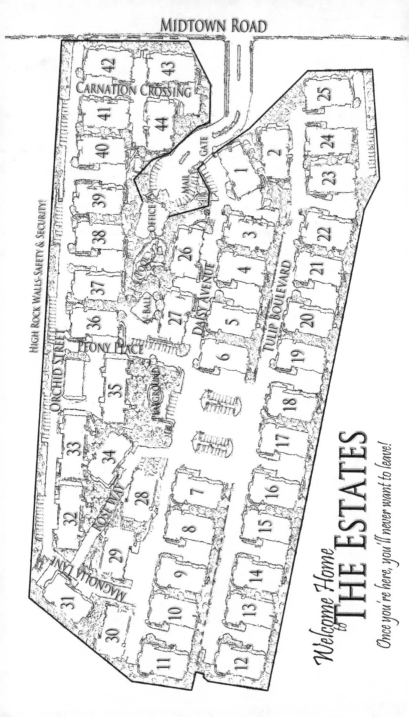

MIDTOWN ROAD

CARNATION CROSSING

42
43
41
44
40
39
38
37
36
35
34
33
32
31
30
29
28

THE ESTATES

Welcome Home to
Once you're here, you'll never want to leave!

HIGH ROCK WALLS—SAFETY & SECURITY!

ORCHID STREET

PEONY PLACE

ROSE WAY

MAGNOLIA LANE

PLAYGROUND

B BALL

POOL

OFFICE

MAIL

GATE

DAISY AVENUE

TULIP BOULEVARD

25
24
23
22
21
20
19
18
17
16
15
14
13
12
11
10
9
8
7
6
5
4
3
2
1
26
27

Neighbors.

Neighbors are people you see every day, but, with the rare exception, you never really know them. You exchange a few pleasant words over the rose bushes, wave hello as you drive past, and then you go on living your life, and they go on living theirs.

This philosopher, Thomas Hobbes? He came up with what he called the Social Contract Theory, which basically states that, in order for a society to develop, we all have to give up those absolute freedoms the barbarians loved so much—stealing, raping, murdering—and agree to play nice with one another. You don't enslave my children, I won't stab you in the face and take your TV. That sort of thing.

With most of the people in your life, that's an easy promise to keep, because you have ties that go beyond the surface, and mutually beneficial reasons to get along. But the only thing that unites you and your neighbors is the fact that you've all chosen to live in one geographically confined area. Packed in like rats, more often than not. Once upon a time, a man of average means could go a whole month without seeing another living soul except the members of his family, but for the last few millennia, we humans have made it our business to dwell in increasingly closer proximity to one another. I don't know about you, but I've always been of the opinion that the more people you have in one place, the lower collective IQs drop. Which might be why we've fooled ourselves into thinking neighbors are a good thing in the first place.

Really though, they're just strangers. Strangers you sleep a few yards away from. You don't know their backgrounds. Their beliefs.

What they're capable of.

But this tenuous thread is supposed to be enough to tie us all together, and keep us from killing one another over untrimmed tree branches and noise complaints.

It's not. Trust me on this.

Because, you see, the thing about Hobbes's theory is, we give up those freedoms—those innate *urges*—but they're still there, bubbling just below the surface.

It took only nine days for the apartment complex where I lived to tear itself apart in an orgy of blood and fire. It made national news. *Time Magazine* called it 'a redefinition of normal society in America.' I don't know about that. I only know I saw a brutality awaken in my fellow man that I'd always believed we'd left behind with our cave-dwelling ancestors.

But maybe I'm being unfair.

After all...we had help getting there.

FRIDAY EVENING

1

I'm pretty stingy with my spring break.

Most of us teachers are. The kids may think they're getting away from us for a whole week, but it's really the other way around.

Don't get me wrong, I had no exciting plans. No hedonistic trips to Aruba or cross-country jaunts of self-discovery. In fact, the hour after I locked the door of my Junior English classroom at D. L. Baker High on Friday afternoon found me waiting patiently for a seven-pound toy fox terrier named Mickey to pick the perfect spot to evacuate his bowels. His usual routine consisted of sniffing every bush and tree trunk—sometimes circling back for a second and third pass—before finally stopping to do his business. I've owned a lot of dogs in my life, but I've never seen one so particular about where he popped a squat. There were some days where I wish Darcy would've taken him along with everything else from our marriage.

Today though, I was just jazzed about the impending week away from a classroom full of eleventh graders. No papers to grade. No cafeteria duty. No trying to make a group of kids who have hundred-dollar jeans and cell phones more powerful than the first computers used to put man on the moon care about how Nathaniel Hawthorne and Tennessee Williams changed the face of American literature. I intended to relax and shut my brain off, and that meant making sure the dog was emptied before I retreated to my precious couch.

Of course, if Mickey hadn't done his usual olfactory inspection, I might never have heard the Squall.

Except I don't think 'heard' is right. 'Became aware of' is probably closer to the truth.

2

At first, I tried to force Mickey to do his business while I stood on the meager concrete patch that served as a patio for apartment 1603, where I moved when my bachelorhood was officially renewed. The tenants in the other units made much better use of this space, with wicker furniture and barbecue grills and potted plants, so they looked like miniature little oases. Quaint in their own way, the efforts of people determined to make their home wherever they happened to be. Mine, on the other hand, was just a big, blank indentation in the side of the building. I'd never been determined to dress it—or anything else in the apartment—up, because I didn't expect to live here long enough. But even after a year, I still didn't have the energy to go look for a new place.

Mickey strained at the end of the leash, trying to pull me forward far enough to smell the bushes on the other side of the alley. "C'mon, can't you please do it here just this once?" I begged. "I promise, nothing smells any better down there than it does right here." He answered by cocking his head back at me and giving a whimper, then went right back to pulling. I sighed and relented.

It was March, but the heat index was already in the low 90's, the humidity bad enough for the sweat to ooze, but not flow. We were supposed to get relief next week, heralded by a round of thunderstorms, but at the moment, it was uncomfortably hot. I held the leash and followed Mickey down the wide grass alley between buildings, grabbing a plastic bag from the dispenser along the way. Two-story brick walls loomed on either side of me, with a row of windows dotting each floor and waist-high hedges lined beneath them. I hummed a Coldplay tune, daydreamed, let Mickey search for that magical spot worthy of his fecal matter, and I can't be sure exactly when it happened, but the next thing I knew, my humming had become one long buzzing note through the nose to match the one coming in my ears.

I tuned back in to my surroundings. The air held an angry, grating, high-pitched whine. I spun in a circle, tangling myself in the leash, until I found the source.

A few yards away, in the middle of the alley, sat a dark green, metal box about three feet high and four feet square. A white sticker on the front said 'WARNING,' and below that, 'Energized electrical equipment inside. KEEP OUT!' The whole setup was anchored into a concrete slab in the ground, a padlock hanging from a hinged door on the front.

An electrical transformer, covered with a steel casing. You know the kind I mean. Or maybe you don't. You see them all the time, but you probably notice them no more than I ever had this one. Before today, if you'd told me one sat ten yards from my bedroom window, I wouldn't have been able to tell you if it was true.

But I noticed now. That electric buzzing was nerve-wracking. I realized I must have been hearing it since I walked out of the apartment, but it slipped right into my subconscious as background noise, got so deep in my head that I was humming right along with it. That I could be ignorant to such an intrusive, irritating sound was both fascinating and frightening. Mickey, oblivious, went right on romancing the flora.

The noise started to throb at my temples. I winced and yanked on the leash, intending to walk Mickey somewhere else. As I turned around, a huge black shape came running at me on all fours. I could only brace for impact as it stood on its hind legs, slapped its paws on my shoulders and slobbered across my face.

"Damn it, Yonkers, get down." I put a hand against the Rottweiler's muscled chest and shoved.

"'Sa matter Jefferson?" The voice came from the end of the alley, where the grass easement ran between the backs of the buildings and the high, decorative rock wall that surrounded the complex. "'Fraid that's gonna be the last kiss you ever get? Or just the best?"

"Schrader, how many times do I have to ask you?" I slapped the plastic sign above the bag dispenser. "Keep. Your dog. On a leash."

John Schrader stepped out into the alley, a cherry red sucker clutched between two knobby fingers in lieu of the cigarettes he kept trying to give up. My neighbor from around the corner. One of three units that shared the building with me. He was a short, hefty, troll of a man, with leathery skin and a pitted face. I always got the impression he did some kind of construction work, but maybe that was an assumption on my part.

"Leashes are for poorly trained animals," he said. "Yonkers, *come!*"

The Rottweiler trotted in the opposite direction of his master, coming around me to sniff at Mickey.

"Yeah, he minds well." I reeled in the leash, dragging Mickey over to me, and scooped him up. "It's dangerous to have a dog his size running free, especially around leashed animals. If they start fighting, there's no way to separate them."

Schrader grunted. "Hell, Jefferson, you want a tampon for that yappin hole in your face? Yonk never hurt a fly."

I didn't answer. I knew from experience that it wouldn't do any good, and besides, that buzzing noise from the transformer felt like it was vibrating the fillings in my teeth.

Schrader, on the other hand, didn't seem affected in the slightest. He tipped his sucker at building 15 across from us and then jammed it in his mouth. "Martha told me somebody new's movin in over there."

"Oh yeah?" I asked distractedly. I could barely focus on his words over that racket. Between that and the heat, I felt dizzy.

"Yep." He nodded his sweat-beaded head, casual and slow, then gave me a snide grin. It occurred to me this was the most we'd ever spoken to one another. "S'posed to be a *woman*. Maybe she can give yer willy a washin."

I smirked. "Why are you so obsessed with my love life, Schrader? I don't see you with a girlfriend over there."

"Whores, my friend." He brought his teeth together, cracking the sucker in his mouth, then tossed the paper stick onto the lawn. "They're cheaper in the long run, and you don't gotta come up with excuses in the mornin."

Yonkers hunkered a few feet away from me and released a stream of solid, brown feces. When he was finished, he trotted toward his master, leaving his gift behind on the grass. Schrader turned to go back inside without any effort to clean it up. That's why I stopped going outside barefoot.

"Hey Schrader!" I called. It was louder than I intended, but I was competing with that squeal.

He looked at me and held up both hands. "Yeah, yeah, gimme a break, I'll pick it up later."

"No, not that." The transformer gave a particularly piercing shriek. My eyes rolled back in my head and I squeezed Mickey to me. The dog wheezed. "I was just wondering... don't you hear that?"

"Hear what?"

"That...sound."

Schrader's eyes were the only thing that moved, back and forth. Looking for the punchline, probably. "What sound?"

I saw no hint of a lie on his face; I was sure of that, even then. But if he wasn't faking, that meant he was as deaf to the noise as I had been when I first came outside. Amazing. "Nothing. Never mind."

He studied me a second longer, than shook his head. "Man, Jefferson...yer crackin up. Ya need to get laid." He retreated inside.

He was right. About getting laid, I mean. But I certainly wasn't the one cracking up.

Not yet, anyway.

I carried Mickey back inside the apartment.

3

Except going inside did no good.

I could hear the electric sizzle of the transformer even indoors, in every corner of the apartment. It was absolutely constant, a solid *zzzzzz* that muscled it way into my ears, and, from there, into my thoughts. Every few minutes, when I felt like the unending monotony of that noise would drive me insane, it would give a renewed surge of squealing energy and that was somehow worse.

I stood, I sat. I considered going out but refused to be run out of my own apartment and besides, I had nowhere to go. I tried to read, then to watch TV, then to work on a model of Night Rider I'd been piecing together for two weeks now, and couldn't concentrate on any of them. That sound—which I finally dubbed The Squall—held dominion over all. My headache continued to get worse.

All in all, a shitty start to spring break.

How long had it been doing this? I'd never heard it over the past year, but surely it hadn't started while I was standing beside it. It wasn't really as loud in my apartment as it had been outside, but it was still invasive. If it had been screeching since I got home, then more likely I hadn't noticed it before, and now that I'd become aware, I couldn't become *un*aware again.

This time, that idea truly frightened me.

I couldn't help thinking: in this modern world, we're bombarded by stray electricity and random energy waves and microscopic amounts of radiation on an hourly basis, but it's all just background noise to us. If you don't believe me, try turning off everything in your house that competes for your attention—TV's and radios, computers and smartphones—and you'll actually be able to hear the power current that roars through your home non-stop. Listen to your refrigerator running. The *whoosh* of your air conditioner. That hum your television makes even when it's turned off. Your fuse box. If you have a home phone, put it on speaker, then set your cell phone next to it and listen to those energy fields fight with one another.

All that invisible interference flowing over and through us, and all of it changing and evolving so fast that modern medicine has no way of knowing what the long term effects are on human beings. I thought of all those stories about how people living under power lines got cancer or birthed mutant children. Who knew what kind of wattage or amperage or, hell, *gamma radiation* this thing was putting out, right down the alley from my bedroom window?

Worse yet, how was I going to sleep tonight?

As late afternoon wore on, I found myself pacing the apartment while Mickey watched. I was jittery and anxious, a feeling that was too familiar, and it scared me. A few minutes later I wondered into the kitchen and rummaged through the cabinets and under the sink, all my old favorite hiding places back when Darcy and I lived at the house. I knew it was ridiculous—I'd never brought so much as a drop of alcohol into this apartment—but going through the motions of looking was just as bad as bringing a bottle to my lips.

I just need something, a pleading voice in the back of my skull said. *Something to take the edge off. That noise is killing me.*

That's just an excuse, I answered. *And you know it.*

In the end, I stuffed shredded cotton balls in my ears and fell into a cramped and uneasy slumber on the couch.

4

And woke up to the sound of my cell phone tweeting from the coffee table.

I nearly rolled off the couch. I'd fallen asleep with the lights off and the sun no longer streamed through the windows beside me. I fumbled in the dark for my phone and finally found it just before it would've gone to voicemail. I answered with a muzzy, "Hey, hello?"

A pause. Then an annoyed sigh from the other end. "Good god, Elliot."

"Darcy." I muttered my soon-to-be-ex-wife's name and ran a hand down my face, wiping away drool and sleep. "What...what time is it?"

"It's 8:30." Her voice sounded muffled; it took me another moment to realize I still had the cotton in my ears. "What are you, asleep?"

I could tell by the way she asked the question that what she really meant by 'asleep' was 'passed out.' As in, *Elliot would rather pass out than have sex.* Or, *Elliot's passed out on his office couch after drinking a whole bottle of scotch, so I better turn him over before he chokes on his own vomit.* Or, the instant-classic, *If I can just wait until Elliot passes out for the afternoon, I should have time to get him and most of his belongings on the lawn, call the locksmith, and leave the restraining order on his chest for when he finally swims back to consciousness sometime tomorrow morning.*

"Yes, I was asleep," I answered. Too defensively. "I'm allowed to sleep in my own home. I don't have to ask your permission for that anymore."

She gave another one of her patented moments of Darcy silence. The kind where you can just hear the judgments clicking away in her brain, as she chooses the perfect sarcasm-edged weapon from her arsenal. "I don't think you ever asked my permission for much of anything, Ellie dear. That's why we're in this situation."

I sighed. She knew I hated when she called me 'Ellie dear.' "What do you want, Darcy?"

"Just calling to remind you about Tuesday. Nine o'clock at my attorney's office, so we can get this finished once and for all."

"I know. I said I'd be there. I don't need a babysitter." I winced as this last came out, remembering how many times she dragged me out of a stupor just so I could make it to work.

She let loose with a brittle, deep-throated laugh. "You bringing that shystering little Jew lawyer of yours?"

"Had to let him go. My savings are almost gone. And, really, I have nothing left for you to take, so I figure we're both just eager for this to be over."

"You got that right, honey. You sure got that right."

Neither of us said anything for a span of at least thirty seconds. I thought about what once was, what could've been, and wondered if she did too.

"Goodnight, Elliot," she finally said, and hung up before I could do likewise.

From the floor, Mickey raised his head and looked at me.

"You miss Mommy?" I asked him.

He tilted his head and chuffed.

"Yeah. Me neither."

5

The Squall had stopped at some point while I slept.

I wandered out onto the back patio and hunkered on the concrete. Shadows coated the alley now, the steel box of the transformer only a slightly darker patch in the sea of black grass. The heat had gone out of the world fast, leaving a pleasant—if somewhat muggy—evening. I looked up at the moon and the stars and tried not to think about how much I wanted a drink.

From above me, I heard the rough cadences of arguing. The words were unintelligible, but I recognized those angry voices. Dan and Joan McCaffery, my upstairs neighbors from 1604. I only knew them well enough to say a passing 'hello' at the mailbox. Individually, they seemed calm and rational, but then again, I'm sure India and Pakistan probably do, too. I could hear their arguments from inside my apartment sometimes, drifting through the ceiling. I always had the urge to knock on their door and ask them to keep it down, but I'd been in their shoes all too recently, and I knew the only thing that made spousal fighting worse was a witness.

You always hurt the ones you love, but you just can't be at your nastiest when you know someone else is listening.

Commotion from the building across the alley grabbed my attention. A slamming door. Clomping footsteps coming downstairs. Someone distantly yelled, "*You leave here, young lady, and you sleep outside!*"

The patio door across from mine opened. A thin girl with auburn curls, a 'Right to Choose!' t-shirt, and a beer bottle in her hand slid out and slammed the door closed behind her. She turned first one way and then the other, indecisive about-facing, then settled for raising the bottle and chucking it at the brick side of the building. It shattered, spraying foam and glass along the alley. The sight of it, the *smell* of it, hit me like a croquet mallet to the forehead. Then she sank into one of the plastic lawn chairs on the patio and buried her face in her hands. I could hear her sobbing.

I wanted to slink away. Might've tried, if it had been anyone else.

"Katie?" I asked quietly. She jumped like I'd screamed in her ear. "You okay?"

"Mr. Jefferson." She swiped at her nose and red eyes. A piece of glass on the patio caught her attention, and a look of horror passed over her young face as she realized what I'd seen. "Oh, Mr. Jefferson, I'm so sorry!"

I held up a hand. "Don't worry about it."

"I'm so embarrassed! I can't believe I...*fuck*!" As this last word slipped out, her eyes swelled. She clapped both hands over her mouth, one on top of the other.

I laughed. "It's okay. Really."

"I was just...fighting with my mom..."

"Don't be embarrassed. Fighting seems to be the order of the evening." I hiked a thumb up at the sweet melodies of the McCafferys' marital bliss.

Katie Adler broke into a smile. Now she looked more like the optimistic kid I had in Creative Writing last year. "Geez. Are they going at it again?"

I shrugged and nodded.

"Man, it's like those two are just looking for an excuse to shank each other. There was this one time before Christmas, I swear I could hear them all the way over at Jacob's building!"

"Yep. Something about her spaghetti sauce tasting like burnt dog hair."

Katie giggled, gripping the torn knees of her jeans with slender hands. Afterward, we stared at one another in silence across the narrow grass alley.

"What are you even doing here?" I asked. "It's spring break. Don't you seniors usually take trips to Cozumel? Get a head start on your cirrhosis?"

"Gotta have money before you can do that. And a mom who's not a total psycho determined to keep you nine-years-old forever."

"That bad, huh?"

She got up, crossed over to my side, and plopped down on the concrete next to me. I scooted over to give a generous cushion of space between us. It's a dangerous world out there for us male teachers.

"It's like, I'm seventeen-years-old, I'm going to college next year, and she won't let me do *anything*." She emphasized this by smashing her fists into her legs just above the knee. "All my friends took a road trip to New Mexico, right? I can't go. Derek Mann asked me out last week. I can't go. She won't even let me stay up past eleven on a Friday night. Ugh, I can't take it anymore!"

"She's keeping you out of trouble. That's a mom's job."

"I know, and if that's all it was, I wouldn't whine about it. I really wouldn't, Mr. Jefferson. But..." She looked at her door across the way, and I saw the glint of tears on her lashes in the moonlight. "She just...picks fights with me all the time. And tonight, she...raised her hand. Like she was gonna... Anyway, I just wanted to do something. You know, to defy her. So, right in front of her, I took one of the beers her last boyfriend left in our fridge. I don't even *like* beer."

She kept crying those silent tears. I wanted to say something, but I had no idea what. One thing I've learned from sixteen years of teaching: the mind of a teenager—particularly a female teenager—is rocky terrain. Most of the so-called 'guidance counselors' at D. L. Baker can't even navigate it.

So I stuck to what I knew. "You still writing poetry?"

She looked at me again. "Sometimes. Jacob says it's a waste of time, 'cause I'll never get paid for writing poetry."

I almost asked why she wasted time with a burnt-out, drug-dealing delinquent like Jacob Tinsley, but in this case, he had a point. "Poetry is...romance. It's elegance. Nothing like it. And you have a talent. Don't let anybody talk you out of doing what you wanna do."

"Yeah, but I don't know what I wanna do," she said.

At least, I think that's what she said.

Because at that moment, the Squall started up again, drowning out her words, humming in fast, cycled waves, like a washing machine full of electricity. I cringed away from it.

She stood up and swept her hair back. "I guess I better go in. The longer I'm out here, the worse it'll be."

"Katie," I said, as she reached the opposite patio. I had to concentrate not to shout over the Squall. If she couldn't hear it either, she'd think I was insane. "You know if you ever need anything, need to talk...my door is always open. At home as well as school."

"Thanks." She stepped inside, then halted. "You know, that's really awful."

"What is?"

"That noise. I hope it doesn't do that all night. See you later."

She closed the door and left me staring after her.

6

I wish I could say that was the end of that first night. But I had one other encounter that needs telling, if I'm to get the sequence of events correct.

After Katie left, I retreated back inside, away from that awful sibilation from the transformer. I was all set to begin pacing the floor when my cell phone went off one more time.

It was close to nine. No one I knew would be calling this late, and the number was blocked. I almost let it go to voicemail, but I was eager for any distraction, and talking to a salesman or wrong number would suffice for a few seconds at least.

"Hello?"

There was no response from the other end for so long,

I began to think the line had gone dead before I answered. Then came a quick, ragged intake of breath from the other party, a somehow reptilian gasp that put me instantly on edge.

"Hello?" I tried again, caution in the word this time. "Darcy?"

The voice that answered was even softer than that gasp had been, withered and utterly sexless. "*Will you heed?*" it rasped. The question had such little inflection, it was more of a statement.

Had to be a wrong number. Or, more likely, a prank. But yet, when I tried to answer, I found my mouth had gone as dry as desert sand. "Heed...what?"

"*The still...small...voice.*"

Sudden terror crept into my heart on silent feet, a formless fear that expanded in my chest like rising dough. "I...I don't understand..."

My phone beeped.

The call had been terminated.

SATURDAY MORNING

1

Sleep was sparse, and ravaged by dreams.

For the most part, I was used to that; two common side effects of recovering alcoholism are insomnia and recurring nightmares, a stage which had passed months ago. But the headboard of my bed—a little double I got at IKEA for a hundred bucks after Darcy threw me out, barely more than a stiff mattress lifted a scant foot off the ground by a skeletal frame—lay right up against the only window in my bedroom, which looked out on the alley.

And the Squall never let up, not for one second, all night long.

I first turned on fans to drown out the noise, but it wove through their steady purr until they actually seemed to be reinforcing it, backup singers to its falsetto shriek. Listening to the radio didn't help, nor did my iPod even with the earbuds shoved so far into the canals I didn't think I'd be able to get them out. I tried turning the opposite way on the bed, my head and feet swapping places, then crawled into the floor to make a nest across the room with Mickey, and finally retreated back to the couch. That noise followed my every step. Each time I got past it, drifting into the thoughtless channel that guides us toward sleep, the damn thing would give a renewed surge, as if lying in wait. The few times I did manage to nod off, I could *still* hear it, a droning backbeat to uncomfortable nightmares.

Some of these were about Darcy; some about school. Nearly all of them had vague elements of sex and violence that left me sweaty and guilt-ridden when I awoke seconds later with the Squall in my ears. I sat in the dark for minutes afterward, trying to determine which parts were real, and which imagined.

When daylight finally came, I was almost thankful.

I got up and moped around the apartment in a pair of boxers. I felt restless and mean. That was the worst thing about the Squall, back at the beginning: it got under your skin, made you anxious, kept you from getting any peace for even a second. Weren't there torture scenarios that involved this kind of constant agitation? I found myself praying it would stop again, if only for a few minutes.

By the time I'd scrambled a few eggs and eaten breakfast, I decided I had to get away.

My jogging clothes were in the back of a drawer. I'd been on a pretty strict regimen right after the separation, when the detox was at its worst. For a while, I was running between four and six miles a day. I slimmed down, toned up, but a lax winter had netted me a few extra pounds. Right now, a nice long run sounded perfect to clear my head.

I found Mickey in the kitchen, humping the shit out of one of his stuffed toys. The ferocity and rhythm of his thrusts looked like he might be close to completion.

"C'mon Mick, you wanna go for a run with me?" This question would normally have him at the door in seconds, but he gave no indication he even heard as his hips whapped against the back of the toy's head. I moved forward, bending over and waving my hands at him. "Okay, stop, I will go insane if my morning ends with cleaning up a puddle of dog ji—"

He lunged at me without warning, transitioning from stuffed animal rapist to ball of growling, snapping fury before I could react. His canines sank into the meat between the thumb and forefinger of my left hand. I howled and jerked away, flinging him halfway across the kitchen floor. He came to rest against the stove door and cowered.

I held my hand up to inspect the damage. It bled from at least a half-dozen tiny holes, aligned in a rough crescent. I don't know if I was more shocked by the pain or the fact that he'd done it in the first place.

"God*damn* it, Mickey! What the hell's wrong with you?"

He edged past me warily, out of the kitchen, and ran for the bedroom once he was out of reach. I caught one last glimpse of him, giving me an angry, resentful glare over his shoulder.

2

I went out the back door. I rarely ever used the front; it was always either onto the patio or through the attached garage. Outside, the sun had started its ascent, but a hint of the night's coolness still lingered in the alley.

A short Hispanic man in a gray jumpsuit stood a few yards away, trimming the hedges with a pair of clippers as long as my forearm. The blades opened and closed in long, slow, almost distracted pulls.

"Javier!" I waved a hand at our maintenance crew supervisor.

He didn't respond. It was only rational to think he couldn't hear me over the Squall, but his robotic motions had daydream written all over them. As I approached, I saw him trim the same bare twig three times.

"Javier!" I waved my hand in his peripheral.

His head jerked around like Mickey's had, but at least he didn't try to bite me. His eyes looked dull for a split second, like I'd woken him. Then they focused, and he brightened as he closed the long clippers and slid them into the branches at the base of the shrubs. "*Sí, hola, Señor* Jefferson."

"Look, Javier, we gotta get the power company or whoever out here about that transformer. I couldn't sleep at all last night."

He frowned. "*Qué?*"

I sighed in frustration, pointed at the green box further up the alley behind him, then at my ear. "The transformer. That noise. *BZZZZZZ!* You hear it?"

Confusion twisted his mouth in different directions. He shrugged uncomfortably. "*No comprendo, Señor* Jefferson."

"Javier...Jesus, you're killing me." I took his arm and led him over to the transformer, then made him squat beside me. This close to the box, the noise got so sharp it became physically painful. It was like being next to the speakers at a rock concert when the microphone picks up feedback. Javier gave no indication he even heard it, but his brow wrinkled as he took in my scrunched face, as though mimicking my expressions might help him understand me.

I cupped a hand behind my ear this time. "*Hear it?*" I shouted. He flinched, but only from the sudden loudness of my voice. "Uh...*escuchar? BZZZZZ!* Very annoying!"

He looked from me to the transformer then back again. I caught a gleam in his eye, as though he were trying to decide if I were making a joke at his expense. I couldn't believe it; the thing was so loud, I could almost feel it, like a stiff wind in my face, and he hadn't even noticed. If Katie hadn't commented on it the night before, I might've believed I was going—as one student wrote in an essay after a unit on Edgar Allen Poe—'stark raven mad.'

Finally, Javier broke out in a smile and nodded. "Ah, *sí, sí*, I fix!"

"Okay." I clapped him on the back. "Good man, *gracias*."

I left him kneeling there and went out to where the alley met the curb at the street to start jogging. As I headed toward the front of the property, following the red fire lane stripes, an orange and white U-haul moving truck passed me going the opposite direction.

3

The Estates at North Hills was never a bad place to live. I don't want you to think that at all.

Most apartment complexes are just an ongoing melting pot, a kaleidoscope of faces, a temporary way station for folks on their way to somewhere else, either upward or down. No one bothers to interact or make the slightest attempt to know their neighbors, because, in a year, someone else will be occupying their space. If truth be told, that's the sort of place I wanted when I started looking for a new residence during the separation: a lonely, anonymous corner of the world where I could lick my wounds, hide my shame, and focus on my newfound sobriety. I only ended up at North Hills because every other complex within reasonable distance of D.L. Baker was the kind of place where you could get shot in the parking lot after dark.

But before the fire, before...everything that happened... the Estates was more of a community, in both look and feel. The complex formed a rough oval shape, sprawled out to the southeast for a quarter mile from where the entrance drive branched off Midtown Road. I never counted, but there must've been close to forty buildings, and very few vacancies. At four units per building—ranging from one to three bedroom models—and an average of three people in each unit...well, those aren't exactly New York numbers, but considering the population density of the earth used to be something like 15 people per thousands of square miles, it makes for interesting societal commentary. That high stone wall surrounded the entire property, and when you came in the broad, wrought-iron entrance gate, you found well-kept grounds, buildings with fresh paint on the wooden siding, and a network of paved streets named after flowers.

If Darcy and I had ever gotten around to having kids— which means if I could've pulled myself out of my listless depression long enough to impregnate her, back when she still had any interest in me—I like to think we would've sought out suburbs like this to raise them in. People sat on their patios—or balconies, for the bigger units on the second floor—and waved when you went past. They walked their dogs, and grilled on their short driveways. Flocks of elementary school children rode bikes or played ball in the street. During the summer, the pool behind the office was packed to capacity every day. Upon move in, I was given a map with the names of each occupant, which is when I discovered that a handful of former students lived in the Estates as well. It made me a little uncomfortable. My impending divorce was public knowledge; my recovering alcoholism a whispered rumor. Just another reason to stay indoors with the blinds closed and draw as little attention to myself as possible.

Luckily, on the spring morning I went jogging, the place was a ghost town. Not unusual for 8 o'clock on a Saturday morning, but the silence felt heavy. Expectant. I took Daisy Avenue up past the deserted pool and weight room, by the office, and on toward the front gate. The electric sensor picked me up when I got close, and the gate trundled open to allow me through. Beyond that was a curved drive that led out toward Midtown Road. I jogged down to the main thoroughfare and ran in place while I tried to decide where to go.

Around the Estates, open flatland stretched in all directions. Across the street sat a strip of field the owner still used to grow hay. The crop had just come in, and, after a week of tractors, balers and the sweet smell of cut grass, the rolled disks were stacked on their sides in a neat line that stretched along the horizon, like giant, sliced sausage logs. A lone cell tower squatted amidst the bales, the farmer undoubtedly paid a huge stipend for the use of his land despite the fact that the complex residents were some of the few serviced by it.

The apartments themselves had only been here four years. The city zoning plans called for an elementary school to be built up the street to the south sometime in the next decade, and a slate of tract housing to attend it. But at that moment, the closest civilization was the gas stations and strip malls that began a few blocks to the north, marking the developed edge of the city.

The Estates were relatively isolated, a mere ten-minute drive from anything you could want or need, but far enough away that you could forget it was all there.

Far enough that the rest of the world could forget about you, too.

4

I arrived back at close to 9:30, after jogging down to the SpeedyWash for a bottle of water, and all the way back. I was wheezing, muscles on fire, but it felt wonderful. The cobwebs brought on by the Squall had lifted from my brain, giving me some renewed enthusiasm for the day.

The leasing office opened while I was gone, and, after a second of debate, I detoured in through the front entrance instead of going through the gate. A soft chime sounded overhead as I pushed through the heavy oak door with its ornate stained glass window. The interior looked like the lobby of an upscale hotel, with velvet couches gathered around a highly polished mahogany table, a full kitchenette with bar next to a pool table in the back, and a twinkling chandelier hanging over the tiles in the entry. Information pamphlets beside the door promised 'luxury living for the whole family.' Luxury was right; even for a small unit like mine, I paid almost as much as Darcy and I did for a two-bedroom house.

"Excuse me?" I called. "Anybody here?"

Silence. I stuck my head around a corner to the right. The leasing agent desks were tucked away in a long alcove with the manager's office at the far end. Usually they were occupied by an office staff of outrageously attractive women. I'm talking modeling agency caliber, which might be where they recruited them. One in particular—this early-thirties blond named Carla with slinky curves and nice calves—I'd caught myself fantasizing about more than once. She was the reason I ended up signing a thirteen-month lease instead of six.

But all the desks were vacant. I could see all the way back

to Martha's private office, and could tell it was empty also.

"Hello?" I tried again, but quieter this time. That unsettling stillness from outside had gotten in here too, a tension so deep it was like waiting for a bomb to go off, the kind of silence you feel guilty for breaking. I waited in it, sweat dribbling down my cheeks and between my shoulder blades, and thought about my strange phone call for the first time since last night. In the all-consuming drone of the Squall, I had been able to put that dry voice and its cryptic message out of my head, but for some reason, the desertion of the Estates management office brought it back.

They could've been out showing the property. Maybe driving around some early birds in one of those little golf carts. Had to be. Definitely.

Except, even if there had been enough early birds to warrant all of them going out, leaving no one behind to mind the store, surely they would've locked the door and put up the 'Be Back Soon' sign.

I drummed my fingers on the foyer table, right between a large flower vase filled with daffodils and those slick pamphlets showcasing the various unit layouts, and told myself to leave. I had planned to check for packages—a giant-size B-wing model I'd ordered from Amazon was due any day—but now I just wanted out of here.

I moved back toward the door and the friendly sunlight on the other side, but a series of clunky, furtive noises came from the kitchenette. I turned.

A waist-high bartop blocked my view of the stove and the bottom half of the refrigerator in the kitchenette. The sounds came again, a squeak and then a rattle. Something hit the other side of the bar hard enough to send concussion ripples through the pitcher of lemonade on top.

I felt silly and a little skittish, but only on the surface. Inside, that feeling of the ticking time bomb continued. Probably just the remnants of a sleepless night and the Squall fucking with my head, but instinct is instinct. That being said, I denied the one telling me to leave and inched my way across the wide space, past the pool table. When I reached the bar, I braced my palms on the lacquered veneer, stood on my toes, and slowly leaned over the top to get a view of the floor below.

An orange creature with a head full of spiny quills popped up, close enough to brush my forehead.

I screamed.

It screamed.

Then it dropped the plate of cookies it was holding.

"Jesus Christ!" Tony squeaked. His hands flapped at the wrist for a moment as though he expected to take off, then he pulled the iPod buds from his ears. "Mr. Jefferson! Oh my God, oh my God, you scared the shit outta me!"

"Ditto," I answered, clutching my chest. "That was more workout than I really needed."

Tony still tried to catch his breath, but now his flapping hands had been put to use, turned so just the tips of his fingers could fan his face. "I'm going to need some serious Botox after the wrinkles you just gave me!"

"I'm sorry about that, I…did you say *wrinkles*?"

Tony rolled his eyes. "Um, yeah, he*llo*? Fear wrinkles? My boyfriend Rodney says every time you get frightened, you gain another toe on your crow's feet. That's why I don't watch any movies rated worse than PG-13."

"Well, score another one for the MPAA, I guess."

The only male member of the leasing staff was a thin guy with a horrible, Jersey-quality spray-on tan and dyed blond hair jutting off the back of his head in thin little quills that must've taken him longer to prep each day than my entire morning routine. He always looked like he'd be more at home in an open-throat v-neck and a pair of white skinny jeans, but the only outfit I'd ever seen him in was the dark slacks and yellow polo all the staff wears.

He pulled a whisk and pan from one of the cabinets and knelt to sweep up the glass and cookie fragments.

"Here, let me help."

Tony held up a hand. "No, it's okay. Really. Didn't mean to get in your face, it's just been a *très* horrible day. I didn't sleep, and residents have been calling all morning, complaining about the absolute stupidest shit. It's gonna be one of those days." He stopped and narrowed his eyes. "You're not here to make a complaint, are you?"

I hesitated, glad that I had already put Javier onto solving my Squall problem. "Nope, all good here. Just checking to see if I had any packages."

He gave another eye roll. Now that he mentioned lack of sleep, I noticed he did have some extra baggage under them. I wondered what I must look like. "Gimme a sec, and I'll go look."

I came around the bar to help him anyway, sweeping while he held the pan. "You the only one here? No Kendall, Stacy…Carla?"

He dumped the debris into the garbage can. "No! Those little bitches left me and Martha here alone while they ran off to Cancun for spring break! They think just because we're the only ones that actually live at the complex, we don't have a life!"

"Wow, that's…yeah. That's rough." I tried not to drool at the image of the three of them in string bikinis, stretched out on a beach somewhere.

He took a deep, theatrical breath, held it, and let it go while smoothing down his shirt. "Again, sorry. Don't mean to drag you into my drama. You said you had a package?"

Before I could answer, the front door opened, letting in a burst of sunlight and the property manager right behind it. "Sorry Tony, I'm so sorry I'm late, I..." Martha broke off when she saw me and grinned, her chubby cheeks rising in twin rosy lumps. "Good morning, Mr. Jefferson!"

I tried to backpedal before she could zero in. This encounter was getting far more social than I had intended. "Morning, Martha. I just stopped by to check for deliveries, but you're both busy, I'll come back later."

"No, no, of course not! Tony, would you take a look in my office?"

He saluted. "Aye, aye, Capitan."

After he walked into the business office, Martha waddled into the foyer. She had a stack of paper under each doughy arm, and she set them both down on the table, pulled off the top sheets, and handed them to me.

"What are these?"

"Two bulletins going out today. You get them before anybody."

I glanced at the papers in my hand. The first was a flyer for the annual Poolside Gala on Wednesday night. I hadn't lived here for the last one, but I had come to understand it was Martha's baby. As I understood, it was an evening block party for the Estates, an upscale backyard cook-out.

"Do you think you'll make it?" She clasped her hands over her huge, yellow-clad bosom. "I'm sure you'll have fun, it's such a classy affair!"

"Carla told me someone vomited in the pool last year."

She waved these words away as if they were bees. "Certain individuals will *not* be welcome back."

"Please say you're talking about Schrader."

"We have dancing, catered food, wine for the adults, the children play on the volleyball court, and everyone stays until the stars come out. Oh, it's such a lovely evening! Please say you'll come!"

"I...I really don't know. I'm not the greatest company these days."

"Nonsense, you're delightful!" She peered at me knowingly over the top of her glasses, one pencil-heavy eyebrow arched. "And it's a wonderful way for a single man like you to meet someone!"

Technically, I wasn't single yet, but if everything went according to plan, I would be by Wednesday. Then again, so far as I knew, all the single women in the complex were over the age of sixty. Maybe in another year of celibacy, that wouldn't look so bad, but for now, I contented myself with daydreams of Carla. Besides, a pool party was exactly the sort of gathering I wanted to avoid. "I really would like to, but since I'm off work this week, I was thinking about taking a trip somewhere."

Her face fell. I can't stand to see an overweight woman dressed like a sunflower get upset. "Oh. All right. Well, we'll be here if you change your mind."

To keep from feeling guilty, I flipped to the next flyer. This one had 'NOTICE' across the top in big black letters. And below that: 'KEEP ALL PETS INDOORS OR ON LEASH! DO NOT LEAVE ANIMALS UNATTENDED!' A paragraph in smaller font stood at the bottom, but I didn't get that far before holding it up and asking, "What's this about? Too much poop on the grass?"

Martha was shaking her head quickly, her eyes wide, round O's. "We've had three pets disappear over the last week! The Patels' little Corgi and two of Miss Dillinger's cats!"

"Well, cats get bored, they run away. Maybe she should keep all fifty of them inside instead of letting them roam the complex."

"Yes, but...that's not all." Martha's hands squeezed one another nervously. She looked over her shoulder at the office door, where Tony had yet to reappear, and whispered, "Last night, Javier found three birds mutilated behind building 9."

I had to fight to keep from smirking. "Oh c'mon now, Martha. *Birds?* One of Miss Dillinger's missing cats was probably responsible for that."

She sniffed at my disbelief. "If so, then it learned how to tie them all together by the neck and then...push *nails*... through their little heads. I called Tate but he said there wasn't much the police could do if it wasn't an owned animal. Anyway, I just wanted you to know so you could keep your dog—what's his name...Mikey?...Mickey?—inside."

Tony returned to tell me that I had no packages, then said to Martha, "Mrs. Ratcliffe is on the phone for you. She says, and I quote, 'that Mr. Happling's monster shits next door are backing up her toilet again.'"

"Oh, for—! Excuse me, gentlemen." Martha hurried into the next room.

This time it was Tony's turn to whisper. "If you don't want a massive increase in rent next year, you'll come to her stupid party. She still hasn't forgiven me for not going last year. And that was the day of my uncle's funeral!"

I sighed as I headed for the door. "I'll see what I can do."

5

I checked yesterday's mail, then took my time walking through the fenced-in pool courtyard. Anything to avoid returning to the apartment. Not only was I in no hurry to get back to the Squall, but, after talking to Martha and Tony, I suddenly dreaded the reclusivity that awaited me. I'd never been a socialite, but I'd always had roommates or girlfriends right up until Darcy and I got together, and a circle of close friends. But in the wake of the separation, it had been entirely too easy to avoid their calls and make up excuses not to see my mother rather than answer questions. After taking two weeks off work to check into a detox facility—an experience I would rather swallow rusty nails than repeat—I attended AA meetings long enough to get the general idea, and then that fell by the wayside, too.

But throughout all this, being alone hadn't bothered me; I told myself I was healing, getting stabilized before I emerged from my cocoon like a confident butterfly, but all I really did was cement my solitude as a way of life. Yesterday, with a mass of heathen schoolchildren in front of me, the prospect of an entire week of flipping channels, catching up on grading, gluing together plastic model pieces, and only leaving to walk the dog had sounded like paradise, but now that I was facing the actual reality, it was more like do-it-yourself lobotomy, with slower results.

For the first time since I woke up on my own front porch with neighbors watching from the street and a court-ordered eviction notice in my lap, I realized I wasn't just alone; I was *lonely*.

Ahead of me, the U-haul moving truck that passed me earlier sat parked at the curb in front of the next building down, the back door up and a metal ramp wedged between the bumper and the concrete. The door to unit 1502—which had been closed as long as I lived there—stood wide open, a rectangle of darkness facing out toward the parking lot. I recalled what Schrader told me last night, about our new tenant.

I cut in through the alley between buildings, taking a quick peek around the cargo space of the truck as I rounded the corner. Nothing but wall-to-wall cardboard boxes, all labeled with black marker in small, neat handwriting, several tall lamps, and one beaten leather recliner. I moved toward my back door, wincing in anticipation for that auditory rail spike through the brain, but relaxed when I heard only golden silence.

The Squall had stopped.

"Way to go Javier," I muttered, standing for a moment to enjoy the sound of bird song.

Turning to go inside, I caught movement from the corner of my eye.

Our new neighbor walked out through her open front door, heading toward the ramp of the moving truck.

I took in what I could from behind. Shoulder-length, dirty blond hair tucked under a backwards Green Bay cap. Lean and toned body covered by a loose white t-shirt and bicycle shorts. Athletic legs, with ankles that bunched almost delicately at each step she took in a pair of black Vans. Not Carla-caliber, but enough to make me slow down for a better look.

Without warning, she tossed a wave over her shoulder. "Hi neighbor!"

I jumped almost as bad as Tony had when I'd scared him, partly because I was caught in the act of checking her out, but mostly because I couldn't figure out how she'd known I stood there. Then I spotted the big round mirror jutting off the front of the U-haul, the one that's supposed to help the driver make lane changes. The cheeks of my reflection reddened.

I managed to get out an awkward, "Heeey," but by that point she'd disappeared up the ramp, into the U-haul's gleaming silver interior.

The door of my apartment waited, just six feet away. I wanted to run inside, close the blinds, and hide.

Instead, I took a deep breath, tossed the mail next to my door, and started after her.

6

If you ask me now, I couldn't tell you why I did it.

I was in no position—mentally, emotionally, spiritually, take your pick—to make any serious attempt at engaging a member of the opposite sex.

But I walked to the edge of the U-Haul door and poked my head around the corner. She squatted with her back to me, straining to pick up a huge cardboard box at least three feet high. I tried not to notice the stretch of blue panties revealed at her waistband.

"Um...can I give you a hand?"

"That depends," she said, without turning around.

"On?"

"If you're better at lifting boxes than you are at checking women out discreetly."

"Oh. Yeah, about that—"

"Look, I'm kidding. Would you grab the other side of this already? I'm about to pop a hernia over here."

"Right. On it." I leapt into the back of the truck and squeezed into position on the other side of the box across from her, getting my first face-to-face look at her. Mid-thirties. Blue eyes below the band of her cap. Sharp nose. Chin to match. Buds of color in her smooth cheeks. Cute. Very cute, actually.

"Beth Charles," she said.

"Elliot Jefferson."

"I'll back down the ramp, you follow?"

"Sounds like a plan."

We carried the box out of the truck between us. The thing was immensely heavy even with two of us; I don't know how she would've gotten it by herself. We made it up over the curb before I said, "Next time, you might wanna hire some movers for the grand piano."

A loud *riiiiip* came from the bottom of the box as the packing tape let go. One of the flaps swung down against my thighs, and then the avalanche began.

I looked down and saw scores of magazines flowing over my sneakers. And not just any magazines; I caught the familiar mastheads of such classics as *Playboy*, *Hustler*, *Penthouse*, and even a few *Juggs* along with an assortment of lesser-known skinbooks, their pages flipping open to reveal a cornucopia of nipples and asses and vaginas.

My eyes went to Beth across the top of the box. Her cheeks weren't just rosy now, they were blood red, and darkening by the second. Her mouth opened halfway and seemed to stick there.

I lifted an eyebrow. "Looks like I'm not the only one that needs to check out women more discreetly."

This got a single bark of nervous laughter out of her. "They're research. For my dissertation. Shit, that's embarrassing."

"You're writing a dissertation? What for, Masters?"

"Doctorate. In Social Psychology."

I tried not to look too impressed as I shifted my foot out of the pile of smut, dislodging a copy of *Penthouse* that landed on the grass turned to a page where the model was bent over a chair and spreading her ass cheeks with both hands.

"So what's your dissertation on, home proctology exams?"

"Very funny, Jefferson. For your information, it's called *Gender Stereotyping By Modern Socioeconomic Standards of Inequality*. Now help me get these up. I don't need the whole neighborhood thinking I'm as big a pervert as you on my first day."

7

It took both of us almost ten trips with arms full of magazines to get the entire pile inside her empty apartment. When we were finished, we both collapsed on the floor amid a sea of pornography and rested.

"Cool," I said, looking around at her barren walls. "It's like the mirror image of my place. Everything's on the wrong side. Very *Through the Looking Glass*."

She shoved aside a mini-mountain of *Playboys* so she could cock an eyebrow at me. "What do you do for a living, Jefferson?"

"I teach high school English."

"Ah, so that explains it." I didn't have a chance to inquire what, exactly, that explained before she asked, "So you're on spring break too, huh?"

"For what it's worth."

She got to her feet. "You want something to drink? I think I have a couple beers left in a cooler around here somewhere."

"Actually, water would be great."

Beth disappeared into the kitchen. I tried not to stare at a fold-out of Miss October from 2007 that looked a lot like leasing office Carla until she came back with two glasses. "It's from the tap, and the ice maker in the fridge hasn't produced its first batch yet, so...*bon appétit*." She offered me one, but as I reached up for it, she snatched it away. "Only if you help me with the rest of that stuff. I have to get the truck back by three or I get charged for an extra day."

I pretended to consider this, even though I had planned nothing less. "Deal."

We drank, then got back to work. The other boxes were lighter; single-person jobs. We passed a few friendly words, but most of the time we were headed in opposite directions with our arms full. I wracked my brain for some way to prolong the encounter, something to say that wouldn't make me sound like a drooling chump, and then I came down the back ramp of the U-Haul with my arms loaded to find Beth talking to Schrader outside her front door. I put my load down at the curb and casually came to stand next to her.

"...need more women like you around here," Schrader was saying. Another sucker stick bobbed between his chapped lips with each word as he leered at her. The guy looked noticeably different since I saw him yesterday. His acne-scarred flesh was sallow, and there were purplish lumps under his eyes the size of teabags.

Beth gave a short salute and backed up, toward her door. "Glad I could be of service."

Schrader took a lurching step after her, his gaze roaming up and down her body. Everything about him seemed predatory. "Yessir. A little eye candy keeps a man young. Ain't that right, Jefferson?"

Beth looked over at me gratefully as I stepped between them. "Sure thing, Schrader. That's what got your name on all those sex offender lists, right?"

He smiled, but somehow that only made him look more ghoulish. He snatched the sucker from his mouth—a sour apple green this time—and tossed it into the bushes. "Oh hardy har. I'm surprised yer even out, with the sun bein up and all. Shouldn't ya still be in yer coffin?"

"What can I say?" I fired back, without missing a beat. "Wherever an asshole makes a fool of himself, I'll be there to watch."

Beth demurely put a hand across her mouth to hide a smile.

Schrader's grin widened. Showed teeth. There was nothing mirthful about it, certainly no humor in his eyes, which looked dead and hollow as they held mine. It all seemed out of character; at least, as much of his character as I actually knew. Our mutual, unspoken dislike had caused us to trade quips ever since I moved in, but this had none of the bored undertones of our usual banter. This was more like baboons beating their chests at each other in a territorial dispute.

And something—probably those rolling expanses of absolute zero in each of his eye sockets, a cognitive 'Out-to-Lunch' sign—told me it could only get worse.

"Or maybe," he began, then licked his lips and swallowed hard, as if the words took effort, "You were just hopin Little Miss Blondie here would do a little *pole vaultin* in exchange for yer gentlemanly assistance."

"Hey!" Beth said indignantly.

"That's enough, John." I grabbed his upper arm and yanked him around the corner into the alley. I expected him to fight, but he came willingly, feet tripping over one another. When I was sure we were out of earshot, I asked, "What the hell's wrong with you? Are you drunk?" But I knew that wasn't the answer before the question was out of my mouth. No one knows the signs of alcohol-induced dickhead syndrome better than me.

Schrader had his head down, and when he looked up, his eyes were red-rimmed but more normal, more *there*. That dumb meanness was gone, replaced by vacant confusion. He muttered something unintelligible, but I could swear at one point I caught the phrase, "*Still, small voice.*"

"What did you say?" I asked sharply.

He shook his head; I couldn't tell if it was a refusal to repeat his words, or if he didn't know what they were. "Nuthin. I didn't say nuthin."

I stared at him. "Look, man...just go home, all right? Sleep it off."

He shook his head—fast and short, almost a spasm of the neck muscles—and then repeated, "Home. Sleep it off." He wandered down the alley in the direction of his door, leaving me to stare after him.

8

Beth waited with her arms crossed on the short walkway to her door.

"Sorry about that," I said sheepishly.

She shook her head. "Don't apologize for him."

"He's not usually like that."

"An asshole?"

"Oh no, he's always an asshole. Just not a creepy asshole."

"Is everybody around here that overbearing?"

"Sort of, actually. It's kind of a suburban version of *Rose-*

mary's Baby, without so much devil worship." I shrugged. "Apartment living doesn't always attract the highest caliber of neighbor. You know how it is."

"No, I don't. I've never lived in an apartment complex. I don't think I've ever even been in one."

I blinked at her. "How's that possible?"

She took her cap off, retucked hair behind her ears, and tugged it down again. "I'm from Oskaloosa, Kansas. There's not an apartment in the entire town. We had *acres*, not units. I couldn't even see my neighbors when I went outside."

"Talk about a change of scenery. You feeling stifled?"

"Suffocated, more like. Moving any further into the city would've killed me. I don't think it's natural to have so many human beings crammed into so small an area, living on top and underneath and around one another."

I nodded. "Like we're all puzzle pieces."

"Or a big, writhing snake orgy." I gave a grunt of laughter, and she continued. "We need space to breathe, to grow, or we just start killing one another."

"Good fences make good neighbors?"

She gave another wry smile. "Exactly."

"So tell me, if this whole city suburbia is so awful, then what are you doing here in the snake orgy?"

"Well, you might be able to stretch your arms without punching someone in Oskaloosa, but that also makes it hard to practice social psychology. Plus I was tired of commuting two hours to Kansas City for work and class. The college here offered me a staff position and some post-grad research, so I took it. I didn't wanna buy a house until I saw how things worked out, and this place looked nice online."

"It really is. Nice, I mean. Hey, you want me to give you the grand tour?"

She hesitated. It was hard to get a read on her, if she was actually as enamored with my company as I was with hers, or merely tolerating me. "I would, I'd really like to get the lay of the land, but, like I said, I have to get this truck unpacked."

As she spoke, a beat-up Honda pulled into one of the row of spaces across from our building, and out piled three muscle-bound young men in their early twenties. Garrett, Rick, and Miles; what I called the Jock Trinity. I'd had them all in junior English four years before, and now they were sophomores at the same academic institution that employed Beth, all riding high on a football scholarship and with the collective IQ of a pickle jar. They shared a three-bedroom in Beth's building—the other half of the ground floor—and threw wild parties about once a month for which Tate, our security officer, was frequently called. I waved to get their attention as they lumbered toward their door with all the grace of a roving pack of gorillas.

"Hey fellas, you wanna make a quick twenty bucks?"

"*Each?*" Rick asked.

"Sure. Do Miss Charles here a favor and carry everything from the moving truck into her apartment, okay?"

They looked at each other, shrugged, and set to work.

Beth was giving me a squinty look.

"It's cool, I know them, they're good guys. They should have that done in a half hour. Forty-five minutes, if they get distracted by the porn."

"It's not that, it's just, um...are *you* paying?" Beth asked. "Cause I don't have sixty bucks."

"Of course. My treat. But you have to come sightseeing through the scenic Estates of North Hills with me."

She lifted an eyebrow. "I guess I could use a break. Lead on."

9

I didn't take her through the whole complex. We kept to the streets, and I pointed out a few amenities, like the playground on the opposite side of our parking lot, or the miniature basketball court in between buildings 12 and 13. The place was starting to liven up, Javier and a few other members of the maintenance crew out tending the grounds, folks coming and going, sitting outside in the rapidly dwindling morning breeze or working in their open garages, kids wandering outside to start their own spring breaks. I forced myself to shout greetings to total strangers, feeling like Jimmy Stewart at the end of *Wonderful Life*, eager to prove, if only to myself, that I wasn't the vampire Schrader implied. Everyone looked sluggish and slightly dazed to me, as if they'd just crawled out of bed and dragged themselves outside. A few people still had on pajamas.

But I was so focused on the enigma of Beth Charles, I didn't stop to think about any of it.

We talked more. It'd been a long time since I conversed with an attractive, eligible woman like that, and I felt woefully outmatched. Considering I had no idea what her intentions were—hell, I still didn't even know what mine were—I was careful to keep the topics light. I asked about the research she did, she asked me about the rigors of teaching high school. We made our way past the pool and the weight room, and I felt so good I even took another trip through the office to introduce her to Martha and Tony, who she'd only talked to on the phone when she rented the place.

By the time we got back, the Jock Trinity had the truck emptied. I ran inside, grabbed my wallet, and paid them their cash.

"So this is my back door here," I concluded the tour. "Schrader lives at the other end—"

"I'll be sure to avoid that one when I go out selling Girl Scout cookies."

"—the McCafferys live above me, and the other unit up there is occupied by a guy named Kirk—I think that's his name—and his family."

"What about my building? Anyone else I should look forward to meeting?"

"Well, let's see, you know the Jock Trinity now. They're on the other side of the wall from you. Then upstairs you have Katie Adler and her mother, Samantha. Katie was a student of mine last year. Great kid, you'll like her."

"I'm sure I will. What about the other unit up there?"

My mouth hung. If Beth hadn't asked, I wouldn't have even thought about it. I had never actually seen the other resident of Building 15; I only knew her name from that labeled map I'd been given upon move-in. She was, perhaps, the only resident of the complex more standoffish than yours truly.

I craned my neck back, looking at the last three windows in the top row along the far half of the building, just in time to see the Venetians in the middle snap back into place.

"That's Mrs. Isaacs. Little old widower, keeps to herself. I think I remember somebody telling me her husband was a preacher. You probably won't even see her."

Beth took in this information with a bob of her head. "All right, Jefferson. I've gotta get this truck back and then unpack some of those boxes before the movers get here with the rest of my stuff. Really, thanks for all the help today. Don't know what I would've done without you."

"My pleasure."

"I'm sure I'll see you around. It'll be nice to have a familiar face."

She walked away, around the corner toward her front door. I tried not to feel disappointed. I mean, what did I expect, that we'd have a wedding ceremony right here in the alley within a few hours of meeting each other? This was just overcompensation, pure and simple.

I headed back inside my own unit. As I closed the back door, my eyes landed on that upstairs window across the alley again.

A shriveled hand poked through the blinds, separating the slats enough for the owner to peer between them. I could see nothing but darkness beyond.

SATURDAY EVENING

1

The Squall was not finished. Far from it.

It started up again about three that afternoon, worse than before. I was drowsing in my recliner, daydreaming about my new neighbor with a rerun of *Law and Order* on the television, and I suddenly realized that the actors' words were nothing but blurred squeals of electricity. Right about then, I heard muffled shouting from upstairs as Joan ripped into Dan.

"Oh, gimme a *breeeeak!*" I moaned. In the corner, Mickey cocked his head. He'd been acting like himself since this morning, but he'd peed in the bedroom to punish me for not taking him out sooner.

I slammed out of the chair and headed to the kitchen, grumbling all the way. If you wanted something done right, you had to do it yourself; *that* would never change. I found the phone book and dug out the customer service number for Via-tel Electric, our service provider for the Estates. I feared I would only get an automated line, and I was right, to a degree. For emergencies, you dialed 1, which sent me to a voicemail system. I left my name, address and telephone number, along with an expletive-littered diatribe describing the racket and what would happen if it wasn't fixed immediately.

Only after I hung up did I pray I hadn't actually referred to it as 'the Squall.' My head already hurt so bad, I couldn't remember. Odds were, they probably wouldn't rush out if they got the idea I was a nutjob.

All I could think about was what that noise must look like in my head, rattling all those little bones in the ear canal. Vibrating my skull. Drilling into the meat of my brain.

I took two aspirin and walked the floor for a while. I tried playing with Mickey, but every time he barked it was like an ice pick in my head and when he snapped at me again, I swatted him hard enough to make him cry out. I fixed a bachelor's dinner, which is anything that microwaves in under three minutes and can be eaten standing over the sink.

My mom called at close to seven. The conversation eventually rolled around to the divorce. She never liked Darcy. On a hunch, I stepped outside and walked toward the transformer while she spoke. The reception on my cell broke up with every step I took toward it. I told her I wasn't feeling well to get off the phone, which was mostly true.

My head. God, the headache was a blinding light shining on the backs of my eyeballs. It made me nauseated. I dry-swallowed another three aspirin and decided to get out for a while.

2

I'd begun grocery shopping on Saturday nights, when the store was its emptiest. I usually waited until nine or ten to go, but I was so eager for a reason to get away from the Squall, I left closer to eight in my ancient Tercel.

The closest Walmart was twenty minutes away, farther into the city. There were lines at the registers, as the last of the regular-hour shoppers finished up their business and the store succumbed to the lull of the late-night crowd. I took my time walking the aisles, happy just to be somewhere quiet. The headache eased up, and I lost myself in the simple joys of shopping for one, when you don't have to worry about what anyone else wants. Even with dinner still sitting in my stomach, I found I was suddenly ravenous. Every shelf my eye passed over caused a flood of saliva in my mouth. I gave in to the urge and packed my shopping cart with every item that caught my attention, more food than I could eat by myself in a month, but I didn't care, there was something almost manically gleeful about that mountain of food in my cart, and I had to fight to keep from cracking open some of it and stuffing my face while I shopped. I got so distracted, I accidentally turned down the aisle that held the packs of beer and wine coolers.

I stopped the cart, somewhat of a challenge now that it had grown so heavy. An unpleasant jolt shot up my spine. I shouldn't be here. Not under ideal circumstances, but especially not now. Anything on this aisle was lighter than the stuff I used to drink—stores like this didn't even sell the level of liquor I used to suck down—but just the sight of those brown bottles with their twist-off caps made my mouth feel parched.

So we're agreed then. One of these won't hurt you, you'll barely even feel it. All it'll do is mellow you out so you can get some sleep tonight.

Now it didn't seem like such a random accident that I'd come down this aisle at all.

My father was an alcoholic. Not a mean drunk, mind you; there's a tendency to associate the two, but not everyone turns into a violent degenerate. He never beat me or my mother, wasn't cold or neglectful, he just liked to escape from life at the bottom of a bottle, and it killed him at the age of 47. Nobody seemed particularly surprised.

I couldn't even remember how I'd gotten started, other than a creeping general malaise that started in my mid-thirties and a growing dissatisfaction with my life and my marriage. For years, I told everyone I was a writer, that teaching was just to pay the bills until I got that big, fat publishing contract, but other than one short story I penned—mostly stole—my senior year of college and sent out to approximately two literary magazines, I'd never so much as put down a word on paper. In reality, I think I just needed another goal after the planned-out string of checkpoints we get early in life—graduate high school, graduate college, find a job, find a mate—and then there's suddenly this vast, open plane where you should feel like you can do anything but most of the time are too scared to do everything. It all just started to feel pointless, and booze became such an easy way to deal. By the time I realized I was carrying on the family tradition, the owner of the liquor store on the way home had my usual daily order sacked and ready to go by the time I got there.

I started to stress about the habit, but that just made it worse. At the very end of things with Darcy, I just about could've drowned in the stuff. I stopped *sleeping* and started *passing out*. Two weeks after she kicked me out of the house, while I was bedding down in the cheapest fleabag motel I could find, I made the decision to quit. Those first few months had been rocky, with more regress than progress, but I hadn't slipped up even once in the last eleven months.

No way had I gone through all that just to have a goddamned malfunctioning piece of electrical garbage drive me back to it.

I turned my overloaded cart around and went back down the aisle the way I'd come.

3

The groceries added up to over two-hundred bucks at the register. By the time I got them out to my car, I couldn't remember why I'd wanted them all. That all-consuming hunger had faded like the last remnants of a dream. I filled up my trunk with the haul, then packed the rest into my back seat.

It was full dark when I arrived back at the Estates, closing in on ten o'clock. Instead of turning in the gate, I took the entrance drive past it to the office, following the path I jogged this morning. A solitary line of utility poles marched up the median, suspending the electric lines that brought power to the complex and, eventually, the malfunctioning transformer outside my building. As I pulled the Tercel into a parking space close to the mailbox kiosk, I traced the cords to where they descended steeply from the last pole into some kind of junction anchor next to the wall. The remainder of the lines must be buried underground.

As I got out of the car, a warm breeze ruffled my hair, carrying the scent of the hay fields with it. In front of the office was a rough half-circle drive, flanked with lush, high bushes, the lawn studded with a few pine trees. The little brick structure that holds our mailboxes stood at the far end of the crescent from the office, just beside the gate. I walked in, opened my metal drawer, removed today's mail and turned to leave again, sorting through junk to throw in the trash can on the way out.

I had my hand on the door handle of the car when a long moan drifted across the drive.

Mail fluttered down around my feet. I left it and scanned the tall row of hedges leading up to the office, where the noise seemed to come from. It had the pitch of a mournful ghost, the kind of wretched keening you imagine Jacob Marley making. The trees on the lawn cast a deep well of shadows that not even the streetlights behind me could penetrate, especially up by the building.

I stood by the open driver's door for another indecisive minute. The night was silent, only the barely perceptible growl of distant traffic to remind me that civilization still existed. Then the noise came again, a wordless groan. Almost painful. I came around the car and walked cautiously across the middle of the semicircular lot. The change in angle gave me a little more clearance to see into the web of darkness formed by tree branches and the office wall. I kept moving until I was almost at the bushes on the opposite side.

Still too far to see anything. Inch by inch, I crept forward along the curving row of bushes, closer to the front door, straining my eyes. Definitely a shape under the tree. Was someone crouched there...?

The hedges next to me shook furiously. I yelped and jumped away. The bushes continued rustling against one another, dislodging narrow spring leaves. Someone hid on the other side; I could see their arms whipping the slender trunks back and forth.

"Who is that?" I demanded, the words barely a squeak. I turned to go back to the car but got no further than a single step.

A figure stood beside my open driver's door, blocking my retreat. At this distance, and with the weak light from the streetlamps, all I could see was a gaunt wraith with the misshapen head of a demon.

Footsteps behind me. Two more hideous forms stepped out from the bushes and stood silently, glaring at me, their rubbery faces stretched with lumps and points and bulging eyes. One of them raised a hand in my direction, reaching toward me. I backed off, my balls drawing up tight and hot against my groin.

I had nowhere to go. If I started back toward Midtown Road, the figure by my car—already a quarter way across the lot—would just cut me off.

So instead I moved toward the office, sprinting through the row of hedges and onto the lawn. The fourth figure that had been crouched under the tree emerged from the shadows and watched me pass. I caught sight of devil horns and giant incisors before I flew by.

I headed toward the far corner of the office, heart squirting injections of acid into my bloodstream. No use trying to get into the empty building, but if I could make it into the complex, there would be people and doors to knock on. I rounded the corner and realized my mistake.

There was no way onto the property from here. On the other side of another pine tree with low hanging branches, the rock wall that surrounded the Estates formed an acute angle against the building's brick side. The wall spread out to my right, solid and impenetrable. And the only gate lay behind me.

The sounds of my pursuers crossing the lawn were crisp in the night air.

I threw myself at the wall, trying to climb over. Even on my best leap, my fingertips barely skirted the top. The rocks embedded in its sides were all sizes and shapes, but they had been smoothed down so none of them protruded enough to use as handholds. Not surprising, I suppose; it had been designed specifically for this reason, to keep people out.

I stood and panted as I tried to figure what to do. Finally, I dropped to my knees and crawled beneath the low branches of the tree. Pine needles showered down. Hands clutched at my ankles, trying to drag me back. I kicked out. My heel struck something hard and bony; there was a grunt of pain. I squirmed as far as I could into the narrow space until I reached the juncture of wall and building and flipped over to press into the shadows.

Four sets of legs stood just beyond the tree, one of them rubbing at its shin. I was too terrified to register that these creatures wore jeans and an array of sneakers.

"*What do you want?*" I yelled.

One of them bent to look in at me; the one with the devil face. Its hand flicked back and then forward.

I caught sight of a white, round object sailing through the short space before it nailed me dead in the forehead, exploding on contact.

Something dripped down my face. I touched the fluid, expecting blood. It was too dark to determine color, but the consistency and smell revealed the truth.

Raw egg.

Laughter echoed as the legs of my tormentors ran back the other direction.

A youthful, hard-edged voice I knew only too well shouted, "Be seein ya, *teach!*"

Long after my fear had warmed to anger then cooled to embarrassment, I used my shirt to wipe the last of the egg off and then crawled from under the tree. The final insult came when I arrived back at the mail kiosk and found that I'd been assaulted with one of the dozen eggs I'd just bought.

The others had been used to turn my car into a mess worthy of Jackson Pollock.

SUNDAY MORNING

1

I'm not sure if you could call what I did that night 'sleeping.'

The Squall continued on its merry way. It began a new pattern, cycling up and fading in quick bursts, like a set of giant lungs. My exhausted mind entered a realm somewhere between sleep and consciousness, a wasteland of fragmented thoughts and too-real dreams.

I remember only one of them.

I stood alone in the alley, with the transformer ahead of me, screaming its harsh song into the night. My fists balled as I stared at it, furious one second and absolutely infatuated the next. Something stirred in me below the belt. I looked down to find a raging erection stretching the front of my shorts.

In the dream, I stretched out a hand. I had never touched the box in real life, but something compelled me now to take tiny, half-steps forward, lowering my hand until my fingertips hovered just over the metal surface. I could sense the power lurking beneath it, like holding my hand over an open flame.

The whole world held its breath. A feeling slipped over me, that all of reality was a show put on for my benefit, like I could reach out through that veil and touch what was underneath.

And this façade felt thin. So thin. A balloon waiting for a needle.

I moved forward, intent on touching it, meaning to caress its steel side and the raw power beneath, and the Squall soared in intensity, in anticipation, and just as my fingers brushed the metal, I was awoken by laughter.

2

I sat up panting, sweat pouring down my face, my heart thudding like the drumbeats of some of the fast metal riffs my students listen to. I waited until it calmed and tried to pull myself back together.

The bedside clock read 9:00 AM. Mickey shivered against me, pressed against my chest and breathing in quick, shallow pants. I ran a hand down his head and along his side, trying to calm him from his own bad dreams.

My body and brain grumbled; my eyes felt like flaming marbles in my skull. At least the Squall was on another hiatus. I wanted to lay back down, bury my head under the covers, and pray the break held long enough for me to get some real sleep.

From the window behind me came more laughter, high and feminine. I twisted around and peeked through the blinds.

Beth stood barefoot just outside my window with her back to me, wearing a pair of white Capris and a pink blouse. Katie stood on the opposite side of the alley, bouncing—and I thought I was hallucinating this—a hacky sack on the tip of her sneaker. The younger girl wore a dark skirt and blouse far too formal for playing sports. She gave the sack an extra hard kick, got her knee up, and knocked it toward Beth, who caught it expertly with the insole of her foot.

I jumped out of bed so fast, the covers got tangled around my ankle and almost brought me down on my face. I threw on some clothes, leashed up Mickey, and rushed to the back door, pausing just long enough to affect the perfect air of nonchalance.

They stopped the game as we stepped out. Katie smiled and waved. "Hey Mr. Jefferson!" Mickey ran to the end of the leash toward her. She bent to rub his ears.

"Morning Katie. I see you met our new neighbor."

"Yeah, isn't she great? She's teaching me to do this... what's it called again? Hockey sack?"

"Don't get too excited. There's a reason that particular craze didn't survive the 90's."

Beth performed a complicated maneuver that involved juggling the beanbag between her heel, head, and off her breasts, then into her hand. Without yesterday's cap, her golden hair bounced against the back of her neck. "You're looking at the high school state champion two years in a row."

I smirked. "Kansas had a state hacky sack competition?"

"What can I say? We're a dexterous people." She glanced over before tossing the bag. "I hope you don't mind me saying so, but you look like shit, Jefferson."

Katie giggled and missed the catch.

I nodded at the girl. "Try to avoid corrupting my students, okay?"

"Sorry. Used to college kids."

"Oh come *on*," Katie groaned. "Like I don't hear a thousand times worse every day."

Beth stood on one foot and braced the other against her leg, affecting a yoga pose. "Come to my school next year and take Developmental Psych, honey. Then we can talk however we want."

"Awesome, I'm so there!"

Katie's exuberance made me smile. The poetry she'd produced for class had always been like that too, optimistic and full of life. A welcome change from the gloom and doom I got from most kids her age. I envied her, at the cusp of so many possibilities.

They kept playing. I watched the ball go back and forth a few times from the edge of my patio and then said, "For your information, the reason I look like roadkill is because I couldn't sleep last night."

"Let me guess." Beth pointed at the metal box at the end of the alley, then screwed up her face and made a grinding-growling sound through her teeth that was a fairly good imitation of the Squall.

"Yeah. Thank god, you can hear it too, huh?"

"Hear it? The thing makes my fillings ache! It's like the illegitimate love child of fingernails on a chalkboard and a car alarm. How the hell could you *not* hear it?"

"You'd be surprised."

"My...my mom can't." Katie's voice changed as she said this, becoming monotone and hesitant. She squatted, picked up Mickey, and hugged him to her while her eyes drifted toward the transformer. "She wanted to know why I was watching TV in the middle of the night. When I told her that noise was keeping me up, she...she didn't know what I was talking about."

Beth's eyes flicked over to me. She raised a questioning eyebrow. I didn't know if it was in response to the girl's story or the haunted way she'd told it. "Katie?"

She looked back around at us, and I saw flat fear behind her eyes, there one second, gone the next.

"Well, something's gotta be done." Beth walked toward

the transformer, bending slightly to examine the casing. My dream came back to me, and I had the urge to call her back. "I can't take much more of this."

"I left a service order for the power company yesterday. Hopefully they'll get someone out here soon. Then again, maybe it's done for good this time."

Beth turned back without touching the transformer. I gave an internal sigh of relief.

A door opened beside me, and Samantha Adler stepped out onto her own patio in a black blouse and ankle length skirt, clutching a bible to her broad bosom. She was big but not rotund like Martha, with a severe face that had passed on none of its traits to her daughter and a volcano of hair that piled in the front and then ran off in wispy threads in all directions. She took in me, then Beth, then glared at Katie and growled, "What're you doin messin around in your church clothes?"

"N-nothing Mom, I was just—"

"I don't wanna hear it."

The girl's mouth snapped closed. She set Mickey back on the ground.

"Morning, Miss Adler." I feigned cheerfulness. I remained one of the few teachers at D.L. Baker who had survived a semester teaching her daughter and not been called in to a conference with the principal about my methods, my classroom, the other students, or any one of a hundred other items that Samantha Adler felt were corrupting her daughter. Most of the time, she made these complaints under the umbrella of religion, but I didn't think she was any more staunch than the parents who imposed their will with sports or grades. They all just treated their children the way they treated the rest of the world: like we were pawns on a chessboard made only for them. "Katie told me she's been applying to colleges. You must be excited."

She sniffed and squinted. "Oh yes, very much so. Of course, I'd be more excited if certain people would stop filling her head with the ridiculous idea she's gonna be some kinda *writer*,"—this word was said with the kind of inflection one might give an exotic strain of herpes—"so I can keep her focused on things that actually matter."

I opened my mouth—to say what I don't know—but stopped when her head darted forward, the cords on her thick neck visibly straining, her face caught in a snarl, and then pulled back to twitch rapidly to the left. The movement was sudden and awkward and oddly silent, like an attack a Tourette's sufferer might undergo, and over with so fast I wasn't even sure what I'd seen.

I looked over at the other two. Katie had her head down, and Beth was politely turned away. I didn't think either of them had seen the spasm.

"Let's go, Katie," Samantha Adler snapped. "We're gonna be late for service."

She strode toward the end of the alley. Katie kicked the hacky sack toward Beth, gave us an apologetic look, and hurried after her mother.

I couldn't help thinking about that tone she'd used when talking about the woman, and that momentary glimpse of fear in her young eyes.

"Katie, hold on!" I ran after her, leaving Beth in the alley.

Her mom was getting into the brown Mazda parked on their drive. She stopped with one leg inside the vehicle and watched angrily as Katie and I stood just out of hearing range on the grass.

"Is everything okay?" I asked quietly.

She raised one eyebrow. "Yeeeeah. Why?"

I took a second to consider. There was no time to approach this delicately. "Your mother. Has she been...acting worse?"

"No," she said, too quickly. Her arms crossed self-consciously over her chest.

"Katie...just remember what I said. I'm here if you need me."

She nodded. Moisture welled up in her lower eyelids. She wiped them away and glanced back at her mother. "I...I can't talk about it now. Tomorrow, okay? I'll come by tomorrow after she goes to work."

"Okay. I'll be here."

"*Katie!*" Samantha bawled. "*Get in this car! Right now!*"

"I gotta go." She hurried over. Samantha Adler stood glaring at me until her daughter was in the passenger seat, then jumped in and backed out of the driveway in a squeal of rubber. I figured that little stunt could get me into some serious trouble if the woman went to the school board claiming I was having private conversations with her daughter, but I'd deal with that when it happened.

For the moment, I was far more preoccupied with that odd facial spasm.

3

"Geez, Jefferson," Beth said as she came to stand beside me. "You're not a very popular guy around here, are you?"

"Tell me about it."

She gestured after the Adler's Mazda. "She's a sweet kid. Think she'll be all right?"

"You mean now, or in the broader sense?"

"Both, I guess."

"Don't know. The sooner she gets out into the world and away from that woman, the better off she'll be."

"That sucks. Some people shouldn't be allowed to pro-create."

"Change 'some' to 'most' and I agree with you." I turned to face her. "You get moved in okay?"

She nodded while stifling a yawn. The slightest hint of coloring showed under her eyes to indicate her own sleep-less night, but she still looked great. I ran a hand through my tangled hair self-consciously as Mickey tried to pull me further up the alley. "Everything's in there, if that's what you mean. I'll probably be unpacking boxes till Christmas."

"You gonna take a break at some point?"

She frowned suspiciously. "Maybe."

"Then how about dinner?"

I was amazed at how easy the question sounded. Prob-ably because I hadn't planned it in the least. Or that I was so tired, I could barely stand up.

She gave me a lopsided grin, but met my eyes as directly as ever. "You really think that's smart, Jefferson? Dating the next door neighbor?"

"Date? Who said anything about a date? I'm talking about dinner here. I'll have you know, any woman that asks me to help smuggle pornography owes me at least one din-ner. Them's the rules."

"Are they now?" She gnawed at the inside of her cheek with a half-grin so unassumingly sexy, my heart skipped an extra few beats. "Look, I'm not saying no, but I can't for the immediate future. I'll be at the school today unpacking my office and meeting coworkers, so I don't know if I'll be up for it. Then tomorrow is orientation all day and right afterward the head of the psych department is hosting a dinner party to welcome me to the staff. I'll be in and out most of the week."

"No pressure." I held up a hand. "The offer's on the table, you let me know."

I turned and pulled Mickey toward my door, deciding to get out with this small victory under my belt. I had a hand on the knob when the Squall started up yet again. This time it sounded like an old 45 being repeatedly scratched on the turntable.

"Yowch." I inserted fingers in both ears that did nothing to stifle the noise. *How was that possible?*

"This is getting ridiculous," Beth said.

"Those of us that can hear it have gotta keep complaining, or they'll never fix it."

She rolled her eyes. "Oh, please. I don't believe you guys for a second that anyone outside of the deaf can't hear that racket. But if it'll make you feel better, I'll call the power company right now."

"Thanks. It would."

"Yeah, well, I'm just glad I'm gonna be gone all day. Maybe I can get some sleep under my new desk."

I gave her one last wave and went into my apartment.

SUNDAY EVENING

1

The rest of the afternoon went about like the day before.

I prepared a monstrously big batch of German potato salad for lunch from my overflowing food stores and devoured the whole thing before I even realized it. It almost seemed to disappear between bites as I mechanically shoveled it into my mouth while watching a golf tournament on ESPN, one second the bowl overflowing, the next my spoon scraping bottom. I honestly had no memory of eating it, no memory of the time passing at all. I might've looked around to see if it had fallen on the floor if my stomach didn't ache and the golf tournament hadn't given way to motocross.

The Squall let up for a short while, and I managed to sack a few solid hours on the couch.

Then night fell, and I went stir crazy.

My AA sponsor had recommended taking up a hobby for times like this, which is why I'd been building models like crazy for the past year. I had fond memories of whiling away hours as a kid, building replicas of Speed Racer and Adam West's Batmobile. It helped to keep me focused during the long bouts of depression that caught up with me after the detox. I didn't even keep them, I just built them and then gave them to students at school. Tonight though, no amount of precision gluing could get me past the grating whine of the Squall. So around nine—when my lips started smacking and I began to smell phantom snatches of alcohol—I knew it was time to get out. I leashed up Mickey and prepared to take a long walk around the complex.

I went out through the garage, squeezing between the Tercel (still stained with the raw egg I hadn't been able to wipe off) and the rows of plastic storage bins I'd never unpacked when I moved in. I stood in the night air and breathed deep, then started off along the side of the street toward the far end of the complex, where the building numbers got higher.

A light glowed from Beth's front window. I paused for the barest of seconds outside, shook my head, and kept right on walking.

2

Mickey tried to sniff every blade of grass, but I kept him moving this time.

It was even chillier tonight, the breeze enough to goosepimple my bare legs and arms. The moon hid behind a thin veneer of clouds stretching overhead from one rooftop to the next. I passed through circles of yellow illumination under the complex streetlights and then into the dark gulfs between.

One of Miss Dillinger's cats darted out from the bushes that lined her building, hissed at us, and took off, but other than that, the streets were deserted once more. The place could've been abandoned if not for the lamps burning behind blinds everywhere I looked. Usually on a night like this, people had their windows open, letting the babble of television drift through the air, but all I could hear now were my footfalls making dry, dull thuds against the pavement. From somewhere above, a caged parakeet squawked from someone's balcony. I slowed my pace to look up at it. The thing was having some kind of fit, throwing itself around its little home to bash against the bars, then stopping every few seconds to rip a beakful of green feathers from its own flesh.

A shiver grew deep in my core before radiating out, like shockwaves from an earthquake.

Just like yesterday morning, there was nothing at all wrong that I could put my finger on.

So why did I still feel so uneasy?

Because it's fake. All of it.

This stray thought must have come from my dream last night, but it instantly felt right. A sudden, unshakeable, almost schizophrenic surety gripped me, that everything I could see was a mask, an illusion of normalcy, a whitewash hiding something dark and terrible. I had never gotten the DT's when I quit drinking, never seen pink elephants or bugs crawling out of the wall, but it wasn't a far stretch to imagine this is what they were like.

My conversation with Beth yesterday came back to me, about how human beings weren't meant to be so packed in, and I felt so claustrophobic I couldn't breathe. God, I was having a panic attack. I turned back toward the apartment, yanking Mickey's leash, and realized all at once that I could hear the Squall again.

Had been hearing it this whole time.

At first I believed it must be my imagination, or that the night was silent enough for the sound to carry on the breeze. But I stood at the gap between buildings 24 and 25, a good three blocks from home, and if that irritating buzz had been loud enough to cause my teeth to grind all the way over here, in my apartment it would've been deafening.

No; this source had to be closer.

The alley opening closest to me was steeped in even deeper darkness. I crept between the buildings like a thief, following the crackling shriek of electricity. I felt mesmerized, out of control of my own body, like one of Odysseus's men heeding the call of the Sirens. I knew what I would find, and my suspicions were confirmed just before I reached the property border.

A transformer identical to the one next to my building, the metal panel on the front padlocked at the bottom to a four-foot square concrete slab. Something underneath that dark green covering—some electrical switch or circuit or relay that I had no understanding of—emitted the same harsh squeal.

The implication hit me like a slap across the face.

"C'mon," I told Mickey, spurring him into a jog beside me. We went around the transformer—careful not to come anywhere close to it—and entered the narrow strip of grass that ran between the rock wall and the backs of the buildings. We turned right, heading deeper into the Estates. Back here, it was pitch black, no streetlights, but I ran all out, following the curving trail as it wound around the periphery of the complex. The action cleared my head, helped me shake off the vestiges of the weird panic attack. Bricks and windows and dead-end streets flashed by in my flight, but I paused long enough to check down each grass alley. Only when I hit the back corner of the property, where the wall made a ninety degree turn and cut me off, did I have enough raw data to form a conclusion.

Every alternating building gap held its own transformer, a network designed to service the structures to either side.

And each one of these dark green boxes gave off its own Squall, all of them singing in unison.

Which meant every last resident in the Estates of North Hills was now being bombarded with the racket that had been driving me up a wall for the last day and a half.

3

Mickey looked ready to call it quits after our mad dash, so I circled around the far side of the property at a slower pace, spotting transformers as we went. I'd never realized just how massive electrical grids had to be for a place like this. Besides the ones in the alleys, I counted several in each of the parking lots and one beside the playground that stood in the middle of the property. By the time I left the noise made by one, I could already hear the screech of the next.

I could find no escape from the bubble of the Squall. It reached to every inch of the complex.

We rounded the corner of building 33, working our way home along the north side. There was movement in the darkness ahead. Without fully understanding why, I stepped into the deepest shadow I could find, reeled in Mickey, picked him up, and peered into the night.

A figure stood at the opening of the next alley just twenty yards away, shoulders slumped, head down. I couldn't pick out any details, but the shape was unmistakably male. I watched as he approached the transformer there, each step deliberate and halting. He paused in front of it—long enough for me to think it was another resident fed up with the constant noise—and then suddenly jumped into motion, like his muscles had been zapped with a few thousand volts. He circled the metal box with arms flailing.

At first I tried to rationalize what I was seeing, but there was nothing rational about it. The figure went around and around the steel box with hands held high, waving random circles in the air and bobbing his head up and down like a bird. He shuffled sideways, so that he always faced the transformer. The movements were so frantic and jittery, it was like watching an old, scratchy movie reel, where the film just wasn't fast enough to catch everything and some of the actor's gestures are lost between frames. Even though the whole act was completely surreal, something about it seemed distantly familiar. A moment later, I realized why.

It looked like the sort of hokey ritual you might see performed around a bonfire by some African or Native American tribe in the movies. An exaggerated parody of a rain dance, perhaps.

The odd movements went on for a good thirty seconds, during which I pressed even further into the shadows, held my breath, and put a hand over Mickey's muzzle. I couldn't tell whose heart beat faster, mine or the dog's. Instinct gnawed at me once more, telling me I did not want this guy to know he had a witness.

...the still, small voice...

Schrader's mumbled nonsense from yesterday. I'd probably misheard him, and my exhausted brain had inserted the phrase from my weird phone call on Friday.

All at once, the Squall stopped. Everywhere. The entire complex fell as silent as the surface of the moon.

The figure's gyrations halted. He stood staring down at the transformer with his back to me—head jerking to the left in a way that reminded me of that old Coke mascot Max Headroom—and then abruptly turned and hurried back down the alley he'd come from.

I eased after him, still holding Mickey, trying to dampen my footsteps against the grass. Even thought I knew it had to be a goose chase of the wildest variety, the urge to understand what I'd just seen overpowered all common sense. I reached the alley in time to see him disappear around the corner of the building on the left, and I slunk down the brick wall and stuck my head cautiously out.

Magnolia Lane ran in front of me on a diagonal, the smaller fork of Rose Way splitting off on the opposite side to form a capital Y shape. A building sat between each spoke of the roadway including the one I hid behind, all three facing inward toward the wide intersection in a kind of mini-cul-de-sac. I spotted my guy jogging across the street, heading toward building 32 on the far side, where light spilled out of an open garage onto the plane of the driveway.

He sprinted inside the bay. My sight line afforded only a shallow sliver of the interior. I expected the automatic door to trundle closed, but it stayed up. A second later, a series of metallic clatters came drifting out.

I would have to go after him if I wanted to see any more, but it was all open ground out there in the street. No cover, no place to run. The moment I stepped out, I would be completely exposed. Some part of me laughed hysterically at the fact that Elliot Jefferson, eleventh grade English teacher, was running around his apartment complex in the middle of the night, like a kid playing spy games, but the rest took this situation deadly serious.

If I turned back, went into the next alley, then came out on Magnolia farther up, I would be at a better angle to see into the garage. The plan was still forming as I spun and ran. My arms ached from carrying Mickey, so I stopped halfway down the alley, threw his leash around a tree trunk, tied it off, and set him down. "No barking," I hissed, and took off again, still fighting the feeling that I was the world's biggest jackass.

By the time I got to the new position, my lungs wheezed. Rows of blank windows faced me from the apartments across the street. I peeked around the corner from my new cover.

My subject stood beneath the overhead light in his garage. Shapeless brown hair, green shirt, khaki shorts a lot like the ones I wore. I didn't recognize him, but he could've been anybody, someone I passed in the office or squeezed by at the mailbox a hundred times. I could barely make out the apartment number embossed along the frame of the garage: 3204.

But I was far more interested in his actions than his identity.

The garage stood empty, clear of vehicles. Tools and pieces of metal mechanical parts were spread across the concrete floor haphazardly. 3204 worked feverishly on a contraption sitting in the middle of the space, first lying down to tighten something with a wrench underneath, then jumping up to throw the tool aside and grab a screwdriver.

I squinted, trying to get a sense of the thing. It appeared to be constructed from an inclined workout bench, maybe one of the Nautilus machines from the apartment gym, a big metal frame with all sorts of mechanical chains and pulleys hanging overhead and stretched around the sides. He'd modified it heavily, split the bottom of the bench seat up the middle and welded a long cross bar against the back. Behind that nestled a conglomeration of so many gears and cogs, it looked like the inside of a clock.

The door from the garage into the rest of the apartment opened. A women in a blue housecoat stepped out. I watched eagerly, ready for her to chastise him or seduce him or even just talk to him, anything that would put this whole thing back in a normal context and make me see how ridiculous I'd been.

But no words were exchanged. Mrs. 3204 came out and stood beside the man as he worked, gazing down at his handiwork as she swayed ever so slightly back and forth, like a palm frond in a gentle breeze. Every vertebra in my spine turned to ice; it was like watching a couple of doped-up mental patients. Then their heads came up in unison, as synchronized as if a bell had been rung, and they turned to go back inside. He punched the button that started the garage door closing on their way out.

I needed to get a better look at that thing, and not just for curiosity's sake. I felt driven, caught up in something far bigger than myself, playing a role that had been cast without my consent. I waited till the garage door was all the way closed and then jetted out onto the street. I passed the alley where Mickey waited, staring at me with his head turned to the side, then sprinted into the wide intersection.

Here I paused, and took a cautious look around. All of the buildings that looked out on my position were dark and still and silent. In any case, I tried to look casual as I approached 3204. I picked out the windows and front door that must belong to him. When I reached the garage, I stood on my toes to look in through the glass panes that lined the top.

The light was out in there, the room a black cauldron. I cupped my hand against the glass and tried to pick out the shape of that machine. I had just about convinced myself to try working my fingers under the bottom of the door and forcing it up, when someone behind me said, "Well, well, *teach*...I never took you for a Peeping Tom."

4

The words dripped with sarcasm. I froze, not just because I'd been caught, but because I recognized the voice that spoke them, the one I'd heard last night while I cowered under a tree with egg dripping down my face in both the literal and metaphorical sense. This was coupled with the realization of just how far across the complex I had ventured tonight.

I turned around. At the bottom of the driveway stood a young man in the very earliest days of his 20's, black hair hanging in his face, patchy beard scruff along his jawline, wearing jeans that were more ragged threads than actual denim and a hooded sweatshirt with a bleeding skull stitched onto the kangaroo pocket. He looked up at me and ran his teeth back and forth across the silver ring in his lower lip.

"Hello, Jacob," I said evenly.

"Then again, maybe I'm *not* that surprised," he continued. "You were always tryin to look up the girls' skirts in that shitty creative writing class of yours."

Snickers drifted from the night over Jacob's shoulder. Building 34 sat in the middle of the Y formed by the intersection of Magnolia and Rose. One of these garage doors also stood open, but the light was off, which is why I'd missed it before. The vague shapes of Jacob's cronies were visible now, sitting on lawn chairs in the dark. I didn't need to get any closer to know the tang of marijuana in that garage had to be eye-watering.

"How you been, Jacob?" I kept my voice light and friendly, just like I'd dealt with Samantha Adler this morning. If he wasn't going to say anything about our run-in last night, neither would I. "I heard you were going to mechanic school in the fall."

"Who told you that?"

"Katie did. I have to say, that's great. You'd be really good at something like that."

"Yeah? Glad you think so. Your opinion means *soooo* much to me."

More laughter. I swallowed and tried to figure out just how bad this situation could get if these fine youths were hopped up on anything worse than weed. Like that cheap, borderline-poisonous crank he used to distribute at the high school.

Jacob Tinsley took a step up the driveway toward me, hands stuffed in the pocket of his hoodie. "So what are you doin on this side of the complex, *Mister* Jefferson?" The emphasis he put on 'mister' drained all the respect from it. "Out here in the dark…creepin around…peekin in my neighbor's window…"

"It…it's not like that. Really." I hooked a thumb over my shoulder. "I was just trying to get a closer look at the thing this guy was building in there. Did you happen to see…?" I let the question trail. He couldn't have seen anything, not if he'd been in his garage. His angle would've been as bad to the left as mine had been to the right.

Jacob tossed his head, flinging greasy locks out of his face so he could glare at me more effectively. That look had been a lot less scary when it came from the back of a classroom, but now… "What Mr. Connelly does in his garage is his own business. Don't ya think?"

I held up my hands in surrender. "Absolutely. Yes, you're right. I was just curious. I'll go."

I started toward the street, moving to go around him. He took a single sliding step sideways and placed himself in my path.

"Oh, you were curious? Well, let's get the dude out here, I'm sure he'd let you take a look. *Hey, yo, Mr. Connelly!*"

"Shh, keep your voice down!" I pleaded, glancing back at 3204's front door. Nothing moved beyond the dark glass of his windows.

"Woah-ho-ho." Jacob grinned with his jaw jutted forward, pushing that lip ring out like a door knocker. He looked over his shoulder, seeking approval from his crew, and received a fresh round of jeering laughter. "You sound guilty. But why would you be guilty if you weren't doin anything wrong? Hmm, now *I'm* fuckin curious."

I rolled my eyes and sighed. "Jacob...do we have to do this now?"

"But it's all for you, man." He shrugged, bringing his hands out of his pocket for the first time. I tensed up until I saw they were empty; eggs were the least of what he could've had in there. "I'm tryin to clear your squeaky-clean good name here. You know, listenin to your side of the story, which is more than you ever did for me. We wouldn't want people sayin you were out here gettin a look at Mrs. Connelly in her panties, now would we?" He snorted, reared back, and hawked a loogie onto the ground at my feet. "Oh no, not you, not Mr. Goody-Two-Shoes. You don't get in trouble, you get *other* people in trouble. Ain't that your style?"

I met his gaze long and hard, letting all the forced joviality drain out of my voice. I said, through clenched teeth, "I was your teacher, Jacob. What the hell was I supposed to do?"

He rushed forward, until his nose almost touched mine. I didn't flinch, didn't back down; something told me if I did, things might go in a very different direction. Instead we stared into each other's eyes for several long seconds, the rest of the world forgotten, until Jacob said, "You ain't my teacher no more, man. There ain't no expulsion and no principal to hide behind. Now we're just two grown men who gotta settle our own shit."

"So grown men hang around in the dark wearing cheap Halloween masks and throwing eggs?"

"I don't know. Do they crawl into the bushes to piss their pants?"

I said nothing, just waited for his next move. I outweighed him by a good fifty pounds, but he had youth and anger on his side. Not to mention reinforcements.

His eyes gave him away when he finally moved, stepping back with one foot in preparation to pivot and bring his fist into my gut.

But before he could, a golf cart came purring around the corner of the building behind us.

5

The sound broke our deadlock. We both turned our heads.

The man behind the wheel of the golf cart was in his fifties, and wore an officer's uniform complete with revolver. He steered the little vehicle in a wide circle and rolled to a stop in the street beside us.

"What in holy shite is going on here, boys?" Tate Maxwell swiveled in the driver's seat of the golf cart, the fabric of his uniform pants squeaking against the vinyl. He swept the beam of a flashlight across our faces. "Tinsley, you making trouble for the decent residents again?"

Jacob jabbed a finger in my face and declared, in the tattletaling voice I'd heard a zillion times in my career, "This asshole's goin around lookin in people's windows, Tate!"

"That's not true. I was just walking by." The words tumbled out before I could stop them.

"You fuckin *liar!*" Jacob screeched.

Tate climbed out of the golf cart and came to stand between us. He was a brawny guy, with well-muscled arms and a neck like a tree trunk. "I'm supposed to believe you, Tinsley? After all the shite you pull around here?"

Jacob's eyes bugged so far out of his head, I thought they might burst. "It's the truth! Ask my boys, they'll tell you!" From his garage came a litany of shouted agreements and accusations.

Tate stood ramrod straight, rolling the flashlight from hand to hand in front of his gun belt, and looked from Jacob to me and back again. "Okay boy, here's how I'm gonna handle this. You wanna accuse Mr. Jefferson, fine, we can stand here all night while I question him and look into it."

Jacob flashed a triumphant grin in my direction. "Sounds good to me."

"*But.*" Tate held up a single finger to cut him off. "I'm gonna have to do my job fully, and bring your judgment into question. Which means my first step is to go in that garage and take a look around. See what I find. And based on how red your eyes are," he pointed his flashlight into Jacob's face again, causing the young man to hold up a hand and turn his head away, "I think we both know what that'll be. Now, you want me to do that, Tinsley?"

Jacob stood for a long moment, jaw working silently in disbelief. The frustrated rage coming off him was almost palpable. I tried to remember if he'd been this angry when he first stumbled into my classroom, nearly five years ago.

And then he pulled himself together and mumbled, "Man, fuck this." He retreated, backing away down the driveway and out into the street. "Looks like you win again, huh Jefferson? My word ain't jack shit against yours."

"Keep walking," Tate told him. "And you better pray I don't catch you and your hoodlum friends dealing on my property."

Jacob stood outside his garage door and gave Tate the finger with one hand and grabbed his crotch with the other. But to me he said, "You got lucky, but you better watch yourself. There ain't always gonna be somebody else to hide behind."

With that, he stomped into his apartment and started the garage door closing.

6

"Jiminy fookin Christ, you made an enemy for life there." Tate mopped at a spot of color on his forehead. I'd only spoken to the man once or twice, always in the office, so I was surprised he'd know my name. For some reason, he pronounced every obscenity that came out of his mouth—and there were a lot of them—in a Scottish brogue. Maybe he thought it made them less offensive.

"Yeah, but that's nothing new."

"What did he mean about you winning again?"

"I got him expelled his junior year and sent to juvie." I closed my eyes and gave a sad shake of my head. "For bringing a gun to school."

"Oh fook me," Tate groaned. "Yep, that'd do it."

"Even before that, he was the type of kid every teacher dreads: bad home life, dealing drugs, fighting constantly, the works."

"Must be hell, him living so close. He threaten you like that before?"

"Hasn't had the chance. I found out he lived here just after I moved in last year. Kept to my side of the complex ever since. Last night he and his boys gave me a scare, threw some eggs, but I'd mostly forgotten about him. Guess he didn't forget about me."

"Ten-four on that. Certainly explains why he'd make up a story like that about you." A crooked little half-smile crossed his grizzled face. "He *did* make it up...didn't he?"

I hesitated. I really wanted to tell someone else about what I'd seen 3204 doing, but the moment had passed, and I didn't trust myself to string the right words together to convey the surreality of it all. Besides, even if I made him understand, what was he going to do, beat on their door and demand to see that thing? Get a search warrant?

"Yeah," I lied again. A flush of guilt made my cheeks burn. "He made it up."

Tate nodded. "Thought so. Sometimes I think they employee me just so I can keep that punk from burning the place down."

"God, I'll bet. What else has he done?"

"Oh, you know how it is, little fooker like him's too slick to get caught." Tate waved a hand in a way that made me wonder how much of Jacob's misdeeds were truth, and how much wishful thinking. Certain cops see a kid dressed like that and just circle like a buzzard. "I'm almost sure he's dealing, but I've never caught 'im. Punk don't have a job, so how the hell else he afford to live here?" He gestured to his golf cart. "Hop on. I'll give you a lift home."

"That's okay. I can walk."

"Please, I insist. That way I know you made it home safe. I leave you here, and they'll just come right back out and start hassling you."

I looked at the alley where I'd left Mickey. How was I sup-posed to explain that I'd left my dog tied to a tree up the street? I'd have to let Tate drop me off, then come back to get him.

"All right," I conceded. I went around to the passenger seat. Tate got behind the wheel.

"What building are you again?"

"Sixteen. Off Tulip Boulevard."

I hoped he would hang a u-turn and take Magnolia so I could at least check on Mickey, but instead he continued up the way we were pointed, on the Rose offshoot. The tiny engine under the hood made a soft electric *whir* that was almost soothing compared to the Squall. Tate whistled a low tune through his teeth as he piloted.

I watched the buildings creep by on my side of the car, spotting the transformers between them, and then said, "If you don't mind me asking, do you live on property?"

"Me? Naw, I got a house over in Bedford, close to work. This is just a side gig for me. Little extra money." He took the next right turn, the cart gliding onto the new street. "You're lucky I came by to do a round tonight. This was my last day before a two week vacation from the force, and the wife took the kids up to her mother's place for spring break. I got a nice quiet house waiting for me. By now I figured I'd be on the couch with a TV dinner, a bottle of Bud, and last night's game."

"So what are you doing here then?"

He frowned. His eyes flicked away from the road and over to me. "There's been some...problems...on property." He rushed to add, "Nothing bad, no break-ins or anything. Just a lotta complaints, arguments, stuff like that. Civil unrest, us cops call it. Martha asked me to swing by a few extra times this week."

"Civil unrest." I let the words sink in, replaying my conversation with Martha yesterday morning in the office. "That include those mutilated birds you found?"

We were back on my street now; my building was visible ahead. Tate seemed to debate with himself, then gave a sideways nod to the rear seat of the golf cart. "Take a look back there."

I spun around in the tiny space. A wool blanket sat bundled behind me, covering a small lump. I grabbed the corner and lifted.

A mess of bloody fur sat beneath, a thing so squashed out of shape I could scarcely identify it.

"Jesus!" I dropped the blanket again and rubbed my hand against my shirt.

"Cat," Tate told me. "Maybe one of Miss Dillinger's. Found it over behind building forty just before I saw you. Looks like someone bashed its head in with a baseball bat."

Acidic fear sluiced through my veins. "Oh my god."

"Don't worry, probably just some punk kid, practicing to be a psycho when he grows up. Wouldn't be surprised if it was Tinsley!"

"Oh god," I repeated. "Shit."

"Hey, you okay?"

"This is fine, you can let me out here." I dove off the cart while it was still in motion and forced myself not to run toward the closest gap between buildings.

Tate braked and called out, "Everything all right?"

I yelled over my shoulder, "Yeah, thanks for the ride!"

"Not a problem! Hey, you let me know if that shithead gives you any more trouble!"

"Will do!"

As soon as he was out of sight, I did run.

7

I crossed the complex again so fast it would've made Jesse Owens proud. The transformers started their shrieking melody again at some point, but I paid no attention. I rounded the corner of the alley where I'd left Mickey at a dead sprint and stumbled to a halt.

The grassy lane was empty.

Mickey was gone.

MONDAY MORNING

1

I stayed in bed even later the next morning, and felt even more exhausted.

I'd finally come home around one in the morning, after combing the complex for Mickey. There was no sign of him other than his leash still tied to the tree, ending in a frayed edge. My first instinct had been to pound on Jacob's door, to sic Tate or the cops on him, but my rational side told me that was knee-jerk. I had no reason to think he'd taken my dog, and accusing him of it would bring up a lot of questions I didn't know how to answer.

Usually Mickey would be up on the bed by now, trying to smell my morning breath. The apartment felt even emptier without him. For most of the last year, he'd been my only companion, the only living creature I could stand to have near me. Martha's flyer muscled its way into my head, followed by a brief but vivid flash of the mutilated feline in the back of Tate's golf cart.

I felt sick.

And thirsty. Jesus, I hadn't wanted a shot of something, anything, this bad in a long time. I could probably have taken a belt of drain cleaner right then, if it would've gotten me drunk.

Outside, the Squall blasted. I popped four preemptive aspirin, threw on clothes, fixed a quick bite to eat (forcing myself not to fix another huge meal to satisfy my growing appetite), then hopped on the computer to make missing dog posters. I couldn't leave Mickey alone out there; whatever happened to him was my fault. I found a picture of him with his ears pinned back that Darcy took at Halloween the year we got him. The bottom of the poster had my first name and cell number. I deliberated, then added 'REWARD,' and printed the damn things until I ran out of paper.

A knock came at my back door as I got up to leave.

Katie stood on the patio, with a bruise across her throat in the shape of a handprint.

2

"It's really not as bad as it looks."

"Thank god for that, because it looks pretty bad."

"Really, it was just...an accident."

"Oh sure. I accidentally choke people all the time."

Katie sat on my couch now, talking while she went out of her way not to meet my eyes. She put a hand over the purple and blue marks across her throat and winced. Looking at the outlines of those fingers on her delicate neck—like the Thanksgiving turkeys they have kindergarteners trace on construction paper—made my jaw clench. She looked around the apartment and said, "Man, Mr. Jefferson, you've been living here for a year? This place looks empty!"

I crossed my arms and used my sternest teacher voice. "Don't change the subject, Miss Adler."

She looked up at me. Tears brimmed in her eyes. "She didn't mean to."

I sighed and knelt on the other side of the coffee table so I could get even with her. "I know, I'm not saying she did, but Katie...this can't go on. We have to call someone and—"

"No, no!" She threw up her hands. "You CANNOT do that, Mr. Jefferson, I-I...I don't give you permission!"

"Well fortunately, that's not your choice. I'm obligated to report any suspected cases of child abuse."

"It's not *child abuse!*" Katie sounded horrified by the term. Of course she was; no one wants to believe they're susceptible to the awful things the rest of the world goes through. We *watch* robberies and homicides on the news, we never *live* them. "That's not what happened at all!"

"Then why don't you tell me what happened?"

She pulled at her lower lip for several seconds before speaking. "We were fighting again last night."

"About?"

"Same stuff as always. Me going out this weekend when my friends get back. It just got worse than usual, that's all. We screamed at each other, and...I kinda called her a bitch... and then she ...snapped." Her eyes drew away as the memory played out in her head.

"She choked you," I corrected.

"Just for a couple of seconds!"

I almost laughed at that. She was full of excuses. I couldn't help wondering why she'd come here in the first place, and then had to remind myself that, with her friends all out of town for spring break, she had no one to talk to. "It doesn't matter, Katie. That's not right."

"But I probably deserved it!"

"Don't you dare say that," I snapped. My tone caused

her to jump. I felt ashamed, but I didn't apologize or back down. If I let her start internalizing responsibility now, the rest of her life would be a series of shack-ups with men who used their fists to show their love.

After a few seconds of the staring contest, she nodded and sniffled. "She's not usually like this. She's been acting kinda...*weird* lately."

"Weird how?" I asked, even though I suddenly had a pretty good idea. The image of Samantha Adler performing that funky spasm yesterday was one of the many images on a repeat playlist in my head.

Katie's brow furrowed as she struggled to find the right words. Her hand stole to the bruise on her throat and stroked it distractedly as she spoke. "It's like...for the last few days, she's been eating."

I shifted uncomfortably. "Eating?"

"Yeah, like...a *lot*. Like everything in the apartment, then she went back to the store to get more. And she keeps getting distracted. Staring off into space, drifting off midsentence, stuff like that. Yesterday afternoon—before the fight—I caught her with her nose against my aquarium, watching the fish like they were the most fascinating thing on earth. And she...sh-she had one hand down her pants...and I think she was...*you know*." The girl's cheeks burned a quick scarlet flush. I knew what she was implying, but when I tried to conjure the image of Samantha Adler masturbating, disgust stopped me cold. Luckily, Katie hurried on. "And she keeps disappearing for a few hours at a time. I don't know where to, I'll hear the door shut and she's missing, but the car's still in the garage. She left again last night after we got done fighting. I waited a few minutes and then tried to follow her, but she was gone. I walked the whole complex and couldn't find her, so I came home. She didn't show up until close to three, and then this morning she wouldn't even get out of bed to go to work. I had to sneak out after she fell asleep."

I sat for a moment, saying nothing as I mulled over her story.

Silent tears spilled down Katie's cheeks. She wiped at them with the heel of one hand. "Maybe…maybe it's that stupid thing outside, the one making that noise. It's probably giving us all cancer or something."

I'd been so intent on the conversation that, for a blessed few minutes, I'd forgotten all about the Squall, let it slip back into my subconscious. Now, as if noticing it all over again had given it renewed confidence, the electric screech came crashing in on me.

Nevertheless, I shook my head. "I know it's awful, but it's not dangerous."

At the time, I think I even still believed that.

She put her hands over her ears and pressed, reminding me of some movie where asylum inmates had done the same thing. "God, it's driving me *crazy!* I have a headache all the time! I just want it to stop! Do you think if we talked to Martha, she could move all of us to an empty apartment until they get it fixed?"

"Wouldn't make any difference," I muttered. "It's the whole complex. All the transformers are doing it."

She reached across the table suddenly and grasped my hand in both of hers. "Please, *please* promise you won't call anybody or say anything about this!"

"Katie, I don't know. If it happens again…"

"It won't, I swear! Look, I just have to make it a few more months and then I leave for college! If I have to, I can even get out of the apartment when I turn eighteen!"

"And go where?"

"I don't know. Wherever. Jacob says I can crash with him anytime I need to."

"No." I shook my head adamantly. "Absolutely not. That's worse than you staying at home."

She frowned. "I know you don't like him Mr. Jefferson, but I've known him since elementary school. He used to protect me from this gang of kids that hassled me every day on the way home. He's a good guy."

"He's a drug dealer, Katie. And he brought a gun to school."

"He says it wasn't his."

I sighed. It was the story he'd been giving for years. "Yeah, well, he's a liar. I saw him take it out of his locker and put it in his bag. God knows what he would've done with it if I hadn't."

That day had been a nightmare, the school locked down, siren blaring over the PA, students and fellow teachers cowering in their classrooms as Jacob was dragged from my junior English class in handcuffs, proclaiming his innocence the whole way. Before the school security officer could get there, I forced Jacob to stand at the back of the room, with his backpack between my feet, where a very loaded 9mm pistol waited. He stood against the dry erase board, bottom lip quivering, trying to explain to me that it wasn't his, it wasn't his, he didn't know how it'd gotten in there, and begging me to believe him. I watched him, took in his desperate, pleading face, and then looked away, out the window.

Before that day, Jacob Tinsley had never been one of my favorite students, but I never would've placed him on the level of monster as Harris and Klebold.

"Mr. Jefferson…" Katie tried again, but I cut her off.

"Look Katie, if you want me to promise not to say anything about your mother, then you have to promise me you'll stay away from Jacob Tinsley from now on."

She nodded reluctantly. I realized the tactic had probably moved me from comforting ear to controlling authority figure in her mind, but, more so than that, I was suddenly acutely aware that I had a female student alone in my home, holding my hand. God, if her mother showed up, I'd be out of a job before the end of the week, if not in jail. I gently pulled away, and her eyes fell across the stack of flyers on the table. She held one up.

"Oh my god. Mickey? When did—?"

"Last night. He…got away from me. I figured I'd put these up today, hopefully someone's seen him."

She stood and grabbed the stack of paper. "Then let's get going."

3

Together, we canvassed the entire complex, and even stapled some to those utility poles leading up to the Estates and a few on the surrounding empty streets. We attached them to the clips that hung beside each garage door so residents could grab flyers and take-out menus as they drove in, shoved them under windshield wipers and left them on doormats. The Squall eventually quieted, leaving us in the silence of a warm, humid afternoon.

When we reached the far end of the grounds, I let Katie take Jacob's building, while I walked around 32. The garage door at 3204 was still closed, but I stayed away from it this time. That whole sequence of events—the contraption Connelly had been constructing, the frantic shuffling around the transformer—seemed like another dream in daylight.

On a weekday, with most of the residents at work, the complex was usually deserted. And indeed, Katie and I saw barely anyone the entire time we were out.

But the place didn't feel empty.

I sensed eyes crawling over us everywhere we went. The sensation grew so heavy I kept turning around to check over my shoulder. I caught a few ghostly faces peering out of windows as we passed, enough to make me feel like the foreign gunslinger in a spaghetti western. Something had happened to this place since Saturday, when I'd taken Beth on the tour. It didn't feel like that happy community anymore; it seemed more like some forgotten corner of the eastern bloc. I half expected to see abandoned cars on the streets and hobos standing in the alleys, warming their hands over burning trash cans. From one open window on the second floor, the unmistakable sounds of rough copulation drifted down— moaning and snorting and a frenzied, almost animalistic growling—and I hurried Katie past without comment. The only live human beings we did see was a woman sitting on the curb bawling with her head in her hands, and two elderly men standing in front of their respective buildings, yelling at each other about something I couldn't get the gist of, one of them tearing chunks of meat that looked almost raw out of a turkey leg bigger than his bicep. Ordinarily I would've asked the woman if she needed help, but as it stood, we gave all these folks a wide berth.

"This is kinda creeping me out," Katie whispered.

"How's that?"

She stopped in the middle of Dandelion Boulevard and turned in a slow circle, staring up at the blank building fronts. "Don't you feel it? It's like there's something in the air. It feels...I don't know...heavy. Angry."

I felt it. Of course I did. But—stubborn, rational creature that I am—I answered, "It's lack of sleep. From the damn transformers. And the heat. Everybody's just irritable, that's all."

"I don't know. What if...what if my mom isn't the only one spazzing out?"

"Civil unrest," I murmured. I meant it as a joke, but the words fell so flat, I might as well be spitting stones.

"Huh?"

"Nothing. It's nothing. We're freaking ourselves out. This isn't a *Twilight Zone* episode, real life doesn't work like that."

Her words kept coming back to me as we walked home in silence. Something was happening; I could sense that pressure all around us, like storm clouds on the horizon. My mind felt like an overflowing garbage bin filled with the crushed up pieces of some vast machine, and if I could fit enough of those pieces back together, the last couple of days would begin to make sense.

We took the pathway along the periphery of the complex back toward home. As we came up the fence line and turned into the alley that separated our buildings—the Squall assaulting us with a new cycle—those answers felt close. Right on the tip of my tongue.

But they were forgotten as two hundred pounds of snarling muscle, fur, and teeth smashed into my chest.

4

I went straight over backward, heels over ass, landing on my back next to the squealing transformer. The ground came up hard and slammed the air out of my lungs. The last of the missing dog posters fluttered down around me like a snowstorm of giant flakes. Lying on my back, I turned my head to look at what just hit me.

Yonkers stood two yards away, head lowered between his massive shoulders, teeth bared. A rumble that seemed as loud as a lawnmower built deep in the Rottweiler's throat and came spilling from his open jaws.

"Yonkers?" I choked out. The Squall pulsed in my ears, making my voice sound wavery. "Buddy, it's me, it's Elliot." I was afraid to sit up, afraid to move. The dog's entire body vibrated with rage. At the sound of his name, his lips drew back even more, showing an extra inch of yellow incisors. I'd never seen that big dumb mutt so much as bark.

Rabies, I thought. *Dear Christ, it's gotta be rabies.*

"Katie, do *not* move!" I yelled, without taking my eyes off Yonkers. The girl stood frozen a few yards from the animal's left haunch, eyes wide. She nodded quickly.

Yonkers snarled and took a step toward me. From my vantage point on the ground, I could see a bloated erection dangling between his hind legs, so long that the tip of the blood red organ dragged in the grass when he moved.

"*Schrader!*" I bellowed. No way I could get off the ground if this animal came at me. He bit at the air and then shook his head back and forth so fast it was nothing but a blur. His front legs wobbled.

I turned over and tried to scramble to my feet.

Yonkers charged.

I was still on all fours when he reached me. His muzzle locked around the meaty part of my right forearm just below the elbow. Teeth shredded skin as powerful jaws crushed down on the appendage.

A scream punched its way out of me, matched by the one Katie let loose. I tried to yank the arm away, but Yonkers locked on like a vise. I managed to get my legs under me and stumbled back a few steps, dragging the dog along. He shook his head, ripping at the flesh. I went loose, allowing my arm to flail with the bite to minimize the damage. Pain boiled through me.

The primal will to survive took over. I swung one leg back and landed a glancing kick in Yonker's side. The blow wasn't much—in fact, the packed muscle on the Rottie's side probably hurt my foot a lot worse—but it caused him to let go and retreat, with a tiny flap of my skin dangling from his mouth. His tongue flicked out, sucking it down his gullet.

I clutched my wounded arm, trying not to let panic control me. Blood was everywhere, streaming down my hand, splashing on my clothes, dripping on the vibrantly green grass like an abstract painting. My vision blurred looking at it.

Yonkers paced in a tight quarter circle around me, shaking his head in short whips. Pink smeared his dark muzzle. I looked behind me. The alley stretched out long; I didn't think I could make it to my door.

But, as I turned back, I spotted a long pair of familiar wooden handles jutting from the bottom of the shrubbery that hugged the building, just a few feet to my left.

I watched Yonkers. The dog twitched all over. His eyes fixed on me and seemed to pulse with the fire burning up his brain.

Katie broke the standoff. She charged past us, sprinting toward her patio door.

Yonker's head came up, zeroed in. He went after her.

"*No!*" I kicked him again as he passed by, landing my toes hard enough in his ass to make him yip. He turned on me instead, coming in low, snapping at my ankles so hard his teeth clacked. I dove toward the bushes like a ball player sliding into home.

Sharp leaves jabbed me. My bloody hands found the hedge trimmers Javier had left here yesterday morning when

I distracted him. I pulled them free and rolled over in time to see Yonkers flying through the air at me.

He landed full out across my stomach, those wicked teeth aimed for my jugular. I managed to use one side of the clippers to awkwardly knock his muzzle away, but I couldn't get back up with his weight on me. The Squall continued to play like a violin in hell, orchestrating our struggle.

Denying the instinct to protect my face, I stretched my arms over my head and angled the hedge trimmer blades back over my eyes, then opened the handles.

When Yonkers swung back to go at my throat again, he was forced to stick his neck right into the glinting metal V formed by the trimmers.

I slammed those fuckers closed with all my strength.

A gush of warm liquid spilled over my face, but it wasn't egg this time. Yonkers still moved, so I jerked the clippers open and chopped them shut again, felt the twin blades bury deep in gristle and bone. The dog thrashed a few more times on top of me and then grew still. I rolled his body off—the head waggled freely, attached by no more than spinal column and a few strands of muscle—and stood, wiping blood out of my eyes.

Katie waited at the end of the alley with her cell phone already out, staring at me coated in crimson with the mostly decapitated corpse at my feet. Beyond her, the Jock Trinity watched from the parking lot, along with an older black man that I didn't recognize. I held out a hand to tell them all to stay back, but before I could say anything, a door slammed behind me. I turned to find Schrader bulldozing out from his apartment. The squat man made a beeline for me.

"John, Yonkers goddamned attacked Katie and me." I went to meet him, pausing once to spit out the coppery tang of canine blood. "I didn't want to hurt him, but he would've killed us bo—"

Schrader never spoke, never hesitated as he reared back and popped me one right across the temple. I sensed it coming and pulled back just enough to keep it from bouncing my brain around the inside of my skull like a racquetball, but it still caused my blurred vision to triple.

He followed after me, throwing out one fist after the other, striking me wherever he could.

"Stop, it wasn't my fault!" I shouted, trying to block as many of the blows as possible. My blood spattered on him at every impact. With the throbbing wound in my right arm, I was practically handicapped.

I got a good look at his face though, on the other side of those mechanical punches. Even though his eyes were as vacant as when he harassed Beth, the rest of his features were alive with mirthful rage, as if taking supreme satisfaction in this.

And just before he landed a blow across my chin that put my lights out for good, the idea occurred to me that this assault might have nothing to do with the fact that I had just killed his dog.

5

"So the dog was missing for how long?"

"No, that dog wasn't missing at all."

"Then what are all the flyers for?"

"I told you, *my* dog is missing, but that doesn't have anything to do with the dog that attacked me."

The EMT—a smarmy-looking kid in his mid 20's—finished wrapping gauze around my arm as I sat on the rear bumper of the ambulance parked in front of my building. A good-sized crowd had gathered and milled at the sides of the street and behind the vehicle in a semi-circle, which confirmed my suspicion that the complex wasn't as empty as it appeared. Beth wasn't there, but I did spot Martha and Tony among the looky-loos. These people didn't have the usual zeal that rubberneckers tend to get; most of them were as dull-eyed as bored churchgoers in the middle of the sermon. I also caught sight of Katie's tear-streaked face over by her building, along with her mother. The girl had put on a thick-collared sweater, one that was sure to be sweltering in this weather but which completely hid the bruise on her throat. Schrader stood by Beth's building in the alley, sandwiched between two cops. His gaze stayed rooted on me as they grilled him.

The EMT secured the bandage, then picked up a mini-flashlight and pulled first one of my eyelids down and then the other to shine the beam inside. "No concussion, which is good news. We can still take you in to the hospital if you want, just to be safe."

"You kidding? With the insurance the school provides, it'll cost me a thousand bucks to hitch a ride with you. If I start feeling dizzy, I'll drive myself. But what do I do about this?" I held up my right arm, which felt like a flaming log below the elbow. Bruises ran up and down my torso from Schrader's attack and the left side of my jaw had swollen where he'd gotten in that last good hit, but the bite overshadowed all the other injuries.

"It's really not as bad as it could've been with an animal that size. He took a chunk of flesh, but there doesn't seem to be any muscle damage. Even the bleeding's slowed. It's up to you if you wanna see a doctor for stitches."

"Yeah, but what about rabies? That dog was acting like a coked-up maniac."

"We've got the body bagged. It'll be shipped to the lab that does the testing. They should be in touch with you within 48 hours to let you know if you need to get to treated or not."

"Great," I muttered, taking bacterial wipes from a box beside him to scrub at the last of the blood on my face and hands. My clothes were a total loss; they looked like the end result of a gruesome slasher film. "Just fucking fantastic."

The EMT turned away, but before I could stand, one of the cops who'd been with Schrader walked up, a guy about my age. He stood before me holding a spiral notebook. The other officer was still with my neighbor, one hand on his shoulder.

"Good afternoon, I'm Officer Claret. How're you feeling, Mr…" He checked the pad in his hand. "…Jefferson?"

"I've been a whole helluva lot better."

"Sir, can you tell me—just briefly—the situation from your viewpoint?"

"Sure. I came around the far corner of the alley down there and Schrader's Rottweiler attacked me outta nowhere. It bit my arm and didn't show any sign of stopping there, so I had to kill the damn thing in self defense. Then he—"

Claret held up a finger from the pad. "Did you agitate the animal in any way?"

"I didn't even know he was there. Like I said, he came outta nowhere."

"And did you attempt any other resolution before you resorted to putting the animal down?"

I gave him a look that suggested he'd been riding miniature school buses his entire life. "Yeah, I tried sending a calligraphied note inviting him to stop tearing my arm off, but, surprisingly, he didn't even RSVP."

Claret frowned. "No need to be sarcastic, sir. It's just that, with the extreme method of…" He groped for the right word. "…*execution*…one begins to wonder if there are other factors at play."

"Well excuse me if I didn't have an opportunity to prepare the lethal injection syringe. And what do you mean, 'other factors?'"

He waved a dismissive hand. Claret was obviously a different breed of officer than Tate, getting off on the officiality of his job. "Continue with your story, Mr. Jefferson."

I eyed him another second before complying. "So after that, Schrader comes out and just starts beating the holy hell outta me. Knocked me unconscious. I don't even know what happened after that."

"One of your neighbors broke up the altercation." Claret pointed at the black guy I'd seen in the parking lot earlier, now standing in the crowd with his arm around a woman and two young kids in front of them.

"Okay then, ask him what happened, if you don't believe me. And that young lady right over there witnessed the whole thing."

"Yes, we've spoken to her." Claret nodded. "She verified the assault was unprovoked. But Mr. Schrader is claiming that the two of you have had an ongoing argument about his dog for some time, and he believes you may have used the opportunity to kill it out of spite."

"*That's bullshit!*" I sputtered. "I've asked him not to leave dog shit on the lawn, but that's no reason for me to butcher him!"

"Then is this a reason?" He pulled a folded sheet of paper from the breast pocket of his uniform and opened it to reveal one of my missing dog posters.

"What are you talking about?"

Claret bobbed his head side-to-side as he spoke. "Mr. Schrader said that you embarrassed him the other day in front of another one of your neighbors. So maybe when your dog disappeared, it was natural for you to assume that he had something to do with it, in retaliation. Maybe he even did, I'm not saying either way. But then maybe you felt like killing *his* dog was the next step in the escalating war you two are in—"

"Wait, wait." I held my arms up and flinched from the pain that rocketed up the right one. "There's no war. You're making all this up."

"I see it all the time, Mr. Jefferson. These neighborly disputes get out of hand fast because you can't get away from the other person. Having an enemy in constant, close proximity to where you live and sleep unsettles a man. It's a territorial thing."

I shook my head adamantly. "I didn't do anything wrong, and I'm not answering any more of these questions. You wanna charge me or something, go right ahead. Until then, what are you doing with Schrader?"

He ran his tongue around the inside of his cheek for a long moment before relenting. "For starters, he's getting a pretty hefty fine for having a dog loose without a leash. As for his physical assault on you, if you decide to press charges, we're willing to take him into custody."

I sat for a moment and looked across the lawn at Schrader. He glowered back, but the anger on his face was much better than the gleeful, dead-eyed mask it had been while he beat me.

I didn't hate the man, I never had. So how the hell had it come to this?

"No, I'm not pressing charges. The man's dog was just decapitated, I'd be a little pissed off too." I gave Claret a pointed look. "But I guess that doesn't sound like the response of a man involved in a savage war with his neighbor, huh?"

The officer rolled his eyes and pulled a card out of his breast pocket. "If you have any more issues with Mr. Schrader, you can contact me at this number. Have a nice day."

He walked away and gave the other cop a wave. This one let go of Schrader, who gave me one last glare, brushed past the cop, and stomped up the alley toward his apartment. The officers got in their patrol car and drove away.

6

The crowd began to disperse. It was like watching kids return to class after recess. They shuffled away, shoulders hunched, casting mistrustful glances back at me, like I was the bad guy in all this. A few of them hung back, perhaps waiting to see what today's entertainment would do next. Martha approached me first, wringing her hands over her massive breasts. "Are you all right?"

"I'm fine," I told her, hopping off the ambulance bumper.

"I'm so sorry this happened. Mr. Schrader will receive a stern warning from management. Any further incidents and he'll be evicted from the complex."

"No, look, don't do anything like that. It was just a misunderstanding."

She nodded uncertainly, but looked relieved. "And Mickey is missing?"

"Yeah. He...probably just ran away or something." She opened her mouth and I put a hand up to stop her. "I don't wanna hear it, Martha. He ran away. That's all."

She sniffed. "Well, I'm just trying to help."

"You wanna help, then make sure the power company takes care of that goddamned buzzing noise. I already called and left them a message, but something has gotta be done."

Her brow furrowed. "What do you mean?"

"That screeching noise from the transformers!" Her utter cluelessness made my jaw clench with frustration. "Even if you can't hear it, surely someone else must've complained by now!"

It took a handful of seconds for her to answer. Then she said slowly, "I have no idea what you're talking about, Mr. Jefferson. We've had a lot of complaints the last few days, but nothing about a buzzing noise, as far as I'm aware." Was there a mischievous gleam in her eye as she said this, or was it my imagination? "I can check with Tony and see—?"

"Never mind. I just wanna go inside and get some sleep. If I can." I brushed past her, but before I could make it into the alley, the black man who had apparently pulled Schrader off my unconscious body rushed out of the remains of the departing crowd to block my path.

"I'm sorry, I can't remember for sure, but…it's Elliot, right?" he asked. He was a slender guy in his forties, dressed in khakis with cargo pockets and a navy polo shirt. "Elliot Jefferson?"

"Yeah. Who are you?" I didn't even try to keep the impatience from my voice.

"Kirk Gordon. I live upstairs in your building."

"Oh, right. Kirk, yeah, I'm sorry." Now that I studied his lean face and gray-flecked hair, I did recognize him. We'd had a brief conversation about a month after I moved in, where we introduced ourselves and talked about me being a teacher, and he'd invited me to a dinner with his family that I weaseled out of. I knew they lived in the unit above Schrader, but not much else. He had the serious, studious air of an accountant or banker, someone for whom logicality was a way of life. "Listen, thanks for helping me out. I think Schrader probably would've killed me if not for you."

Kirk nodded sternly. "Truth be told, I don't think you're exaggerating. He kicked you twice while you were laid out before I could get there, and looked like he wanted to keep going. Even took a swing at me after I pulled him off. Then it was like he… woke up or something. Stood there blinking at me for a few seconds and then stomped off until the police got here."

"What can I say, I tend to bring out the best in people. Thanks again."

I started to go around him, but he hurried to keep in step with me. "I overheard you talking to Martha. About that horrible noise from the electrical boxes."

"You can hear it?" I realized the transformer in our alley must be even worse for him, since it was even closer, just under his windows. In fact, the only person under heavier bombardment by our piece of the Squall would be Schrader, followed by Garrett, Rick and Miles on the opposite side.

And then Mrs. Isaacs, the old lady sequestered all alone in her upstairs unit, directly across from Kirk.

Comparatively speaking, Beth, the McCafferys, the Adlers, and myself all had it pretty easy.

Kirk nodded in response to my question, but his eyes were troubled. "Normally, I'd be inclined to think you're crazy for even asking a question like that…except Teresa—that's my wife—she can't seem to hear it either." He discreetly cut his eyes toward the short black woman he'd had his arm around earlier. She stood further up the curb, out of earshot, listening to the boy and girl that might have been ten and six, respectively. They were cute kids, pointing excitedly at the ambulance as they chattered to their mother. "Or more like, she doesn't notice. Because it...I don't know, it sort of..."

"Blends in with all the other background noise," I finished for him.

"Yeah, that's it! That's exactly it. And no matter how much I try to point it out, she and the kids don't seem bothered in the least." He sighed. "We've been out of town. Took Jaime and Jamilla out of school a few days early and went to Florida for spring break. Disneyworld, Universal...if there's a theme park in that state, we saw it. The kids loved it, but I think I wore out two pairs of shoes from all the walking. Anyway, we got back last night, and the whole complex seems different somehow. We've lived here three years, and all of a sudden, there's this...this *vibe*... You have any idea what I'm talking about?"

Almost Katie's exact words, coming from this man. I swept a hand down my chest at the bloodstains coating my shirt. "You're talking to someone who just decapitated a dog. Yeah, I've noticed things are a tad bit off around here."

He looked startled for a second, then a smile slowly unfurled across his face. He began to chuckle. The laughter spread to me. It felt good, normal somehow, a way to expose our mutual fears—worries, suspicions, whatever we called them—to the naked light of day. I just hoped we weren't trivializing what gut instinct was trying to tell us.

"All right neighbor, nice talking to you." He offered his hand, which I shook. "Feel free to come by if you need anything."

"You do the same."

He moved around me, heading toward the opposite side of the building where his front door must be, and I continued on toward my patio, wanting nothing more than to escape from other people.

My wish was not yet to be granted.

As I reached the edge of my patio, a voice behind me growled, "Stay away from my daughter."

I spun. Samantha Adler hunkered in one of the chairs across the alley, lying in wait for me, clutching a huge, leather-bound Bible in one hand. Her other lay on the tabletop in front of her, fingers jumping every few seconds so that the nails clicked against the glass.

"The Good Book says that a rebellious teacher spouts foolishness, Mr. Jefferson, and I believe you to be a rebellious teacher. One that is leading Katherine astray."

"What does the 'good book' say about crushing your child's trachea?" As soon as the words were out, I instantly wished I'd kept my big, fat trap shut. I already had far too many enemies in 'constant, close proximity' to where I slept.

But Samantha only gave me a venom-dipped smile. "I don't want her mixed in with you, with all the trouble you're bringing down on your head." Her voice was slow, each word measured, but her eyes jittered in their sockets. "She's a good girl, a very good girl, and she will eventually heed the voice. As soon as she cleanses her impurities so she can open her ears and *listen*."

My mouth swung open. I gaped at her.

Having said her piece, Samantha Adler stood up and retreated into her apartment.

MONDAY EVENING

1

While looking for more aspirin, I found an expired bottle of Percocet in the back of my medicine cabinet from when I'd had gall bladder surgery. Staring at the label—which showed a three-year-past expiration date—I couldn't figure how I still had them, especially after the move. If nothing else, I should've gotten rid of them during the detox. AA stresses how easy it is to go from one addiction to another. One fellow member—a guy that went from chugging vodka to compulsively swimming laps until his BMI dropped into negative digits and his skin was like tissue paper stretched over his skeleton—called it 'monkey swapping'.

I held the bottle in my hand for a long time, turning it over and over in my palm, and finally decided that my need was legitimate. Alcoholism can only define you for so long, I guess. I downed one to dull the fire in my arm, then took one more to make sure I could get to sleep.

But I flushed the rest. Just in case.

Then I called the power company again, and this time got a live operator. She, at least, admitted they'd received a few other complaints about the noise and assured me we were on the repair list and a technician would be out as soon as possible. And, even though her tone came across a tad exasperated—as though I was some uptight prick calling to bitch about a penny overcharge on my bill—it made me feel better just hearing her say it, like the laugh Kirk and I had shared. The world seemed on its way to making sense again.

I showered, careful to keep my bandaged arm from getting wet. I scrubbed blood out of every crease, wrinkle, and fold of my body, though whether it was mine or Yonkers's I couldn't say. All that pink-tinged water swirling down the drain reminded me of the opening of *Psycho*. The warmth felt heavenly though. By the time I finished, the Percocet had taken effect and the Squall's endless grind sounded far, far away. I almost went to sleep standing up.

However, when I laid down on the couch to try for a nap, my own rapid fire thoughts held me awake.

Something had to be done about Samantha Adler. That much was clear. The woman had lost her mind. What she had said to me, in that straight forward, no-nonsense tone... it was utter insanity.

Wasn't it?

Just like Schrader yesterday? And your mystery caller Friday night? Cause it seems to me that they're all spouting the same *insanity.*

An old, well-worn quote from Robert Pirsig popped into my head: when one person suffers from a delusion, it's called insanity; when many people suffer from a delusion, it's called religion.

I sensed that veil again, the one that had been laid over the world like a drop cloth to hide some awful truth. The idea of lifting even a single corner to peek underneath terrified me, but it felt like the only way to get answers.

That image remained with me as I finally drifted off.

2

I dreamed again, terrible nightmares that had me thrashing and flailing back to muddy consciousness every few minutes. In one of these, Beth and I were having a picnic in front of the complex management office, under the trees where Jacob and his crew had chased me on Saturday. I knew it was a date, in that way you just inherently sense things in a dream, but it didn't feel anywhere close to a first date. An intimacy existed between us, the easy familiarity of a relationship that's gotten comfortable, but still new enough to not be stale. A smorgasbord of food lay before us, and we lay side by side on a blanket, wolfing down gigantic sandwiches and egg salad out of a basket like a scene from a Norman Rockwell painting, and the quality of the dream was so crisp, so *stark*, I could smell pine in the air. It was sunny out, a beautiful day, but as we ate, the light faded in hiccuping degrees, and a cold wind began to whip the tree limbs above us into a frenzy. We became trapped on an island of light in the midst of chaos. Further out in the darkness, shadows moved, encircling us, dancing to strange rhythms, chanting in alien tongues. Beth leaned into me, shivering, and said she was scared, but I wasn't, I wanted her, and when I began to kiss her neck and slide my hands up her waist, she struggled. Noise roared in my ears, a blaring, strident, white-smear of sound that was part storm and wind and part electrical shriek. But within it was a voice, a barely audible voice, and it was telling me to heed, to give up and give in, that surrender was the greatest feeling in the world. And, as I began to savage Beth, to tear at her clothes and skin, to beat her and fuck her all at the same time, I could only agree.

3

I woke long after sundown, shuddering in a puddle of ice cold sweat. The effects of the Percocets had worn off fast, but there was still enough in my system to give a hazy quality to the lamplight beside me. I could taste the gooey, mayo-heavy residue of egg salad in my mouth from the dream. I sat still for a minute, waiting for my racing heart to calm. The Squall had quieted again, but above me, I could hear Dan and Joan going at it, the wordless rumble of their angry voices trading back and forth between his bass and her falsetto, like the tide at the beach going in and out.

I felt like absolute shit. Once again, I'd been kept on the ragged edge of sleep instead of getting in deep, where I could recharge my batteries. The expired Percs hadn't been enough to overpower the Squall. If anything, they'd made me even groggier. I couldn't remember ever being so tired in my entire life.

This couldn't go on. I had the attorney's office in the morning, and I needed my wits about me. For the first time, I considered going into the city and finding a motel room. My conscience tried to argue, told me it would be like abandoning Mickey, but I felt positive the situation would look clearer—saner—after one solid night of sleep.

As I sat there trying to wake up and steady my nerves, my cell went off, with an unknown number. I hesitated for a moment, but since it wasn't actually blocked, I answered.

"*Poor Mr. Jefferson,*" the person on the other end crooned in baby-talk cadences. "*Did him wose his wittle doggy?*"

"Shut the fuck up, Jacob," I grunted.

Teasing, raucous laughter. "I don't remember you talkin like that in the classroom, teach. We mighta got along better if you had. Well, that, and if you weren't so fulla shit it was leakin outta your ears."

"How'd you get this number?"

"You plastered it across the entire complex today, re-tard."

I grimaced at my own stupidity. "Did you take him? If you did, just give him back and I swear it won't go any further."

This seemed to amuse him even more. "What is it with you and blamin shit on me, man? Seriously, it's becoming, like, a *habit*. But you know all about habits...don't you?"

"*You goddamn worthless dirtbag!*" I roared. I prided myself on patience with my students, diplomacy, but being wheedled about my addiction by this shithead pushed me to an edge I always managed to stay well away from in the classroom. "*Did you take him or not?*"

"*No, I don't have your fuckin dog!*" he shouted back. "*But I hope whoever does cuts off his head, like you did to that Rottweiler!*"

I hung up. My heart pounded against the underside of my ribs.

But when the phone rang again almost instantly, I snatched it back up.

"*You listen to me, you little shit—!*"

"Woah, Jesus! Bad time, Jefferson?"

It took me a moment to place the new voice. "Beth?"

"That depends. You call all the girls little shits, or is that honor strictly mine?"

"No, I...I thought...you were my ex-wife. It's nothing. Sorry about that." The words were out before I could think better. That certainly wasn't how I would've chosen to tell her about Darcy. I ran a hand down my face, trying to wake myself up enough to handle this conversation.

"Ah," was all she said on the subject. My cheeks burned when I realized the fury she'd heard in my tone. Not just a divorcé, but a divorcé with a temper. This would be the point when she started backpedalling, finding excuses, avoiding me when we saw each other around the complex.

"So what's up?" I asked, trying to sound overly cheerful to compensate.

"I just got home and saw your flyer on my door. You find your dog?"

Had I left a flyer on Beth's door? I didn't think so, I didn't even remember going around that side of her building, but maybe Katie had. "Um, no, not yet."

"Well, that sucks. You okay?"

"I...I really don't know. It's been a long, strange day."

"You wanna get out for a while?"

"What, now?"

"Sure, why not? We're both on spring break, right? Unless you need to take the false teeth out and get into your nightgown."

"Nope, I'm up," I lied. "I'll be up for hours."

"All right, meet me in the alley in five. And wear those cute little running shorts of yours."

4

I wasn't up for this. I should've told her I had to be up early. If anything, I should be out looking for Mickey again, not panting after my attractive new neighbor. But I jumped off the couch, slapped my face a few times to knock the last of the Percs out of my weary brain, and changed into my running clothes. It was just after eleven when I stepped onto the patio and locked the door behind me.

The alley lay steeped in darkness; a chill worked over me as I stood and stared at the spot just a few yards away where I had killed Yonkers. It was too dark to see color, but I imagined splashes of red in the grass anyway. The entire episode replayed in my head, what it felt like to close the shears around the dog's neck...

"Hey." Beth came around the corner of the building, wearing running shorts of her own, and a sleeveless yellow t-shirt short enough to reveal the lower third of a taut midriff. She looked so good—in an easy, casual sort of way—that I was left a little breathless. I recalled my dream, that closeness between us, and suddenly the idea of slipping an arm around that narrow waist seemed entirely normal. I wondered what she would do if I tried.

She saw the bandage on my arm and the bruises on my face and asked, "What happened to you?"

I decided to tell the truth, before she heard it somewhere else. "Schrader's dog attacked me, and I had to put it down. Then Schrader put *me* down."

"That guy just gets more and more appealing." She grabbed my chin and turned my head back and forth to get a better look at the bruises in the distant glow of the closest streetlight. A flicker of a grin crossed her pink lips. "Wait a minute. This wouldn't have anything to do with you so gallantly defending my honor the other day, would it?"

I shrugged. "Could be. I lost a lotta blood, you know. Almost died."

She smirked. "Well, I wanted someone to go with me to check out the weight room, but if you're not up to it, I guess I could go alone..."

I gave my arm a waggle to prove it still worked, and managed not to grimace at the pain. "All systems go."

We made our way through the complex once more, a nighttime version of the tour I'd given her. The evening had bloomed muggy and hot, and the streets were just as still and expectant as earlier this afternoon. Beth wanted to know about Mickey's disappearance, and I gave her what details I could before turning the conversation to more neutral areas, like her new job. She was so eager to talk, it struck me she must be even more lonely than Katie; new girl in town, far away from home, and I just happened to be her first acquaintance. Whether that would prove good for me in the long run was anybody's guess.

At the weight room, I used my key to open the door. The long, rectangular space abutted the rear of the office and contained a myriad of top-of-the-line workout machines. I'd come down a few times over the winter, when it was too cold to run outside, but only late at night when I knew the chances of seeing a neighbor were slim. One long wall was all mirrors, the other a bank of windows that overlooked the pool. I started the timers for the lights and ceiling fans.

All of the workout benches sat side-by-side down the middle of the room. Beth hopped on one that looked like something from a medieval torture chamber and started adjusting straps and pulleys.

At the far end of the row was a blank space on the floor where another of the machines should've been. I wondered if it now sat in the garage of 3204, part of whatever science fair project he was building in there.

I moved toward the line of treadmills against the windows, stepping on one just behind Beth, but I didn't turn it very high. Between blood loss and sleep deprivation, I was scared I might faint.

After a few minutes, she met my eyes in the mirror over

one straining bicep and asked, "So how long you been divorced?"

I raised an eyebrow. "Is it time for this conversation already?"

"Don't blame me, I'm usually not rude enough to blurt out personal questions, but, hey, you brought it up."

I had always wondered what it would be like to discuss Darcy with another woman, but that didn't mean I was eager to find out. "If you must know, tomorrow I will officially be a born-again single."

"No shit, really?"

"Yep. I go in to sign the last of a long train of paperwork tomorrow at nine a.m. sharp." My bowels gave a sudden clench at the ordeal ahead of me. As if I didn't have enough to think about.

"You surprise me, Jefferson," she said, switching her curls to the other arm. "You don't strike me as the divorce-sort-of-guy."

"What sort of guy is the 'divorce sort'?" I asked, genuinely baffled.

"Nowadays, it's the more old-fashioned ones who try to force their wives into outdated models of matrimony."

"You're generalizing," I said. "Typical sociology major. Trying to solve everyone's problems collectively."

She laughed, but it turned into a grunt of effort as she finished up her set. "It's true though. Seventy percent of divorces are initiated by women. Better education, jobs, fewer children, all make for a willingness in the female to leave a relationship they might've once stayed in. Who initiated yours?"

"She did," I admitted, without adding that said initiation consisted of dumping my unconscious body on the front porch and changing the locks.

"How long you actually been separated?"

"Almost two years."

I saw the face she made even though she tried to hide it. "Why wait so long for the divorce then?"

The questions had the rapid fire succession of a cross-examination. "Are you psychoanalyzing me?"

"Just wanting to make sure you've had enough time to get through at least Stage 4 of the emotional divorce process." She watched me run for a moment and then added, "Although, judging by that anger, it might be more like Stage 3."

"I'm not really...*angry*," I said. Although I was getting slightly annoyed at Beth's presumption.

She seemed to sense that she'd put me off. "Sorry. I didn't mean to pry. It actually started out as a compliment."

"No, it's fine, really. It's not like we were putting off the divorce while we tried to work things out. We were both very, very ready for it to end. But it just sort of drug out and drug out while we waited for the house to sell so we could divvy up the settlement. We ended up taking a bath on the price just so we could be done."

"Wow. Okay, in that case, I can understand a little lingering animosity."

"We don't hate each other or anything. We really don't. It's just..." I tried for several seconds to think up the words to describe mine and Darcy's complicated relationship, and by the time I realized what an impossibility that was, the silence had stretched out to awkward proportions.

So I jogged, and Beth switched machines, to one where she lay on her back and worked her legs in wide vees. I watched the pool behind me in the mirrors, the lights on the outside of the building reflecting off the midnight blue water, and then I noticed that her reflection gave me a generous view right up her shorts every time she opened her legs.

I looked away fast, but the damage was done. My eyes were drawn back. I watched the swell of her inner thighs as the muscles flexed, and the quick burst of white panties revealed between them during each stretch. Blood pumped through my groin, inflating my dick like a party balloon before the clown starts turning it into a giraffe, and suddenly my run on the treadmill became an awkward duck waddle.

Good god, what are you, thirteen-years-old, you pervert? Sure, it had been a long time since I'd been with a woman, I just never imagined being reduced to this. Guilt washed over me, but not enough to make me look away.

"Then just tell me this," Beth said suddenly, "and I promise I won't bring it up again until at least our tenth date: would you say it was more your fault or hers?"

I was startled—especially by her use of the word 'date'—but still couldn't drag my eyes off her crotch. Thankfully, she stayed focused on the ceiling as she worked. "Huh?"

"You know, it's like after you have a car accident, and the insurance company asks you, in your opinion, who was at fault? You said she initiated the divorce, but that doesn't really mean anything. What I wanna know is, would you say you're more to blame, or her?" Beth gave a grunt as the reps began to tax her. "But if you really want to, I'll let you plead the fifth. For now."

"Oh. It was definitely mine," I said dazedly. My erection had stiffened to a hot, swollen lump at my waist, so large it was painful. Sweat broke out across my forehead and cheeks, and not because of the jog. What was wrong with me? This was more than just pent-up horniness; I felt hypnotized suddenly. The dream came back to me again, but the awful ending this time, the way I'd brutalized her, and a flush of excitement spread outward from my stomach.

"At least you're honest," Beth said, but I was barely paying attention anymore. My jaw grinded as I watched her sit up on the workout bench. Everything she did fueled this fire in me, as though each move had been calculated to seduce. She was far more attractive to me than any of the women in her porno research collection. I wanted her, wanted to fuck her, I could see myself in graphic detail pinning her to the floor in this very room and tearing her clothes off as she struggled beneath me. In fact, I *wanted* her to struggle. And it wasn't just about the sex either; I wanted to hurt her, to make her cry.

In my thirty-six years on the planet, I had never had such a sick, misogynistic fantasy about any woman, ever. Even now, it didn't feel like me creating these urges, but something being fed to me, like watching a movie. Something that utterly sickened the refined, evolved identity we paste on for the world, but delighted the lizard brain beneath to no end.

I suddenly felt dangerous. Like a wild animal crouched amidst jungle foliage while it studies its prey.

As she continued to talk, I stumbled off the treadmill without even bothering to stop the belt and scooted past her sideways, so she wouldn't see the bulge in my running shorts. It took every ounce of willpower for me to stay on course for the door.

"Where are you going?" she called.

"Back. Not feeling well," I answered over my shoulder. I didn't dare turn around to look at her again.

"You okay? Want me to come with you?"

"*No!*" I blurted. "Just…pushed myself too hard."

"Well, what about this pool party thing on Wednesday? I

promised the woman in the office I'd go. You maybe wanna meet up there?"

"Yes. Absolutely. See you there." I was halfway out the door as I said it.

5

I felt like a monster as I lurched through the complex streets toward home, a werewolf perhaps, or maybe Henry Jekyll, mid-transformation into his mindless alter ego. That comical misspelling from one of my many forgotten students burned in my brain: *stark raven mad*. When I saw the approaching headlights of a vehicle, I veered off the road and sprinted into the pitch black grass alleys along the outskirts of the property.

The Squall began again, ringing out from every transformer I passed. My senses felt heightened; each peal galvanized me. Threads of red shot through my vision. And I was dizzy too, overtaken with an unfocused savagery that made me want to hit or hump everything I saw. My cock was a burning steel rod, a clogged pipe ready to burst if the pressure wasn't relieved.

...the still, small voice...

I reached the mouth of the alley next to my building and fell to my knees beside the warbling electric box, just a few yards away from Schrader's front door. A series of images rose unbidden in my head: Yonkers charging at me...my ravenous trip through the grocery store...3204's strange, jerking dance around the transformer, like some primitive villager worshipping an idol. That veil over reality began to slip away, and the world around me grew dimmer and less real with each passing second.

The Squall hit a deafening fever pitch, singing in a thousand insectile voices that sounded like the one in my dream, pleading for me to give up my inhibitions and indulge in what I wanted to do.

And right then, there was only one thing I wanted to do.

I slipped my shorts down, oblivious to everything around me, pulled my dick out, and began to tug furiously.

the still...small...voice...

It took only a few strokes before the orgasm exploded through me like a stick of dynamite in my groin. Seminal fluid flew in ribbons, the hardest I'd ever come in my life, a Krakatoa of ejaculate. It spurted across the metal side of the transformer like some perverse baptism. My eyes rolled back in my head. I let out a choked moan from the unbearable pleasure and tried not to faint.

stark raven mad, I've gone stark raven mad...

When it was done, I felt more in control, more myself. And deeply ashamed. Had I just publically masturbated? I couldn't even recapture the feeling that caused me to do it, and the Squall was just the Squall again, nerve-wracking and horrible. I staggered to my feet, tucking myself back into my shorts before someone saw me, and became aware, all at once, that it was too late for that.

I looked up and to my left, toward the upper unit on the end of building 15.

The drapes were open up there, and a faint glow from within outlined a tiny, hunched figure in the window, looking down on me.

Then it withdrew, fading into the darkness.

TUESDAY MORNING

1

The rest of the night was a vague soup of bad dreams. When my eyes fluttered open the next morning, nothing made sense. I could barely remember my own name. Thank Christ I had set the alarm the afternoon before, or I would've slept right through.

The events of last night crept back up on me as I showered. In the light of day, it almost felt like another dream. I still couldn't remember what had possessed me. And running away from Beth? Jesus. At least she hadn't seen me rubbing one out in the alley.

As for the old lady...well, so what? She never left her apartment; who would she tell about the weirdo in the next building yanking his crank outside in the middle of the night? If she called the cops, I would deny it.

Maybe I should've been more worried—not just about Mrs. Isaacs, but everything I'd experienced over the last four days—but I found it all easy to dismiss in the shadow of the hellish experience looming ahead of me.

I was getting divorced today. The prospect opened a well of loss that I'd kept buried deep for the last year. If I didn't focus on the next step, and then the one after, I would never get through it.

In some clean slacks and a dress shirt, I looked almost presentable. The bruises on my face had darkened and spread a bit, and, when I changed the bandage, I found the dog bite looked oozy and raw. My arm had a dark crevice in it about an inch wide and half as deep where Yonker's teeth had torn out a strip of jerky. But the bleeding had stopped as promised, so maybe I could squeeze by without stitches.

Rabies shots were another question entirely.

As I came out of the bathroom, the Squall started up, as reliable as Old Faithful, the pattern this time irregular and more grating for it.

"Motel tonight," I resolved. "Just get through today first."

If I had known this was my last chance to get out, I would've packed a bag right then, and left without looking back.

2

Five minutes later I pulled out of my garage and stopped on the short stretch of driveway. The sun hung low enough to cast deep shadows across the complex. I could hear the Squall even in the car with the windows up and the radio playing NPR; in fact, it seemed to be intertwined with the words as they drifted from the speakers, like an audio parasite. I tuned to some rock, secured a cup of coffee in the holder, and when I turned back to the wheel I realized someone stood right beside my door.

A burly guy in a navy-blue suit waited in the driveway that ran parallel to mine, on the threshold of the open garage door. Dan McCaffery, that marital matador from upstairs. The man was my age but bigger, wide-shouldered and muscular, with a thin layer of fat on top. The body of a high school football player gone to pot. He stood with shoulders slumped, a briefcase dangling from one hand by a few fingers, like a man waiting on a subway platform. He worked for a small auto liability law firm, although I didn't know it at the time.

I rolled down my window. "Dan? You okay?"

He didn't answer. I realized his eyes were fixed on something over the roof of my car. I turned to look the opposite direction, out my egg-streaked passenger window.

Another ambulance sat parked up the street, almost out of sight where Tulip Boulevard receded toward the far end of the complex. It could've been the one that treated me the day before. The sirens were off, but the lights made slow, almost lazy turns, painting the sides of the buildings in silent flashes of red and orange that reminded me of autumn leaves. No crowd this time; it was too early for that. As I watched, two EMTs came out of a unit wheeling a gurney with a covered form on it.

"Christ, what now?" I whispered, mostly to myself.

"Dillinger," Dan croaked from my left. "That's her apartment."

I pictured the blue-haired spinster, a surprisingly big-boned woman whose front stoop was littered with saucers of milk in various stages of curdling because no one had ever told her that cats and dairy products were an image of myth. "Poor gal," I said, remembering the torn form in the back of Tate's security cart. "Probably had a heart attack. All those cats are gonna starve to death in a week."

"Fuck that old broad, and fuck her fleabag cats."

I looked back at Dan, shocked by the sudden vehemence from a man I barely knew. His eyes rolled down to me. I saw, for the first time, the dark circles under them, the color of a ripe bruise. He grinned ghoulishly and snarled, "It's all just nature taking its course. And I think the same goddamn motherfucking thing is gonna happen to my cunt wife. *Real* soon."

"What...what do you mean?"

That creepy smile melted, as if forgotten. His head gave a few quick twitches, then his face glazed over in a way I recognized all too well. "Nothing. Nothing at all. Just jawing. I think...I think I might be a little under the weather." He tilted his head back and looked at the pale morning sky, as though meaning this literally. "Maybe I should call in to the office today."

"Yeah...you do that," I agreed.

Dan gave a tired nod and went back inside his apartment.

3

A sign had been posted at the front gate of the Estates, reminding everyone about Martha's Poolside Gala tomorrow night. Beth said she would meet me there, but not even the prospect of seeing her again was enough to get me excited about attending. As I sat waiting for the gate to open, my attention drew away.

Next to the notice, on the face of the rock wall that encircled the property, someone had spray-painted a crude but effective face, a brooding visage in brazen slashes of red, a figure with furrowed brow and angry eyes and the hint of a scowling mouth. A single word stood below it, in large, looping graffiti letters.

HEED.

My hands shook on the steering wheel. The letters seemed to stand out in three dimensions.

I sped through the gate and down the driveway to the street, only wanting to be away from it, and found that my nerves actually calmed. In fact, the further I got from the complex, the better I felt in general.

Partly it came from escaping the Squall—so my perpetually agitated brain could finally take a rest—but I think it was also because I was returning to the real world, where sanity reigned. Out here, beyond the wall of the Estates of North Hills, there were no neighborly feuds, no missing dogs, no weird undercurrent of anger and fear in the air. The last few days seemed flat and dimensionless when viewed out of context, like watching a poorly acted TV show.

It was 9:18 when I reached the attorney's office downtown. I'd arrived late after all, but I felt so good suddenly— so relaxed and mellow—I didn't really care. Darcy's legal lapdog was set up in a two-story brownstone that faced the freeway. The Headley and Kern law office owned the entire building. I relished the fact that this would be the last time I would have to sit in a room with Jerry Kern.

The receptionist gave me directions to the conference room. Darcy waited outside the door with a cigarette in hand, even though I was positive this was a non-smoking establishment.

I hadn't laid eyes on her in just over eight months. She'd put on a few pounds, but she wore it well. Darcy had always been all curves and hips, an hourglass with just a suggestion of a tummy no matter how much she worked out. She'd pulled her dark hair back in what I used to call her 'no-nonsense ponytail,' the one she wore to work when she needed to be taken seriously. She had on a black skirt that showed at least a half foot of tan thigh above the knee and a green blouse tight enough to push up even her mammoth breasts into a valley of cleavage. All for my benefit, undoubtedly; one last look at what I would never have again.

An angry scowl dragged at her lips, but it fell off in a hurry when she saw me. She asked, with what sounded like actual sympathy, "Jesus Christ Elliot, are you all right?"

"I'm fine, yes."

"What happened?"

"Long story. Got into a fight with one of my neighbors."

"*You?* In a *fistfight?*" She snorted laughter.

"What so funny about that?" I asked, trying not to let her spoil my newfound good humor.

"I would've thought that went against your precious ethics. Isn't that what you preach to all your students, that violence never solved anything?"

"It's not something I planned. One second you're talking, the next you're fighting."

"Oh, spare me, Ellie dear, you'd need an instruction manual to make a fist." She breezed forward before I could move, stuck her nose practically against my neck, and inhaled like a Hoover. This was how she'd tested me for booze when I first started drinking, before I stopped caring enough to hide it and she stopped caring enough to check. She pulled away from me again, a disappointed frown pursing her lips at not having anything to lord over me, and then dove into another insult to cover it. "Anyway, I'd be willing to bet an extra ten grand in the settlement you just stood there while the other guy pounded on you like a lump of Play-Doh."

"Neither of us has ten grand, Darcy." I shrugged and gave a good natured grin. "And unfortunately, I can't solve all my problems like you, because I don't have a gaping twat."

Her nostrils flared. "You certainly didn't know what to do with mine, asshole. Maybe if I'd used it as a beer cozy, you would've paid it a little attention."

Next to her, the door opened, and the weak-chinned, perfectly-coiffed head of Jerry Kern poked out. "Excellent, you're here. Come right in and we'll get started. This won't take long."

Still fuming, Darcy breezed through the conference room door, and I followed in her wake.

This was off to a better start than I'd hoped.

4

In the end, it was an anticlimactic affair, but enough to kill my good mood. We sat on opposite sides of a board room table, not so much as looking at one another, while Kern passed us document after document, explained what they were, and told us where to sign. Most of it declared legal ownership of property and funds we'd divided a year ago. I mechanically scrawled my name on each one and tried not to think about what they really meant.

This is the way the marriage ends, not with a bang but a waiver.

When it was all over, I shook Kern's sweaty palm while he leered down Darcy's top, then left the building. I stood in the parking garage next door for several minutes, staring out over the city from the third floor.

"Feels different, doesn't it?"

I turned. Darcy waited behind me, unlit cigarette in hand.

"What does?"

"The fact that we're officially unshackled from each other."

I was so busy searching for the barb in her words that it took me a second to realize how right she was. Not only did I feel lighter—less burdened on an undefined, cosmic level—

but even looking at her now, I sensed that the old wellspring of resentment between us had almost magically run dry. We were divorced people now, exes, vicious creatures that had undergone metamorphosis and who would, theoretically, come out more beautiful on the other side.

If our marriage had been a boil, it was lanced now, and the poison drained.

She came over, leaned against the concrete wall of the garage and fumbled her lighter out of her purse. I swiped it from her hand and did the honors, offering her the flame. She stretched her neck out and thrust the tip of the cigarette into it.

"What comes now?" I asked. "For you, I mean?"

She sucked at the cigarette until her cheeks caved in. "Elliot...I'm seeing someone."

The gentleness with which she said this shocked me more than the declaration itself. Darcy hadn't taken such care with my feelings since we first started dating. She suddenly couldn't meet my eyes as she blew smoke toward the concrete rafters.

"That's great," I told her. "How serious is it?"

"Very. I met him at work, he's a good guy." An insult lay buried in that short descriptor that she hadn't intended: he was a good guy, and I had been anything but. "The company is talking about transferring him to Chicago. If they do...I'll probably go with him."

"Wow. That is serious." I was further surprised to see tears standing in the corners of her eyes. "Darcy? What is it?"

"I'm just ashamed." She waved away a cloud of cigarette smoke lingering in the air between us. "I wanted to tell you about him sooner, but I was afraid you'd get mad and complicate the divorce. Which is pretty shitty of me, because I know you're not like that. You did a lot of awful things—we both did—but vindictiveness was never one of your negative character traits."

I lifted a shoulder. "Hey, if some other schmuck is dumb enough to get you outta my hair, more power to him."

She laughed, then wrapped one arm around my torso and pulled me to her, resting her chin on my shoulder. I thought I could feel her crying, but when we pulled apart, her eyes were dry again. "Enough about me. What are your plans for the wide open future?"

"Me? I think I'm just gonna...coast for a while."

"You and Mickey, huh? Eligible men out on the prowl."

I bit the inside of my cheek. "You know it."

Darcy finished the cigarette and I patiently waited just to prolong the encounter, knowing that when it ended, there was a more than fair chance I would never see her again. She dropped the butt, mashed it out with the pointed toe of one shoe and said, "To be honest, you don't look too hot, Elliot. Even besides the bruises. Your eyes are swollen, and you're so pale I kept expecting you to fade away the whole time we were in there. Just tell me, are you drinking again?"

"Not a drop in almost a year."

"Then what's wrong?"

Dan McCaffery's gaunt face floated through my head, the first time I'd thought about home all morning. "I'm just a little under the weather."

"Don't feed me that," she snapped. "This isn't like you, not even when you *were* drinking. Your cheeks were always pink and rosy back then. Is it drugs, cancer, what?"

I studied her, thinking it might be nice to hear someone else's opinion on that surreal other world the Estates had become. I didn't want her to tell me I was crazy...and yet I really did.

"Well...you see...there's this noise..."

5

I talked for fifteen minutes, told her everything that had happened since I got home from work Friday afternoon. Well, almost everything. Beth's part in the story was downplayed (Darcy might be ready to discuss her new love interest with me, but I certainly wasn't), and I kept the details of my midnight masturbation session to myself. To Darcy's credit, she listened to it all without interrupting, even when I got to the part about Mickey's disappearance.

"What do you think?" I finally asked her.

"I think you need some sleep."

"So you don't believe me."

Darcy frowned, her thin eyebrows drawing together. "What's to believe? It all either happened or it didn't. And I have to assume it did, because the alternative is that you're completely and utterly delusional." She gave a small, secret smile, as though something about this struck her just as funny as the idea of me in a fistfight. Rather than be offended, I chose to take comfort in that. "I think the real problem here is that you're so exhausted, your imagination is taking some liberties with the facts. You make it sound like you're in the middle of one of those horror novels you love so much. *Attack of the Body Grabbers*, or something."

I stayed quiet. She nailed it exactly; the last four days were imbued with the fevered paranoia of Heinlein or Finney, except I didn't believe what was happening at the Estates—if, indeed, anything actually was happening—to be a thinly veiled allegory for Communism.

"Look, all these things have easy fixes." Darcy began checking off each of my problems on a separate finger. "The power company will come and fix this noise if you just keep complaining. Someone will find Mickey and bring him back. Call CPS on this Adler woman and let them take care of her kid. And the rest of your neighbors—the guy who hit you, and that idiot teenager?—they can all go fuck themselves."

"But what about everything else?" I asked. "All this stuff about…you know…'heeding the voice'…" I got a chill just from repeating the words.

"It was just a prank phone call. Probably by this punk that's out to get you. All the rest…you either imagined or misunderstood, I guarantee you. After a good night's sleep, you'll see that."

I sighed. "God, I hope so."

She pushed away from the wall; I realized our pleasant little interlude had come to an end. "Promise me you'll get away from the place for a few days. You can stay with me if you want."

The idea was tempting, but I shook my head. "Thanks for the offer, but you know we would murder one another before the sun came up. Let's not ruin this friendship before it begins."

"Fair enough. Feel free to call me if you need to talk." She reached up and ran the back of her hand down the un-bruised side of my face. "Take care of yourself, Ellie dear."

It was the first time I actually liked her snide nickname. "You too."

I stood in the garage and watched as she walked away, this woman that used to be my wife. The whole encounter felt good, like an actual ending. Closure, they call it in AA.

I just wish to God it really had been the last time I ever saw her.

6

If getting away from the complex had made me feel incrementally better, driving back toward it had just the opposite effect. Exhaustion stole into my bones, so heavy my eyelids drooped. My stomach twisted as I turned into the long driveway and pressed the button on my keychain clicker that started the gate sliding open.

Javier and several members of his maintenance crew were on the other side. When I pulled through, I saw they were making a token effort to wash that painted face off the rock wall. They stopped to glower at me as I passed. I suddenly wondered if they all lived on property.

The Squall was audible almost immediately. Somehow, the fact that I'd been away from it all day only served to make it worse now. I gave one of the transformers the finger. It was about time for another call to the power company.

Like Darcy said, I truly believed I just needed to get away for one night, and things would start looking normal to me again. I had reached that point where sleep begins to supercede all other concerns. Everything else would just have to wait.

It was closing on one in the afternoon when I pulled into my driveway. The complex streets were deserted, but when I opened my door, the sound of mean-spirited laughter reached me over the hum of the Squall. I turned and looked across the short rows of parking spaces, toward the playground on the far side.

The Jock Trinity leaned casually against the iron jungle gym bars over there, watching a group of seven or eight elementary school kids gathered around in a rough circle in front of them. I couldn't tell if they were playing ring-around-the-rosie or some form of duck-duck-goose, but there was a lot of excited movement and their heads were bowed as they looked at something on the ground. Garrett, Rick and Miles clapped and cheered as the kids' feet moved, raising to stomp or rearing back to kick, like chorus line members in a performance of *Riverdance*.

Then I caught a glimpse of tiny flailing hands through the tangle of the children's legs and sprinted toward them.

"Hey!" I shouted, drawing on years of experience in stopping hallway brawls. "You kids break it up! Stop that!"

The younger ones scattered in all directions when I was still a few yards away, loosing peals of shrieky laughter. One of them looked back at me as he ran for the corner of the closest building, his lips caught between a smirk and a snarl. Just before he turned away, I could've sworn I saw the left side of his face draw up in a stroke victim tic.

The boy they'd been thrashing couldn't be more than eleven or twelve. He lay curled in a fetal ball, head tucked into one armpit. I knelt down beside him and looked up at Garrett, Rick and Miles, who hadn't moved from their spot when the others ran.

"What the hell is wrong with you three?" I demanded. "Were you just gonna let them kill him?"

They stared at me without a word, an identical sheen of dull malevolence reflected in their eyes. My mouth slammed shut before I could berate them further. These were not the slightly dopey young men that I knew. There was something almost feral about them today, as if at any second they would show their teeth and start growling. Rick's head gave a minute twitch to the side. That motion had begun to remind me of a rattlesnake's tail. They looked me up and down, Miles popping his knuckles menacingly, then all three of them uprooted themselves from the jungle gym in unison and sauntered away, back toward their apartment.

I turned my attention to the boy on the ground, still hunched up with his knees against his chest. I put a careful hand on his shoulder, afraid to move him in case anything was broken. "Hey, you all right?"

The kid uncurled and sat up beside me, blinking dazedly behind thick glasses with one cracked lens. A gash across one of his temples leaked a pencil-thin line of blood down his face. Captain America glared at me from the t-shirt over his narrow chest.

"You all right?" I asked again.

A sudden panicked grimace crossed his face, the look of someone who has just remembered something important. His hands went to one hip of his jeans, where he grabbed at the pocket there.

"Oh no!" he cried. He flipped over on his hands and knees and began to dig through the cedar chips that made up the floor of the playground. "Where is it? *Where is it?*"

I started to ask him if I could help, when something caught my eye. A prescription pill bottle lay against the rubber boundary of the yard. I picked it up—loose pills rattled inside—and glanced at the label.

Phenobarbital. The patient name was Paul Bergman.

I held up the bottle. "Is this what you're looking for?"

He looked up. Relief smoothed his small forehead. He reached for the bottle, but I held it away.

"Please, I *need* those!" he begged.

"Are you Paul?"

He shook his head. "That's my dad! I'm Rory! Give them to me, please!"

"These are your father's?" I gave the medicine bottle another shake, trying to remember what I knew about Phenobarbital. Not much, but enough to know it wasn't something I'd feel comfortable letting a child run around with unsupervised. "Then what are you doing with them out here?"

Instead of answering, he gave a nervous look over his shoulder, around the empty complex.

"Why were those other kids hurting you?" I asked softly. "Were they after these?"

"No, they...t-they've already changed..."

I gaped at him. "What do you mean? How did they change, Rory?"

"You don't understand!" he wailed. He surged forward, colliding with me, and snatched the bottle from my hand. Still on my knees, I didn't have the leverage to stop him. By the time I'd recovered, he was halfway across the playground.

"Hey, wait! I need to talk to you!"

I ran after him, surprised to find myself dizzy and winded almost at once. Constant exhaustion can take a quick physical toll. Ahead was the building around which the other kids had disappeared, but Rory didn't follow them. Instead, he headed toward the row of hedges along the front and dropped down behind them. I reached them a few seconds later, just in time to see his tiny sneakers disappear into a square ventilation grate about two feet wide in the side of the building. The opening was far too small for me to fit.

"Rory," I called out after him. "My name is Elliot Jefferson. I live in apartment 1603. You can come and talk to me anytime you want, okay?"

No answer from the dark shaft, but I could hear echoed breathing.

I turned around and headed back to the playground, but stopped halfway across, beside the jungle gym, when I realized that the blinds in every window of the surrounding buildings were open, and my neighbors stood in all of them, watching me.

There were people of all ages and colors, even a few kids younger than Rory Bergman. Some were alone, some crammed in together behind one pane of glass, some shoveled food into their mouths while others were hardly even dressed—one woman, a not particularly attractive one, fondled her bare breasts absentmindedly—but all of them stared down at me with the blank, silent aggression I'd seen in the faces of the Jock Trinity and Schrader and Javier's work crew. Had they been watching while Rory got the shit kicked out of him by their children, like spectators in a Roman coliseum, hungry for blood as the slaves below fought for their amusement?

Civil unrest. The phrase suddenly seemed elegant for its simplicity.

Despite the heat of the day, gooseflesh crept up my arms and along the back of my neck.

Was this even real? Or was my perception skewed? The world seemed too bright suddenly as I looked around at them all, an abstract watercolor. I dropped acid once in college, at the insistence of my roommate, and hated the loopy, out-of-body sensation that came over me. But that's how I felt now, as if this was all another of those fever bright dreams, except I wasn't asleep, I hadn't been truly asleep in days, and my mind had finally had enough, it seemed.

Yonkers really did give you rabies, and now it's setting in.

I knew that was ridiculous, but in that queer moment, anything seemed possible. I forced my legs to carry me back across the playground and on toward home. Once inside the apartment, I turned the deadbolt on every door. If this was a head trip, I had entered the paranoia portion, and my skin practically itched with the feel of all those eyes on me.

Early afternoon sunlight stabbed between the blind slats, spinning dust motes across the living room. Each ray seemed to sear my eyeballs. Wasn't light sensitivity a symptom of rabies also? I bolted into the cool darkness of the bedroom. Retrieved my suitcase from the closet. Snatched clothes from drawers and hangers and tossed them inside with haphazard abandon. I intended to see the Estates in my rearview within the next five minutes, and I wasn't sure I would ever come back.

Outside, the Squall screeched on, rising and rising and rising to impossible heights, a screech that no human should've been able to hear, a dagger straight through my weary brain. I clapped hands over my ears, but, as usual, it did nothing to dampen the sound. Goddamn it, how was that *possible?*

And...so help me God and Jesus and all the saints...beneath its droning whine...I could hear a voice whispering my name.

That heat from last night built in me again, that dangerous, violent yearning, full of all the darkest urges I had scarcely even admitted to myself. I was crazy after all, stark raven mad, I knew it in that moment, but I also knew if I could only leave this place, I might feel better. Escape, that was all it would take. I just had to bully through this like I had alcoholism. Tuck my head between my ass and kiss my legs goodbye, as we used to say. Wait, was that right? I didn't even know anymore.

Focus. One step at a time. Get your clothes and get out of here. I reached back into my dresser for a few pairs of socks...

...and then found myself standing in the cramped kitchen of my apartment wearing nothing but underwear, with my penis hanging over the top of the waistband like a dead snake and blood dribbling down my arm.

TUESDAY EVENING

1

Dissociative fugue disorder.

I wouldn't hear that term for a few weeks yet, until my lengthy recuperation in the hospital, but that would eventually be the label the doctors gave my mental lapse when they started coming up with explanations for the incident at the Estates, writing articles for their medical journals so they could feel like they'd tamed the madness and assure the world that something like this could never happen again.

At the time though, I could only blink in confusion. The transition had been utterly seamless; one second standing in the bedroom cramming everything I could grab into a suitcase, the next mostly naked in the kitchen, and I couldn't even remember walking through the apartment to get here, let alone how I'd gotten undressed. I forced myself to stand as still as possible while I examined the scenario.

For starters, I was filthy, my bare chest and arms smudged with dirt. Nonsensical designs had been painted all over me with what appeared to be condiments: yellow mustard zigzags across my chest, red ketchup spirals on my belly, purple trapezoids outlined on my upper thighs in grape jelly. My shriveled dick was ringed in barbecue sauce that got all over my hand when I tucked it back into my underwear; the tangy smell of it almost made me gag. I looked like a creative kindergartener left untended for too long. Or one of those Australian Aborigines. That comparison set off a distant ping in the back of my head that I didn't have time to explore.

Fresh blood dripped from my left arm. The bandage had been torn off, the dog bite beneath raw and leaking. Scarlet dripped onto the counter in front me, where a heap of half-eaten food and empty wrappers sat. I reached out with my clean hand—or rather, my non-bloody hand—and sifted through the pile. The contents of my newly overstocked fridge and pantry had been mostly devoured, the remains smeared across the Formica and up the walls. And, judging by the painful bloat to my belly, I was the one that had done the devouring.

"What the fuck?" I murmured. The disorientation terrified me. I'd never sleepwalked in my life, but that was all I could compare the experience to.

Then I turned to the rest of the apartment, and felt far, far worse.

The entire place was trashed. Everything I owned—what little there was—had been smashed, stomped, shredded, and strewn about the room, including most of the clothes I'd just packed. The garbage can had been dumped on the carpet and the contents ground in, the upholstery of the couch torn to shreds, the screen of my television completely obliterated. Pieces of my laptop were everywhere. The model I'd been working on was pounded flat. The devastation was absolute, and frightening for its intimacy.

But what scared me most was the fact that, beyond the windows through which sunlight had just been streaming, the world had slipped into night.

My watch was gone. I craned my head around, frantically seeking something that would tell me the time. The digital clock on the stove reported 8:42. My jaw fell open as I stared at it. I stayed that way long enough for my tongue to dry out.

Assuming it was still even Tuesday, I had somehow lost almost eight hours. Hours during which I had obviously been busy, because there was no denying I was the culprit behind this rampage. I strained, trying to remember, trying to catch a glimpse of what it had felt like to do these things, but there was nothing, not even a blank spot in my memory, as people with split personalities sometimes claim.

Just that quick blip from there to here, as easy as changing the channel on the TV.

It was about that time, as I stared in wonder at my handiwork, that I realized the apartment had been silent this entire time.

The Squall was on another hiatus.

And then a terrible idea leapt into my head, one that sent icebergs floating through the canals of my heart.

Had the Squall actually stopped?

Or could I just not hear it anymore?

2

My inner vandal had been at work in the bedroom also, wrecking my bookshelves and shredding one of my cheap, foam pillows.

I started by cleaning and rebandaging my wound, and used a washcloth to wipe off the edible body paint. The mustard left jaundice-colored stains on my flesh. My reflection in the mirror was haggard and pale as milk; I looked sick, *deathly* sick, *terminal-cancer-patient* sick. My stomach was so full I felt like an anvil sat on top of my guts, and a head-ache pulsed at my temples. I dry swallowed three aspirin, but wished I had kept the Percocets. Of course, what I really wanted was alcohol: a beer, a few swigs of Jack, anything to steady my nerves enough to let me think. I ignored the urge and threw on my last surviving pair of jeans and a t-shirt that had been ripped from the hanger in the closet and dropped in the floor.

I had to find help. Get to a doctor. Screw packing, I just needed to *go*. Whether it was rabies, the noise from the trans-former, or even just good, old-fashioned insanity, there was obviously something wrong with me. Last night I'd been com-pelled to jack off in the alley; tonight I'd entered an amnesiac state during which I'd destroyed my own apartment and eaten enough food to feed a third world country. It's like I really was becoming a modern-day Hyde. I couldn't let this continue unchecked; I might be a danger to myself and others.

Once I had my shoes on, I went to the table next to the garage door where I keep all the pocket belongings that go with me when I leave the house, then realized my keys had been in the slacks I wore to the lawyer's office. I finally found the destroyed pants wadded up in a corner under the bed, amid the remains of my copy of *Catcher in the Rye*. My phone was still in the right front pocket, but my wallet and car keys were gone.

I performed a quick search of the entire apartment, then a more thorough one, followed by a completely panicked one. The keys were gone, stolen by my alter ego. He'd even taken the spare set I kept in a coffee can on top of the fridge. For fifteen minutes, I stood in the middle of the living room, turning in circles as I examined every inch of the space like a *Where's Waldo* drawing, and tried to figure out what he—

that is to say, *I*—would've done with them. In the end, the apartment was pretty small. They had to be here somewhere, unless I'd goddamn consumed them during my food binge.

Or unless you left *the apartment.*

I stopped my pirouettes and went to the back door. The deadbolt sat unlocked; I was sure I'd closed it just before I began packing. Feeling heavy with dread (and several pounds of groceries), I opened the door and stepped out onto the patio.

The night air felt still and warm, with so much humidity the sweat burst from my pores almost immediately. That rain they'd been predicting for the end of the week was on its way, and it would be bad when it finally got here.

The crushed ketchup bottle from my fridge lay on the concrete patio like a giant, plastic slug, proof that I'd been outside at some point during the black out. I prayed to God I'd left on this excursion before I stripped down to my skivvies, but considering I must've painted myself before dropping the bottle out here, I didn't think that probable. Which meant I'd gone running around the complex naked and smeared with food, like some geriatric lunatic. Christ, what else had I done? Worse, who had seen me do it?

In any case, I had myself in checkmate. Continuing the search was pointless. If my keys had left the confines of the apartment, they could be anywhere. I had to start thinking about other options. Calling a cab to the emergency room seemed like the best one. Once I got there, I could insist on a full examination—MRI, CAT scan, blood test, whatever.

I turned to go inside, but was stopped by a piercing scream.

3

The cry—high-pitched and unmistakably female—sounded muffled, but still close enough to startle me. It could only have come from one of the units overlooking the alley. Katie leapt to mind. Then that keening, fearful shriek came again, and I traced it to the window above my patio.

Dan and Joan's apartment.

There was a sharp crack, like the breaking of a huge tree branch. A flash of reddish light burst behind the blinds up there, bright enough to momentarily burn my retinas.

I could identify that, too.

Gunshot.

I recalled my neighbor's ghoulish face this morning. His mumbled declaration: *I think the same goddamn motherfucking thing is gonna happen to my cunt wife.* Real *soon.*

And then all my other problems were forgotten as I raced around the corner of the building and across our driveways, where my car was still parked, locked and useless to me, and then around the far side of the building, where the entrance to unit 1604 was located. By the time I got there, the exertion of running had pumped my supersized dinner into my throat; I paused long enough to take a long vomit in the bushes and felt instantly better, then stepped back to survey the scene.

Above their front door, the McCaffery's balcony overlooked the short, stub-of-a-street meant to give access to the garages on this side of the building. Their porch light was on, but everything inside appeared to be off, the balcony closed and dark. I stood on the mat outside their door (*Bless This Happy Home* it read, and I'm guessing the McCafferys weren't much for irony), wiping puke off my lips and trying to catch my breath as I raised my fist to knock and then lowered it again.

Did I even want to get involved in this? As it was, I had jumped into too many other people's business these last few days. Besides, what would I say if he actually answered the door? *Dan, can I borrow a cup of sugar, and oh, by the way, did you happen to just kill your wife?*

Nevertheless, I had a responsibility to do *something*. I'd heard his threat earlier and dismissed it as more of their usual vitriol for each other. I got out my phone to dial 911.

"That won't do any good."

I jerked and spun, then spotted a shape on the next doorstep over, a few yards away. "Kirk? Is that you?"

Kirk Gordon stepped forward, just enough for me to make out the ghost of his face. With his porch light off, his dark skin practically blended into the shadows. As one of the few people who still seemed relatively normal around here, I was relieved to see him.

"You okay, Elliot?" he asked, motioning toward the bushes where my vomit still dripped from the leaves.

"Just a little food poisoning." I pointed at the door of 1604 and lowered my voice. "Kirk, this might sound crazy, but I think...well, I think the guy in this apartment shot his wife a second ago."

"I know. My bedroom is right on the other side of the wall from theirs. Teresa and I have had ringside seats to every title bout those two ever put on. It sounds awful to say, but we used to joke that Dan and Joan would've made a great reboot of the Honeymooners." He got a funny look on his face as he said this—half smile, half teary frown—but it was so dark over there, I couldn't be sure. "So I heard it all. Those two were going at it again, yelling and screaming, then...*blam!* To the moon, Alice." Kirk licked his lips nervously. His glasses reflected the McCaffery's porch light in twin flares. "One way or another, I'm pretty sure their show just got cancelled."

"Then we have to call the police."

"Already did. The dispatcher told me after the Estates's office closes, the courtesy officer is the designated responder."

"*What?* This isn't some noise complaint, we have an emergency!"

"That's what I told them, but they said they've had so many calls from the complex lately, as of this morning Martha gave strict instructions only to dispatch on Tate's say-so."

I grimaced, thinking of all those scowling faces in the windows earlier this afternoon, the angry vibe yesterday as Katie and I walked the complex putting up flyers. Civil unrest. The cops were tired of coming out this far from the city for bullshit reports. I couldn't blame them, but the fact that we couldn't get any help made me suddenly feel marooned on an island. "Okay, so where's Tate?"

"At home. But they called him, he's on his way."

"What about Martha? You know what apartment she's in?"

"Nope."

"Jesus Christ." I pointed at the McCaffery's door again. "He could've killed her in there."

Kirk shook his head matter-of-factly. "She's not dead."

"How do you know?"

"Because I can still hear her on the other side of the wall. Sounds like she's mumbling. Or praying. He may've shot her, but she's still very much alive." He swallowed. It seemed to take some effort for his scrawny neck to get the saliva down. "For now, anyway."

"Christ," I repeated, and ran a shaking hand through my hair. "So what do we do?"

"I don't know about you, but my mother didn't raise me to ignore a woman in trouble." He raised his arm. The burnished steel of a large revolver glinted in the light. The sight of the gun made me go numb. "That's why I'm gonna try to help her. You're welcome to come, if you want."

I gaped at him. "Kirk….we can't go in there."

"Why not?"

"Because if you get up to his apartment and start shooting—"

"I'm not gonna hurt him if he doesn't make me," Kirk said quickly. "I just wanna see that she's taken care of until help arrives."

"Yeah, and suppose he does make you? Suppose you get into a firefight and he shoots you, too? Or worse yet, you shoot him? You break into his residence, it'll be *you* that goes to jail."

"It's not breaking in if we suspect someone's in distress. We can say we just went in to render aid."

"Oh, sure. You busted in there with that hand cannon to perform CPR. I'm sure the cops will buy that."

His lips pulled into a frustrated frown. "We're living in a community here, Elliot. We have an obligation to help our neighbors, to make sure that community stays safe."

"Tell that to George Zimmerman."

Kirk flapped a hand in irritation. I wondered how long he would've stalled out here if I hadn't come along, trying to work up the nerve to go through with this. "Enough talk. You don't wanna help, then stand outta my way."

He came forward, crossing the stretch of grass between his porch and the McCafferys. When the light from the porch bathed his face, I saw the puffiness around his left eye, the skin so swollen it pushed his glasses crooked on his face. His pigmentation was too dark to see the bruising except on his eyelid, which looked glaringly red.

"What happened to you?" I asked. In my head, I saw the bruise across Katie's throat, those delicate, finger-shaped swirls of blue and green. The marks Schrader had left when he tenderized my torso.

"Nothing." Kirk shrugged the question off and brushed past me to stand in front of the door where I had been moments ago. I thought he might put his shoulder to it, like cops in a movie, or maybe just shoot out the lock, but instead he gripped the knob and turned it experimentally.

The door popped open, swinging away into darkness. A whiff of something rotten drifted out.

He looked over at me, the fear in his eyes naked. "You coming or not?"

I looked around the complex. The streets were empty, all the blinds closed in the windows facing us. Even so, I was positive I could feel eyes watching once more. "After you," I told Kirk.

He hefted the revolver and eased through the doorway.

4

I'd never been in any of the second floor units. The narrow landing beyond the door was only a few feet of tile before the stairs began. We stood at the bottom for a long moment, gazing up the interior staircase, which receded into darkness somewhere near the top. I had the urge to call out—that was what you did when you entered someone's home unannounced, after all—but knew the element of surprise would serve best.

Kirk put his foot on the first tread. I whispered for him to hold on, then got my phone out, switched on the flashlight app, and used the tiny camera bulb to light our path. It wasn't a focused beam, like a regular flashlight, but rather a glow that extended about two or three yards in front of us.

We continued up the stairs, taking them one careful step at a time. That smell—a badly rancid stench—got stronger as we climbed. The only sound was a curious, soft gurgling that seemed to emanate from near the top of the stairs, where the hall dead-ended in an abrupt left turn. It sounded like someone choking out their last breath around a mouthful of blood. When we got close, Kirk signaled for me to cover the light up. He came to a stop with his back against the staircase wall and held the snub-nosed gun pointed upward in both hands just in front of his face. As ridiculous as it made him look, I was suddenly aware that I had no weapon at all. He looked at me, nodded, and swung around the corner fast, bringing his gun out to sweep the area beyond the upper landing. My heart thudded, waiting for the shootout to begin, but Kirk only jerked his head to the side after a few seconds, indicating for me to join him.

I crept up to his side and looked around, using my phone like a lantern. The stairwell opened onto the living space. Unlike Beth's unit, the McCaffery's apartment had a totally different layout than mine, which was now directly below our feet. And it was better decorated too, more like a place where people lived rather than just existed. A leather sofa sat in the middle of the room, facing a wall-mounted plasma screen across from us, and some expensive looking rugs and artwork, including a freestanding abstract sculpture beside the couch: three thin, red spikes growing from a wide base that stretched up to waist height as they gradually curled around one another. It looked pretentious to me. The gurgling I'd heard came from a long aquarium along the wall to our left. Its aerator released a stream of bubbles from a tiny treasure chest on the bottom. A recessed florescent light in the tank's lid cast a dim pallor over the room. Several large fish observed us as we crept past.

Kirk led the way once more, never hesitating; I had to give it to the man, he might look like an accountant, but he had a set of brass balls on him. He checked every room and possible hiding place with brisk, almost military precision, detouring to the left of the couch to check the adjoining den, opening a door that turned out to be a coat closet, and then heading around to the opposite side of the room, toward the kitchen and dining nook. Nothing seemed out of place, no signs of a struggle, but that only served to heighten my discomfort. It had been perhaps ten minutes since I'd heard the scream and the gunshot; what had Dan been up to since then? I had the sudden image of the car accident attorney setting up trenches and booby-traps throughout the apartment like a suburban Vietcong, buckets of boiling water to fall on us or nail-studded mop handles that would spring out to impale us when we walked through a door.

On the way across the room, we passed an end table with several framed photographs. I picked up one of the happy couple and studied it in the flashlight. Joan McCaffery was a slim, pretty, short-haired blonde with big eyes, teeth, and breasts, a trophy wife in all but age. Even though I'd heard some foul-mouthed denigrations from her in the months I'd lived below the two of them, in this picture she looked happy, vibrant and full-of-life. It was the last push I needed to go through with this, to make sure I did everything in my power to save her.

"*Psst!*" Kirk stood in the kitchen doorway, waving to get

my attention. I came to join him, and found a scene I was already too familiar with.

A tornado had torn through the McCaffery's kitchen, leaving a trail of garbage and half-eaten debris strewn across the tile floor and counters. I saw an open box of Little Debbie cakes, nothing remaining but empty cellophane and a few crumbs. Gnawed hunks of raw t-bone lay spoiled on the stovetop, the source of the apartment's odor. Spilled corn flakes crunched underfoot. An open can of spaghetti sauce had been used to scrawl archaic symbols on one wall, around a glowering face.

"You think they were fighting in here?" Kirk asked softly.

I nodded, but I didn't think that at all. An awful certainty crept over me, a connection too obvious to ignore.

Kirk moved away, heading toward the apartment's only hallway, and I followed. Together, we checked another closet, a spare room full of exercise equipment, and then moved on to a closed door at the end of the hall, the master bedroom. We pressed our ears against the thin, compressed wood. As he'd told me outside, a constant, breathless mumbling was audible on the other side.

My companion's eyes were round O's of fear. He squeezed the revolver's handle, pointed at my phone light, and then put a hand on the doorknob. His lips moved, counting down: *one, two, three.*

He turned the knob and flung the door open. Together, we brought gun and light to bear on the room's contents.

I got only a brief impression of the McCaffery's bedroom, for it was the tableau directly in front of us that demanded our instant attention.

A blood-soaked body lay stretched out on the floor in a red puddle. The face had been obliterated, presumably by the pistol that lay beside it—just a caved-in hole filled with gleaming white bone chips and a stew of blood and brains—but based on the size and shape, it was obviously male.

Even so, I probably would've been able to deduce that it was Dan because his wife was straddling the corpse's chest, completely naked and gyrating her way to an orgasm.

5

In the light from my phone, Joan's full breasts—implants, I figured—bounced high enough to almost hit her chin as she rode her deceased husband, the nipples standing stiff and proud. Her contorted position looked painful: legs spread wide and back arched in such a way that she could press her genitals down against Dan's cloth-covered crotch. She moved back and forth so fast, I figured she must be getting fabric burn on her pussy. The whole scene would've been straight out of a porno, if the male's face hadn't been missing and the female wasn't drenched in his blood.

Her eyes were closed in ecstasy. She remained completely unaware of our presence. A stream of guttural gibberish poured from her mouth, the inflection rising higher as she moved toward climax.

And, God help me, I was disgusted to feel a pleasant shiver of motion inside my jeans.

Kirk, on the other hand, made a low gagging sound.

Joan's eyes popped open at the sound, but they were utterly blank, devoid of the slightest shred of intelligence, and ringed with dark circles. Her head jerked toward us. She snarled, revealing a mouth full of glistening, perfect teeth. She looked far more animal than human, like a lion crouched over a dead gazelle on the Serengeti, blood smeared across her lower torso. Any perverse attraction she might've held for me blew away as I stared into her empty face.

"Joan...get off him." Kirk pointed the gun at her. I couldn't tear my eyes away from her to look at him, but he sounded remarkably calm and composed.

Her head gave a single fast twitch to the side.

And then she came at us.

Her speed was uncanny. She didn't go for the pistol on the carpet that, it would later be determined, she'd used to shoot her husband; I think by then, she was too far gone to even remember how to use it. Instead, she launched forward, scrambling on all fours off the body, then jumping to her feet and blazing toward us, shoulders hunched and breasts jiggling. The sight was so surreal, the rational side of my brain had trouble believing it was happening.

Kirk tracked her with his gigantic pistol, but hesitated to fire. He'd come here expecting to face a man and, in the end, he just couldn't shoot a woman, especially a naked one. Joan knocked the revolver away and smashed him across the face with the heel of the other hand, all in one fluid motion. His head flew to the side, a burst of scarlet spilling from his mouth. He fell against the wall and slid into the floor, eyelids fluttering closed.

Joan stood just a few feet away from me. I could smell the tang of blood wafting off her, could see her small, pink nipples and the waxed curve of her groin as she spun in my direction. Her dull eyes burned with rage. My courage withered.

I tried to back away, but one hand flashed out. Long nails ripped through my shirt, raked furrows in the flesh beneath. I gasped. She screeched triumphantly. It was the sound I'd heard from outside, in the alley. I turned and fled, leaving the unconscious Kirk behind, thinking of nothing but escaping the insanity of this place.

She caught up with me in the living room, leapt onto my back. Teeth sank into the side of my neck hard enough to draw blood. I cried out and stumbled, spilling both of us onto the leather couch in a tangle of limbs. We ended up on our backs with her beneath me. My phone tumbled across the floor, throwing shadows in all directions. I tried to spring back up, but Joan wrapped her legs around my midsection, clutching me to her. Her thin arms became a whirling pin-wheel of pain. She pounded and clawed at me anywhere she could reach, a furious rain of blows to rival the beating I'd taken from Schrader yesterday. And all the while, her hips bucked under me, as though she were trying to fuck me and kill me in equal measures.

I protected my face and throat with one arm and drove an elbow into her skinny side, once, twice, three times, putting all my weight behind it. Her breath *whooshed* out; there was a snap that had to be her ribs breaking. I escaped the em-brace of her bare legs, slid into the floor, and tried to crawl away. Joan was up again in less than a second, not slowed by her injuries in the least. She snatched one of my legs and dragged me away on my stomach, back toward the darkness of the bedroom.

In a panic, I grabbed at the carpet, the couch, the coffee table, anything that might help me get free, but she felt like three hundred pounds of muscle on a ninety pound frame. The strange sculpture with the curving spikes came into view on my left. I curled an arm around the base, but the damn thing just slid across the floor with me.

At the same time, Joan let go of my foot and leapt at my back, meaning to finish what she'd started.

A shriek sounded above me, then tapered into a piteous moan. I rolled over to find Joan McCaffery—my neighbor of almost a year, but a woman I'd never said more than a polite 'hello' to—impaled on her own abstract artwork. The spikes had been angled enough to pierce her chest just below her naked breasts, propping her up like some gruesome department store mannequin. Rivulets of blood snaked their way down the sculpture.

Her eyes rolled to meet mine. They cleared; I saw it happen, like a fog bank withdrawing from a sun-dappled meadow. She blinked rapidly, her eyes darting from my face, to the spikes jutting out of her, and back again. Her mouthed opened and her tongue waggled inside for a second until she finally whispered, "*Heed t-the still…small v-voice…*"

Joan went limp, and both she and the sculpture crashed to the floor beside me.

6

Tate arrived just a scant few minutes later—wearing civvies but driving an actual patrol car this time—to find myself and Kirk sitting on the curb in front of the McCaffery's place, him with an ice pack, me with a clean towel pressed to the bleeding bite wound in my neck. The courtesy officer didn't believe us when we told him what happened, just stared at us for a full minute with his mustache pulled to one side in an uncertain smile until he went upstairs and saw for himself. He came running out of that apartment like a marathon sprinter and got on the radio with his dispatch. Ten minutes after that, the entire complex street was clogged with squad cars, ambulances, and even a morgue truck. Crime scene techs scurried back and forth while cops milled around outside the building, one of which turned out to be my good buddy Officer Claret. He seemed to relish ordering us not to move until a detective arrived on scene.

Great, cops to detectives. I'm working my way up the criminal justice ladder.

It turned out to be a balding man named Hammond with an exaggerated underbite. He had a lengthy conversation with his uniformed brethren before approaching us. Claret, in particular, seemed to have a lot to say, gesturing at me the entire time.

We stood up when Hammond came over. After introductions, he simply said, "Tell me what happened."

Kirk and I hadn't had time to discuss what we would say, but in the end, it didn't matter. The truth was on our side. We took turns explaining our actions, interjecting when the other forgot something or adding details when needed. I stuck to the facts, careful to keep my own growing suspicions out of the recounting.

Hammond paced in front of us as we talked, nodding along. He didn't miss a beat during our description of how we'd found Joan dry-humping the corpse of her murdered husband, but when we reached the part where she'd bashed Kirk, Hammond asked, "She came at you *naked?* Completely unprovoked?"

"Well...I had the gun pointed at her," Kirk admitted. His words were a bit slurred from his battered jaw.

"And that didn't make her think twice?"

"Not a bit," I answered. "We told you, she was acting insane. Totally irrational. Like..." *Like she was in a trance,* I almost said. *Like she'd just consumed everything edible in her apartment, murdered her husband, and would've woken up in the morning fresh as a daisy and not remember a shred of it.* "Like an animal," I finished instead, hoping the sudden flush of guilt didn't show on my face.

"I understand you've been having that problem a lot lately, Mr. Jefferson." Hammond gave me a pointed look. My heart started to pound until I realized he was talking about Yonkers. "First a dog bite, now a human, huh?" Hammond shook his head, then turned back to Kirk and traced a circle in the air with one finger around my neighbor's swollen left eye. "She do that too?"

Kirk met the detective's gaze unflinchingly and said, "She did. Hit me across the face once, knocked my glasses off, then punched me again right here as I was going down. Didn't she, Elliot?"

He turned to me. Behind the lenses of his glasses, his eyes pleaded.

"Uh, y-yeah," I stammered. I didn't know what game Kirk was playing, but if he got caught in this lie, I wanted to make damn sure I had an escape clause. "It was so fast, but...I'm pretty sure that's how it happened."

The detective regarded him for another moment, then said, "All right, go on. How'd Mrs. McCaffery die?"

I finished up the story with my struggle in the living room with Joan, trying to keep my voice clinical and dry, but by the end, tears had crept in. The clouds of shock cleared from my head and I understood the cold, hard truth of it: I had killed a woman. Even if it wasn't what I had intended, I was responsible for the extinguishing of a human life. An avalanche of guilt crashed down over me. I couldn't even finish telling Hammond how she'd been impaled. The memory of her dying as she dangled above me would be competing with Yonkers's decapitation to see which one could give me the most nightmares.

"That it?" Hammond asked coldly when I stopped talking.

"What else do you want? Two people are dead, for Christ's sake."

"Just making sure you don't wanna change your story."

Story. I didn't like the sound of that. "It's the truth."

"It is," Kirk added. "I saw it."

Hammond's brows drew together beneath the long stretch of his forehead. "I thought you were unconscious."

"Just for a second. I came to and got out there in time to see the end."

Another lie. I'd had to wake him up and help him out of the apartment while Joan lay bleeding out on the carpet. Kirk glanced at me again, lifted an eyebrow. The message was clear: *you help me out, I help you out.*

The detective stared at us skeptically, his abnormally long jaw grinding in a way that made him look like a bulldog. "So you claim her death was self-defense?"

"It *was* self-defense!" I said angrily. I threw the bloody towel at his feet even though it was myself I was mad at, for predicting this would happen and following Kirk anyway. "What do you think, we went in there meaning to kill her?"

Hammond's cheeks began to redden. "I don't know. That's what I'm trying to figure out."

"We just wanted to help!"

"Then you shouldn't've gone in there at all. You're not officers, you had no right to enter a private residence."

"Yeah, well maybe if we could've convinced you assholes to come out here and do your job, we wouldn't've had to take the law into our own hands!"

That one probably went too far. Those red blooms on the detective's cheeks spread to his forehead as he growled, "Interesting you put it like that, Mr. Jefferson, because that's exactly what you two idiots did tonight. It's called *vigilantism,* and it's highly illegal. Yes, it appears this woman killed her husband—Officer Maxwell has vouched for you on the fact that they fought like cats and dogs—but even if she attacked you like you claim, you two have turned this situation into a royal clusterfuck just by sticking your noses where they don't belong. At the very least, you'll be lucky if you're not brought up on manslaughter charges." He honed in on me as he said this last bit, then added, "And *you've* got the added bonus of having been in altercations with two different neighbors in as many days, Mr. Jefferson. That looks extremely wonky to me. So let me ask, what do you two have to say for yourselves?"

"Hold on, hold on!" I waved my arms in frustration at the buildings around us—buildings from which, I might add, not a single soul had ventured to watch as they had the day before, even with a sea of slowly revolving red and blue lights in the parking lot. "Look, you have to understand, there's more to all this! Something is going on here…!"

My arms dropped back to my sides. I couldn't explain the situation here at the Estates to Hammond like I had to Darcy; if I started blathering about the odd behavior I'd observed—all the people twitching and talking about voices, that angry undercurrent in the air, my missing minutes, and, yes, even the Squall—he would think I was nuts. And I still couldn't even convince myself that I wasn't, let alone a detective who seemed intent on making me the villain.

"What?" Hammond prompted, with a questioning brow raised. Even Kirk stared at me. "What's going on?"

I lowered my gaze. "Nothing."

Hammond continued to eyeball me. That jaw of his surged forward over and over again, like the prow of a ship slicing through waves. "Maybe we should discuss this in private, Mr. Jefferson. Tell you what, let's step into your apartment so we can go over this one more time."

"*No!*" I blurted, unable to keep the panic from my voice. I composed myself and said, "I just...I'd rather talk out here." I wasn't prepared to handle questions about my destroyed home. *Jesus, I've got so much to hide, it's no wonder he thinks I'm a criminal.*

And then, all at once, I saw just how bad my situation really was. I couldn't let him or anyone else find out about my black out, or those potential manslaughter charges would start looking preferable to what they might throw at me. Any lawyer worth a brass-plated nickel would be able to tear me apart on the stand if they knew I had a big, violent gap in my conscious memory just minutes before I was involved in a homicide. They'd have me painted as the next Richard Ramirez in a heartbeat.

Which meant I couldn't go to a doctor. Not until I'd been cleared of this mess with the McCafferys.

A smug grin spread across Hammond's face, a *gotcha* sort of smile. Before any of us could speak again, the door to the McCaffery's opened and the first of two covered gurneys was wheeled out by EMTs and steered toward the coroner truck. I didn't know whether it was Joan or Dan. Neither Kirk nor I looked for long.

"What happens now?" my neighbor asked solemnly. "Are we under arrest?"

"Not yet. For now, I want full signed statements from both you, and pictures of all your injuries. Including any that you had prior to tonight. And don't be surprised if we bring you in for further questioning." That smile returned to his face. "Who knows? I might even be back with a search warrant."

I asked, "How long till we know if we're gonna be charged with something?"

"That's up to the DA's office after we present our find-ings. But if I were you...I wouldn't plan on leaving town for a while."

7

By the time we finished jumping through all their hoops, it was past midnight. The Squall stayed silent the entire time, not so much as an electronic peep. At least, I hoped it was silent. I found myself watching the faces of the officers and crime scene techs as they came and went, looking for any signs of auditory annoyance. It would've been the perfect opportunity to get some sleep, but I suspected if I've been at home, by myself, that noise would come right back at full volume. Paranoid, I know, and probably another road sign pointing the way to mental instability, but I couldn't help believing it.

At one point, Jacob's car drove by, blaring heavy metal music. I could see him behind the wheel as he slowed to weave through the emergency vehicles, wearing that skull hoodie again. He spotted me and stopped to watch long enough to ascertain that I was on the wrong side of the law equation—suspect rather than victim—then drove away laughing.

And then everyone else departed one by one, leaving Kirk and I standing alone on the complex street and a barrier of yellow police tape across the entrance to 1604. Officer Claret was last to leave. He tipped us a smug salute as he drove toward the gate.

"This is bad," I told Kirk. It was the first time we'd really had a chance to talk since wandering out of the McCaffery apart-ment, and we'd been too dazed to speak then. "*Really* bad."

"I'm sorry, Elliot. It's my fault. I should've listened to you."

I shook my head. "We did what we had to do. And I think we can both agree, that wasn't one of their typical grudge matches. If the police wanna paint it that way, it's better for us, but...Jesus, Kirk, what the fuck was wrong with her?"

"I don't know. God help me, I don't know."

We were quiet for a moment, and the Squall suddenly rushed in to fill the void. Both of us winced, but part of me was just relieved to hear it. As long as I was conscious of it, then I figured I was okay.

But what if I had another of the mental jumps right now? Where would I wake up this time? Mexico? A jail cell?

Straddling Kirk's mutilated corpse?

That one was bad enough to make bile creep up the back of my throat.

"You started to tell Hammond something," Kirk said, distracting me from my own morbidity. "Was it what we talked about yesterday? The bad vibes?"

"Yeah, but...it's more than that, too." I rubbed at my weary eyes. "People everywhere are acting strange. Not like Joan, nobody's that bad off. But some of these folks just seem...off. Aggressive, sort of spastic."

"It's the people that can't hear the transformers, right?"

I took a second before answering, and decided to play devil's advocate. "It's gotta be a coincidence. How can hearing—or not hearing—a sound change your behavior? Your personality?"

"Coincidence." Kirk's tongue traced around the inner edge of his lips, as though tasting the word, and then jumped topics as smoothly as an experienced driver shifting gears. "Last night, I woke up and Teresa was gone. I usually take a tranquilizer to sleep—I've tried Ambien and Lunesta but that newer junk leaves me too loopy in the morning, so I stick to plain ol' Valium—but when we finally got around to unpacking the luggage, my prescription was gone. I guess I must've left them in Florida. Anyway, I was restless, sat up in bed about two in the morning, and saw her side was empty. I checked the apartment. Nothing. But the front door was unlocked. So I went outside, and walked around the building in the dark."

This story sounded familiar to me, and then I knew why: Katie had said almost the same thing about her mother. For the first time, it seemed odd that not even Kirk's tiny wife had come outside during our ordeal with the police. "Was she...at the transformer?"

"No, sir. Not her. But those three college kids from across the way were. They were gathered around it on their knees. Just staring at it, like it was a TV set."

I squirmed. That meant Garrett, Rick, and Miles had been out in the alley last night, and so soon after me that my semen had probably still been wet on the transformer's metal casing.

Kirk continued, pointing at the far end of our building that ran up against the property wall. "I stood in the shadows by Schrader's place and watched them. A few minutes later, the door to that upper apartment in the next building opened, and Teresa came out, along with that Adler woman and a few other folks I didn't recognize."

"Wait a minute, the upper...? You mean *Mrs. Isaacs* place?"

He nodded. "Which is weird because, as far as I know, Teresa's never even met that old woman."

That silhouette in her window last night, watching me while I fell to my knees in the alley and satisfied the undeniable urge to get off. But, if Kirk was to be believed, she hadn't been alone up there. Teresa Gordon and Samantha Adler—who, according to her daughter, had been disappearing for hours at a time lately—had been up there with her, along with more of our neighbors. "So what did you do?" I asked.

"I watched them for a few minutes while they talked in the alley. I couldn't hear what they said, but they seemed real chummy. And all the while, those college boys are hypnotized by the transformer, swaying back and forth right beside them."

"Like a druid ceremony," I uttered.

"Yes! That's exactly what it felt like! Then, when it seemed like the party was breaking up, I ran home and hopped into bed. Pretended I was asleep when she came back." A strange look passed over him, the expression he'd had earlier when he mentioned the joke with his wife. "She didn't say one word about it today. I don't even know if she remembers."

"Kirk...none of this makes a goddamn bit of sense."

"I know that," he agreed miserably.

We stood for another minute, letting the Squall assault us. Neither of us seemed interested in leaving. Kirk looked up at the night sky and that shiner around his left eye—the one he'd blamed on Joan McCaffery—gleamed in the moonlight.

"Katie Adler thinks that noise is giving everyone cancer," I said offhandedly. I wanted to broach the subject, get his reaction, and then decide if I should tell him what had happened to me. "Not that it explains everything going on around here, but..."

Kirk sucked in a sharp breath and once more jumped to a new subject. "You know who Charles Whitman is?"

The name sounded familiar, but I shook my head.

"He's the man who climbed that tower in Texas back in the 60's and shot all those people."

"Oh yeah. Killed his wife and mother too, didn't he?"

"That's the guy. Not a lot of people know this, but before his rampage, he left specific instructions that an autopsy should be done on his body."

I frowned. "Why?"

"Because near the end, he felt like he wasn't in control of himself. That he was doing these things against his will. So they did an autopsy. And do you know what they found?"

I stared at him, not wanting to hear the answer, yet needing to. "What?"

"A brain tumor. One that had been pressing against all those vital areas up there for who knows how long. And yes, there were a few doctors that put forth a theory that it could've altered his behavior. Enough to make him violent. Now I ask, can you imagine what that feels like, to watch yourself doing all these horrible things against your will— murdering your loved ones in cold blood—but being unable to stop yourself?"

I found that I could imagine it. Entirely too well.

"Why are you telling me this, Kirk?" I asked, my voice husky.

"Just to show you that maybe it's a better explanation than you think." A single tear coursed down Kirk's cheek from the swollen eye. Suddenly, I felt sure I understood why he'd lied about that bruise. "I intend to get my family out of here. Tonight, if possible. You should leave too, Elliott." He turned and started toward his front door.

"Kirk, wait," I called after him. He stopped on his darkened porch but didn't turn around. "Your wife...she did that to you, didn't she?"

He shook his head and said over his shoulder, "Nope. My son did."

Kirk Gordon went inside and shut the door.

8

My hands were shaking so bad by the time I got back to my apartment, I could barely get the door open. Memories of detox and the days immediately after rocketed through me, when raw need had consumed me. Sweat coated my forehead; my nerves were shot. When I pulled the back door closed, the sound of the bolt settling in the strike plate startled me as much as a gunshot. I just barely got to the toilet in time to heave up the last remains of my binge earlier in the evening.

As my head hung over the lip of the bowl, staring down at the swirl of mostly digested food that now looked like a Jackson Pollock painting, all I could think about was Kirk's Charles Whitman story, told in his clipped, matter-of-fact, unembellished way.

He felt like he wasn't in control of himself. That he was doing these things against his will.

I was no stranger to that, either. I'd become the king of *doing things against my will.*

And what if I wasn't the only one?

Joan's face burned in my brain, first plastered with a snarl, her head twitching to one side like those obnoxious SNL characters Will Ferrell and Chris Kattan used to play, and then how it was at the end, when her eyes cleared and she looked completely confused about how she'd gotten there. Was it actually possible that she'd murdered her husband while in the midst of a trance? If so, that meant she was innocent. She might never have convinced a jury—even if they believed her, she'd be in the same boat as every mentally handicapped killer—but she certainly didn't deserve to get run through with modern art by the likes of me.

Of course, the flip side to this theory was equally horrifying: had I looked like her during my own black out, growling like an animal and trying to hump everything in sight?

I couldn't keep rationalizing or denying the truth: something was happening to the residents of the Estates of North Hills. As young Rory Bergman had put it, in the simple but effective parlance that only children can command, they were *changing*.

And so, it appeared, was I.

Going to the police was out. If I went to the doctor and they were able to find something physically wrong with me, maybe I'd have a decent shot at convincing someone what was happening, but if I received a clean bill of health after admitting my black out, Hammond would roast me slowly over a legal spit.

So listen to Kirk and just leave, like you had planned to anyway.

I could do that, even without a car. Just walk out of here right now with nothing but the clothes on my back. Call Darcy to pick me up once I was away from here. Hell, maybe I could hitch a ride with the Gordons.

Of course, I would be leaving Beth and Katie here to face this alone.

In case you haven't figured it out, Ellie dear, you're not responsible for them. They're just your neighbors, and you've been doing your best to avoid them ever since you moved in. So get out of here, and save yourself while you can.

I pulled my head out of the toilet, leaned back against the bathroom wall. The Squall pounded at my temples like an invading army with a battering ram. That's what it wanted, I was sure of it, to get inside my skull, to pull my gears and levers and control me like a puppet. Imagination or not, I could almost hear that voice beneath it, a soothing lull encouraging me to submit, to give in, to heed…

That dropped-acid feeling slipped over me again. The world suddenly felt like it was being sucked down a giant drain. My senses sharpened; the light above the sink grew in brightness until it was almost blinding. I sprang to my feet in a panic, grabbing at the counter, the doorjamb, the edge of the bathtub, as if these things would somehow anchor me to the here and now. It was going to happen again, *blink!*, and I would suddenly be somewhere else after having committed some other atrocity, like the guy in the werewolf movies who wakes up in the woods with the partially-eaten body of a deer beside him. I closed my eyes and fought, focused on the Squall with all my will, and when the noise began to waver in and out, I inserted my tongue between my teeth and bit down as hard as I could. A gush of warm blood filled my mouth, but I felt a little more like myself.

The Squall made a new noise, an odd, musical chirping, and then I realized it was my cell. I dug the thing out of my pocket and answered, not caring who it was, just eager to hear another human voice.

"*Hello?*" The word was thick around my swollen tongue. "*Oh god, hello, who's there?*"

"Don't fight, Mr. Jefferson." I recognized the voice immediately as the ancient rasp that had called me on Friday night.

"Wh...what?"

That creaking murmur spiraled upward in pitch, emphasizing words like an evangelical preacher. "The change is *coming*, Mr. Jefferson. The still, small voice has been given to *deliver* us into the Promised Land. You *hear* its words, but you *refuse* to submit. Cleanse yourself of impurities and you will be able to *heed*."

"No," I said. "No, I won't. I won't ever heed." My own voice sounded childlike as I answered gibberish with gibberish.

The person on the other end of the line seemed to consider this. "If you will not come with us willingly, then you must stay out of the way. You're meddling in affairs far greater than yourself, Mr. Jefferson."

"Who are you?" I whispered. Blood thundered in my ears, leaked from the corners of my mouth like red drool. I felt as lightheaded as a balloon.

"I can be kind," the voice purred. "I can give you what you want, if you agree not to interfere."

"I...I don't understand..."

"Look in your freezer."

My breath caught in my throat. Through the bathroom door, I could see all the way past the bedroom to the kitchen beyond. The refrigerator sat tucked between two counters in there, its white exterior as bare and white as the surface of the moon.

I'd left the back door unlocked while I was upstairs with Kirk. The realization hit me, coupled with a mounting terror.

"Go on," that decrepit voice urged.

Taking tiny, frightened steps, I inched my way through the apartment until I stood in front of the fridge. The smaller door at the top was the freezer. I grasped the handle and would've given anything not to open it, but apparently I had as little choice in the matter as I did in wrecking my apartment.

I pulled. The seal broke with a crackle. A breath of cool air leaked out around the edges.

The door swung open, and I cringed in anticipation of whatever lay inside.

A few frozen dinners lay at the back of the rectangular space; apparently I hadn't gotten to them during my unconscious pig out. But just on the other side of the door, front and center in the small space, as if on display, was an entire unopened bottle of Jim Beam.

The brown liquid inside quivered under a layer of frost. I'd used to keep them in the freezer just like this, so they would be cool even before they touched ice.

Every molecule in my body lurched toward that bottle.

I gasped. My hand reached out, without my consent. Fingertips caressed the chilled glass, insuring it was real.

"That's for you," the voice croaked in my ear, startling me so bad I almost dropped the phone. I had forgotten that I held it.

"Why are you doing this?" I asked in a tremulous squeak.

"You've had a hard couple of days, Mr. Jefferson. This is your reward for getting through them. Stay out of our way, and there will be more to come."

The phone went dead. I put it on the counter and picked up the bottle, then unscrewed the top. When the smell hit me, all the spit in my mouth dried up.

A reward. That was the only part of the conversation that seemed to matter. Alcoholics latch on to any excuse, and this was logic I couldn't argue with.

Just a little. To take the edge off.

Outside, the Squall continued its harsh lullaby.

I put the bottle to my lips and drank.

WEDNESDAY
MORNING

1

Daylight pierced my eyelids like a needle. I moaned and then whimpered as the sound traveled from my mouth into my ear and drilled into my brain.

When I worked up the courage to open my eyes, I immediately wished I hadn't. My vision swam in lazy, nauseating corkscrews. A washing machine had been turned on in my stomach. I raised a hand to shade my eyes against the merciless sun, but it felt like my brain synapses were coated in molasses.

I recognized this feeling. All too well.

Judging by the light quality, it had to be late morning. I lay in the tangled ruins of my bed, still dressed in blood-stained clothes, the front of the shirt shredded by Joan's nails. I had no clear memory of coming in here, but it wasn't like when I didn't remember trashing the apartment. This type of blackout was an old friend, which was perversely comforting. I rewound my memory and found I couldn't recall much of anything past splitting up with Kirk. Anything past that gradually blurred into a dirty fog.

It took an indeterminate amount of time for me to turn my head. A near empty bottle of Beam lay on the pillow beside me, in a sizeable puddle of whiskey that smelled like it had already been rejected by my digestive system once. My stomach lurched as the acidic smell hit my nostrils, but there was nothing left in there to vomit up.

Relapse. Holy hell, I'd had a *relapse.* The dreaded word was whispered around the AA meetings like a normal person would say *genocide.*

Nearly a year of sobriety, down the drain. Self-loathing washed over me.

I was weak. Pathetic. Useless.

Yet I still yearned to pick up the bottle and drink the last of the liquid sloshing around the bottom.

I couldn't even remember where I'd gotten the damn thing. A gift from my alter ego, perhaps? Or maybe he was even the one that drank it, and then stuck me with the hangover. I imagined myself walking into a liquor store in nothing but my underwear and loosed a peal of gut-felt laughter that almost split my head in two.

Then I realized there might be more elsewhere in the apartment, waiting for me like trip mines, and my belly turned sour.

I sat up, made my way shakily across to the bathroom. Dry heaved into the sink a few times. Tried to look at myself in the mirror, but caught a whiff of my breath and went back to dry heaving. I had to call my sponsor, a guy whose name I could barely remember. He would want me to come to a meeting ASAP, confess my sins, my *relapse*, and then beg forgiveness from the congregation. Maybe they would have some advice on how to stay sober when your deranged split personality is the one tempting you. Then I would have to wait and see if I needed to detox. God, I didn't want to go through that again, the clammy sweats, the shivering, the—

There are more important matters to deal with than your fall off the wagon, jackass.

I stopped in the midst of splashing water on my pale face. Jesus. The Squall. My return to the land of booze would have to wait until I could find a way to warn people about my suspicions. And I had to get the apartment cleaned up, in case Hammond made good on his implied threat to return.

But I would start in the living room. I didn't trust myself to be anywhere near that unfinished bottle while I felt this awful.

After putting back on the clothes from yesterday, I headed toward the bedroom door, intent on whipping up something for an alcohol-induced headache before I started putting the place back together.

Instead, I walked directly into Mickey's dangling corpse.

2

I couldn't see what I'd run into at first, but I threw my hands out and shoved it away even as I stumbled back against the wall. My palms came away crusty and red where they'd made contact. I looked up, and a harsh, choked sob escaped me.

Mickey hung from my ceiling fan by a nylon cord tied around his neck and looped over the metal base of the unit, strung up exactly at eye level so I'd be sure to smack into him when I came out of the bedroom. Our collision had caused him to swing at the end of the neon yellow rope, his fuzzy head lolling from side to side like it had in life when he tried to work something out. His tongue protruded from one side of his mouth, bloated and purple from his strangulation, but even if this hadn't killed him, the disembowelment would have; his small body was slit down the middle like a ripe melon, spilling a runny mess of guts that reached almost to the floor. Judging from the smell and blackened, rotten patches on his sides, it looked like he'd been dead for a while.

My throat constricted again in preparation to gag, but I forced it not to. The world turned watery as grief flooded my eyes. My little dog's face looked accusatory, as though asking me why I had let this happen to him. I wheeled around, heading back into the bedroom to find my phone so I could call the police.

You sure you wanna do that? The question, from the depths of my own brain, sounded sly.

Yes, I goddamn well did. I didn't care what Hammond did when he got wind of this, I just wanted whoever did it to pay.

And what if you're the one who did it?

I froze in the bedroom doorway. No. That wasn't possible. Even if I'd actually had another blackout, I had to believe I wasn't capable of something like this. I *needed* to, for my own sanity.

Oh really? So you haven't killed any other canines lately? Or people, for that matter?

A cheap shot.

Even so, I numbly went to the kitchen instead and got a knife to cut Mickey down, telling myself it was because I didn't want him becoming part of some investigation, bagged up and taken away to an evidence locker or a coroner's fridge. I looped one bloodstained hand through my dog's collar so I could take his weight once he was loose. It was only then that I found the scrap of gray cloth tucked in between his fur and the leather. I pulled it out and unfolded it.

A vinyl skull grinned at me.

Just as it had before, from the front of Jacob's hoodie.

3

Black rage settled over me like a coating of radioactive dust after a nuclear explosion, fostering a determination that drowned out even the pain of my massive hangover. My dog had been killed, but what really made me furious is that I'd believed, if only for a moment, that I was to blame. All I knew then, as I stalked out of my apartment with the gray swatch of cloth clenched in one hand, was that the little son of a bitch had gone too far, and I would make him pay.

That anger hadn't abated in the slightest in the few minutes it took me to cross the eerily quiet grounds and stomp up onto Jacob's doorstep. His mat was much more suited to the owner than the McCaffery's had been: a giant hand with middle finger upraised, and the phrase 'Step Off, Bitch!' I picked it up and flung it out into the street—a petty victory—before pounding on the door with the bottom of both fists.

Just when I got ready to raise my foot and smash at the lock with my heel, the chain on the other side rattled. The door began to swing open, and Jacob's irate, sleep-slurred voice drifted through the crack. "Man, what the fuck do *you* w—?"

I rammed my shoulder against the door, shoving it all the way open. Jacob stumbled back, his eyes widening in shock. He was barefoot, dressed in plaid pajama pants and a stained Slipknot t-shirt, his greasy hair rumpled on one side. I grabbed him by the front of his shirt and threw him against the wall of the entryway.

"*You asshole!*" he squawked, his voice cracking so much on the last word, he sounded like a child. "You can't do this, man, you can't just bust into my place and—!"

"Shut up," I snapped. It took every inch of willpower I had to not just pummel him, to keep from wrapping my fingers around his scrawny neck and squeezing. He tried to shove me away, but I pinned him to the wall with my good forearm against his throat. The ring in his lower lip quivered. "You're gonna do something you never did in school, and *listen to every goddamn word I have to say.*"

In response, he pistoned a fist into the soft tissue of my belly and then slid from my grasp while I coughed. He tried to run back into his dark apartment, but I knew if I let him get in there—where he might have any manner of weapon—I was finished. I lurched forward and grabbed him by the shoulders, then yanked him back. His feet tangled with mine and he went down, landing on his back against the hard tile with a grunt.

"Stay down," I wheezed, standing over him.

His eyes jittered with what I at first took to be hate as he looked up at me. "You're a dead man, Jefferson," he spat. "I was just fuckin with you before, but I guess you couldn't take a joke. If you think I'm gonna let you walk away after you break into my place and lay hands on me, you're fuckin crazy. Consider the stakes raised, motherfucker."

"A *joke?*" I gave a breathless chuckle. "I'm so tired of listening to your sad sack, bullshit excuses, Jacob. You're not innocent and you know it." I threw the gray cloth in his face.

"What's this?" he demanded, picking it up suspiciously with two fingers.

"The only thing I need to get your ass sent away for good this time. Proof."

His hands shook as he sat up and held the fabric out in front of him. He squinted at it like his eyes wouldn't focus, then shook his head. Not like the twitches I'd seen so many others in the complex give, but a genuine headshake, as if to clear his mind.

"You're high," I deduced. I hadn't seen how glazed his eyes were when they bounced around before, but I could now. "Even better."

He ignored me and held up the cloth with its slick skull design. "Where'd you get this?"

"You know exactly where I got it. On my dog's body, which you strung up in my living room. Are you the one that's been killing all the animals, you little psycho?"

"Dude, I didn't...I never..." His tone started out subdued, almost bewildered, as though trying to convince himself. And that certainly could've been the case. For all I knew, his memory was just as wrecked as mine, but I wasn't willing to accept excuses. Not for him. He gnawed at his lip ring, then shook his head again—forcefully this time—and said, "No. No way, man. You're just tryin to frame me. Again."

"Oh, would you shut up with that tired old crap? I didn't frame you, Jacob. You brought a gun to school."

"No, I did NOT! Just cause it was in my bag doesn't mean it was mine! And you know you didn't see me take it out of any locker, you fuckin liar!"

I didn't answer that accusation.

Mostly because he was right.

I actually *hadn't* seen him take the gun out of his locker.

When the police began to investigate, they hadn't been able to find anything to link him to the weapon, not even a single fingerprint, and it looked like the prosecuting attorney was actually beginning to believe his ridiculous story about rival drug dealers planting the pistol on him. So I made a small revision to my story, and claimed that I'd seen him take it out of his locker and put it in his bag.

Because, even if I could entertain the idea that the gun wasn't his for the barest of seconds—which I couldn't—he was still a useless scumbag, a blight on society, handing out poison to kids that still had a chance to make something of themselves, and I figured my school would be a better place without him.

So I lied. Didn't even have to testify, just signed an affidavit. And he got sent to juvie.

And I hadn't lost a single night of sleep over it since.

Now, looking at me from the floor, he said, "Yeah, see? You know you did. You framed me then, you framed me with Tate the other night, and now you're doin it again."

"Then where's your hoodie, huh? You were wearing it last night when you drove by the McCaffery's, I saw it. So where is it now?"

One hand went to his chest, as if he expected to be wearing the garment. His ran his upper teeth back and forth across his lip ring. "I...I don't know, man, lemme go look..."

Jacob started to get up. I pushed him back down with my foot and snatched the torn cloth out of his hands. "I don't think so. We'll let the cops search for it. Between this and whatever drugs you've got in here, they should be able to put you away in a real jail this time."

I pulled out my phone and made sure he saw it as I punched in '911'. A look of panic crossed his narrow features, which I took supreme satisfaction in.

My finger hovered over the Call button as a familiar female voice called out from the depths of the apartment, "Jaaacob?"

Without invitation, I left him in the entryway and walked further inside, distant echoes of last night playing in the back of my sore brain. It was just as dim in here as it had been at the McCaffery's, despite the fact that it was close to noon. Thick woolen blankets had been nailed across all the windows to seal out even the smallest shred of natural light, making the place look like a shuttered crack den, but with the illumination from the open front door, my eyes adjusted quickly to the gloom. The cloying stench of ganja hit my nostrils as I entered the living space.

This unit layout was much smaller, maybe half the size of mine. I made my way past cheap wicker furniture and squatted next to a beaten leather couch, where Katie lay sleeping on her stomach in a tank top, under a rat's nest of blankets. The sight of her passed out like some common junkie in a flophouse caused my heart to sink.

I put a hand on her bare shoulder and gave it a gentle shake. "Katie, c'mon, get up, right now. I'm taking you home."

Her eyelids slid halfway open, revealing the same glaze I'd seen in Jacob's. She gave me a dreamy smile. The bruises on her throat looked like dark slashes in the gloom. "Hiya, Mr. Jefferson. Is it time for class already?" She was out cold again before she'd even finished speaking, and this time I couldn't get her to wake.

On a glass table beside one end of the couch sat a small pile of white powder with green flecks in it. I swept a hand across it in frustration, scattering a cloud across the dingy carpet. "Goddamn it, Jacob, what is this stuff? What the hell did you give her?"

"What she asked for." Jacob stood at the edge of the entryway, leaning against the wall with his arms crossed.

"You poisoned her," I insisted. "Slipped it in her drink so you could take advantage of her, or something."

Jacob barked derisive laughter. "Shit, you're just determined to think the worst of me." He took a few steps forward, sneering as he said, "You know what? Adler ain't the angel you want her to be. Truth is, she's been buyin from me for weeks. It's the only way she can deal with her mom. See,

I'm *helping* her, cause you sure as shit ain't. Then, last night, she showed up here at like one o'clock, said the old bitch had scared her bad. Outta the kindness of my heart, I offered up my couch. Even gave her a little sleep aid. On the house, seein as how she's such a good customer." His nostrils flared. "And once she's up, I'm sure she'd be happy to tell you that I was here *all fuckin night.*"

His words knifed through me, but I didn't let it show. "I don't believe you. She would never take this garbage willingly. She's too smart for that." I turned and tossed the blankets off Katie, slid my arms under her thin body, and lifted her off the couch. She must've weighed less than a hundred pounds. Her skin was clammy, her hair damp with sweat. "I'm taking her out of here and then calling the police. We'll let them get to the bottom of this."

"I don't think so." Jacob blocked my path. "She stays. You wanna call the cops on me, go ahead, but you don't get to pick and choose who goes down for what. She's gettin busted right along with me."

I hesitated a split second, which was probably my undoing. "Move outta my way, Jacob."

He shook his head once. "In fact, why don't *I* call the cops? You're the one breakin into other people's places, after all. I'm sure they'd *looooove* to see you again after last night."

We stood for a long moment, glaring at each other over Katie's limp body. She moaned in my arms. Finally, I turned and put her back down on the couch, then pushed past Jacob on my way out.

"This isn't over," I said, once I was back outside.

"You bet your ass it isn't," he agreed, and slammed the door behind me.

4

I considered everything Jacob had told me as I trudged back home.

It killed me to imagine Katie using his discount-bin pharmaceuticals, but could I honestly blame her? I knew about the temptation to chemically escape one's reality. I wondered what her mother had done last night to finally drive her away for good. As much as I hated to leave her in Jacob's care, perhaps that was the safest place for her.

That is, if he was telling the truth, and he really hadn't killed my dog. The jury was still out on that one.

I dreaded returning to the apartment, where Mickey's corpse waited, but the Squall started a fresh cycle on the way there. I was caught between two different transformers, battered from both directions. I looked around almost hysterically, seeking escape in case I blanked out again, before realizing that I felt nothing.

The noise was still horrible, and it made my alcohol-battered brain ache, but besides that, it felt more like it had the first day I'd discovered it: an overly annoying electrical buzz. No more drugged lightheadedness, no more sensation that the world was slipping away.

In fact, it almost sounded *tolerable*.

As I stood there marveling at the change, my phone went off, with the last call I would ever get on it.

"Hello, I'm—each—on." Static skewered the connection, each word saddled with a reverberating echo that made the woman on the other end sound like she was speaking from inside a cave.

"I'm sorry, can you repeat that?" I asked, walking around in a circle to find better reception. It had to be interference from the Squall, but when I looked at the phone display, I saw that only one of the signal bars showed. With that cell tower across the street, my reception had always been perfect. "Can you hear me?" I asked.

The voice faded back in. "Yes, I said I'm trying to reach Elliot Jefferson."

"Speaking."

"Mr. Jefferson, this is Lauren Peters from Plainview Animal Clinic. We did the testing on the dog that attacked you?"

"Oh, my god, yes!" I glanced down at the bandaged lump on my forearm. "Thank you for getting back to me so fast."

"Not a problem. Cases involving human endangerment always have priority."

Human endangerment. Instead of my life flashing before my eyes, it was the entire last half hour of *Ol' Yeller*. "So when should I expect to start foaming at the mouth?"

She laughed. "You'll be happy to know, the animal did not have rabies or any other communicable disease. As long as the wound site doesn't get infected, you should be fine."

"Hold on." I wanted to be relieved, but I think at some point over the last 24 hours, I had come to realize that rabies wasn't responsible for my death match with Yonkers. "You didn't find any reason for him to attack like that?"

"There's really no telling. Even domesticated dogs are still animals, and they can behave in unpredictable ways. All I can tell you is that physically there was nothing wrong with him."

"Are you sure? Nothing at all, nothing out of the ordinary?"

She hesitated for a split second.

"What is it?" I pressed. A hard ball had formed in the pit of my stomach.

"It might be hard to explain."

"Try me."

"Are you aware of how we test for rabies?"

"You have to cut the dog's head off, right?" I grimaced. "I guess that part was pretty much already done for you."

"That's a simple way to put it. Basically, we need a brain tissue sample. I took it from this specimen myself. We don't actually do the testing here—we have to send it to a state lab so they can keep track of any potential outbreaks—but as soon as I opened the animal up, I knew it couldn't be rabies."

"How come?"

"Because when rabies is at such an advanced stage that it's causing behavioral changes, it's also sure to be encephalitic. That's brain swelling. You can see it spread pretty evenly across the hippocampus, the limbic areas, the medulla and cerebellum."

My brain buzzed with all those big words. "And in Yonker's case, you didn't see that?"

Again, that pause. "Not exactly. One area was quite enlarged, but since I've never seen rabies attack it so specifically, I really didn't think much of it."

"What area was it?"

"Are you familiar with the amygdala?"

"I must not've gotten to that chapter in *Gray's Anatomy* yet."

"The short answer is that the amygdala has a lot to do with...well, let's say emotional responses. It's also been linked to seizures and epilepsy in canines. There are even some rare cases where a dog has sustained lesions to the area that cause it to attack. From the description of the behavior in the report, I thought that might be a possibility, but there wasn't any evident damage, just...the enlargement."

My mouth went dry. I had to swallow several times before I could speak again. "Miss Peters, can you tell me...do humans have one of these amig...?"

"Amygdalas?" She seemed perplexed by the question. "Yes, we do. Serves pretty much the same function."

"Are you doing any other tests? Anything to find out how this could've happened?"

"The owner requested the animal be returned, and, since the body is clean, my hands are tied. But don't worry, sir. Like I said, this isn't anything you could catch. Just keep the wound clean, watch for signs of infection, and you should be fine."

"Okay," I told her, "but this is really important. I think I know what might've caused—"

A double-beep indicated the call had been terminated. When I checked, I saw that my phone no longer had any signal at all.

5

My first stop was Kirk's apartment. I knocked on the door almost as hard as I had at Jacob's, but I hoped to find them long gone after his declaration last night. Further down the building, police tape blocked the entrance to the McCaffery's unit, but I noticed someone had used red paint on that cheery doormat since last night, to recreate the brooding graffiti face that had been on the complex wall yesterday. I actually shivered at the sight of it, despite the heat of the day.

But Kirk's door did open, and it was his wife standing in the entrance. Teresa Gordon had an angular face, with much lighter skin tone than Kirk, framed by tight coils of hair that hung to her shoulders. The crown of her head barely reached to my neck, but I took an almost involuntary half step back, as though the door had been answered by an angry dragon. I didn't know what to make of Kirk's story about her midnight rendezvous at Mrs. Isaacs's, but this tiny woman might be every bit as dangerous as Joan.

"Is Kirk home?" I blurted, denying the sudden urge to add, *Can he come out and play?*

She regarded me coolly. "I'm afraid he's not feeling well."

"What's wrong with him? I just saw him last night."

"That's really none of your concern, Mr. Jefferson. Perhaps he was out too late getting into trouble with you."

"Can I just talk to him for a second? It's urgent."

This time her response came coated in ice. "He's asleep. But I'll let him know you came by."

She started to close the door, but I stuck my foot in the crack to hold it open. There was no time to play games anymore. "Teresa, listen to me. I don't know what's going on with you and the other people that can't hear the transformers, but if you value your family's safety, you have to get them out of the complex immediately. Do you understand me? Just get in the car and go."

Teresa Gordon gave me a knowing grin. Her head twitched to the side, that grin momentarily morphing into a horrible rictus. "I'm sure we'll be fine, Mr. Jefferson. I would be more worried about myself, if I were you."

She used a heel to shove my foot out of the way, and closed the door in my face.

6

I considered going back to get Katie, but knew Jacob would never make the mistake of letting me into his apartment twice. Trying to warn him would be equally fruitless. That is, if he even needed a warning; I still didn't even know if he could hear the Squall or not. And Beth wasn't home. I figured she must've been at the college, which meant she was safe for the moment. I aimed to have the lid blown off this thing long before she got back.

So I jogged toward the front of the complex. I would leave the Estates immediately, on foot since I had no way to drive, keep running until either my cell had a signal or I found a phone that worked, and then call the police, the fire department, the mayor, the National Guard, and have the grounds evacuated as a health risk. Now that I knew there was actual medical evidence for my trance, Hammond couldn't use it against me. I had no doubt that this was what had caused Joan McCaffery to snap, just like Yonkers.

It took only minutes to reach the wrought-iron fence that encircled the pool courtyard behind the office. As I passed, I saw a low, metal platform had been erected beside the shallow end, and long tables with decorative tablecloths were laid out in rows on the pebbled decking to either side. I had to stare for several seconds before I understood.

Preparations were under way for Martha's party in a few hours. Before, the idea of attending a poolside affair with a bunch of fellow residents that I had no interest in knowing had sounded like hell, but now, after this nightmarish week, it seemed totally ludicrous and unrelatable, a bizarre ritual from another planet.

And that date with Beth is gonna have to be rescheduled.

My heart and head both thudded sickly by the time I came within sight of the front drive. With my level of exhaustion, it might take longer than I estimated to reach a phone. I slowed to a walk just before I reached the gate, gasping to catch my breath.

Which is a good thing, because I might have run into the bars otherwise.

The sensor mounted at the top didn't open the gate. I stood there stupidly for a few seconds, waving my hands in front of the electronic eye. If my keys hadn't been MIA, I would've tried opening it with my remote. In frustration, I worked my fingers into the gap between the bars and tried to shove the thing aside, but it stuck solidly in place on the sliding track. Metal spikes lined the top, reaching a good four feet over my head, with no way to climb over.

The walk-through gate stood to my left, a metal mesh door set into the stone wall that gave residents access to the mail kiosk. I went over, punched in the three-digit code on the push-button lock above the handle. It wouldn't budge either.

The first creeping fingers of dread began to massage my guts.

All I could do now was stand there like a jackass and wait in the hopes that a car with a functioning remote pulled up soon.

Or cut through the office.

I turned and examined the management building. It suddenly looked far more ominous to me than it had the last time I'd walked through, on Saturday morning. I was surprised, and yet not surprised at all, to find a gigantic version of that unnerving graffiti face—the mascot of those clandestine Heeders—spray-painted on the vinyl siding around the rear door, so it looked like the entrance lay right in the middle of that leering mouth. Lights burned inside, I could see them through the windows, but no people were visible. Carla and the rest of the gorgeous office ladies were still away for spring break, I remembered, leaving only Martha and Tony to worry about.

I crept across the short stretch of lawn, to the back door. The scowling eyes of that huge face glared down at me, like the entrance to some carnival funhouse. I cupped my hands over the glass panels in the door to cut down the glare and looked inside.

What I could see of the interior—the main room, and the tiny kitchenette—was deserted. I couldn't tell if there was anyone in the management alcove, where the desks for the leasing agents sat. But I could see the front door from here, a wide, heavy oak slab with a metal push bar in the middle and a window through which the circular front parking lot was visible. The last obstacle between me and freedom. If I went fast, I could be across the room and out the other side in fifteen seconds, rid of the Squall once and for all. I suddenly felt like a con in an old prison movie, attempting escape past the warden's office.

I pulled open the back door, wincing at the squeal of hinges. Air-conditioning wafted across me, chilling the beads of sweat across my forehead. I crossed the threshold, stepping into the graffiti man's mouth. I cleared the pool table and moved fast toward the exit, looking only straight ahead, arms out in front of me and ready to push the metal bar that would release the latch.

It didn't move when my palms struck it. I pushed, put my shoulder to the wood and shoved as hard as I could. The door was locked. Like a fish in an aquarium, I could see the regular world through the window, tinted in shades of light blue and yellow from the stained glass, but I couldn't god-damn get to it. Panic hit me, so severe I contemplated just smashing the window and squirming through.

"Mr. Jefferson?" Tony's lilting voice from the alcove. I turned to the left and saw him sitting at his desk, brow creased as he stared at me, a new crop of wrinkles in the making. "Did you need something?"

"Why is this door locked?" I demanded.

"Martha said to keep it closed today unless a resident specifically needs it opened. We've had a bunch of reporters calling all day. You know, about…what happened last night. And I've been in and out all morning getting ready for the party. Not that anyone's in the mood anymore. Personally, I think it's in *très* poor taste." He frowned as he examined me and asked, "Is everything all right?"

"No, it isn't," I snapped. I didn't want to escalate this, especially if poor Tony wasn't part of the conspiracy taking shape in my head, but I couldn't let myself succumb to the belief that it was all as innocent as it seemed or I'd be doubting my sanity again in no time. "I need to leave. Unlock this door right now and let me out."

"O-okay, of course." He started to come around his desk, digging in his pocket to remove a key ring.

"Stay there, Tony."

I turned toward the new voice. Martha stood behind me; where she'd come from, I didn't know. I had spoken to the property manager just two days before, right after my fight with Schrader, but it looked like those two days had been as hard for her as they had for me. She wore no makeup, and the only color in her sallow skin was the purplish hollows under eyes, which clashed badly with her yellow work shirt. Her usual joviality had vanished. She stood with hands on her massive hips and glared at me with the same vacant antipathy as the coliseum of spectators after I'd rescued Rory Bergman.

Tony halted halfway across the offshoot at her command, and turned his head awkwardly back and forth between us.

"Open this door," I reiterated. When neither of them moved, I slammed both hands against the latch bar behind me; Tony jumped, Martha did not. "I want out! You can't keep me here, I demand you let me out!"

"I'd be more than happy to," she said flatly. "But first, there's something I'd like you to see. Please come with me, Mr. Jefferson." To Tony, she added, "Why don't you go to lunch?"

"But I needed to—"

"*Leave*, Tony."

She waddled past me, into the long offshoot. I stood there a moment longer, trying to decide if I should run. Once I took that step, gave into the panic, something told me whatever little control I had over this situation would quickly evaporate. And even if I did take off, where would I go? Unless I really wanted to leap through one of the windows like an action movie star, I would be forced to flee back into the complex.

Since I couldn't think of a viable alternative, I followed Martha past a bewildered Tony, toward the far end of the alcove.

7

Martha's office was a square little more than ten feet wide, mostly taken up by her desk, whose entire surface held framed photos of her husband and three children. A transformer sat right outside the only window on the other side of the desk; the buzz of the Squall was almost deafening, like sitting on top of a constantly vibrating fault line. The idea of remaining in here for more than a few minutes turned my testicles into shriveled raisins. Martha stood by the door while I entered, then shut it behind me. "Have a seat."

I did, easing into one of the chairs in front of the desk. I kept my eyes on her as she came around to sit behind it, ready for anything.

"I planned on getting in touch with you later today. But since you're here, we can get this out of the way now." Martha squeezed her bulk into the leather office chair as she spoke. I almost couldn't hear her over the Squall. My hands found the edge of her desk and squeezed hard enough for my fingernails to leave crescent indentations in the lacquered top.

Then, for some reason, the taste of that Jim Beam splashed across my taste buds, and the noise dampened almost instantly, dying down to a mutter. I was so grateful for the relief I didn't look a gift horse in the mouth.

"Martha...you have to call the police," I pleaded. "That noise from the transformers...I know you can't hear it, but it's making everyone sick. I can prove it. The whole complex needs to be evacuated."

She regarded me over the top of her desk, through the raccoon-mask of circles around her sunken eyes. "As you've probably seen, we've had some vandalism around the complex the last few days," she began, not acknowledging a word I'd said.

My jaw tightened. "Yeah, I've noticed. Please, you have to listen—"

"But I'm guessing you *didn't* notice the cameras the management company had installed on property last week." She smiled at the blank look I gave her. "They were intended to catch whoever is behind those awful animal killings, but they've served just as well to help find our amateur artist. Then again, who knows? Maybe they're one and the same."

"Okay, great. What does that have to do with you keeping me here against my will?"

Martha swiveled to face her computer, moved the mouse, typed something on the keyboard. Then she turned her monitor to face me with one pudgy hand, having to move pictures of her equally obese family out the way to do so. A picture of the darkened pool and back door of the office waited on the screen, taken from a high vantage.

"This is camera footage from early yesterday evening, just before that unfortunate business with the McCafferys." Martha used the mouse to move her cursor over to a play button at the bottom of the screen.

I turned my gaze away from her, focusing on the screen as the movie began.

And just about fell out of my chair as I saw myself creep into frame, wearing nothing but underwear and decorated with food condiments.

8

The figure in the video clip moved like a prowling animal as it came into view beside the pool, hunched and low to the ground, half-scampering on two legs, half-loping with its fingers brushing the ground, like a chimpanzee. It stopped just before reaching the building and lifted its head to the night, as though listening. The action looked scarily primal. At one point, it glanced directly at the camera, and there was no mistaking my own face, still slightly swollen from Schrader's fists. One side of my mouth drew up into a silent growl while my head jerked to the side.

In Martha's office, I tried to speak, but only a reedy whisper passed over my lips.

The other me, the one in the video, moved toward the office and squatted beside the door, like a filthy, mongrel dog. For the first time, I saw he held something in one hand, a short metal tube, and as he held it up to the side of the building, I recognized one of the miniature cans of spray paint I used on my models. He began to paint a towering circle around the door, scurrying up a nearby lamppost with creepy agility to complete the top, and then set about the other details of his masterpiece.

When he was finished, he had created the leering face I'd walked through to get into the building just a few minutes before. He crab-walked backward and sat admiring his handiwork for a few moments while absent-mindedly stroking his cock over his underwear, then turned and leapt over a nearby row of bushes, out of frame.

At least now I knew what I'd been up to last night during my lost hours.

9

"That...t-that wasn't...me..." I couldn't even muster the energy to get the lie out. Of course it was me, the evidence was undeniable. But everything I'd done on that video, every action, was as alien to me as if I'd just watched myself performing brain surgery.

"Come, come now, Mr. Jefferson," Martha scolded. In mocking undertones, it seemed.

"Look, this is what the Squall is doing to us!" I blurted, not caring if she understood my term for it or not. "It's turning us into...into *that!* I blacked out last night, I don't remember doing any of this! And I think it happened to Joan McCaffery, too! This is exactly why we have to call the police!"

"Be my guest." Martha gestured past the minefield of framed photos, to the phone on the corner of her desk closest to me. "By all means, call them. But when they arrive, I'll be forced to show them this video."

"Yeah, so what?"

She ran a chipped red fingernail down the side of her monitor, the motion seductive. "Well, the recording...coupled with your involvement in Joan McCaffery's death... and, of course, what you've done to your apartment..." Martha grinned demurely, batted her eyelashes and licked her lips, just before her head jerked to one side. "I think the police would have no choice but to arrest you."

I jumped to my feet and brought a fist down on her desktop, mostly to hide my fear at how much she knew. The pictures fell like dominoes, the glass cracking in one of them. Martha didn't even flinch. "You think you can intimidate me? You go ahead, show them whatever you want, tell whatever lies you need to! Because once I get a doctor to examine me, to do an MRI or a CAT scan to see what that noise is doing to our brains, it won't matter! They'll figure out the truth, and then whatever you and Samantha Adler and all the other Heeders are up to is finished." I snatched up the handset.

"Good heavens, I don't know what you're talking about," Martha said quickly. "But I do know it will take the police at least a few hours to listen to your story—if they actually do—and even longer for them to substantiate it with these tests you think you need. And during that time, well...who knows what might happen to Katie Adler?"

I paused with my finger on the 9 key and stared at her.

"Her mother is so violent," Martha continued. "Poor Katie might be hurt without you here to keep her safe. Or what about our newest tenant? Your little girlfriend? She seems like such a clumsy woman. Just an accident waiting to happen."

"Don't," I said softly.

"Then hang up that phone, Mr. Jefferson. Hang it up, and sit down."

Looking back, I wish to God I had just called anyway.

But at the time, I put the handset back on the cradle and dropped into the chair like a sack of stones.

Martha made a come-hither gesture in the air with her hand. The door opened behind me, and I twisted around to see Rick, the middle third of the Jock Trinity, enter the room and stand brooding in the doorway with his muscular arms crossed. "Rick, please show Mr. Jefferson out of the office."

"Why are you doing this?" I asked.

"You'll understand soon. Everyone will."

"What does that even mean? Just tell me what's going on. You can't keep me here!"

"We'll see."

Her answer chilled me. "But Martha…this is insane. This isn't you. The Squall is making you act like this. You need help, we *all* need help."

"And we're getting it. You will too, if you just cleanse your impurities and *heed*."

She signaled to Rick again, and the young man's hand fell on my shoulder. I got up numbly and walked through the door with both of them following. Martha stopped just outside her office and said, "I suggest you return to your unit for now, Mr. Jefferson. I have a party to prepare for, and I don't have time to babysit you. If you try to leave the complex again, or cause any more problems with the other residents, it will be me calling the police. And I can't promise you where things go from there."

I stared at her in utter disbelief, her final threat echoing, then stomped out of the office and through the offshoot, heading toward the back exit.

Behind me, Martha called out, "Oh, and do be careful with what's left of your unit, Mr. Jefferson. I think you've already lost your security deposit…"

WEDNESDAY
EVENING

1

I went home.

What else could I do? I believed every word Martha had said, that if I attempted to leave, she—or more likely *they*—would turn me into a fugitive, so that no one would listen to a word I had to say. I didn't care so much about that, I knew I could eventually convince someone of what was happening in the Estates, but as for the threat she'd implied about hurting Katie or Beth…I couldn't take any chances. I might be the only person who could get the truth out, but I wouldn't sacrifice them to do it. If I left the complex, I would have to either make sure they were safe, or bring them with me. My preference was the latter.

But let the Heeders think they'd beaten me for now. I could feel eyes watching from every window as I trudged back home, trying to look as dejected as possible, but all the time the wheels turned in my head. Thanks to the animal clinic, I knew how this was happening—trauma to some mysterious part of the brain called the 'amygdala,' brought on by the Squall—but I had no idea what endgame the Heeders were working toward (*You'll understand soon…everyone will*) or why certain people seemed to be immune.

The only thing that terrified me more than the malicious, twitching mannerisms of Schrader and Martha and Samantha Adler was the sight of myself in that video, crawling around on all fours like some asylum-ridden halfwit and painting their propaganda everywhere. Almost as bad as Joan had been.

Once behind a locked door though, I tried my cell phone again. I wouldn't call the cops until the Heeders had no one to hold over my head, but I could try to reach Beth through the college and convince her not to come home. If I could keep her out of their clutches, then I would only have to worry about Katie.

Still zero bars though, no reception. My thoughts went to the cell tower across the road, the only one close enough to service us this far from the main hub of the city. And my budget had been so limited since I'd moved into this place, I'd never paid for a landline or Wi-Fi connection.

Fortunately, I knew where Beth would be in just a few hours. Where the whole complex would be.

To kill time, I set about the arduous task of cleaning the apartment from top to bottom. No sense giving Martha further ammunition against me. I fixed everything I could, bagged up what I couldn't, put new sheets on the bed, and hung up my surviving clothes. I sealed up Mickey's body and laid him in the garage until I could get him buried properly, then scrubbed the bloodstains from the carpet until they were a pale, pink blur.

I approached the bottle of Beam as though it were a biohazard. Using two fingers, I picked it up by the neck, held it at arm's length as I walked to the kitchen, and started to pour it down the drain—really, I did—but stopped just before it would've dribbled out.

By this point, the Squall had worked my nerves over yet again. I could feel it worming its way into my head, setting fire to my nerves.

That moment in Martha's office came back to me, when just the thought of the liquor had been enough to quell the sound.

With shaking hands, I brought the bottle to my lips. I waited a moment for something to stop me, some cosmic force to show me I couldn't possibly be right, and when nothing happened, I took an experimental swallow.

The whiskey hit my stomach like liquid fire, and then my head a split-second later. God, that was *good*. Not just the taste, but that comforting, creeping numbness. I had missed it so much, figured I would always miss it, even if I managed to stay clean for fifty years. For just a moment, I didn't care about sobriety or the Squall or anything else; I just wanted to chug the rest of this fine Kentucky redeye. Drowning my problems had always worked before, and none of them had ever seemed as big as what I faced now.

But I forced myself to stop—prying the bottle away from my lips after that one heaven-sent shot—and listened.

The transformers sounded...different. Still there, but muffled. Distant. So far, I hadn't been able to achieve that no matter what I stuffed in my ears. And I didn't feel dizzy or out-of-body. In fact, I felt more grounded and normal than I had all week, aside from the slight buzz I now had going.

I stared at the bottle. About a fifth of the liquid remained. I denied the urge to take just one more swallow, that was all, just *one more*, and instead poured the rest into a mono-grammed flask that Darcy had bought for me when we first started dating. I didn't know why it helped—hell, maybe it was just wishful thinking—but I needed every ounce of strength I could get.

After that, I actually stretched out on the couch and got some genuine sleep, unhaunted by dreams.

But only for a bit.

Because at seven o'clock I put on a pair of shorts, sneakers, and a Hawaiian print shirt I'd worn on my honeymoon in Florida, then headed back down to the office to attend the annual Poolside Gala.

2

I had spotted Beth coming home about a half hour before, which meant the gate had let her through. The real question was if she would find herself trapped when she tried to leave again, or if the house arrest was meant only for me. If it didn't extend to her now, it probably would once I filled her in on what I knew.

Even though I saw her car pull in to the garage, I didn't dare go out to talk to her. I would only get one shot at this, and I wanted her to be as close to the exit as possible when I made my move. We could try for the office, or I could just boost her over the wall as a last resort. Maybe Katie would be there too, and I could get them both out together.

Until then, I would attempt to blend in. And be ready for anything.

I could hear the music even over the Squall by the time I reached building 10, a turntable-heavy dance remix of "Who Let the Dogs Out?" My buzz had blossomed into a full-blown tipsy thanks to a few more pulls from the flask, so neither the song nor the electric squealing got on my nerves in the least.

The volleyball court stood abandoned, the sand packed and dry from the heat. Beyond that, a warm glow hung over the pool courtyard. The temperature had hovered in the low nineties as the sun set, but a strong wind had sprung up from the north since this afternoon, smelling of rain. The sky in that direction was smeared with clouds. I hoped Martha's precious party got flooded.

When I reached the fence surrounding the pool, I found tiny floodlights placed outside the perimeter, lighting the place up like a Hollywood premiere. A DJ had set up his equipment on the stage I saw earlier, with a portable dance floor laid out in front of him, but no one was on it. The tables were laden with plastic wine glasses and a selection of cheeses and finger foods. Colored lights blazed beneath the crystal clear pool water, shifting every few seconds from red to blue to green. Fake lily pads floated on the surface, with a lit candle in each one. Even before the Squall, I had expected hot dogs and streamers, but this affair was truly as elegant as Martha had claimed, like a wealthy country wedding.

The guests, however, were not.

I studied them through the fence as I made my way toward the gate that separated the pool courtyard from the rolling green lawn behind the office, which seemed to be the preferred entrance to the party. There were around fifty or sixty folks milling around the pool and the grassy strips to either side, with more drifting in all the time. Almost none of them talking, some even scowling around angrily, others just staring at the ground as though transfixed by their feet. None of them looked like they wanted to be here. Even the few children among them seemed subdued. A smaller group stood hunched over the food table, shoveling handfuls of tiny sandwiches and biscotti cookies into their mouths, barely even chewing before they went in for more. In the darkest corner of the yard, beneath some overhanging bushes, a couple in their mid-forties had their tongues jammed down each other's throats and hands under clothing, oblivious to the world. The woman had one leg hiked up around her partner's hips and grinded against him in a way that reminded me instantly of Joan McCaffery.

And that tension I'd been feeling all week was back with a vengeance. It seemed to be focused right here, over this miserable soiree, another kind of storm just as ready to break as the one forming in the sky overhead. I figured the Heeders must be going through with this party just to keep up appearances, but, if so, they weren't doing a very good job.

A quick scan revealed no one I knew besides Tony—who stood uncomfortably by the stage in a maitre d's outfit, his skin so orange it almost glowed in the dark—and Javier, standing beside the entrance gate with arms crossed, like a night club bouncer. No Beth, Katie, or even Kirk. Martha stood opposite Javier, in a frocky blue dress far too formal for the occasion, greeting more sullen attendees arriving ahead of me.

Suddenly, I didn't want to go in there. I started to veer away from the gate.

Then I remembered why I came here in the first place, and stayed in line.

Martha's eyes widened when she caught sight of me. I tried to figure out what I would do if she wouldn't let me in. When my turn came, Javier stepped forward as though to block my path, but she waved him back and wrapped her doughy arms around me. "I'm so glad you could come, Mr. Jefferson! It's wonderful to see you making an effort to join our Estates family!"

"Wouldn't have missed it," I muttered.

As she pulled away, I looked down into her face and saw the hardness in her eyes, despite the friendly smile and singsong tone. "Go right in, but mind your manners, you naughty boy! We wouldn't want to have to send you home without supper, now would we?"

I swallowed and shook my head, then went past her and entered the party.

3

Heads swung in my direction in perfect unison as I passed through the gate. Not all, not even most, but enough so that the odd synchronization made me feel like an outsider in the *Village of the Damned*. I saw empty eyes and scowls, heads ever-so-slightly twitching to the side. I wondered if one of them was Connelly from 3204. Javier followed me through and stood with several other members of the maintenance crew, glowering at me. I marked every face as a Heeder and headed toward an empty spot near the food table. If I could sort out who was and wasn't a danger, maybe I could find some help.

The "Dogs" remix ended, and the DJ—a lean black guy in a driving cap and sunglasses—leaned in to his microphone. "Okay folks, let's play somethin to get this party goin, or you're gonna put *me* to sleep up here." A fast, Calypso-flavored rendition of "Celebration" started up.

I watched the DJ as he went about his mixing. Here was one person definitely not under the spell of the Squall. What would Martha do if I started causing a scene right now, in front of him? Shouting out everything I knew, perhaps. How far would they be willing to take this absurd charade of normalcy?

It doesn't matter. Until Katie and Beth are safe, you're gonna say nothing and keep a smile on your face. I felt like a contestant on some bizarre reality show, playacting for cameras I couldn't see.

The food on the table beside me—the few trays that hadn't been touched by the frantic grazers, that is—looked tempting. My belly gave a prolonged rumble. I hadn't eaten since my unconscious gorge yesterday, mostly because my appetite had been nonexistent. But I wasn't about to put anything from this offering in my mouth.

The Squall blended in with the music blasting from the DJ's speakers, giving an ear-splitting warble to Kool and the Gang's vocals. I pulled out my flask and took a swig. There was no guilt in it this time, no inner turmoil or sense of betrayal. Sobriety had been put on indefinite hold; the bar was open and drinks were on the house. As before, the alcohol had the oddly curious effect of stabilizing me against the Squall, like sandbags forming a floodwall, but with my empty stomach, it also hit me hard and fast.

The flask, which had been full when I emptied the Beam, was down more than a third from those quick nips. The glow around the floating candles began to soften around the edges. Jesus, I'd better make an attempt at moderation, or I'd be blitzed before I knew it.

A hand fell on my shoulder. I spun around, ready to fight.

"Woah, fookin hell, you're jumpier than a horse in a glue factory." Tate, fully uniformed, took a step back and held up his hands in mock surrender. "I guess that's understandable, though."

"Sorry," I told him, then, as his last statement caught up with me, "Wait, what do you mean, it's understandable?"

"Well, after last night." He looked around and then whispered, "You know...Joan and all."

"Right, right." I said. For a second, I'd dared to hope that he knew exactly what was going on.

I couldn't even believe he was here. He didn't live on

property, couldn't be affected by the Squall. It was an opportunity I couldn't afford to waste. I prepared to start babbling at him, then saw Martha watching us from the gate over Tate's shoulder. She smiled and wagged her finger mock-menacingly at me.

"I wanted to talk to you about all that shite anyway," Tate continued, drawing my attention back. "I called Detective Hammond today. Tried to put in a good word for you and Gordon. I don't think for a second any of that was you boys' fault. Frankly, it's a fookin wonder Dan and Joan didn't kill each other a lot sooner. Pardon me for speaking ill of the dead, but I can't even tell you how many times I've been called out to their place for a double D. Domestic disturbance, I mean."

"Try living underneath them," I said.

He nodded. "I can imagine. Anywho, you'll be happy to know, I won Hammond over. I think you two are off the hook."

This morning, that information would've thrilled me, but now I wished an entire S.W.A.T. team would swoop down from a helicopter to arrest me. But I mumbled, "Thanks. I appreciate that."

His mustache wiggled on his upper lip as he glanced around the party again. "You wanna know the truth, I don't know what the hell's going on around here lately. I've had so many calls this past week from feuding neighbors, I haven't gotten a moment's peace on my vacation. After the situation with the McCaffery's last night, I had to drive back out here at four in the morning to keep two ladies from beating one another to death over a car parked three inches over the median."

"Civil unrest."

"You got that goddamned right." This last curse came out 'god-doomed' in his fake brogue. He snorted. "Martha tried to tell me I didn't have to be here for this, if you can believe it. I told her no fookin way. I mean, for chrissake, we had three deaths on the property yesterday! *Deaths!* And it's a good thing I insisted too, cause most of these folks look ready to snap."

I studied the party guests again, now close to a hundred people. Two men on the far side of the dance floor looked to be having an argument, reminding me of the old guys I'd seen when Katie and I walked the complex. There seemed to be a few normal types here and there, looking as uncomfortable as I felt, but everyone else still eyed one another angrily. A few more people had bellied up to the smorgasbord; they elbowed one another roughly whenever they got in each other's way. I couldn't see the couple in the bushes anymore, but a few other spontaneous make-out sessions had broken out.

"Who was the third?" I asked suddenly.

"What?"

"You said three people died yesterday. Dan, Joan, and who else?"

"You didn't hear about Miss Dillinger?"

"Oh. Yeah." I had forgotten all about that solemn, silent ambulance yesterday morning. It felt like a lifetime ago. "What happened to her, anyway?"

"Broken neck. Poor old gal fell down the stairs. Ya ask me—which ya didn't, but I'm gonna tell ya anyway—she had no business living on the second floor, with all the medication she was on."

For some reason, that made me think of Rory Bergman, and his bottle of Phenobarbital. I hoped the kid was okay.

Tate grimaced. "Probably tripped over one of those cats of hers. And, if that wasn't bad enough, the ingrates chowed down on the body. I heard the little shites went nuts and even attacked the paramedics when they came in."

The two men on the other side of the dance floor graduated from angry words to shoves. Tate sighed. "I'm on the verge of telling Martha to take this gig and shove it. The hassle ain't worth the piddly stipend they pay me." He walked away to break up the fight, and I took another nip from the flask, then turned back to the party just in time to see Beth enter the pool gate.

4

It was the first time I'd seen her since that disastrous night at the complex gym. The ground lights illuminated her from behind, giving her an almost angelic glow. She'd worn a sheer green spaghetti strap camisole, covered by an almost see-thru white overshirt tied at the waist, and a pair of hip-hugging jeans with sandals. Her blond hair curled delicately at the shoulders. Conservative, yet stunning. For just a moment, I got so distracted staring at her that I forgot all about my current predicament.

Beth spotted me and gave a cheerful wave. She angled through the crowd toward me. I stayed where I was until she was a few feet away, then stepped forward to meet her.

My knees buckled as the whiskey caught up with me in a rush. My thoughts had still been more or less clear, so I hadn't realized just how far gone I really was. I toppled forward like a downed tree and would've faceplanted on the patio if she hadn't stepped in to catch me.

"Woah!" she said over the music. "Jesus Jefferson, you that happy to see me?"

"Sorry." I awkwardly used her as a prop to get back on my feet, grabbing a generous helping of boob in the process. My head swirled, and the party blurred momentarily before drifting back into focus.

She straightened her shirt, readjusted the groped breast in its bra cup. "Looks like you got started a little early on the wine tasting, huh?"

I imagined I could hear judgment in the question, the sort of needling Darcy had been such an expert at. Embarrassment flushed my cheeks. I couldn't believe I'd managed to get drunk when I most needed my wits about me. Par for the course for Elliot Jefferson. The litany of old excuses formed in my throat.

But Beth grinned wickedly and stepped around me to the food. "Guess I better catch up. Can't let people say you drank me under the table."

Before I could stop her, she grabbed a glass of wine and downed almost the whole thing in one swallow. She gagged and made a face.

"What? What is it?" I expected her to puke blood.

"Ugh, it's apple juice! I was promised there would be alcohol at this thing."

"Apple juice?" I stared at the collection of glasses. A couple of stray ideas tried to connect in my bleary brain.

Was it possible Martha and the others knew that alcohol helped block out the Squall?

Beth lifted an eyebrow. "So how are you so blotto?"

I glanced around. We had drawn Martha's undivided attention; she stood at the gate, ignoring the stream of hollow-eyed entrants, and pointed us out to Javier. I dug the flask out of my pocket and held it low. "Don't let the screws see you," I advised. "Something tells me it'll be confiscated."

Beth snickered and took the flask. "I feel like I'm at prom." She ducked as though tying her shoe and discreetly tossed her head back, taking two huge swallows, the kind only a drinking amateur downs of an unknown beverage.

I needed her firing on all cylinders for what I was about to attempt, but if a few belts buffered her against the Squall it would be worth it. She came back up grimacing and shook her head. "Wow, you go for the hard stuff, Jefferson."

I grabbed the flask, screwed back on the top, and then took her by the wrist. "C'mon, I have to talk to you. Right now."

Stepping more carefully this time, I started to lead her away, around the far side of the pool and toward the office. Once we were out, it was a scant fifty yards to the gate and the front wall of the property.

But we hadn't taken more than a few steps before Javier and his crew broke from their positions and started moving to cut us off. The crowd around us seemed to thicken, slowing us down, but whether it was by design or my own imagination, I didn't know.

Above us and to the north, the first grumble of thunder rolled lazily across the sky.

"Wait, hold on, what's the rush?" Beth offered resistance, dragging us to a stop.

My tongue flopped in my mouth. "I told you, I need to talk to you. In private. It's important!"

Beth groaned, oblivious to the Hispanic men slowly surrounding us. "I don't wanna talk, Jefferson. It's way too early in our relationship for any conversation that sounds so serious. Let's just...have some fun, okay? Ooo, ooo, come dance with me!" She pulled me in the opposite direction, toward the small stage instead. It was either go with her or separate, and since two of the maintenance workers had already cut around the pool and stood between us and the exit, I went with her.

We passed by Tony, who gave me a fearful glance, and then I found myself on that deserted dance floor, standing stupidly as Beth shimmied around me.

Darcy and I had taken a ballroom dancing class a long, long time ago, but I had never been much for the formless, to-the-beat gyrations the club hoppers performed, even if Beth looked young and sexy while doing it. Plus, as drunk as I was, I knew I would end up on the ground if I tried anything too elaborate. Javier caught up to us, stopped on the edge of the dance floor, and glared. I looked around for Tate, but couldn't see him. Surely they wouldn't try anything with him here.

"All right, the white girl knows how to have some fun!" the DJ announced. Beth whooped, still unaware that we were the only two dancing, undoubtedly a little tipsy herself. "This one's for her and her man!"

He started playing a slower R&B song, one I didn't know. Beth snuggled up close, put an arm around my upper back, and laid her head on my shoulder, right about where Joan had bitten me. I let my hands creep around her waist, which felt damn good against mine. Together, we took shuffling steps as I led her in a slow circle across the dance floor, her providing enough support to keep me from an inebriated sway.

"Mmm, this is nice," she murmured. It *was* nice. There was no denying that I liked her. A lot. I would've gladly kept her in my arms all night, but now other angry faces turned toward us, one at a time, drawn like flowers toward the sun. My muscles stiffened as that tension in the air spiked.

Time to stop letting myself get distracted. I had to tell her, so we could work together to get out of here.

"What do you know about the amygdala?" I murmured in her ear, pronouncing the word carefully, so my alcohol-heavy lips didn't slur it.

Beth picked her head back up and gave me a quizzical look. "That's a mighty hefty topic. Or is that some sex thing I don't know about?"

"I'm serious." I glanced over at Javier. "And just...put your head back on my shoulder. Pretend we're not talking."

She kept squinting at me, an uncertain smile dancing on her lips. "You just keep finding new levels of weirdness, Jefferson."

"Humor me."

She did, and we went back to dancing, me careful to guide us away from the glares at the edges of the floor. "So?" I prompted.

"I could give you the textbook definition, but the easiest way to explain the amygdala is the four F's."

"Four...F's?"

"That's how one of my professors told us to remember it." She tapped each of her fingers against my neck as she listed them. "Fear, feeding, fighting, and fucking. The amygdala is essentially the physical component of Freud's id."

It was a different answer than I'd gotten from Lauren Peters of the Plainview Animal Clinic, but still over my head. "Can you tell me what it does? In layman terms?"

"What it does?" Her breath was electric against my ear. God, I felt so dizzy. I wanted to down the last of the booze and then find a quiet place to curl up with her. "It sort of...I guess you could say it's an emotional gateway. One that uses fear of consequence to regulate all those dirty little impulses we don't want the rest of the world to know about."

We came to a stop on the dance floor. I couldn't help it; my feet would no longer obey. The alcohol in my stomach turned cold and sour. "Like what?"

Beth raised her head again; this time I didn't stop her. "It's what keeps you from, say, scarfing an entire pizza because it tastes good, or raping every woman you see just because she's attractive, or tearing someone's head off when they bump into you on the sidewalk." Her brow drew together. "Too little stimulation of the amygdale, and you're an unfeeling zombie; too much, and you become a primitive with no self-control."

Primitive.

The word hit me hard. Wasn't that exactly what I'd thought when I saw Connelly dancing around the transformer that night, and when I'd woken from my blackout to find my body painted in condiment swirls, like some bohemian from a forgotten tribe?

I looked around the party again, at all those angry faces watching us. The gorgers had almost polished off the last of the food, like Joan and I had the contents of our respective pantries. And, beneath the bushes where the couple had been before, the initial stages of an orgy appeared to be unfolding.

Suddenly, I understood what the Squall was doing to all of us at the Estates.

It was turning us into cavemen.

5

I stood there, dumbfounded, feeling the scowls of my neighbors as more jagged pieces of the puzzle came together, too blatant for even my alcohol-sluggish brain to miss: Mickey and Yonkers attacking me...Schrader's brutal savagery...my own indiscretion in the alley two nights ago... even my ravenous trip to the grocery store way back on Saturday. All this time, the Squall had been monkeying around in our collective subconscious, reprogramming us, causing those who couldn't hear it to oversatisfy our basest desires: food, sex, and confrontation.

Beth must've seen something on my face, because she asked, "Jefferson? Elliot? What is it, what's wrong?"

My jaw waggled when I tried to answer. The party seemed very far away, the Squall impossibly loud but fading in and out through the music, like bad radio reception.

That voice...that horrible, whispering voice buried deep down in the noise...

Suddenly, I was looking at Beth from the far end of a pitch black pipe. I scrambled for the flask in my pocket.

And had it knocked out of my hand before I could even unscrew the cap.

"Shame, shame. You ain't supposed to have that, now are ya?"

Jacob stood on the dance floor next to Beth, shoulders hunched, eyes sunken craters.

"Leave me alone," I grunted. The words sounded a thousand miles away. *Kill him, kill him*, the voice of the Squall—the still, small voice—chanted in my head, an invitation as appealing as cold margaritas on the beach. I scanned the dance floor for the flask even as the world continued to dim around me.

"But I'm just tryin ta help out a buddy." Despite the mirth in Jacob's voice, there was none on his face. He looked just as gone as I felt, spaced out, unfocused, and swaying slightly. He put a hand on my shoulder and shoved. There was barely any force behind it, but I wobbled back a step anyway, arms out for balance like a man on the trapeze. A murmur ran through the gathering crowd that sounded almost anticipatory. The DJ cut off the music, leaving us all to bathe in the Squall. "It's the least I can do after the visit you paid me this morning."

"What's going on?" Beth asked. "Elliot, who is he?"

"Oh looky here." Jacob swerved toward her, unsteady on his feet. "This your new girlfriend, Mr. Jefferson? Gotta say, she's a lot pretty than the picture of that cow you used ta keep on your desk." He turned a vicious smile on me. "You know, the one that left your worthless ass?"

"Get away from her." The blood in my veins turned to hot engine oil. My vision was down to a pinhole. I could feel myself slipping away just like before, and, when I did, I would probably murder Jacob Tinsley, just as my upstairs neighbor had murdered her husband.

That is, if he didn't kill me first.

Jacob hiked a thumb at Beth. "Guess you haven't told her about your little problem, huh? You used to think you were so cool about it in school, sneaking off to the bathroom, popping mints, but everybody knew. We could smell the booze from the back of the class."

Beth crossed her arms protectively over her chest. "What's he talking about?"

Before I could answer, my eyes landed on the flask, sitting in the shadow of the crowd at the edge of the dance floor. I lunged for it, landed on my knees, and stayed hunkered on the ground while I got the cap off and then drained what was left. The heat of the drink made me swoon, but the world snapped back into place. I looked up to find Beth watching me, her eyes wide in surprise and maybe even a little disgust.

A few steps away, Jacob was laughing. "Fuck man, look at you! You got it worse than any junkie I ever saw!"

At that moment, I didn't need the Squall to goad me into killing him. I came up swinging, but my reflexes dragged. Jacob ducked under my flailing fists. He came in low, wrapping himself around me in a bear hug that lifted me off my feet, and drove me across the floor. I could hear Beth screaming, but I ignored her as I pawed at his face. My fingers found the ring in his lower lip.

I yanked.

Jacob screeched and dropped me back on my own feet just before we would've plowed into the crowd. He stood there, brow raised, holding the front of his jaw in one hand as blood seeped between his fingers. I looked at the ring pinched between my thumb and index, still with a scrap of flesh caught on its barb, and let it fall.

"Where's Katie?" I demanded. "Is she still at your apartment? *Tell me, goddamn it!*"

Jacob moved his hand away from his face, revealing the tear in his lip through which gums were visible. Blood cascaded down his chin. Rage bloomed in his eyes, as bright as a torch, and he came at me again, fist cocked back to slam me in the face.

And then Tate was there, shouting for us to break it up, grabbing Jacob by the arm and pulling him away from me. The young man turned and took a swipe at the cop, who met the attack with a full body tackle. The two of them tumbled off the edge of the patio, falling into the elegantly-lit pool with a tremendous splash.

Their bodies hitting the water seemed to signal a snap in the midst of our audience, a crack so loud, I at first took it for more thunder. But no; that tension in the air—the heat of potential violence that had been hanging over the complex since Saturday morning—had finally broken.

And then the Poolside Gala turned into a full-fledged riot.

6

It started somewhere in the crowd of angry onlookers, a spark of violence that swept through all but a few of the complex residents. No structure to it, no orderly pairing off to spar like bare-knuckle brawlers; those under the influence of the Squall just turned to whoever they could get their hands on and went berserk, punching, kicking, biting, and scratching. I saw one man grab another and try to plunge his thumbs into his victim's eye sockets, stopped only by a woman that sank her teeth into his forearm. The tables were overturned, the last scraps of food spilled across the concrete, where a few people hunched on the ground and ate them while shoving each other away. Even in the sexual frenzy beneath the bushes—now a group of close to twelve individuals, all at various stages of disrobing—the participants growled and clawed at one another.

This is what had been just beneath that veil across the world, the thin veneer of civility that we cling to.

Almost one hundred men, women and even a few children, all doing their damnedest to kill one another, succumbing to those urges that good ol' mankind has pursued since our jungle days.

And Beth and I were caught in the middle of it.

Through the scuffling bodies, I spotted Tate and Jacob surface in the shifting colors of the pool, wet and shivering to gawk at the insanity. The DJ backed away from his booth in horror, then grabbed as much of equipment as he could carry and ran for the closest gate.

I figured he had the right idea. If I wanted to get Beth out of here, now was my best chance.

"*Run!*" I yelled at her.

At first, she was too stunned to comprehend, but when I took her hand and pulled, she followed willingly. But there was really nowhere to go. The entire courtyard was packed. We were still looking for a hole in the crush of bodies when a command boomed above the sound of the riot.

"*STOOOOP THIIIIIS!*"

Even at a shouting volume, the voice was an ancient purr. But it was utterly undeniable, like a mandate from the heavens. The fighting around us tapered off. Bruised, snarling faces turned toward the speaker.

On the other side of the gate through which I had entered earlier stood a stooped, bone-thin woman, her face sagging and crowded with wrinkles and silver hair tucked up into a neat bun at the back of her skull. She was dressed crisply, in a dark blue linen suit with a skirt that reached down to her narrow ankles; the kind of church attire my grandmother had once worn. Both hands hovered near her flat breasts, clutching each other in a vice-like grip. Her eyes skewered through the assemblage, seeming to take the time to meet each person's gaze until it was so still in the pool yard I felt like I'd gone deaf. Even the Squall ebbed for this woman.

Mrs. Isaacs. I had only ever seen her silhouette, but I think I would've known it was her even if I hadn't.

Behind her, she had an entourage consisting of Samantha Adler, Schrader, and the Jock Trinity, among others. The members of her midnight sewing circle. They stood behind her in a double row, like schoolchildren behind the marm, some of them with blank faces, others—like Katie's mother—wearing a smug, superior little grin. Martha held the gate open for them with the penitent flair of a red carpet unrolling before royalty, then fell into line at the end.

Isaacs walked through the crowd with measured steps. The throng parted in front of her almost reverently. She looked back and forth between them as the silence grew thick enough to taste.

"*Thiiisssss*," she hissed, drawing the word out so that it rolled over the crowd and echoed off the wall of the office, "is *not* the way. Giving succor to the Beast within leads only to *destruction* for us all. Turns us against one another. But we have been given a *new* path."

I recognized that awful, dead voice. My mystery caller. A flood of memories broke through last night's blackout dam in my head, the phone call, the bottle of whiskey in my freezer. She had been the one to leave my gift. My skin prickled as the haunted conversation came back to me, how she told me to stay out of their way.

"*Freedom* is what you crave," she continued, still moving slowly through the crowd like some teacher from Biblical times. "*Freedom* from the constraints that modern civilization has placed upon you. We have complicated our existence with all of these…these *talking noise boxes* and so-called *modern conveniences*, but I assure you, a simple life—a life of basic human need—is a life of *happiness*."

A snatch of that old Disney song played in my head, the one where the talking bear advises one to seek out the bare necessities. I knew Transcendentalist dogma when I heard it; the units on Thoreau and Whitman, with their emphasis on living in the moment and seizing the day, were always easy for the kids to grasp.

This old woman understands, I realized.

Somehow, she knew—*on a conscious level*—about the Squall, and what it was doing to us.

Isaacs had a hard glint in her eye as she told the crowd, "We stand on the cusp of a great new *era*, an age where you can have that life…if you but *heed*."

"*Heed*," her followers murmured.

Her words had a mesmerizing lilt to them. I broke my gaze from her and looked around at the assemblage. Many of their heads nodded in agreement, some almost mechanically. And why not? She was telling them exactly what they wanted to hear, whether they realized it or not. I knew how seductive that voice inside the Squall could be. I glanced at Beth, and she looked back at me with glassy fear in her eyes.

Isaacs wasn't finished yet. She continued her sermon as she walked on a spiral course around the dance floor. "The good Lord has given us a gift. He has chosen to speak directly to us, to show us the way. You have heard His still, small voice all week. It speaks to you even now. Listen!" She paused, tilting her head so that her ear pointed to the sky. "Do you hear?"

"Yessss..." A whisper of hesitant assent rolled across the crowd. Many of them mimicked her pose. The Squall surged upward for just a moment, becoming an eye-wateringly high-pitched buzz, then faded away again in time for her to speak.

"And will you *heed* its command?"

"Yes." The murmured answer from the crowd was still soft, but began to grow toward the end as more voices joined in.

"Will you give up the trappings this world uses to drag you down, and live the simple lives that your mind and body crave, without giving in to the Beast?"

"Yes!" Louder this time, more sure. She was weaving a spell over them, a hypnotic litany that brought a spark back to their vacant eyes.

She was uniting them. Focusing them. Like she'd been doing with the others all week, turning them into the people I thought of as Heeders.

"There are those who would stop you," Isaacs declared. She prowled the edge of the dance floor now, the members of her entourage strung out behind her. "There are *interlopers* in our midst even now. They could be anyone: spouse, sibling, child, or neighbor. They are *weary* from the burdens of this world, yet they refuse to lay them aside. Some of them can still be saved, if they are willing to cleanse themselves. But for those that refuse to heed…you must be willing to rid yourselves of their influence if you are to walk the unencumbered path."

"*Yeeees!*" they shouted in unison, loud enough that Beth's hand clamped down on mine.

Isaacs stopped walking. She turned to face the dance floor at last. Her black eyes fell upon mine. She pulled her bony hands apart and crooked one finger at me. "There stands one of them, unwilling to heed. What will you do?"

The crowd swung toward us again, their faces dull at first, but quickly transforming back into a collection of snarls. They gnashed their teeth and clawed at the air as they closed in. Beth screamed again, pressing back against me.

With a burst of rumbling thunder, the sky opened up and dumped rain.

7

The spring downpour came in a crushing wave all at once, one second nothing, the next a raging monsoon. Raindrops as big as dimes pelted my exposed skin, so hard and cold they hurt, wetting me to the bone in an instant and rattling against the pavement.

The water also seemed to break the spell that Isaacs had cast on the partygoers. They forgot about us and looked around in confusion, a few of them crying out in consternation at the rain. Then they covered their heads and ran for the gates en masse. Beth and I had no choice but to move with them or be trampled. I craned my head around as we hurried away, looking for Tate over my shoulder, the one man that might be able to help us, and instead saw the old crone standing her ground as rain coursed down her face and unraveled her bun of silver hair. Beady, jet-black eyes followed us until I lost her amid the stampede.

People streamed out of the pool yard and then broke into different directions, running for home. The rain had gotten so thick, it was impossible to see more than a few feet ahead. Flooding already choked the gutters to either side of the street, the sudden influx of water too much for our storm drains to handle. Crooked tines of lightning arced over our heads, accompanied by a constant growl of thunder and a freezing blast of wind left over from winter.

Beth and I didn't speak, but we kept holding hands as we pelted down the street toward our apartments. I knew we should be running the opposite direction, trying to find a way out in the confusion, but Beth was in a panicked flight to find shelter and I was too drunk to do anything but follow. When we reached the alleyway between buildings, I stumbled toward my porch, but she pulled me in the opposite direction. "*No, come with me!*" she yelled.

She got her front door open, and we burst through, me skidding on the tile in my wet sneakers. Beth slammed the door and threw the deadbolts as I climbed to my feet and leaned against the wall, panting and shivering.

"What the hell was that?" she demanded, looking out the window that faced the street. Through the driving rain, I could see a few dark figures running for cover. The staccato sound of it beating against the windows and the sides of the building didn't drown out the sound of the Squall at all. "Those people went fucking nuts."

"Something's wr-wrong with them," I wheezed. The room spun sickly and the Squall screeched on. I realized that, sometime between my brawl with Jacob and fleeing the Gala, I had lost the flask once more.

"You're goddamn right something's wrong with them! It looks like another group is gathering in that playground on the other side of the parking lot, just standing there in the rain!" She whirled to face me. "Half the complex was on the verge of tearing each other apart! Then that old woman, with all that nonsense...Jesus, it's gotta be some form of mass hysteria!"

"N-no...no...their heads, the Squall, th-they..." I pushed away from the wall, desperate to make her understand, and some fundamental, load-bearing structure inside me—surely a combination of alcohol, exhaustion, and fear—let go. I collapsed into a soaked, shivering heap on the tile.

"Oh my god, we have to get you dry." She offered her hands. With her help, I stood again, but my whole body quivered. I was completely soused inside and out, my thoughts a sludgy whirlpool. Beth led me through her living room, which was still cluttered with unpacked boxes, and into her bedroom. She left me standing beside her four-post bed while she retrieved towels from the bathroom, and started rubbing me down.

"Y-you...you're w-wet, too," I told her. Her thin clothes clung to her body like a leather jumpsuit.

"We'll worry about me later. Here, take your shirt off." She helped me unbutton the floral print and slipped it off. The garment dropped into a soggy pile on her carpet. A small gasp escaped her when she saw the landscape of wounds and bruises my body had become.

"N-not as bad as it looks," I said through chattering teeth.

"Who *bit* you?" she asked, fingering the circle of tiny slashes on my shoulder where Joan had gone vampire on me.

"Avon lady. T-they really get mad when you place an order you c-can't pay for."

She reached around behind me to wrap the towel over my bare shoulders. "Elliot...I just don't understand anything that happened out there. That kid that started it all...he was one of your students?"

I nodded, but I was afraid it looked too much like a twitch. I couldn't stop shaking.

"And what he said before, about you...?"

"Is a l-long story, that doesn't really m-matter right now." I took her gently by the arms to make her stand still and look at me. I didn't think I could get my brain and body to cooperate long enough to explain the whole story, so I settled for, "Beth, I think th-those people are dangerous."

"No shit." Moisture gathered in the corner of her eyes that wasn't rain. "Tell me what's going on. What do you know?"

"Not m-much, but enough to tell you that you need to get out of the complex and go for help. Right now. I don't think the gate will open and I'm afraid for you to try ramming it with your car, so I'll g-give you a boost over the wall. You'll have to go on foot."

"What? No, that's crazy! If you think we're really in danger, then let's just call the police!"

"Do you have a landline?" I asked eagerly. "Or Wi-Fi?"

She frowned. "I haven't had time to get any of that hooked up yet. Why?"

"Because cell service is out."

"No it isn't, I used my phone right before..." She pulled her cell out of her pocket and found it as useless as mine. "How—?"

"I think they d-did something to the tower that services this area. They're isolating us, t-trying to cut us off from the outside world."

"For Christ's sake, who is *they?*" Beth asked, her voice getting shrill. She pounded a fist against my bare chest. "None of this makes any fucking sense!"

"I c-can't explain it to you now. Tate, the courtesy officer, he just saw all of that. Hopefully he's calling in reinforcements, but we can't sit around waiting for them. You just h-have to go. I need to know you're somewhere safe."

She paused to consider this, her hand still on my chest, short strands of wet hair plastered to her forehead and hanging in her face. "No. I'm not going anywhere without you. And neither one of us is in any shape to go back out in that." She moved aside and lifted back her bedspread. "Here. Strip and get in."

I gaped at her.

"It's the fastest way to get you warm," she explained. "We'll stay here for a while until the rain stops, and you can tell me exactly what's happening. Then we'll figure out what to do."

I wanted to argue with her. I wanted to tell her there was a chance I was every bit as dangerous as those people out there. But I was so tired, and that bed looked as inviting as a cloud.

She turned off the light, allowing me some modesty to pull off my shoes, wiggle out of my sopping wet shorts and underwear, then burrow beneath her blankets. Beth took my wet clothes away. A few seconds later, I heard a dryer starting.

When she reappeared in the doorway, she was naked, too.

The light was too dim for me to get more than a vague sense of her firm B-cups and the dark triangle between her legs. She came around the bed and slid into the opposite side next to me. I expected her to keep her distance, but she scooted across without hesitation, until our bodies were right up against one another, and laid her head on the pillow beside mine. She draped an arm across my chest; one of her smooth legs came up and wrapped around my waist, grazing my genitals in the process. I could feel her heart thudding against my shoulder.

"Are you warm?" she asked. Her voice sounded husky.

I couldn't answer. I was still shaking, but it had nothing to do with the cold anymore. My cock grew beneath the covers, against her leg, and I didn't know if I should be embarrassed or not. The dream tried to seep into my head— that awful nightmare where I'd savaged her, surely a fantasy unleashed by the Squall—but I pushed it away.

Her lips found mine. They tasted of cherries or strawberries, some fruit-flavored lip balm. Her tongue pushed against mine with such urgency. My hands sank into her hips, pulling her even tighter against me, raw need overtaking us. God, this was another dream, it had to be, and if it wasn't, then we were fools. But I didn't stop her as she rolled over on top of me, straddling me, still kissing me until my blood boiled. I ran my palms across her breasts, stroked the small pebbles at their centers. One of her hands stole down between our bodies, caressing the iron bar that now grew from my groin, and maneuvered it inside her.

After that, I don't remember much, but I know I slept afterward.

THURSDAY
MORNING

1

I awoke to the sound of pounding at the front door.

At first, when my eyes flew open, I couldn't remember where I was. The room—turned into smears by watery morning sunlight—looked like my bedroom, but I didn't recognize anything in it. Then Beth stirred beside me, and everything rushed back.

She sat up, looked around blearily, seemed to notice me. Confusion flashed across her face, there and gone. She flushed a deep crimson, like she had when her porno mags had spilled out of the moving box, then pulled up the sheet to cover her breasts.

A little bit late for modesty.

The frantic knocking at her door came again, so insistent my bowels tightened. Nothing good ever came from a knock like that.

Beth slid out of bed, giving me a flash of nude backside. A worn yellow robe hung from the corner post and she put it on fast, cinching the front as tight as a chastity belt. "I'll be right back," she said.

"Where are you going?"

"To answer the door."

"*What?* No, don't do that!"

"Why not?"

"Because it could be anybody!"

"Yeah, that's the point of answering. Ed McMahon can't give you the giant check if you don't."

I stared at her in disbelief. "Do you remember nothing that happened last night?"

Beth flapped a hand dismissively. "It's fine, Jefferson. I'm sure it wasn't…you know, what we thought."

She strode from the bedroom while I threw aside the blankets. I recognized that response. She was attempting to rationalize it all in the light of day, like I had for so long. I had to protect her until I could convince her of the danger.

My clothes were still in her dryer, but a pink t-shirt sat on top of the dresser. I pulled it on—the hem reached just below my ball sack—and ran after her.

In the living room, Beth was turning deadbolts and reaching for the knob.

"*Wait!*" I shouted. My imagination conjured Isaacs on the other side of that door, her skeletal frame perched like a vulture.

But it was Katie that stood on the threshold, with tears in her eyes.

"I'm sorry, I didn't have anywhere to go and Mr. Jefferson isn't home and…" She caught sight of me over Beth's shoulder—standing in the girl's tee that was far too tight, cupping my groin with both hands—and her jaw dropped.

Beth sighed and held the door open. "Come on in. I'll get Captain Dignity his clothes."

2

I stood in the laundry room and changed back into the ensemble I'd worn last night while Beth went into her room and shut the door to get dressed. The coldness coming off her now was palpable. Had I done something wrong, or was this standard morning-after jitters? Last night probably had less to do with my animal magnetism and more to do with alcohol and adrenaline, so maybe she was fuzzy on the details.

There wasn't time to worry about it. The Squall was in one of its softer cycles at the moment, a gentle but steady hum, but it could start digging in again at any moment. I had to get out of the complex with these two right now. As I waited for Beth in the hallway, I checked my phone one more time. Still no network, and the battery was just about drained, too. Soon it would serve as a nice paperweight.

When Beth emerged, she gave me an awkward smile and started to go past. I put a gentle hand on her arm.

"Hey..."

She shook her head adamantly. "I don't wanna talk about it."

The brusqueness surprised me, but when she tried to slip away, I stopped her again. "That wasn't what I was gonna say." I closed me eyes, feeling embarrassed heat flush my cheeks. "Do you...do you have anything to drink here? Liquor, beer, anything at all?"

The question sounded even more pathetic than I'd feared. And it should, because, if there had ever been any legitimacy to my belief that alcohol was my only weapon against the Squall, it was quickly becoming just another excuse to drink. I needed a shot of something, anything, I didn't care if it was cough syrup, this raw craving in my gut must be obeyed, and, god, I had just monkey-swapped one destructive voice for another, hadn't I?

Even though my hands didn't shake and my lips didn't smack, Beth took one look in my eyes and saw that need. Her nostrils flared in that expression of disgust she'd given me last night, when I'd scrambled for the flask on the dance floor. That face reminded me so much of Darcy, the two of them could've been twins. "It's a little early for a Heinie, don't you think?"

"I don't...it's not...you see..." I realized, but it was too late for explanations. Even if she knew the facts as I did, she'd seen the truth in that one moment of weakness. I had never felt lower in my life, not the day Darcy kicked me out, not the first time I stood up in AA and declared my addiction.

"That kid last night. Your student. He was telling the truth then? You're...what? An alcoholic?"

I just stood in the narrow hallway a few inches from her and wished I could fade away.

"Jesus, I sure can pick 'em," she said, and walked out.

This time, I let her go.

3

By the time I slunk into the living room, Katie sat hunched on the couch with Beth beside her, holding her hand. The bruises on her throat had faded to a mottled yellow that was barely discernible from her skin tone.

I hurried to the window and looked out. The rain had stopped and the morning was sunny and bright, almost stingingly so. Not a soul was on the streets.

"I don't know what to do," Katie said, in a bewildered tone. Her eyes were so wide, I wondered if she were in shock.

Or stoned.

"What happened?" Beth asked her.

"I...I came home this morning...I've been away the last couple of days, and—"

"You mean you've been at Jacob's," I interrupted, perching on the edge of Beth's beaten recliner.

"How...h-how did you...?"

"I was there, Katie. Yesterday morning. You were passed out on his couch. You've been using that garbage he sells, haven't you?"

Katie's face turned fire-engine red as she dropped her gaze to her lap. "I'm not, like, an *addict* or anything. I just needed something to get by. You don't know what it's been like, living there with her..."

"I don't care about that. You promised you would stay away from him."

"I didn't have anywhere else to go!" she blurted. "The night before, my mom woke me up at like two in the morning! She was shouting all this crazy stuff, about how I should listen and obey, and that if I didn't, she would make me listen! She...s-she was really scaring me, so I just...I just ran! I came to your door first and knocked for a long time but you didn't answer!"

That would've been right about the time I was unconscious from a near lethal injection of whiskey. Any other protests curled up in my throat and died.

Beth had gotten a box of cereal bars from her kitchen. My stomach growled at the sight of them; I hadn't eaten in almost 36 hours. She offered them to Katie, who declined, and then to me. I took two and wolfed the first down without chewing.

"Go on, sweetie," Beth urged, stroking the girl's long, auburn hair.

Katie continued, giving me one last guilty glance. "Jacob let me stay there, just until things chilled out. So this morning, I came back to see how my mom was, but I can't find her anywhere and th-there's blood all over the place..."

"Blood?" I echoed around a mouthful of food.

She nodded. "In the kitchen, the living room... I-I tried to call the police, but my cell phone won't get any bars."

"What about your landline, did you try that?"

"I couldn't get it to work either." Katie bit her lower lip. "All that stuff I told you, about the weird things my mom's doing? Jacob said there's other people in the complex acting just like her."

"Yeah, and he's one of them." She frowned, and I said, "He came after me at the pool party. Started a fight."

"He did? I knew he left for awhile. When he came back, his lip was bleeding, but he barely remembered anything. He...he's been high a lot lately."

As far as I was concerned, everything she said had confirmed my suspicions. Now I just had to make her see the truth. "Listen, I know what's causing all of this, and it's probably gonna get worse. We have to leave, right now."

"It really is the electric boxes, isn't it?" Katie's fingers curled in her lap, her hands clenching into fists so tight the knuckles went bloodless. "They're doing this."

"Yes. That sound is affecting people's brains just like you said, and—"

"Not this again," Beth groaned. "Aren't we done with this bullshit?"

I turned on her, suddenly angry. "You saw what happened last night. You said yourself it was some kind of mass hysteria. The Squall is what caused it."

"What happened last night?" Katie asked, looking back and forth between us.

Beth ignored her as she spoke to me. "Mass hysteria doesn't work like that. There's always a point of origin—a patient zero—that experiences an initial delusion and then spreads it to others. Okay, yes, exhaustion can make you more susceptible to suggestion and that noise has certainly kept us all from sleeping, but I sincerely doubt it's the cause. If anything, what we saw was brought on by that old hag who riled everyone up."

I wondered what she would say if I told her that 'old hag' lived less than twenty yards away from here. "Trust me, it's not her. She's just getting the others to...I don't know...work together somehow."

"All right then, let's test your theory." Beth jumped up from the couch and began rooting through the unpacked boxes stacked along one side of the room. She found what she wanted in a long, rectangular one and came up holding a chewed wooden baseball bat.

She started for the door.

"What are you doing?" I asked.

"I'm gonna beat the holy hell out of that transformer until it shuts up. If there's no more noise, then there shouldn't be any more problems, right?" Beth yanked her front door open and stepped outside.

I didn't know how much difference destroying one transformer could make if the others were still going, but Katie and I were up from our seats and after her in a flash. Outside, the grass was still damp from the rain, but the water on the streets had dried up.

"Hold on, hold on, let's think about this." I tried to grab Beth's arm. The idea of her touching one of those green metal boxes still gave me chills. "It could explode or something. You could get electrocuted."

"I don't care." She nimbly stepped out of my reach, walked around the corner of the building into the alley, and came to such an abrupt halt I almost ran into her. Katie and I came around both sides of her to see what she was looking at.

At the far end of the alley, a hefty man in a white, Via-Tel electric jumpsuit knelt down in front of the padlocked door on our transformer with a toolbox in one hand.

4

He sensed us standing there and looked up. He was a big bear of a man, with a Grizzly Adams beard that stretched from one ear to the other by way of his wide jaw. A fearsome specimen, but he gave a friendly smile when he saw us and raised a hand.

"Mornin folks!" he called, his words barely audible over the Squall. "Just here to do some work on the transformers. Shouldn't affect your power, but if it does, it won't be for long."

I drifted toward him in a daze, leaving Katie and Beth at the mouth of the alley. He seemed like a mirage to me, a hologram. If I touched him, surely my hand would go right through. I wanted it too much for it to actually be real. "That noise…" I got out, before my mouth went dry.

"Yeah, it's a doozie, idn't it?" He flipped open the lid of his box and began laying out a variety of tools on the grass, right about where Yonkers had attacked me. A name patch on his jumpsuit read 'Avery.' "Every once in a while, the voltage ratio gets screwed up and causes a flux like that, but this has gotta be the worst one I ever heard." The techno-speak was nonsense to me, but I stood close enough now for him to turn and give me a friendly slap across the chest with the back of his hand. I jumped, but he didn't seem to notice. "No wonder we got so many complaints from this complex, huh pal? We thought you guys were just a buncha pansies, so we set it as a pretty low priority!"

I wanted to hit him and hug him. "How did you get into the complex?" I asked. "Wasn't the front gate closed?"

Something about my awed demeanor must have finally struck him as odd. He stopped in the process of removing a ring of keys from his belt and raised one bushy eyebrow at me. "We got the override codes. In case of emergency." We stared at each other a moment longer until he gestured at the box. "You mind? I got a lotta these to work on today. I stopped here first because the initial complaints came from these units, but it looks like every damn transformer in the whole place is doin this."

"Oh! Yes, please, go right ahead," I invited. The Squall continued to shriek, with what sounded like an angry undertone. *Your minutes are numbered, my friend.* When that sound finally shut off, would all the Heeders just suddenly wake up, with no memory of what they'd been up to? I hoped it would be that simple.

I spun around to Katie and Beth with a huge grin on my face, ready to proclaim that everything would be all right, but instead the door to Mrs. Isaacs's apartment flew open right beside me.

5

The crone marched out, surrounded by the honor guard from last night, eight of them in all. They reminded me of a scrimmage line as they spread out around their leader, even the shortest of them a good foot taller than her. I heard Katie gasp behind me when her mother stepped into view, but Samantha Adler gave no reaction. The whole group came to a stop on the grass just a few feet away from Avery and me. Schrader stood like some military officer—ramrod straight, with his hands clutched behind his back—and glared in my direction.

"What is going on here?" Isaacs demanded. She wore a different colored suit of the same conservative cut, her hair once more pulled back and up into a pristine bun. This close to her, I could see the leathery texture of her skin, like cracked mud at the bottom of a dried-up pond.

My new friend Avery looked a little creeped out. He lumbered back to his feet, two-hundred-and-fifty pounds if he was an ounce, and not just in his gut, but evenly distributed over his big frame. "Folks, I'm just here to fix the transformers. Get rid of that buzzing noise for you."

"It is not a *noise*," Isaacs snapped, slipping back into her aggrandizing preacher's tone. She looked around at her cadre of followers. "You see? *This* is what I foretold! The outside world has come at last, with their *complications* and *onus!* They mean to silence the still, small voice of our Savior because they *cannot* abide its truth!"

"Woah, woah. What is this?" Avery shot me an uncomfortable glance. I felt sorry for him, coming into the movie so late, but I still took a few slow steps back toward the alley opening, putting distance between me and him. An awful sense of dread had filled me.

"The time is *now!*" Isaacs shouted through clenched yellow teeth, the words ringing off the sides of the buildings to either side. I'd never heard anyone with such a forceful voice; it didn't even seem possible that her diminutive figure could house lungs big enough to produce it. "Those that will not *heed*, must be *purged!* If you wish to keep the freedom that you have tasted, then now is the time to *fight* for it!"

Schrader moved first, taking a single step forward. His

arms moved from behind his back, and it was only then that I understood he wasn't clasping them, but trying to hide what was in them.

A long-handled fire axe.

My breath caught at the sight of it.

"Hey, what the fuck? What are you doing? Stay back! Get away from me!" Avery, the friendly neighborhood Viatel rep, backed away as Schrader advanced on him with the same manic gleam in his eyes as when he'd come at me with his fists. Schrader held the axe handle with both hands at an angle, so the head floated in front of his face. The repairman's attention was so focused on that glinting, triangular blade, he didn't even react as two of Isaac's other apostles—one of them Rick, the other a man I didn't know—slipped around to either side of him. He moved backward still, stumbling over his toolbox, working his way around the transformer's steel shell to keep it between him and Schrader. I wanted to help, wanted to shout, but I stood there useless, only able to watch as they closed in on the poor man.

Then Rick and the other guy leapt at Avery from both sides, grabbing his arms and pulling them in opposite directions to hold him in place. He struggled, big enough to crush them one-on-one, but he couldn't pull either of his hands free without help from the other. Schrader continued toward him, raising the axe head back and over his shoulder. It all seemed to happen in slow motion.

And then it sped up in a big fucking hurry as Schrader brought the blade whistling down, burying the edge right in the middle of Avery's chest with a wet *shlunk* sound.

The repairman gave a scream that Beth and Katie echoed. A red stain spread across the front of Avery's white jumpsuit. Then Schrader wrenched the axe free and then the wound gushed blood, spraying across his attacker and anointing the green transformer that had accepted my seminal sacrifice just a few nights ago. As it had then, the Squall surged upward in a gleeful trill.

Schrader swung again, a crossways blow this time that just about sheared off the top of the other man's head. Avery collapsed.

"*Now!*" Isaacs shrieked, holding her clawed hands toward the sky. "*The time is now! PURGE THE WEARY!*"

And, if I had to pinpoint, I would say that's the exact moment when Hobbes's precious Social Contract disintegrated for us, and the Estates went from apartment complex to war zone.

6

My paralysis broke. I whirled and sprinted toward the open end of the alley, where Beth stood horrified, holding the bat in one hand and covering's Katie's face with the other. "*Go, go, run!*" I shouted at her. A glance over my shoulder revealed Garrett and Miles breaking formation from Isaacs's coven of enforcers to come after me, but I had a long head start.

Beth turned and tried to do as I said, but Katie stood in place, sobbing and clutching fistfuls of her long hair like she wanted to rip them out. By the time Beth got the girl moving, I had reached them. The three of us exited the alley.

And ran headlong into chaos.

The streets and yards that had been empty minutes before were now filled with people fighting for their lives, a riot whose enormity staggered me. But this wasn't the sort of directionless anarchy we'd witnessed at the pool last night; it looked more like a peasant village under siege by a group of Vikings. Cries and shouts bounced between the buildings as weapon-wielding groups chased down their neighbors and tackled them to the ground, where they were savagely beaten or even—God help me—raped right out on the vibrantly green complex lawns. In one panoramic sweep of the buildings across the road, I saw both helpless women *and* men brutalized by twitching, hollow-eyed gangs, knocked unconscious with clubs and shovels, or stabbed with kitchen knives. Some of the victims begged, others fought back, but they were no match for the sheer number of their enemies.

It was the most unreal thing I've ever seen, a shot from a big budget disaster movie. All around us, doors were kicked down so those inside could be dragged into the street. As we stepped off the curb—no longer running, completely lost in horrified amazement—a man in the next building over crashed through a second floor window and screamed on his short trip to the ground. He was immediately set upon by two women that began hogtying him with electric cords. In the playground, the squad of psychotic elementary school kids attacked a man who kept trying to escape right up until they dragged him down into their midst.

I was so busy taking in the insanity, I completely forgot we were still in the middle of it.

The screech of brakes from my left snapped me back to attention.

"*MOVE!*" I shoved Katie and Beth forward as a Mustang careened toward us. A man clung to the hood and bashed at the windshield with a brick. The driver swerved back and forth across the street, trying to shake off his attacker. We surged forward, trying to get out of the way, but if the car hadn't veered to the left at the last second, we'd have been hood ornaments. As it was, the front bumper tore away the tail of my shirt.

Garrett, however, was not so lucky. My former student had just reached the street behind us when the Mustang jumped the curb and pulled him under its wheels before crashing into the corner of my building with a concussive boom. The front end of the car crumpled. The person on the hood flew forward to slam against the wall. I couldn't tell if the driver was hurt, but Garrett's screams drifted out from the undercarriage.

Miles had been cut off on the other side of the car, which billowed smoke from under the bent hood. He tried to climb over, but flames whooshed up, forcing him back. The whole car was engulfed in seconds, a fiery barricade across the mouth of the alley. Before the smoke became too black to see through, I caught a glimpse of Isaacs and her minions at the far end of the alley. The old woman's eyes burned like coals.

"Mr. Jefferson, *come on!*"

Katie's voice, shrill with fear. She and Beth were across the street, heading toward the next opening between buildings, which appeared to be clear. I sprinted after them and caught up just before they entered the alley. A growling man stepped around the corner to grab Katie, but Beth struck him a hard blow across the head with the bat. He fell in the street and we ran on.

"Keep going, don't stop," I told them as we ran along the exteriors. Most of the coup seemed to be happening along the main thoroughfares of the complex; the inner alleys remained empty as we crossed to another narrow opening, heading toward the center of the grounds. "We have to get out of the complex."

"I can't run anymore," Katie wheezed. She was young and pretty, but not nearly as athletic as Beth or me. And my lungs were already burning from all-out flight.

The far end of the passage let out in a row of trees meant as a dog walk, with even more buildings on the other side. Somewhere ahead, terrified screams continued to tear through the morning, along with what sounded like a chainsaw. And, of course, the Squall; that motherfucker sang from every corner of the Estates, like a church bell calling the parishioners to worship, making it hard to think. I signaled for the girls to stop and rest.

"They killed him," Beth gasped, as she leaned against the building and held her side. Her face was etched in horror. I knew how she felt; I kept seeing Avery in my head, with Schrader's axe buried in his chest. "Jesus Christ, they're killing everyone."

This is what Isaacs had been putting together the entire time, I realized. The reason for her public appearance last night, when she entranced those who weren't already under her thumb. Her command in the alley had been the signal not just for her group to take action, but for Heeders everywhere to rise up against those unaffected by the Squall, to root us out once and for all. "Still thinks it's mass hysteria?"

Her face hardened as she looked at me. "Yeah. I do."

Rather than argue, I poked my head around the corner. Way down at the end of the dog walk, three people dragged a fourth across the grass by the legs. Their victim kicked and screamed, but was still very much alive. I remembered the man we'd seen being tied up, the others that were knocked unconscious.

Maybe they weren't killing everyone after all.

So what were they doing with the ones they didn't?

"That was my mom," Katie whispered. She shivered uncontrollably; shock looked more likely all the time. I stepped over and put an arm around her shoulders. She buried her face against me.

"That was not your mom," I told her. "They're being manipulated. Controlled. Once the Squall stops, she'll go back to normal, I promise."

I only suspected that to be true, but the reassurance did the trick. Katie looked up and asked, "What're we gonna do?"

"We're gonna leave, and get help. All we have to do is find a way to escape." I felt a kernel of anger at myself, for not having forced Beth to leave with me last night, when we might've had a chance.

"What about these other people?" Beth asked.

"We can't do anything for them." I thought of Kirk as I said this. "They'll have to fend for themselves until we can get the police."

They both nodded in agreement. I led the way when we started running again, but kept the pace slower this time. I took us down alleyway after alleyway for the next few minutes, weaving through the complex in whatever direction let us avoid major streets. We still heard a few shouts, screams, and, once, a crazed bout of laughter that made my bladder want to let go, but for the most part, the action seemed to die down. I didn't take it as a good sign.

At last, we emerged onto Peony Place. Around the corner and a mere two blocks up, we could see the front gate of the Estates and Midtown Road beyond. A body lay sprawled across the concrete in front of the iron bars, blood all over its back.

The girls followed me as I eased around the corner and started warily toward the gate.

But we all froze as a shriek of "*Purge the weary!*" echoed across the street behind us.

7

I looked back.

A mob of ten Heeders stood in the street a block away, a teenage girl even younger than Katie at the front of the pack, pointing in our direction. They were armed with instruments both blunt and sharp, like villagers in a Frankenstein movie, one of them with an honest-to-god pitchfork. From their positioning, they must've been placed specifically to guard the gate.

They charged, waving their weapons in the air, mouths twisted into snarls. We were closer to the gate than we were to them, but making it there would do us no good if it was still locked.

"*That way!*" I shouted, indicating the far side of the office, where there were more alleys to lose them in. The three of us cut across the volleyball court, the sand still wet and hard-packed from the rain, and past the pool yard, where the trashed and sodden remnants of last night's party were still strewn across the patio.

The crowd followed. Their footfalls were a rumble, but otherwise they were eerily silent. Katie started to fall behind. We would never be able to escape them like this, I saw that now, but we were out of options.

"*Hey! Over here!*"

One of the office windows was open, close to where the complex wall met the side of the building. Tony leaned out, beckoning frantically to us. I couldn't think of another scenario where I would've been so happy to see his fake-baked face. We ran along the office down to him.

"C'mon, hurry, don't let them see you!" he pleaded. I gave Katie a boost through the window, and Beth slithered through on her own right after. With Tony's help, I climbed high enough to get a leg over the sill and then sprawled painfully across the foyer tile on the other side.

Tony slid the window down and then ducked. I moved next to him and peeked out. The mob pelted past without stopping, looking for us between the buildings beyond.

"Thanks," I told him.

"I've been hiding all morning." His usually chipper voice was rough and raw. Sweat stains spread beneath the arms of his canary yellow work shirt.

"Yeah, I know, we have too. But we can get out through here, right?" I headed across the foyer toward the front of the building without waiting for an answer, helping Beth to her feet along the way.

Tony bounded along at my heels like a yapping dog. "No, wait! You can't go! The...the door's locked!"

"Don't you have the key? Never mind, it doesn't matter, I'll break the goddamned window if I have to." I reached the door I'd tried to go through...Jesus, had that only been yesterday?

Then I looked out and saw the problem with my plan.

Sawhorses had been placed across the entrance drive. A poster board sign hung from one of them. From this angle, I couldn't read it, but since it faced anyone that might be coming from the street, I guessed it must've said something about the office being closed.

A car sat parked just inside the barricade with three men milling around next to it. They stood as close to the wall as possible, where they would still be within range of the Squall.

Lookouts. They would see us the second we stepped outside. I pounded a fist against the doorframe.

"What now?" Beth asked, hefting the bat beside me.

"I have someplace you can hide!" Tony took my arm and pulled me back toward the depths of the office. "Come with me, they'll never find you! *Hurry!*"

I hesitated, even though I really didn't see any other choice. My head throbbed with the makings of another Squall headache. I wanted out of here and away before it could do worse. But even if we got off the Estates grounds, we still had a nearly three mile run to reach help. We wouldn't make it if we were being chased the whole way. Perhaps it would be best to lie low until we could think of a way to sneak out.

Beth and Katie waited for my decision. I submitted to Tony's frantic tugging and followed him past the management alcove, into the rear hallway that led to the restrooms. He stopped at an unmarked door and produced a key ring to unlock it, leaving the key in the knob.

A faint alarm bell pinged in the very back of my head.

"It's a storage room," Tony explained. "No one ever goes in here but me. I've been using it all week." I didn't have time to ask what he meant before he swung the door open. A wave of fetid air rushed out, the stench enough to make us all gag.

"What is that?" I choked out. The interior was pitch black, and filled with the angry buzzing of flies.

"There's a broken sewage pipe in the wall," Tony explained. "That's why no one uses it. Just get in!"

"What about you?"

"I have another place, don't worry!"

Katie grabbed my hand. "Mr. Jefferson, I don't wanna go in there!"

"Just hold your nose, sweetheart," Beth told her.

Tony ushered Katie and Beth inside first, then I stepped through, running into them in the dark. In here, the smell was so concentrated my eyes began to water. A fly landed on my cheek and then buzzed away again. I was on the verge of telling Tony we would have to find somewhere else when he flicked on a light switch.

In front of me, Katie screamed.

Tony's storage room was a rectangular closet with metal shelves of various cleaning supplies, but it wasn't any broken sewage pipe causing the smell. Animal carcasses in various stages of decay lay across nearly every surface, decorated the walls like paintings, or dangled from the ceiling by ropes around their necks, all with their intestines spilling out of gaping holes. Birds, squirrels, rabbits, small dogs, even a chicken. But mostly cats, the kind that Miss Dillinger had in ready supply before they'd killed her.

The truth hit me immediately: we had just found the Estates's animal mutilator.

8

"Do you like my collection?" Tony stood in the doorway, gazing around at the putrefying corpses with a large hunting knife in one hand that I'd never seen him produce. "I've always wanted to do this—always had this, I don't know, *urge*— but before last week, I was too scared. Then, suddenly…I just didn't care anymore. Cause the voice told me it was okay."

"Oh my god," I whispered. Now I recognized the dull look to his eyes. If he'd been under the Squall's spell since the very beginning, he'd done a damn good job of hiding it.

Tony giggled, but then his face darkened. "Mickey was part of my collection, you know. But then *she* made me give him back to you. I don't think she likes my collection very much. She said I started too early, that it would get us caught. That's why I've been hiding, so maybe she would forget about me. But now…if I give all three of you to her…maybe she'll let me keep them."

He stepped back, reaching for the door.

"No!" I ran at him.

Tony sidestepped like a bull fighter, letting momentum carry me past, and shoved me into the opposite wall so hard I saw a burst of stars. I spun, expecting the knife to be flashing at me, but instead found Tony slamming the door closed and turning the key in the lock. A split second later, Beth and Katie pounded on the other side. He turned and jiggled the knife at me with a limp wrist.

"Don't do this," I pleaded.

"You should heed too." Tony advanced, holding the knife out. "It makes things so much simpler. If there's something you wanna do…you just do it."

He illustrated this by slashing out with the knife. I stepped away, but he kept coming, driving me back down the hallway toward the foyer. I looked for an opening and grabbed his thin forearm, holding the knife aside while I drove my knuckles into his nose. The crunch—and gush of blood—were so satisfying on such a visceral level, it made me a little worried for my own sanity.

Tony stumbled back, face shocked for a moment before transforming into a rage-filled grimace. He screeched and came at me again with the knife held over his head, Norman-Bates-style. I made myself wait until he was close, then grabbed his arms and brought my knee up hard into his stomach. His wispy body folded over with a grunt. He curled into a ball on the floor and I kicked him one more time, for Mickey.

Then I heard the footsteps behind me, and something crashed down over my head.

THURSDAY EVENING

1

I heard the Squall even before I came to, yowling like an angry mountain cat. In that murky stretch of my barely conscious mind, it seemed that noise was all-encompassing and eternal. It had always existed, had been a part of me since the day I was born, and it would be here long after I was gone.

God, how I loathed it.

"Mr. Jefferson, please, wake up!"

Someone shook me.

My eyes opened, but everything around me was so dim, I could barely tell the difference. I seemed to be indoors, lying stretched out on a hard, flat, fuzzy surface that my hands finally identified as carpet. A blurry shadow hung over me, lightly slapping my cheeks.

"Katie?" I blinked the world back into focus and then, as I recalled our predicament, I snapped, "Are you okay? Where's Beth?"

"I'm here." Her delicate features appeared beside Katie, blond hair glowing ghostly pale in the wan light. "And yes, we're both fine. Manhandled a little by the nutjobs that found us in Tony's slaughterhouse, but nothing permanent." I sighed in relief and tried to sit up, but something in the back of my head throbbed sickly. "Be careful. You have a knot the size of a baseball on your scalp where they beaned you. I was afraid you'd wake up with brain damage." Beth tried out a weak smile. "You know, more than usual."

I managed to get upright with their help, then leaned against the wall beside me with my eyes closed, waiting for that rotten ache to subside. This was a different sort of pain from my hangover yesterday, less nauseating but more dizzy. The Squall pulsed behind my eyelids in tune with my heartbeat. "How long was I out?"

"Not long. Just enough for them to bring us here."

I coaxed my eyes into opening one more time so I could get a good look at where 'here' was. A bare, rectangular room stretched out in front of me, a bar countertop to the right surrounding a tiny kitchen, a tiled hallway on the far end of the room leading to a door. I recognized the layout just as I had at Beth's place: another unit like mine, probably one of the unfurnished models. The door to the back patio stood just to my right.

"Where are we?" I asked Beth. "Which apartment is this?"

"I don't know."

"What building?"

She shrugged.

"Didn't you see when they brought you here?"

"That mob picked Katie and me up and carried us, like bags of laundry. I didn't exactly have time to draw a map."

I started to ask why they had dumped us here when I realized we weren't alone. Around the room, other people huddled in small groups on the floor and a few sat alone in the corners, no more than black outlines that all seemed to watch as I got shakily to my feet. More neighbors, I deduced, those on the wrong side of the Squall, but lucky enough to have survived the hostile takeover this morning. What had Isaacs called us? The Weary? They certainly looked it now, hunkered in the dark. The interior door leading to the bedroom was open across from the kitchen, but I couldn't tell if anyone else was in there.

Why were they all just sitting here, instead of trying to get out? And why was it so dark? That little bit of illumination came from the windows along the wall at my back. It was bright enough that it could only be sunlight, but milky and scant. As I turned to examine the windows, I understood why.

Something had been placed over the glass on the outside, allowing only a few strangled rays to filter through the blinds. I pulled the slats apart so I could get a better look.

Wooden boards were nailed across the window in tight rows, leaving only tiny cracks and chinks, barely big enough to see the alleyway through.

Before the girls could stop me, I brushed past Beth and yanked open the patio door. Sunlight poured through in a sudden burst, blinding me until my eyes could adjust. I could see the alleyway and the building on the other side, but there was no way for me to get to them.

Beyond the threshold, a cell door had been constructed out of rebar. The narrow steel bands stretched across the outside of the doorframe in a crisscross pattern, the spaces too small for anyone to fit through. I took one in each hand and first gave them an experimental shake, then strained to move them. The damn things were welded together, not even rattling. I reached an arm through the grid and followed one to its end. The rebars were attached to flat metal posts, which were then anchored to the brick exterior of the building. My probing revealed hinges on one side and a heavy padlock on the other that, when removed, would allow the bars to be swung open.

"There's no way out," Beth said quietly over my shoulder. "We already looked."

I didn't answer and I didn't take her word for it. I tore through the apartment to see for myself, frantically checking every possible exit. The front and garage doors were likewise sealed, except there the bars were permanently in position, without even hinges. Every window was boarded over, and didn't even budge when I raised the glass on the one in the bedroom and kicked at the barrier over and over again in a panicked rage, as the inevitable reality of the situation sank in.

We were prisoners.

And renovation this extensive hadn't all been completed this morning.

The Heeders has been planning this for a while.

Katie followed me as I went through these fruitless motions, along with a couple of the other people that had been sitting in the floor, but the others just watched in a bored, distant way that made me think they had probably already tried this. But I didn't stop. I couldn't. Claustrophobia gripped me, spiraling out of control even though I knew I should hold it together in front of Katie. I finally ended up back at the patio door, wailing through the door of our communal cell.

This lasted only a few seconds before two men that had been standing just out of sight around the corner of the building stomped onto the patio. One was burly, dressed in an urban camouflage jumpsuit, the other a scrawny guy in jeans and a t-shirt. The one in the jumpsuit looked familiar, just another half-glimpsed neighbor from around the complex, before it went to hell. Both of our jailers had purple bags under their eyes and held long hunting rifles, the first firearms I had seen since the cleansing began.

"Shut up," Camo growled, in a voice whose soft tones somehow made it all the more dangerous.

"*You can't keep us here like this!*" I shouted. Which, I admit, was amusing, considering that forcible imprisonment was the least of the illegal deeds the Heeders had committed today. "*You let us the fuck outta here, right now!*"

In response, he shoved the butt of his rifle between the bars of the door, striking me hard in the stomach. The air went out of my lungs in a grunt as I stumbled back into Beth. Next to me, Katie wept softly. Another young woman pressed into the farthest corner of the room did the same.

Camo reached through the bars and grabbed the handle of the real apartment door. "Keep this closed or—"

He didn't get to finish his threat. There was a commotion behind him. Over his shoulder, I saw two more men marching up the alleyway, carrying a third under the arms so that his toes dragged the grass and his head lolled against his chest. Then, as they pulled him onto the concrete patio, his head rolled to the side enough for me to see his face.

"Kirk!" I called out.

He gave no sign that he'd heard me as his captors carried him to the door. For all I knew, he might've been dead, hanging limp from their arms while Camo undid the lock and swung the grate open. I wanted to rush the exit, but the skinnier guard in the t-shirt kept us covered with his rifle, shouting for us to get back. The other two brought Kirk inside, dropped him in a heap on the floor, and retreated. Both doors slammed behind them, leaving us in darkness again.

2

We gathered around Kirk on our knees. I turned him over onto his back as gently as I could. The smell of piss and shit hung heavy around him, worse than Tony's closet of death, so ripe I had to force back an involuntary gag. His lips were chapped and cracked, and his eyes so heavy-lidded, I couldn't even tell they were open until he croaked, "Hey Elliot."

"Christ, Kirk. Are you all right?"

"Water. I need...water."

Katie ran to the kitchen tap and filled up a plastic disposable cup from a package that had been left for us on the counter by our gracious hosts. We helped Kirk sit up, ignoring the stench of his soiled garments. He grabbed at the cup twice and missed, squinting hard, before Beth took his hand and guided it to the plastic. I realized his glasses were missing; he was near blind. He held the cup in both hands and tried to gulp the contents, but Beth made him slow down.

"What happened?" I asked.

He tried to talk, choked on water, and coughed long and hard, the sound like a maraca in his chest. "The night we got back from Dan and Joan's place, I confronted Teresa. Told her I knew she was hiding something, and that I was leaving the complex with the kids. I started to pack a bag, and the next thing I know, Schrader and two other guys are in my apartment holding me down. They kept me gagged and handcuffed to my bed for two days. Figured they'd forgotten me until they showed up again this morning."

"Ah, god, man, I'm so sorry. I went to your apartment and your wife said you were sick. If I had known..."

Kirk waved a hand weakly. "You probably would've just ended up next to me." He drained the last of the water, then craned his neck to take a look around, still squinting. "Where are we?"

"I was gonna ask you the same thing." I said. "Could you tell anything at all when they brought you in? Which building or just where in the complex? Anything at all?"

He shook his head, but from a group in the middle of the floor—five people, the largest by far—another man said, "I'm pretty sure it's building 28 on Daisy, just past the intersection with Rose. Right smack in the middle of the complex."

I gave him a grateful nod. "Thanks."

He slid close enough for me to get a look at him in the dim light—a chunky guy in a sweat-stained t-shirt, bald on top but with his remaining hair pulled into a ponytail, and a bloody gash down one cheek—and offered his hand. "Ron Banfield, 4101."

"Elliot Jefferson, 1603. These are my neighbors Kirk, Beth and Katie." We shook.

"I'm pretty sure this ain't the only apartment they set up like this either," Ron continued. "I saw them takin people to a few of the other buildings around here."

I thought about Avery the repairman, with the axe buried in his chest, and all the other atrocities I'd witnessed during the Heeders' assault. "Then we're the lucky ones."

"Why are they doing this?" The girl that had started crying with Katie stayed pressed into the corner, both hands splayed along the wall to either side. She had grass stains across the front of her blouse, and blood crusted under a swollen nose. "Why are they keeping us here? *What do they want from us?*" Each question was more shrill than the one before. She started to slide down the wall, sinking into the floor, and sobbed, "Oh god, my sister...s-she tried to *kill* me..." Beth made a move toward her, but she shied away, turning her tear-streaked face to the wall.

Ron whispered, "When they brought her in, a couple of guys held her down right outside the door and..." He broke off, eyes darting to Katie, and I decided immediately that I liked the guy. "We heard her screaming, but we...we couldn't do anything."

I examined the girl in the corner again. She might've been twenty-years-old, but not by much.

"They'll let us out...won't they?" a plaintive male voice asked from the darkness.

"Whatever they have planned, I don't think that's part of it," I answered. "We have to get out of here ourselves, as soon as possible."

"How bad's the situation?" Kirk asked.

"They've barred every door and window, and have guards posted at the exit."

"There has to be another way. An air vent. Something."

"All the vents are too small," Beth said softly.

A middle-aged woman with a bruise on her forehead raised her hand like one of my students, a habit some people never grow out of. "Doesn't anyone have a phone to call the police?"

Ron pointed to the people he'd been sitting with and said, "I don't know about the rest of you, but they took everything we had before they locked us in here." I felt my pockets to confirm this and found them empty also. "'Sides, the phones've been out since yesterday. Internet, too. I missed quite a few guild raids."

"I just don't understand this, it's absolutely insane!" someone else shouted. "What's wrong with them? Why are they acting like that?"

"Mr. Jefferson knows!" Katie said eagerly. "He knows why this is happening!"

All eyes in the room turned to me.

"That true?" Ron asked. "You really know somethin about all this?"

"If you know, you need to tell us!"

"Tell us, Elliot." Kirk agreed, leaning his head back against the window sill. "Tell us anything you know."

It was Beth I looked to first, standing with her arms crossed a few feet away. "You ready to listen?"

She sighed. "Why not? Unless someone has any ideas on how to get outta here, that's all I really can do at the moment."

The other faces drifted closer to me through the gloom, fear and desperation lining their features. "Maybe we should *all* compare notes," I said.

3

There were sixteen of us, in the beginning of that nightmare. Nine men and seven women of various ages, the youngest Katie, the oldest a guy named Delbert with gray hair who groaned every time he moved and then apologized for his joint problems, all of us beaten and banged up to some degree.

The Weary of cell block 28.

The electricity to the unit was out, either by accident or design; we couldn't even turn on the few recessed lights that came built into the unit. So, after giving Kirk a chance to clean himself up in the bathroom, we gathered around in a circle on the carpet like kids telling ghost stories in the dark. All except the girl in the corner, who refused to join us. I think talking helped ease the panic that constantly gnawed at us while we waited to discover our fate.

Before I would divulge what I knew, I had the others introduce themselves and tell their own stories, figuring the more they collectively acknowledged on their own, the less I would have to convince them of. They were all pretty much identical with the exception of Beth, who had been gone from the complex most of the week. The Squall had kept each of my fellow prisoners from getting a moment's peace since they'd noticed it late last week (Thursday or Friday for most of them, but Carolyn, the woman with the welt on her forehead, swore she started hearing it as early as last Wednesday), and then they had watched as their loved ones—or, for those who lived alone, their neighbors—began to act strange. Overeating, oversexed, and belligerent seemed to be the common symptoms, although everyone had their own unique, shocking urges also. Those with families had already made the connection between the odd behavior and not being conscious of the Squall. Most of them had watched quietly as those around them grew steadily weirder, withdrew from society, stopped going to work, and then there were the ones that also started disappearing in the middle of the night, and talking about voices that needed to be heeded. Each believed they were alone in the situation, except a few that had been present for the melee at the pool party.

Kirk ended story time with our adventure in Dan and Joan's apartment, a few calm tears leaking from his good eye as he told us about how his son had punched him for taking away a bowl of raw hamburger the boy had been trying to consume like a rabid wolverine, how he'd grown scared of his own wife and children over the last few days. Finally, he looked at me again and said hoarsely, "I intend to get my family back, Elliot. If you know what's making them act like this, it's time to goddamn start talking."

"It's definitely the Squall," I confirmed. Every time someone had mentioned the noise—most of them now using my name for it—the entire group had winced and glanced around nervously, as if hearing it all over again. After the excitement this morning, it had once again relented, dropping to a low drone, like a person falling asleep after a big Thanksgiving dinner. "At least, that's one of what seems like two components at work here. If you can't hear it, it gets into your subconscious and affects this part of your brain called—"

"The amygdala," Beth finished for me, from the opposite side of the circle. She had seemed to purposely move away from me when we sat down. "That's what your questions were about last night, weren't they? Why all those people are acting like a bunch of troglodytes."

"What's a trog...one of those?" Katie asked.

"A caveman," I interpreted. "And yes, that's exactly what's happening, although some of them seem to be worse off than others." I gave them a brief rundown of my encounter with Yonkers, showing off my oozy forearm for a visual aid. "The lab where they tested him for rabies called me just before the phones went out yesterday. They said he definitely didn't have it, but this part of his brain—the amygdala—was swollen. Based on what you told me, I think that noise is overstimulating it in these people."

"I don't understand!" Carolyn's voice was shrieky with panic. "What does that mean?"

"It means the Squall has freed these people of inhibitions. Allowed them to live out their darkest desires."

"Like it's tapping directly into their ids," Beth added, mostly to herself.

"No sir." The old codger—Delbert—shook his head heavily. "There must be more to it than that. I watched my wife of

42 years rip off her clothes and attempt to...*have relations*... with another *woman* at that party last night. I refuse to believe that's some kind of...of secret fantasy for her."

His denial made me think of the violent urges I'd had with Beth, in the workout room. They had shocked me...but they had also appealed to me on some deep inner level that only knows hunger. It isn't pretty when we're faced with the needs of our subconscious. "Believe what you want. But I think that these people...they're not even aware of what they're doing."

"How do you mean?"

"Well..." I chose my words carefully. "It could be like a trance, something they might not remember if...*when* they snap out of it."

"Oh malarkey! You mean to tell us they're all hypnotized or something?"

"I don't know if that's exactly how I'd put it," I said defensively.

"You couldn't make a person do those things against their will! It's just not possible!"

"There was an experiment," Beth began, speaking with her eyes on the carpet in the middle of the circle, "where they exposed test subjects' brains to electromagnetic fields, then presented them with theoretical scenarios and asked them to determine right from wrong. They found, almost invariably, that the subjects' decisions were based on *outcome*, rather than *intent*. For instance, they were given a situation where a man allows his girlfriend to cross a bridge he knows is unsafe, but she makes it to the other side in one piece. The control subjects found it...well, reprehensible. The test subjects found it acceptable, since ultimately there was no harm done." She swallowed hard. "In other words...these people lost their sense of morality."

This was met with stony silence for a moment until the girl in the corner—who hadn't so much as told us her name yet, asked timidly, "Are...are you a doctor?"

"Social psychologist."

"What's your point, missy?" Delbert asked.

"Just that we have very little understanding of the human brain. There's a lot of buttons up there to push, and nobody knows what any of them do."

"Charles Whitman," Kirk murmured.

Beth raised her eyes to me. "I didn't believe you before, and I'm sorry for that. Maybe if you had actually explained, I would have. In any case, I still think there must be more to it than just a simple noise for it to affect people like this."

"I'm more interested in why it *hasn't* affected us," Ron said, pulling on his ponytail distractedly. "Gotta be somethin that makes us different."

"Yeah, and you'd need a battery of medical and psychological tests to figure out what it is."

"So you haven't been?" I asked Ron hopefully. "Affected, I mean."

"Other than the fact I haven't had a decent night's sleep in a week?"

"No, I mean, *really* affected. Like them."

He raised a bushy eyebrow. "As in, have I felt the urge to round up my neighbors and start my own personal Auschwitz? Cause let me tell ya, if I had, I'd probably be on the other side of that door right now."

"It might not be as obvious as that," I pressed. "It might be... strange urges or lost time. A...a sort of...jump in your memory. Think hard. None of you has experienced anything like that?"

They all shook their heads, leaving me with a sudden pit in my stomach as heavy as a wrecking ball.

Kirk's good eye bored into me. "How do you know all this, Elliot? What are you not telling us?"

I hesitated, but only for a moment. There was no reason not to lay out everything we knew if it might help.

"I think...it started happening to me."

The effect of this admission of was like telling them I'd been exposed to Ebola. An uncomfortable murmur went through the group. They all looked horrified except for Beth, who watched me with her brow furrowed thoughtfully. Ron—sitting on the other side of Katie to my right—went so far as to break the circle and scoot a few feet further away, as though I might go berserk at any moment. Which, now that I think about it, isn't that irrational.

"What do you mean?" Katie asked.

"It started with these cravings. Getting really hungry or really...frisky. They came and went. Then, on Tuesday night, just before Joan killed Dan, I had this spell where I just blanked out. Wrecked my apartment. I don't remember any of it, but I saw some video and...let's just say, I looked like I would be pretty amazed by the discovery of fire."

"Why didn't you say something?" Kirk sounded angry now. "Or try to get some help?"

"Because I didn't know what was happening. Not for sure. And by the time I did, it was too late. I've been trying to get out of the complex for two days now, but they kept finding ways to stop me." I licked my lips. "Besides...I thought I had it under control."

"With the flask, right?" Beth was still studying me.

I nodded. She was putting pieces together a lot faster than I had.

"What flask?" Kirk demanded.

I squirmed.

"Tell them," Beth said, "about your little disability."

"What does that have to do with—?"

"*Just do it,*" she snapped. Her tone was short, but at least it wasn't as disgusted as it had been back at her apartment. "We don't have time for your insecurities."

Now everyone leaned forward expectantly, waiting to hear what I had to say. I gave them a wave and said, "Hello everyone, my name is Elliot Jefferson, and I am an alcoholic. There, satisfied?"

"Yeah, I am." A sudden devilish grin spilled across Beth's face. "Because alcoholism has been known to damage one very specific part of the brain. Care to take a guess what it might be?"

I sighed and said what I think I had known all along, on some level.

"The amygdala."

4

"Hold up," Ron said. "Are you sayin alcohol...what? Made him immune to that noise somehow?"

"No," Beth answered, "I'm saying the damage to his brain caused by long-term alcohol abuse *might* be a factor. It's just a theory. There's no way for me to know anything for sure."

"But before yesterday, I hadn't taken a drink in more than a year," I said.

"That makes even more sense. The fact that you were in recovery could explain why you didn't succumb immediately, and why your symptoms were sporadic. The existing damage provided a shield that the Squall kept trying to find a way around, and then, when you started drinking again, it helped to strengthen that shield."

"Oh, the irony," I muttered. "If only my ex-wife could hear this for herself." My tongue turned to sandpaper as I remembered how that whiskey had tasted going down. "I think the Heeders know about it also. That's why they made sure the party last night was dry."

"But that doesn't explain the rest of us," Kirk argued. "I haven't touched a drop of alcohol in fifteen years."

"I don't drink at all," Delbert added.

Rory Bergman sprang into my head, clutching his father's prescription bottle.

"Valium." The answer hit me so hard and fast, I almost shouted it. Kirk looked startled. "You said you take Valium." I looked to Beth. "Could that do the same kind of damage?"

She shook her head. "Not really. Not specifically the way alcohol does."

But I leaned forward, unable to let go of this theory that had suddenly gripped me. "Martha in the office, and Katie's mom; they both mentioned something about 'cleansing our impurities.' It sounded like crazy talk, but…"

Beth squeezed the very tip of her narrow chin. "If the mechanism that causes this change is dependent upon neurotransmitters to and from the amygdala, then—again, speaking theoretically—anything more powerful than, say, aspirin—something that screws with state of consciousness or body chemistry—if taken regularly, could be enough to distort or block the signal."

"Translation, Spock?" Ron asked.

"Drugs. She's talking about drugs," I answered eagerly. "What about everyone else? Be honest. Anybody on anything? Prescription or otherwise?"

"And cigarettes," Beth added. "For all we know, nicotine could do it, too."

The answers came back fast, mounting in excitement. Delbert had a prescription for his joints. Ron had been taking Ritalin since he was twelve. Carolyn was on thyroid medication. Katie reluctantly admitted to her recreational drug use, which she claimed had only been going on for a month. Three of the others were lifelong smokers. The list went on until the truth was undeniable.

Those unaffected by the Squall had all been artificially changing their body chemistry.

5

At this point, the powwow adjourned, so some of the attendees could use the apartment's sole restroom. They lined up in the empty bedroom to take their turn in the adjoining bath, all of them speaking and arguing in hushed whispers. Katie went with them.

Without power to run the air-conditioner, the afternoon's heat had become stifling in the closed space. I eased open the back door again, just enough to let a breeze blow through, and stood there to enjoy it. Without the Squall going full blast, and operating on a full night's sleep at Beth's place, I actually felt physically better than I had in days. Kirk and Beth joined me.

"You really think it's as simple as that?" Kirk asked. "Why we're in here instead of out there?"

"Let's keep our voices down." I glanced through the cracked door. I couldn't see our guards beyond the patio, but I had to believe they were still there. "Maybe we should let them think we're still in the dark. It might be our one advantage."

"It's not much of one." He turned to Beth. "What happens when the medication is out of our systems? You know, when our body chemistries return to normal, or whatever? I haven't had a Valium in almost a week. Does that mean I could become one of them?"

Beth's shrug was helpless, and a little frustrated. "I have no idea. It could be that we have an advantage since the drugs made us aware of the Squall, and now that our systems are clean, it's going to take a little longer for it to fade into the background again."

The answer didn't satisfy him. He turned to me next and demanded, "What happened when you drank from this flask of yours?"

"It dampened the Squall. Downgraded it from intrusive back to just annoying. And when I started losing my self-control, it gave it back." The irony of describing my drinking that way was worthy of the best O. Henry.

"Maybe I didn't leave my Valium in Florida, after all. Maybe Teresa took it."

"I think you'd probably find that happened to a lot of people's medication. We can't be the only ones out of the whole complex whose body chemistries were altered enough to block out the Squall. The numbers just don't add up."

Kirk nodded. "So that's it then. We get those people out there to drink alcohol or take some pills, and they'll stop acting this way."

I didn't bother to point out the many flaws in this plan. Like, for starters, that we had neither. "It's much simpler than that. We just have to get them away from the Squall."

He snapped his fingers. "Now that's an idea! If we could cut power to the complex somehow..."

Another fantasy, considering we were locked in a thousand square foot prison. "Kirk, I know you want to save your family, but—"

"No." His good eye narrowed. "I *am* going to save them. Which means I'll do whatever it takes to make sure I don't become one of those animals." He stalked away from us and plopped back down in the middle of the floor.

Beth and I stood in uncomfortable silence for a moment.

"You didn't say what you were taking," I told her.

"That's because I'm not on any medications, and the only alcohol I've had in the last few weeks was from your flask last night."

"Then why...?"

She waved her hand to cut me off. "Look, this thing was probably ramping up for weeks, blending in with the background noise and then slowly getting louder, because if it'd started out as annoying as it's been all week, I think even those people out there would've noticed. But it got in their heads and did whatever the fuck it's doing to their brains, and the rest of you were saved because of your diluted blood stream." She stopped, took a sudden, sharp breath. "But I moved in after it started, and I've been gone most of the week. I've had such limited exposure, that noise hasn't been able to slip into my subconscious. Which means I would really like to get out of here before it can."

Across the room, Ron lumbered out of the dark bedroom doorway and asked me, "What was the second?"

I looked away from Beth with some effort and responded, "Second what?"

"Component. You said there were two components at work. One was this Squall. What was the other?"

I closed the patio door again. The others drifted back in to the room also, waiting for my answer, but we didn't bother to sit cross-legged on the floor this time. "The voice. The still, small voice they keep talking about. Several of you mentioned it."

"That old woman kept screaming about it," Carolyn said. "Mrs. Isaacs."

"She's horrible!"

"I know. Those people out there, they may not be able to hear the Squall like we do, but that woman has got them convinced they're hearing something *inside* it, a voice from above that's giving them commands, like the goddamn Son of Sam." I didn't bother mentioning that I had heard this voice for myself; I had been looked at like a serial killer enough for one day. "They would probably all be out there attacking and fucking one another instead of us, just like at the pool party, but she's brought them all together under the banner of some pseudo-religious experience. The Heeders have become her own personal cult. And I think she's been planning this from the beginning, waiting until she had enough followers to take over the complex."

Delbert shuffled closer. "To what end?"

"To keep anyone on the outside from knowing what's happening. All of this today was a bid to ensure their new life of moral freedom continues unhindered."

The old man made a derogatory noise through his teeth. "They can't keep something like this quiet."

"Oh yeah? And just why not? Think about it: this place is geographically isolated and self-contained. They've already managed to sever communications. You couldn't ask for a better setup."

"But you can't just make an entire apartment complex disappear and not expect someone to notice!" Carolyn joined the argument.

"That's just it, it hasn't disappeared. As far as the rest of the world is concerned, the Estates of North Hills is still ticking along like always, and the apartment manager and most of the residents are still right here to play house and make everything look normal if they need to."

"What about that man they killed?" Katie asked. "The one from the electric company. Won't someone come looking for him?"

"They might, but I'm sure they'll be able to buy themselves at least a few days by having Martha and Tony say he never showed up here. After all, there won't be any reason not to believe them."

"But someone will miss the rest of us eventually!" Carolyn insisted.

"That's what I'm hoping. So let's try to figure out how soon that'll happen. Friends, relatives, coworkers; when's the soonest you think any of them will start looking for you?"

"My kids call from Ohio every Sunday morning like clockwork!" Delbert proclaimed proudly.

"Yeah, and your wife will still be there to pick up the phone this week and say you have the sniffles and can't talk right now," Ron told him. "That is, if she's ain't busy havin an all-female scissor-thon with the rest of the crazies out there."

"Shut your crude mouth!"

"Okay, enough," Kirk barked. "We don't stay civil, we're no better than them."

I nodded. "But Ron's right. The Heeders will just lie to anyone that comes looking for us. And if our spouses or children are the ones telling the lies, they're gonna be pretty damn convincing. So what we should really ask is, how long before someone gets worried enough to contact the authorities?"

We went around the room again quickly, but the outlook was grim. Ron was a total recluse; the only people that would miss him were his fellow online gamers. Like Delbert, most people had Heeder family members that could speak on their behalf to any friends or relatives that came calling. Katie's friends would start coming home from their spring break trips soon, but she didn't think they would worry until school started back up. Work was no better; some hadn't been to their jobs in a couple of days with everything that had happened in the complex, some worked at the kind of high-turnover hellholes where no one would care if they just disappeared, and the rest lived with people under the influence of the Squall that could just call in sick for them.

No, our best hope lay with the people that lived alone, for whom excuses from strangers would arouse more suspicion than flat out disappearance. This group included Beth, who figured her new coworkers would start looking for her a lot sooner than her family back home in Kansas; Carolyn, who had a boyfriend that would be expecting a call tonight; and, of course, yours truly. My own mother would be worried if she didn't get the obligatory phone call at some point this weekend, and if I didn't show up for class on Monday, the head of the English department—a woman I'd known for eight years, that had fully supported me when I went to AA—would start trying to hunt me down. The idea of being locked in this dark, hot apartment until then made me want to open my wrists with my fingernails.

"So that's it then," Kirk said. "We're on our own for now."

"But just remember," I told them, "they're holding us here because they're afraid. This is a delicate balancing act they're attempting. If we get the word out, this thing gets blown open, and their little party is over."

"There's just one thing about it that doesn't quite make sense," Ron said, tugging at his ponytail again. "If all this is about keeping us quiet, then why not just kill us? They took out a buncha other people this morning. So why'd they leave us alive and go through the trouble of locking us up?"

For the first time in our meeting of the minds, I didn't have an answer.

And it terrified me.

6

After our last talk, the group broke up again into smaller duos or trios, some to continue the debate, some to commiserate. A few folks took to pacing, while others curled up on the floor against the wall to sleep, their exhaustion overcoming their fear. Katie and Beth tried to coax the brutalized girl—whose name turned out to be Laura—from her corner.

Sitting still would've been the worst kind of agony for me. I needed action. So Kirk, Ron and I went over every inch of the apartment again, looking for anything we might have missed.

Each room was empty, nothing but walls and carpet, which we ripped up to look underneath and found cold concrete flooring. Even the refrigerator and the lid to the toilet tank had been removed. Beth was right about the heating and cooling vents, they were barely big enough for a skinny ten-year-old to fit through, but we pried them open anyway to look inside the ductwork. We could see daylight at the end of one of them, past a sharp turn, but couldn't figure how that helped us. The coverings over the windows and doors were solidly in place, and ramming our shoulders against the wood resulted in bruises and another threat from the guards. Unless we could break through a wall or ceiling to one of the other units, we wouldn't be escaping.

Next we turned our attention to anything we might be able to MacGyver into a weapon, with the intent to attack the guards if we ever got the chance. Suggestions included nooses made from our clothing, bending the vent coverings into metal spears, and pulling up the thin wooden rods to which the carpet was tacked to use as improvised caning rods. At the garage door, a metal wrench sat next to the water heater, tantalizingly out of reach beyond the bars of our prison. In the end, we decided it might be best to just rush them and try to get the guns rather than tip our hand by hiding weapons, and recruited two of our fellow male prisoners to help. One of them, I remember, was a guy named Simon, but the other has long since slipped my memory.

But afternoon turned to early evening, and still we sat. The interior of the apartment cooled a bit as the sun went down, but by then, all of us were hungry and irritable. A few went to the door and begged the guards for food, and were told again to shut up. Ron and Delbert snapped at one another, arguing over the stupidest things. Many of the women burst into tears at random intervals. All except Beth, who played nursemaid to the rest. I tried to pull her away so we could talk alone—about the situation, about us, I didn't care, I just needed to be with her for a few minutes—but she shrugged me off.

If there was one upside to that never-ending day, it was the fact that the Squall remained in a down phase. It was barely more than a tingle in the back of my mind most of the afternoon, forgotten for the first time since Friday. I heard a few of the others express hope that it was coming to an end, that all of this was about to be over, but I knew that son of a bitch too well by now to believe it.

And then, around what must have been five-thirty or six, the very edge of dusk, we heard keys rattling outside the patio door.

Kirk jumped to his feet and stood with hands fisted, ready to fight. Even starving and mostly blind, this scrawny, middle-aged black man was one of the most fearless individuals I'd ever met in my life. However, one look at the faces of Ron and the others told me they'd lost whatever balls they had. I was still willing to try, but when the door opened up, six men walked into the room instead of two, more than we could hope to fight, and all of them armed with handguns and rifles.

Everyone shrank away. Physically, they looked even worse than we did: backs humped, shoulders hunched, faces drawn and haggard. Their clothes were in tatters, stained with either dirt or blood. And they twitched and jerked constantly now, like palsy victims, the jumping muscles in their necks making it look like something was alive just beneath the skin, and fighting to get out.

"Get up!" one of them barked. He was balding and hefty, the kind of guy that looked like he rode ATVs on the weekend with a Coors in one hand. "All of you! Right now! Form a line!"

Those not already standing got up and drifted hesitantly to the middle of the room. One of our fellow prisoners tried to ask what they were going to do, and got pistol whipped across the side of the head for it. Everyone else hurried their pace and lined up without speaking.

Kirk stayed where he was, staring hard at the man in charge. His eyes flicked to the hunting rifle.

I put a hand on his arm. "Not now," I murmured.

He hesitated a moment longer, then stomped toward the line. We took up positions at the head, with me leading and him just behind.

The leader growled in my face, "You follow us outta here and stay in a goddamned line." His breath smelled rank, rotting meat and sour stomach acid; or maybe that was just him in general. "Anyone tries to run, you'll be shot without warning. Now fucking move!"

I was prodded forward by one of the other men. We all started walking behind their leader. The rest of the pack waited at the door for us to pass by so they could take up positions at the middle and end of the line. One of them leered at the girls, licking gummy lips. Laura began to cry softly.

We went through the door onto the patio, stepping outside for the first time in eight hours. Even the last rays of early evening sunlight dazzled my eyes after being in the dark all day, but the fresh air tasted wonderful. We were forced down the alley to the closest main road, where we got a look at the new and improved Estates of North Hills.

7

The Heeders had been busy while we wasted away in our cell.

The fallout from their takeover this morning was still visible—broken windows and kicked-in doors looked out from almost every building, debris and trash lay scattered everywhere, a few dark patches of dried blood on the concrete, the whole place looking like an urban battlefield—but the renovations were what really caught my eye. For starters, that frowning graffiti face was everywhere now, spray-painted on the sidewalks and across the buildings fronts like the one I had done at the office during my trance, the Heeder equivalent of *Kilroy was here*. Cars had been parked at every intersection, to function as barricades, I presumed. As we marched through the middle of the deserted complex with our armed escorts, I caught glimpses of the rock wall between buildings. Makeshift scaffolding had been erected along the inside perimeter, cobbled together from cars, two-by-fours, ladders, crates and pipes, whatever they could find. Men patrolled along the narrow junkyard catwalk, backlit by the setting sun, surveying the hayfields beyond the wall like guards on a prison tower. I spotted a few more on several of the second-story rooftops where they would have a higher vantage point, carrying shotguns and watching us warily as we passed.

The whole complex felt like a guerilla base or POW camp now, the kind of place you'd find deep in a South American jungle.

"Jesus, we're never gettin outta here," I heard Ron mutter from somewhere behind me.

I hated to admit it, but the situation was much worse than I'd feared. Their level of organization chilled me.

They quickened the pace until we were practically jogging. Someone else got cracked for not keeping up; I found out later it was Delbert, and they'd broken his arm. A couple of other groups joined us along the way, more frightened faces of all ages that fell into step on either side of us as we were herded toward the front of the complex.

Finally, the buildings in front of us cleared, revealing the long, rolling lawn behind the office that adjoined the pool and volleyball court, the one Beth, Katie and I had fled across this morning. A huge crowd milled here, perhaps three hundred people, enough to dwarf the body that had attended the Poolside Gala. The entirety of the Heeder army, all of them just as filthy as the men who'd brought us here, most likely from their day labors transforming the Estates into a penal colony. They turned to face us as we arrived, and the corners of every mouth pulled up in the same god-awful, lip-twitching grin, like they were all distant relatives that had maintained the slightest resemblance.

"*Keep moving!*" our drill instructor shouted.

We were shoved forward, into the waiting arms of the Heeders. The crowd parted in front of me, giving us a narrow path up the middle. As we walked through their midst, we were pelted with rocks, trash, whistles and catcalls. The gleeful taunts were almost deafening. I felt Kirk grab hold of the back of my shirt to keep from being lost in the crowd. I tried to duck my head and just keep moving, but hands came from all direction to clutch at me, tear my clothes, shake me, and slap my cheeks until I was dizzy. Leering women— some wearing nothing more than bras and bikini bottoms— lurched forward, pressed against me full-body, and dry humped my leg for several seconds before disappearing back into the mob. It was like being swept down an angry river, with no relief or escape, and barely any room to breathe. My chest grew hot and tight with anxiety. Every few seconds, a familiar face loomed out of that blurry sea: Javier...Rick...Martha. Tony, with his broken nose swollen and red in the middle of his face. He loosed a wad of phlegmy spit that hit me on the cheek.

But the children were the worst by far, those feral snarls terrifyingly out of place on their young faces. One Hispanic girl that couldn't have been much older than ten wormed out of the crowd, put a hand between my legs, and squeezed so hard my vision turned purple. She shrieked laughter and jumped away.

Just when I thought this treatment would never end, the crowd thinned. We had reached a clear space on the lawn in the center of the crowd. Ahead of us, more prisoners waited on their knees in a square formation, facing one another. The sun was down by now, inky shadows stretching across the entire yard, but the corners of this area were lit by open flame torches on poles. Tiki lamps, if you could believe it. There was something mildly amusing about the fact that their tribal ambience had come from the garden center of Home Depot.

I came to a halt, and the group piled up around me. A man with a crossbow pointed at a broken section of the square and ordered us to join the rest.

Beth leaned forward and said in my ear, with remarkable calmness, "They're gonna kill us."

I gaped around at the kneeling prisoners, most of them weeping and shivering, and the screaming, crazed people standing over them, waving various weapons and pumping their fists in the air. I had seen videos of Klan rallies and Nazi gatherings—places where hate was celebrated and the worst of mankind was on display—and this had the same sort of frenzied, angry feel.

Was that what this was? A public execution?

Had they spared us before and kept us locked up all day just to slaughter us together now?

Why not? Ritualistic sacrifice certainly sounds like their idea of a fun night.

"*Mom!*"

I heard the shout above the din of the crowd. Katie had broken away from the line and ran toward the closest edge of the square, where Samantha Adler stood with her hands clasped over her bosom, still the picture of piety even though she now wore a torn cocktail dress at least two sizes too small, one that bulged awkwardly from fat deposits and barely covered her below the waist. That tiny, knowing smirk was still on her lips, but it turned into a grimace every few seconds as her facial muscles jerked tight. The girl reached her mother and threw herself at her feet, then reached up to clutch the woman's hands.

"*Please, Mom, please help us, don't let them hurt me, I'll do anyth—!*"

Samantha jerked free, put one bare foot against her daughter's chest, and shoved. Katie fell back on the grass, where two other men rushed to hold her down. "*Teach her to heed!*" Samantha growled.

They forced Katie flat to the ground, one of them holding her hands, the other straddling her chest as she kicked and struggled beneath him. This one pawed at her small breasts through her shirt, then leaned over and ran his tongue up her neck. The Heeders in the crowd cheered him on; would've kept cheering, I'm sure, even as he raped her in front of them. But when he started to scrabble at the drawstring waistband of his stained sweatpants, I charged.

I bashed into him hard with my shoulder, tossed him a full yard away from the girl, then turned and kicked the one holding her hands in the chest. The crowd's happy cries never wavered; they just loved violence in all its forms, and didn't care if it was one of them on the receiving end. Katie scrambled away, hiding behind me as she got to her feet.

"*You people are insane!*" I screamed at the Heeders. I wanted to leap into their midst and just rend and tear anyone I could get my hands on. Probably would've been cheered for that, too.

Something hit me in the lower back, right at the base of the spine. Pain shot through me. I tried to turn, but my legs failed and I landed on the ground on all fours.

"Heya, Mr. Jefferson. Looks like it's my turn to teach you."

I looked up into Jacob's grinning face.

8

I *knew* it.

No matter how Katie defended him, no matter how much innocence he feigned, there had never been a doubt in my mind that Jacob was one of them. He may not have killed Mickey, yes, maybe I'd been wrong about that one, but not about the fact that the little fucker was evil through and through. And now, here was the proof.

Jacob leered down at me, his lower lip a scabby mess where I'd torn out his lip ring the night before. He clutched a rifle in both hands, the one he'd just used to smash me from behind. Now he turned the barrel on me and pressed the end against my forehead. I stared up at him without blinking, daring him to pull the trigger. Even now, looking back, I honestly don't know whether I wanted him to or not.

"Jacob, please, don't!" Katie pleaded. "You're not one of them, you can't be!"

"I heed the still, small voice," he said mechanically, then shoved my forehead away with the rifle barrel. His eyes were unfocused, pupils floating in bloodshot whites. "Now get over there, or you're gonna see what happens when I actually do have a gun."

My back screaming, I stood and moved toward the others, taking Katie with me. We were all directed to line up, completing the square formation, then forced to kneel as the rest of the crowd continued to hoot and jeer. I took a quick look around at the others in the torch light. All told, there couldn't be more than forty of us, forty people still in control of themselves, still unaffected by the Squall, and I saw doom reflected in each of their eyes. They had all arrived at Beth's conclusion.

As absurd as it seemed, we were going to die here, on our knees in the suburban apartment complex where we paid too much rent each month, killed by the collection of strangers that society had dubbed our neighbors.

Katie took one of my hands. Kirk took the other. The gesture was repeated around the square, the prisoners joining hands with each other until we were an unbroken chain. I had the hysterical urge to start singing *Kumbaya*.

Then the Heeders fell silent. The only sound came from the flicker of the torch flames, and the soft buzz of the Squall beneath, no louder than a mosquito around my ear. The crowd drew aside once more, and this time the matriarch herself appeared, with Schrader at her heels. The man had another lollypop jutting from his mouth; it dawned on me that if he hadn't quit smoking, he might be on his knees with us.

Isaacs wore one of her prim, dour church frocks, the only one of the Heeders that didn't look homeless. She tried to enter the interior of our square, but was stopped by the line of held hands. She stared down at them, patiently waiting, until Schrader came around her and kicked at the arms blocking her path with one booted foot until they let go. Then Isaacs continued on, into the middle of our ring, and stood looking around at us.

Her eyes flashed in the torchlight, as reflective as a wolf's.

"This won't help you," she rasped softly. The angles of her face were so severe, the leathery skin so shrunken, you could just about see the outline of her teeth through her sunken cheeks. "This show of solidarity. You must understand, there is no *you* anymore, just as there is no *we* or *us*. In the paradise you are being offered, the only pronoun you need concern yourself with is *I*."

Isaacs walked slowly around the square as she spoke, looking down at each of the captives in turn. "And the 'I' has needs. Basic, human needs, granted by the good Lord Himself. It *hungers*, you see. Not just for food, but for blood, for...flesh." A dry grin crossed her face, but I noticed it stayed firmly in place, wasn't a constantly squirming mess like the rest of them. "These urges—these hungers—are natural, but for the past few millennia, we have done nothing but try to bury them deep within ourselves."

The rest of the Heeders murmured their agreement, just as at the pool party, but she ignored them. That show had been theirs, to strengthen their resolve, but this one was entirely for the benefit of the uninitiated.

Isaacs arrived at our corner of the square. She stopped in front of Ron, just a few places down the line from me, then reached out and stroked one of his stubbled cheeks with gnarled, bone-thin fingers. "You are weary. Yes, I understand that. The world *grinds* at you and *grinds* at you until you are dust long before you ever enter the grave. You spend so much time worried about the weights draped over your shoulders that there is no time to satisfy the *I*." She turned her head, swept her gaze across us, and those cat's eyes seemed to pick me out. "But the Lord has chosen to show us the way out of this endless maze. To give us yet another chance to enter the Promised Land, which our ancestors have failed at time and time again. He uses an unconventional method to convey His message, a still, small voice that calls to your *I* even now, but, because of the impurities you feed yourselves, you have been given a deaf ear. This voice offers you complete freedom, and everything you could ever want. Not money, no, nor flashy cars or big televisions. Those are the trappings of the world, the distractions that drag you down and mire you in a cesspool of trivialities. No, my friends; this voice offers you what your heart *truly* desires."

"Which is murder, right?" I spoke before I even knew I intended to. The words were startlingly loud in the crisp evening air. Every face joined Isaacs in turning toward me. "That's what we all want when the filters are taken off, don't we? To kill? And rape? Maybe a little gluttony? Torturing animals to death, that's a good one, huh? Who knows, maybe someone out there in the crowd has always wanted to flay an infant. Because there are no lines we can't cross with what you're proposing. Isn't that right, you old hag?"

Across the square, Schrader came at me with that brutal, mechanical swiftness, but Isaacs raised a hand to ward him off without taking her eyes from me. She moved closer and then squatted down in front of me, the movement surprisingly fluid for a woman her age. I felt Katie's hand contract in mine.

Isaac's face hovered inches in front of me. This was the closest I had been to her, and every wrinkle looked as eternal as a crack in bedrock. She smelled more pleasant than the others though; I caught a whiff of lilac-scented perfume as we faced one another. Her gaze was like a battering ram, but I didn't show the slightest sign of weakness.

"There are lines," she whispered, her voice like loose gravel being crunched underfoot. "There are *always* lines. Without them, there is anarchy, and anarchy does no one any good. The Beast lurks in all our hearts the same way our Savior does. He constantly seeks to escape, to run roughshod over everything we attempt to build here. We must take our freedoms in moderation, to satisfy the *I* without letting it control us completely, or all is lost."

It was the second time she had mentioned the 'Beast,' but it made no more sense to me now than it had at the party. "I don't care how you rationalize it, or how pretty you make your propaganda," I said, "it's still madness. And you're just the queen of the loony bin."

Isaacs gave a tight-lipped grin. She rose and said to the entire group. "We were forced to eliminate many brothers and sisters today. It was not their fault that they could not heed, no more than it is yours, but their deaths were necessary. Yours, however, are not. We have decided to give you one last chance to cleanse yourselves, and to heed the still, small voice. Until that time, you will remain here as our guests. Once we are all disciples, then, and only then, can we plan for the future."

So that was it. The reason for our imprisonment.

We were an experiment in conversion.

Isaacs swept back out of the square, Schrader falling into line behind her, but stopped just before entering the mass of Heeders. She said, without turning, "And in case you needed further encouragement not to resist…"

Her words signaled another part in the crowd just to her right. Eight men entered the ring of torchlight, lugging a huge, unwieldy contraption full of gears and chains and jutting metal parts that I recognized immediately.

The science project from 3204's garage.

And lying full length on the padded workout bench in the midst of its mechanical parts was Tate.

9

The courtesy officer still wore his full uniform, although the long sleeves had been torn away from his navy blue shirt, revealing pale skin and a faded Navy tattoo on the left bicep. The angle of the bench kept him partially inclined and sitting up, like a hospital bed, but he was bound to the clockwork machine by a series of tight chains across his chest. His bare arms were stretched out to either side and lashed to thick metal rods by leather straps around the wrists. The pose's similarities to crucifixion were not lost on me.

His head had been fixed firmly in place also, by a reflective silver bowl clamped over the top of his skull and strapped under his chin by a steel brace. The crown was welded to another of those metal rods, which arced over him and then fed into the back of the machine. The whole thing looked like some kind of steampunk dental chair.

Tate's eyes rolled wildly in their sockets. He tried to speak when he saw us, but a cloth gag over his mouth made the words unintelligible. The men carried him inside our square and placed him in the middle. The iron feet of the machine sank into the lawn several inches. Tate's boot soles hung just about level with my eyes, giving me a front row seat to whatever was about to happen.

"*The Weary must be purged!*" one of the attendants bellowed, sounding like that boxing announcer who got famous with the rumble line.

"No, don't hurt him!" I pleaded, but the enthusiastic roar of the crowd drowned me out. I tried to get up, but this time Kirk held me back.

The man who'd shouted hit a button on the side of the contraption and then stepped back.

In the clockwork guts of the machine, something began to move. Parts shifted with a grumble, cogs clicked against one another, pulleys ratcheted tighter. The crowd moaned in anticipation. We watched, trying to figure out what the hell was happening in the bizarre mousetrap, until finally the entire system jerked taut, quivering with the strain, and the metal rods holding Tate's arms and head began to extend.

"Oh shit," I groaned. "It's a goddamned torture rack."

Each grinding turn of the gears caused the bars to extend an inch at a time, telescoping outward. Tate's arms were pulled further out to either side, his head lifted away from his chest by the brace under his chin. The tension wasn't enough to hurt yet, but more than enough for him to get the picture. He wailed through the gag and thrashed, but his bindings were too tight for it to amount to much.

His fear fueled the crowd to new heights of frenzy. Some of the Heeders began to dance, some to shake like they were in the throes of an epileptic seizure, while others rubbed and ground against one another like dirty dancers. Through the crowd, I saw Martha drop to her thick knees, unzip the pants of a man I was fairly sure wasn't her husband, and begin to give him a hearty blowjob, all while keeping her eyes on the awful scene unfolding in the middle of the lawn. As sick as it made me, I couldn't help flashing once more to my fantasy about Beth.

Deep inside ourselves, where the sun never shines, we all know that sex and violence taste better together than chocolate and peanut butter.

Tate's arms and neck had stretched just about as far as nature would allow, and still the gears kept turning and the rods kept growing. The officer's screams had gone from panicked to pain-stricken.

Beside me, Katie flinched. I pulled her to me, forced her to turn her face against me. On the other side of her, I could see Beth doing likewise with Laura. "Don't look," I said. I wished I could follow my own advice, but I couldn't let myself turn away. To do so would be to let Tate face his demise alone.

His limbs resembled pulled taffy after another few seconds, his neck impossibly elongated. Something snapped in one of his arms with a crack, audible even over his cries and the caterwaul of the mob. Tears leaked from the man's eyes. A red seam appeared below his chin as the flesh's elasticity reached its breaking point. Rivulets of blood snaked their way down to his chest, the torchlight lending them a black sheen.

And then, with a champagne cork pop, Tate's arms and head separated from his body in an arterial gush of blood, the latter trailing a short length of spinal column behind it like a tail.

The crowd around us gave the type of cheer you would usually get when the home team scores a touchdown.

And, as the blood drained from the officer's severed head and his disconnected arms dangled from the ends of the rods like sausages in a butcher shop window, I lowered my head and did something I hadn't done since the very earliest of my AA days.

I prayed.

FRIDAY MORNING

1

That night was the most hellish of my life.

After watching Tate's horrible end, we were led back to our cell. Several people from other groups tried to run—just broke from the line of prisoners and sprinted up the street toward nowhere in particular, a gut response to what they'd just witnessed—and were gunned down without hesitation. The shots cracked across the empty streets, echoed between buildings, but they still sounded dismayingly soft out in the open. Unless someone driving by heard them, they wouldn't carry to anyone who could help us. The rest of us marched on numbly.

When we arrived at the apartment, a few people helped Delbert splint his broken arm, but other than that, no one spoke. We were too traumatized for that. Hell, we could barely look one another in the eye. We huddled in the dark, as far away from each other as possible, our empty stomachs growling, and listened to Laura sob.

Then, perhaps ten or fifteen minutes after the door closed behind us, the Squall started up again.

And when I say started up, I mean *started up*.

It didn't just return to full volume; no, everything that had come before was merely an appetizer to this main course. It was so loud this time, thundering through the entire apartment, we couldn't even tell which direction it pulsed from. The very air seemed to swim with it, like we weren't just hearing it, but breathing it in, absorbing it through it our skin. The Squall became a piercing, throbbing whistle that made it feel like the seams of your skull were slowly being forced apart as your brain swelled from the grating irritation of that sound. And that's what it was doing, of course, finding ways past the shields we had unknowingly created against it, rubbing against our amygdalas like sandpaper, causing that strange lobe of our brains to bloat.

I've had so much time to think since then, to reconsider, and I'm almost sure this was why it had been so quiet all the previous day.

It was conserving energy. Preparing for one big push, this all-out assault against the last few people standing in the way of its total domination of the Estates.

I know what that implies. That it was coordinating with the Heeders. That it had a will.

That it was alive.

And, God help me, even now, I can't say that it wasn't.

2

Sleep—even thin and light—wasn't an option. We were like heroin junkies going through withdrawal: shivering, tossing and turning on the hard carpet, pacing around the small unit. One guy stripped down to his underwear, wrapped all of his clothes around his head so tightly I didn't see how he could breathe, then curled up in a ball and covered the bundle with his arms. I would have also, if I thought it would help. The unrelenting barrage—coupled with our starvation—was an effective brainwashing tool. Each of us suffered in our own personal hells throughout that endless night, isolated in our own heads, unable to think about anything else, afraid to even *try* thinking about anything else, because we all understood that once you stopped noticing the Squall, once it got past your defenses and slipped into your subconscious, then it was all over, you packed up your mental bags and checked out of your own head and whatever was left went out to join the Manson family.

Somehow, it reminded me of that first night, a week ago, when I desperately tried to find a way to sleep. Now I was too afraid to even do that much, because I knew any form of unconsciousness I did achieve would be plagued by horrible nightmares.

So I waited. Waited for the world to drain away again. To hear that horrible, buzzing voice whispering all the things I secretly wanted to hear. I just hoped I would blank out fast again, like before.

When the first weak rays of sunlight speared through the chinks in the window coverings, they found us all sprawled in the floor like the aftermath of a killer party, exhausted and miserable but still ourselves. The Squall gave a particularly high-pitched squeal and then cycled down into its usual needling shriek. The relief was like cool water on a blister. I blinked and stared at the ceiling while my senses readjusted until, a few minutes later, the door of our cell creaked opened and a large cardboard box was shoved through.

I forced myself to turn over, climbed to my hands and knees. A few other people stirred in the empty living room, but I lay closest to the back door. I crawled forward, every joint a dull throb, then pulled back one flap on the box and cautiously looked inside.

It was food. A random, hodge-podge collection of sliced sandwich meat, crackers, half-finished cereal bags, apples and oranges, and several boxes of granola bars. The leftover contents of someone's pantry. I suddenly wondered if the Heeders would send expeditions for food when their stores ran out. I couldn't envision them calling for pizza or Chinese.

Ron appeared beside me, purplish bags under his eyes, and scooped up an apple. "Thank god."

"Stop," I told him. "Don't eat that. What if they put something in it?"

"What would be the point?" He considered the shiny skin of the apple for a moment. "If they drug us, it just makes us less susceptible, and if they wanted to kill us, it would be a helluva lot easier to just walk in and shoot us than to poison us."

I couldn't argue with that. I watched as he bit into the apple, then, as more people drifted over, I fished out a few granola bars, an orange, and a handful of meat and backed away.

Katie lay in another corner, curled up on the floor beside Beth. She groaned when I tapped her.

"C'mon, kiddo. You have to eat something."

She sat up, wiped tangled hair out of her face, and accepted a granola bar without comment.

"How do you feel?" I asked.

She shrugged, rested her chin on her knees, and nibbled at the food. Beside her, Beth scooted up against the wall. I offered her the orange, but she declined. Her eyes were so bloodshot, it was impossible to tell where her corneas ended and the whites began. "What do we do now?" she asked grimly.

"I don't know."

"We have to get out of here."

I crammed a few deli-thin slices of turkey in my mouth and chewed once before swallowing. My belly told me it wanted more. "I agree."

Her eyes widened in frustration. "Then what's the plan?"

"Beth, I don't have a plan. We've been over it and over it. There's no way to escape, short of rushing the guards next time they open the door. And even if we get out of this apartment, what then? You saw what it was like out there. They have actual sentries posted everywhere. They've turned this place into a fortress."

"So the alternative is to sit here until we become one of them, or until they get bored and strap us into their torture chair?"

Before I could answer, Katie whispered hoarsely, "I have to go to the bathroom." She got up, tucking her meager breakfast into a pocket, and started for the bedroom. Everyone else had looked our way when Beth raised her voice. Her whole body quivered with tension.

"Calm down," I told her. "We're close enough to the edge as it is."

"I can't take another night like that," she said. "I just...I *can't.*"

"I know, me neither. We just have to stay alive until help comes." I reached out and took her hand, which she promptly jerked away again. She turned her head to study the wall. After a moment of silence spun out between us, I asked, "Look, did I do something wrong?"

"What?"

"Did I upset you somehow?"

She rolled her eyes, a snarky expression that reminded me of Darcy at her worst. "Jesus Christ, Jefferson, is this junior high study hall? What are you talking about?"

She was right, this was far from the right time for this dis-
cussion, but I pressed on. "It's just, things between us were
moving along pretty well, and then, after the party, we...you
know...and since then, you just seem perpetually pissed at me."

Her scowl grew even heavier, shadows carving lines
through every crevice and wrinkle. "That was a mistake. To
tell you the truth...I don't know what came over me. It just
happened, and I think we should forget it."

The words stunned me. She seemed like a completely different person. And I couldn't help being paranoid that finding out the truth about me had put her off.

*Or maybe you should keep in mind that you met her less
than a week ago. For all you know, this could be her MO
with every guy she fucks. Regardless of whether or not she
gets imprisoned with them the day after.*

Everyone else milled around the breakfast box as Ron
doled out the food like a ponytailed Santa. After going
through the line, Kirk limped over to our corner, using his
shirttail as a bowl for dry cornflakes. He sat down cross-
legged beside me and began moving the cereal from shirt to
hand to mouth, as automatic as an assembly line, just forced
nourishment without any enjoyment.

"I felt odd last night," he said distractedly. "Kind of
loopy. Like I feel just before the Valium kicks in and drags
me down into sleep. Is that what it feels like, when you start
changing into one of them?"

"Yeah. Sort of. I didn't actually change into one of *them*.
I think it was closer to the way we found Joan."

"What's the difference?" Beth asked.

A split-second flash of me in the video on Martha's computer. "More...primitive. Animalistic."

"What about Tate?" Kirk asked. "He doesn't live here.

Somebody will report him missing. His family, the other cops. *Someone.*"

"Not for a couple of days, at least. He's on vacation from the force, and his wife took the kids out of town."

"Then we're gonna have to make a move soon. We can't afford to sit and hope that someone eventually comes looking for us. We won't make it that long."

Beth waved a disgusted hand in my direction. "You're wasting your breath on him."

The first real stab of anger hit me. "You know, if you have any ideas, feel free to share them."

She opened her mouth, but the rattle of the lock on our cell door stopped her. The people still standing next to the food box scurried away, like a frightened sheep herd. This time, three armed men—all different from our execution escorts last night—entered and stood in the shaft of blinding sunlight coming through the door.

A collective gasp rose up as we got a look at them.

All three were shirtless and barefoot, wearing only ragged jeans or, in one case, a pair of mud-caked khakis. But their bare skin had been streaked with what looked like ash or soot, random slashes of dark war paint that reminded me of my condiment body art. Random smudges and archaic symbols decorated cadaverous cheeks, hunched shoulders, and sunburned torsos. Primitive tribal tattoos crawled up their necks and arms. The image of predatory savages was broken only by the guns in their hands, instead of spears.

They looked around at us for a moment, eyes dull but angry, then one of them—an especially jittery specimen with an inverted triangle painted across his forehead—raised a hand and singled out Kirk, Simon, and Katie, who stood peeking out from the bedroom doorway with Laura.

"Them," he grunted. "Bring 'em."

The other two Heeders lumbered forward. Katie tried to backpedal as one of them caught her wrist and pulled her out into the living room. Laura clutched at her, but the son of a bitch backhanded her across the cheek and giggled at her cry of pain. The other one went to Simon, squatting against the wall with an orange wedge forgotten halfway in his mouth, grabbed his hair and yanked until he got to his feet. Triangle walked toward where Kirk, Beth, and I sat.

I shot to my feet. "Wait a minute, what's going on, where are you taking them?"

He didn't pause, just took Kirk's arm and hauled him up. Cornflakes spilled across the carpet. "You had yer group therapy, now it's time for yer one-on-one's," he said with a twitching sneer as he drove Kirk back across the room. The other two followed with their captives.

"*Let go!*" Katie screamed, struggling as the Heeder dragged her toward the door. "*Somebody help, don't let them take me!*"

I sprinted across the room, trying to get to her, but Triangle put out the barrel of his rifle to block my path. "Touch her, and I'll put a bullet through yer fuckin kneecaps. Then I'll stick my dick in every hole she's got while you watch."

I would've pushed past him anyway, but by then, Katie was almost through the door. We watched helplessly as Kirk and Simon were taken out right behind her, and the iron bars were slammed closed.

3

We went back to waiting.

The seconds dragged out into minutes, the minutes into

hours. I couldn't think about anything except Kirk and Katie being dismembered by that machine. Outside, the Squall went through intermittent periods of remission every fifteen to thirty minutes, followed by blats of pure white noise. Almost as though it were probing, trying to find the right frequency to break us. We constantly checked one another, asked if everyone felt all right. A few people reported the kind of symptoms Kirk spoke of, but not me; I never even felt lightheaded. I could only figure all the alcohol I'd consumed in the past 48 hours had given my immunization a boost, but how long would that last? Ron tried to raise morale and take our minds away by organizing some games—the guy could barely sit still, which was, I suppose, why he was still on Ritalin in his thirties—but most of us stretched out and tried to catch what sleep we could in the few minutes of peace.

Our living quarters quickly descended into third-world conditions. An apartment of this size wasn't meant to contain so many people for such extended periods. The place began to stink from the packed, sweaty bodies, so we took turns showering in the bathroom. Without electricity, the water was chilly, and we had to either air dry or just put our clothes back on and sit around damp. The meager supply of toilet paper we'd been provided ran out, but by then the toilet had stopped up from overuse anyway. Carolyn got sick, began puking up reams of sweet-smelling bile, and took over the bathroom.

And then, about three hours after Kirk and Katie left, we were visited by a new set of war-painted Heeders, and this time Delbert and another woman were taken.

Our numbers continued to dwindle as the day wore on. Noon came and went. The rest of us sat around and stared at one another and waited for our turn. We developed a Pavlovian response of gathering as far across the room as possible every time keys jangled outside, cowering as we waited to see who would be chosen next, but we still made no effort to fight. We were dead on our feet, nerves frazzled from constant exposure to the Squall. Laura suggested locking the back door to the apartment and holding it closed next time they tried to come in, but I said the amount of time this bought us probably wouldn't be worth the resulting punishment. They eventually served us a late lunch, a paltry offering of a half loaf of bread, meat, and cheese, but since there were only seven of us by this point and Carolyn remained locked in the bathroom, it was enough to go around.

I had just finished forcing the last couple of bites down my throat when we heard voices outside. This was different; we'd never heard them speak before they came to take a group away. Ron cracked open the door and looked out. "The guards are changing or something. One of them just handed the keys over to somebody else. Shit, here he comes!"

He barely had time to jump away before the cell bars creaked and the inner apartment door opened, allowing a lone figure to enter.

Jacob clutched the rifle he'd threatened me with last night. The kid was bare-chested also, with black smudges under his eyes like a football player and lightning zigzags scrawled along the shelf of his muscular ribcage, obscuring a couple of real tattoos. His gaze roamed the room until it found me. Then he pulled the iron bars shut behind him, reached through, and snapped the padlock closed again.

Locking himself in with us.

4

My guts clenched like an accordion. The phrase 'fish in a barrel' suddenly took on a whole new meaning for me. Isaacs might want to keep us around until we joined the family, but her wishes meant nothing to a group with severe impulse control problems. Frankly, I was surprised one of the other foxes hadn't been tempted to sneak into the henhouse before now.

Whatever the kid had planned, I would come out on the losing end. The two of us locked in a room was a dream scenario for him even before he became a medically-certified psychotic; now the prospect must've been too enticing for him to pass up. I would have to make a move before he did and just hope someone backed me up.

But whatever expectations I had for this situation dried up and blew away when he reached in the pocket of his sagging, torn jeans, pulled out a gallon plastic baggy half-full of a familiar white powder, and held it out to us. "You guys need to take this shit. Right now."

All of us blinked at him for a span of long seconds, but it was Ron that actually voiced our mutual, "Huh?"

"C'mon!" he urged, glancing outside. One long corkscrew of war paint began above his ear and curved down his neck. "I don't got time for you to be dumbasses. I been lookin for an excuse to get the guards to leave all day so I could get to you, but they'll be back soon." When still none of us moved, he shook the baggy and said, "Jesus Christ, *take it!* Snort it, swallow it, whatever, just keep some in your bloodstream and it'll keep you from changin!"

"You're...not like them?" Beth asked cautiously. She drifted toward him, and the rest of us followed.

Jacob gave an irritated sigh and moved aside so he could close the back door to the apartment. "No, I ain't. I'm just playin along until I figure a way to get out."

"Holy shit, for real?" Ron asked. "Then let us out!"

He and several others moved forward, crowding anxiously toward Jacob, who lowered the baggy and raised his rifle to ward them off.

"Get back, man! I can't do that! You guys get seen, it's my ass on the line."

"But this is our chance to escape! We can all go together!"

Jacob shook his head emphatically. "Look, lettin you outta this apartment ain't gonna do jack shit, because there's no way off the property. Those psychos're watchin every inch of the wall, and they got Martha and an entire platoon coverin the front gate like it's the border of Mexico." He winced as some sudden memory prodded him. "I mean, when they're not stuffin their faces or fuckin one another in ways I didn't even think was possible."

"You have a gun!" Ron insisted.

"Yeah, and they got fifty guns. I can't fight 'em all. Sorry, man, I'll do everything I can for you, but I just can't afford to let you guys blow my cover."

"Oh, this is horseshit," I groaned. But as I did, I couldn't help noticing that, even though he looked like shit—face sallow and haggard beneath the paint, the tear running down the side of his lower lip still crusted with blood—he certainly wasn't doing the jitterbug like the other Heeders. "He's one of them, trust me. This is some kinda trick."

Jacob snorted. "Of course. Why am I not surprised? I risk my life to help you, and you don't believe a word I say."

"Maybe that's because the last two times I saw you, you tried to kill me."

"Don't be such a drama queen, Jefferson. I didn't try to kill you at the pool, I only tried to give you a much-needed beat down. There's a difference. And I did that because you're an asshole, not because I'm one of them."

"You two know each other?" Ron asked.

I ignored him and said to Jacob, "Oh really? Is that why you got the *Lord of the Flies* makeover?" The kid touched his cheek self-consciously, smearing the makeup there. "And you were sure chanting and cheering like one of them last night. And bashing me with a rifle when I tried to save Katie."

"All just to fit in, man."

"That's fucking stupid, Jacob. If what you're claiming is true, why wouldn't they know it?"

"*Well, whadda you think, they got a fuckin crazy detector?*" Jacob's eyes widened as he realized how loud he'd shouted this. He dropped his voice to a harsh whisper. "Listen motherfucker, I don't know what's wrong with those people or what that noise is doin to them, all I know is that they got no way to tell for sure if you're hypnotized or not. The only reason you people are in here is because you're *not* chanting and cheering. If you just do what you're told, keep your head down, mumble some shit about how great this *still, small voice* is, throw in a few twitches every once in a while, then you're all good. When shit started goin down yesterday morning, I just blended into the madness. I seen people actin weird all week, so I knew how to put on a show. At first, I didn't know why I wasn't one of them, but then I heard that crazy bitch talkin about people with 'impurities in the blood' and I figured it out."

Even though I knew it would be the most hypocritical statement to ever leave my lips, I said, "Then I guess it's lucky for you you've been on drugs for the past five years, huh? Validation for all the choices you've made in life."

Jacob's lips wrinkled back, the bottom one exposing clenched teeth down to the gums. "You know what, I've been on a continual goddamn high for nearly two days now. I haven't slept, I'm close to crashin out, I've seen shit that makes my nightmares look tame, and I don't need your attitude, you cock. You don't want my help, fine, I'm gone. There's people locked up all over the complex I gotta try to get to."

He turned to the inner door and pulled it open.

"Wait, don't go!" Laura pleaded. The others echoed this, making me feel ill.

"Hold on," Beth added, and when Jacob paused she said, "If it's so easy, then teach the rest of us the same routine, and we'll all pretend. Better to be out there where we have options."

"But don't you see, *it don't matter!* Even if you convince them, you'll just be outside instead of in here, listenin to that noise, until you turn into one of them for real. And the only way to keep that from happenin is to stay fucked up." He shook the baggy again. Now that I was closer, I could see those green flecks throughout the powder, ground up bits of whatever stimulant he used.

Ron reached out and took the bag, holding it in both hands like he'd just been given the holy grail. "What is this stuff?"

"My own special blend of herbs and spices. Use sparingly, my man; a little goes a long way."

Beth leaned closer to examine the contents and asked, "Couldn't you just bring us some cough syrup?"

"Not a chance. That old bitch is sendin people through every apartment to get rid of all pharmaceuticals and alcohol. Shit, she even outlawed soda and coffee. Afraid caffeine might be enough to break the spell, I guess. I just barely managed to get my stash out of my pad before they raided the place." His gaze picked me out one more time as he pulled a keyring from his pocket and reached through the bars to release the lock. "I gotta go before they come back. Long as you ration that, it should last all of you until I can get back with some more. I get a chance to escape, I'll bring back help."

He started to walk through the door, but I said, "Jacob."

The boy looked back at me, his dark eyes flashing.

"Do you know where Katie is? What are they doing with the people they take?"

Jacob swallowed heavily before answering. "I don't know, man. I just heard somethin about them wantin to put pressure on you guys. That's all I know."

He went out onto the porch, locking the bars behind him.

5

"How do you know him?" Ron asked.

"It doesn't matter." I held out a hand. "Here, let me have that."

Ron raised an arm to give me the baggy. "You gonna ration it out?"

"No, I'm gonna wash it down the sink."

He reeled the bag back in before my fingers could close on it and cradled it protectively against his chest. "What? No, you can't do that! Didn't you hear him, this could stop us from turning into them!"

"It's bathtub crank, Ron. Even if he was telling the truth, would you really wanna take that stuff?"

"If it kept me from becoming one of those lunatics, I'd take arsenic." Several others voiced their agreements.

I balled my hands and put them to my eyes. I was being ridiculous, I knew it, but even after everything we'd been through, when hope was the most valuable commodity we owned, I still stubbornly refused to believe that anything good could come from Jacob Tinsley. "Yeah, well, I'm not gonna let you destroy yourselves the way that idiot has."

"That's really not your decision to make," Beth said softly.

"Yeah," Ron agreed. "You don't wanna take it, you don't gotta, but everyone else should get the same choice."

Before I could say anything else, he pulled the zipper at the top of the bag, reached in, and took a small pinch of the white powder between thumb and forefinger. He held it in front of his face for a long moment, studying the substance, then muttered, "Bottom's up." His thumb moved to the opening of his nostril as he inhaled sharply. "Wooooah, *mama*. Anybody know of a 5K I could run?"

The others moved in for their own hits, some snorting, some putting a small quantity on their tongue. All except for me and Beth, who shook her head when offered the bag and walked away.

FRIDAY EVENING AGAIN

1

Sometime later that afternoon, I blanked out for the first time.

After the bag of Jacob's homemade blow made the rounds, they hid the remainder in the ventilation shaft, and the mood in the apartment soared. Real conversation started for the first time that day, infused with actual laughter. Those morons were high, giggling like high school kids who'd just gotten their hands on pot for the first time. Ron practically bounced off the walls. The Squall continued to cycle, but they were oblivious.

Meanwhile, I bottomed out. Their merriment annoyed me, so I crawled into the empty bedroom to escape. My eyelids started to flutter, but sleep remained elusive. Once I caught myself staring at a stain on the carpet and drooling on my own chest.

And then, one second Ron stood in front of me, pounding at the bathroom door and demanding Carolyn let him in so he could take a piss, and the next, my vision seemed to jump. Ron disappeared, the bathroom door opened, and the shadows in the room deepened, spearing out from the dark corners and crevices like they were spring loaded.

I jumped up, cold dread caressing my neck and cheeks. Judging by the light quality, several hours had just passed in a heartbeat. But had I actually succumbed to the Squall, or just fallen asleep? The world hadn't wavered, and I hadn't heard any voices, but this didn't feel like waking up, it felt like before, in my kitchen.

The bare walls seemed to mock me as they pressed in closer. I pulled at my cheeks, rubbed my eye sockets until I saw bursts of fireworks.

Outside, the Squall ground on, as patient as ocean waves carving a cave into solid rock.

I was just about to find the others and beg for some of Jacob's concoction, when a commotion started in the other room.

Kirk had returned.

2

By the time I got out to the living room, the cell door was already closed and locked again. Kirk had an arm around Ron and Beth's shoulders, hanging completely limp as they helped him further into the room. Behind him, Simon and another woman that had been taken from our group lingered by the door, dazed and shaking. The woman had a black eye and a bloody lip that hadn't been there when she left. She burst into tears under our scrutiny and sank into the floor. Laura went to see about her. Simon held one hand in his opposite armpit, the shirt around it stained with fresh blood. He ducked his head and slipped past all of us into the bedroom without a word.

Ron and Beth made it only a few more steps with Kirk before his weight became too much. It was everything they could do to get him lowered to the floor without dropping him. I rushed over to help, and got my first look at what had been done to him.

His face was beaten so severely, the skin had begun to crack under the swelling. Both eyes were narrowed to bulbous slits, his right cheek sunken in such a way that the facial bone had to be broken.

And the injuries didn't stop there. His shirt hung open, revealing the xylophone stack of his ribs covered by a minefield of tiny cuts that oozed blood. He gasped sharply as they laid him back, raising a hand to clutch at his side.

Kirk wheezed, "Careful. Pretty sure...I got a busted rib. But at least they gave my glasses back." He patted his shirt pocket.

"What did they do?" I demanded. Rage filled me like a kettle forgotten on the stove, ready to boil over. "Kirk, where did they take you?"

"My family," he mumbled. Tears squeezed out between his swollen eyelids and spilled down both cheeks, but he began to chuckle. That rough, helpless laughter haunted me then, and still haunts me now. "They took me to see my family, just like I wanted..."

Beth tore off the sleeve of her shirt and wet it down in the kitchen sink. She knelt on Kirk's other side and gently set about cleaning the blood from his chest. "Tell us what happened."

"They brought me back to my apartment, let me go in alone. Teresa was there, and the kids. They were themselves again. Normal. God, it was like a dream." Kirk reached out, found my hand, and squeezed, but his grip was so very weak. He had barely eaten anything in the past four days. "They hugged me, told me it was all right, that they were all better. But...it was just an act. They sat me down on the couch, the kids climbed in my lap, Teresa laid her head on my shoulder...and they told me I had to heed. That I had to listen for the voice to speak and do what it said, so I could be with them forever. I refused, tried to get them to snap out of it, but then they got mean, said some...awful things. And when browbeating me didn't work...those other bastards came in, forced me into a chair from my own dining room table, and tied me down."

"They...they tortured you?" Ron asked fearfully.

"No," Kirk answered, wincing as Beth dabbed at the wounds across his chest. "They let my family do it." A rattling cry drifted from his mouth. "My own children...they cut me...hurt me...and laughed about it. They *enjoyed* it. And my wife...she..."

He couldn't finish, but I don't think any of us wanted him to. I wondered if this experience had lessened his resolve to save them. Beth stroked his forehead, and, after a few seconds, his strangled sobs tapered off, either into sleep or unconsciousness.

"I think he has a fever," she said.

Ron started to get up. "I'll get that powder stuff."

I caught his arm. "What the hell for? You think it's magically gonna heal him?"

"No, but he's gonna need some! If nothing else, it'll help with the pain!"

"Maybe, but you're not gonna force it on him while he's out cold. You want everyone to get a choice, then he does, too. Besides, if they're bringing people back, it needs to stay hidden."

Laura, looking pale and shaky, came over to us then and reported pretty much the same story about the woman by the door, that she had been cajoled by her husband, then teased and tormented before moving on to physical torture.

I looked around at those of us who hadn't left the cell today. "That's why we weren't taken to any of these 'one-on-one therapy sessions.' Most of us don't have any family here they can use against us."

"But why torture?" Ron asked. "They know we can't just decide to be like them, not until we're clean."

"Because that's how they get their jollies. Cruelty and sadism."

Beth had that expression on her face again, the one that indicated the hamster wheel was turning upstairs. "There could be more to it than that."

"How so?"

"I don't know if I really explained how the amygdala works. It all has to do with fear."

"Those guys don't seem scared of anything," Ron said.

"I know, and that's the point. The reason we're not all living like savages all the time, taking what we want, whenever we want it, is because we've learned to be afraid of the consequences. Both individually and collectively, as a society. That's really what the amygdala does, when you get right down to it. I can't explain the specifics—this part is more physiology than psychology—but the amygdala serves as a kind of processing center for fear. It's literally the place where we learn to be scared, and turn that emotion into adaptive behavior. Burn your hand on a stovetop, and you make damn sure you never do it again. Maybe that's all the Squall is really doing: taking away their fear and guilt."

"But how does that fit in with what they did to Kirk?" I asked.

"Because the swelling of the amygdala could be indicative of overstimulation to the point of shut-down, to remove that roadblock of fear. If so, then what better way to get it working—and possibly blow it out entirely—than to make someone really afraid?" She glanced down at the bloody pulp of Kirk's face. "Say, by letting their own flesh and blood abuse them?"

The magnitude of what she was saying hit me all at once. "They're trying to jumpstart the change."

Beth nodded.

"How would they know to do that, unless they understand exactly what's happening to them?"

"Maybe they do. Or maybe it's just instinct, like salmon swimming upstream. In which case, this process is far more developed than it has any right to be."

None of us spoke. Except the Squall, which continued gibbering in a language we didn't understand.

Yet.

"Oh man," Ron moaned. "I think I need another toot from the stash."

For the first time, I began to agree with him.

3

Over the next hour or so, as our second night in captivity fell, our other missing cellmates were returned to us one and two at a time. All of them in shock, all of them badly injured from torture sessions performed by their loved ones. Cuts, bruises and burns were triaged. Katie's fingernails had been ripped from her right hand by Samantha Adler herself. She told me her mother had used a pair of pliers, all while stating that she wished her daughter had been aborted.

The only one who didn't return was Delbert.

By the time we'd treated everyone as much as possible without any medical supplies, dinner was brought to us, no more than several boxes of crackers and a jar of peanut butter. I imagined we were getting down to the dregs with the way the Heeders loved to gorge themselves. We all ate enthusiastically, except for Carolyn. Even Kirk sat up and had a few bites.

With the food gone, Ron went to the ventilation shaft and pulled out the drug bag.

"What is that?" Katie asked. Like most of the others, she barely had any voice left from screaming her throat raw.

"All of you need to know what we found out," I said.

We quickly related the story of Jacob's visit. The knowledge that we had a spy on the inside caused a burst of excited questions.

"I told you," Katie exclaimed, a weak smile lighting up her entire face. "I told you he wasn't one of them. He couldn't be, with all the drugs he's on."

"I'm sure his mother would be so proud."

"So that's it," Ron concluded. "All we have to do is hold on, and this stuff will help us do that. We took some earlier and, man, that noise didn't bother me at all!"

"And if we make it out of this, we can all go to the methadone clinic together," I muttered.

"Excuse me," Kirk said quietly. Beth tried to help him stand, but he waved her away and headed toward the bathroom, his steps slow and decrepit.

When he was gone, Ron frowned at me. "Man, I don't know what your deal is with that Jacob kid, but you gotta ease up."

"My deal is that he's a burnout loser who you're all treating like the messiah. He's a chronic liar, and he ruined his life with the stuff in that bag."

"Yeah, but...weren't you an alcoholic?"

"That's different."

"Is it?" Beth asked. "Or is the real issue here that this is all hitting a little close to home for you?"

I took a deep breath before continuing. "I'm not stopping any of you from taking it, and I'm not saying I'm not going to. I just want us to consider other options besides voluntary drug addiction."

"Consider all you want," Ron said. "Just leaves more for the rest of us."

He unzipped the bag, took another snort. Others came forward hesitantly, a majority of the group, but Beth hung back once more.

I stared at the green-spotted powder. I was surprised to find how badly I wanted some, not just because I'd been so terrified earlier when time had seemed to jump, but because I hoped this stuff might be able to scratch the itch that alcohol always had.

Monkey swapping, in other words.

I reached into the bag.

From the bathroom came a terrible, soul-wrenching shriek.

Several of us ran for the bedroom, but I beat them there. I tried the bathroom knob, found it locked, and then rammed my shoulder into the flimsy wood until it cracked apart and flew open.

There was just enough lingering light to see Kirk, standing in front of the mirror above the sink and screaming uncontrollably. He turned to face us as we crowded the doorway. I saw the blood pouring out of both ears and the long, needle-thin sliver of wood from the carpet trim we'd pulled up and understood immediately what he'd done.

"*Oh god!*" Kirk wailed. "*It's still there! That fucking noise is still there! Don't you see, it's not a sound, we were never really hearing it at all!*"

He pressed red-gloved hands to his temples and squeezed till his forehead bulged grotesquely.

"It's broadcasting directly into our goddamned *heads!*"

4

Kirk was a pathetic sight as we led him back out to the living room and forced him to lie down, all the while mumbling that he had to do it for his family, had to try, to make sure that he didn't become one of them. Laura and Katie were tasked with cleaning him up.

The rest of us didn't even get a chance to talk about what his revelation meant before someone opened the cell door. Ron just had time to toss the narcotics baggy into a kitchen cabinet as Schrader walked in. Snarls of gray hair covered my neighbor's leathery chest in a carpet so thick, it looked like he had on a sweater, and dark ash covered his skin in a jagged double helix all the way up his arms and neck. A pair of jeans converted into ridiculous frayed cutoff shorts covered him below the waist. The axe he'd used to kill Avery dangled from one hand, still stained with blood.

"Jefferson," he growled. He brought the axe up and pointed it directly at me. "Let's go."

Giving Beth and Katie one last look, I followed him out into the night.

5

Not a single light was on anywhere in the complex as we walked through the dark avenues. Every once in a while, I would see the flicker of a torch as someone scurried by on one of the cross streets ahead, like a sleepy old west town, but other than that, all I had was wan moonlight. Even the city-run streetlamps had been busted out. There had been a power outage right after I moved in last year, and I remembered the Estates looking black and somber like this.

"*That* way," Schrader grunted, whapping me in the shoulder with the side of the axe to get me to take the next turn. That was the extent of our conversation since we'd left the cell, him driving me like livestock.

"Where we going?" I finally worked up the nerve to ask. In the dark, on the unfamiliar side of the complex, I had lost all sense of direction.

"If I wanted ya to know that, I woulda told ya, now wouldn't I?"

"I don't know. That logic sounds a little complicated for you, Schrader."

He snorted as he guided me down a new turn. "Mr. Funny Man. Yeah, you always thought you were so amusing, tellin your little jokes and puttin me down. Just a regular comedian. Well, we'll see how funny everything is when you're cleansed and heeding."

"That's never gonna happen," I snapped, but the only thing I could think about was my blank out earlier in the day. "You're not right in the head, man. None of you are. When you snap out of this and realize what you've done—"

Schrader grabbed me by the back of the neck, squeezing so hard I thought, for just a second, that he'd put the blade through it. He pulled me back against him, brought the axe head under my chin, and snarled in my ear, "You know what I found out since all this started, Jefferson? I like hurting people. I like it a lot. My ex-wife, I used ta slap her around some, but somethin always made me stop just when things were gettin good. Now, I don't have ta stop. The still, small voice has set me free, and Mother Isaacs knows how to make use of me. So, between you and me, I hope you don't heed. Cause she's promised you to me if you don't, and I'm plannin on wipin that shiteatin grin off your face once and for all. Get a little revenge for ol' Yonk. So...whattaya say to that, Funny Man?"

I couldn't really speak without pressing my Adam's apple uncomfortably close to the axe, but I still managed to get out, "Maybe we have something in common after all. Sounds like we were both shitty husbands."

He grunted and released me. "Turn, Jefferson. Right up that alley. You know the way."

I looked at where he pointed and realized, for the first time, where we were.

Schrader had brought me home.

6

The burning car had been removed from the mouth of the alley between buildings 16 and 15, but the evidence of its crash was still present. The brick façade at the corner of my building, right at the edge of my garage space, was crushed in, the grass beside it scorched. The only reason I could see these details was because the orange glow of torchlight flickered from deep inside the alley.

As we approached the opening, I heard the murmur of voices speaking in unison. No, not speaking; there were no words in this, just a toneless hum that matched the intensity of the Squall. Then Schrader shoved me around the corner, and I saw where it was coming from.

At the far end of the alley, a group of maybe twenty people were gathered around the transformer, some of them holding torches and swaying back and forth, others performing the jerky, spasmodic dance I'd witnessed 3204 doing earlier in the week. Their shadows leapt and cavorted against the buildings. And all of them matched that high-pitched buzz through their noses, like an autistic child that just needs to make noise. They couldn't hear the Squall (according to Kirk, none of us could), but some part of their brains must be aware enough that they were able to produce this imitation.

As Schrader and I drew closer, I felt like a photographer for *National Geographic*, sneaking up on a hitherto un-known tribe in the rainforest.

I moved toward my own back door, which I'd last walked through Wednesday night, when I left for the pool party, but Schrader herded me away with the axe. "Not there, idiot. Mother Isaacs wants to see you."

A steely cold slipped beneath my skin as I understood what he meant.

He pushed me toward the group worshipping at the end of the alley. They didn't stop as we approached, gave no no-tice they even saw us; they were too busy staring at the green shell of the transformer with completely blank expressions. The dancers wore even less clothing than the Heeders we'd seen today, loincloths fashioned out of rags and skirts and pants. A few of them were even naked, daubed in nonsense symbols and designs with a rainbow palette of paint, like college kids at a rave. Javier was in their midst, the mainte-nance man's penis flopping in the breeze as he twisted and jerked. Just beyond them, the makeshift scaffolding began against the complex wall, with patrolling guards stopping to watch the worship.

Schrader led me around them, to the door of the unit across from his own. He opened it and pushed me through.

There were stairs on the other side, as there had been at Dan and Joan's, but lit by warm overhead lights, the first electric illumination I'd seen in almost 48 hours. We ascended one after the other, my heart pounding. This was the lair of the kingpin, the belly of the beast; I could only imagine what depravity I was about to walk into.

But as we reached the top of the stairs and entered the apartment proper, it was more like coming through the door of my grandmother's house, complete with the mingled odor of mothballs and dry earth.

Isaacs's living space was quaint and decorated in elderly fashion, with doilies on the coffee table and a crocheted blanket on the back of the ancient couch. Threadbare throw rugs covered the floor. As my eyes moved across the room, they finally landed on a heavy oak shelf to my left.

I started so hard, I fell back into Schrader, who shoved me roughly away.

On the shelf space sat a collection of mostly black-and-white photos, most of them of a much younger woman that could only be Mother Isaacs herself. But, from a few of these pictures, a hatchet-faced man with unfriendly eyes scowled out at me, never smiling, always dour and brooding, and, even though I'd never met him, I recognized him all the same.

His was the face that had been painted all across the complex.

7

The graffiti was a rough approximation, but it had captured the harsh lines of this man's face so well, it could've been one of these photographs blown up to epic proportions. I studied each picture in mute silence, the sounds of the jungle conga line drifting in from outside.

I had drawn this man's face during my trance, despite never having seen these.

You copied it, I assured myself. *You copied it from the one on the complex wall.*

I wanted to believe that, because the alternative—that the Squall had somehow inserted that face into my brain, like a post-hypnotic suggestion—was too awful to contemplate.

"My husband," a scratchy voice informed me. Isaacs stepped out of the shadows of the back hallway and entered the living room with crisp, measured steps, like she was part of an invisible wedding party coming down the aisle of the church. Unlike the other Heeders, she was still immaculate and fully clothed, wearing a spotless black dress with frilly cuffs that looked like it would have been at home in a Thomas Hardy novel. She held her hands out when she saw me.

"Mr. Jefferson, how good of you to come." It wasn't the proselytizing voice she used on the masses, but it still grated almost as much as the Squall. "Please have a seat. John, make us some tea, won't you?"

"Yes, Mother," Schrader agreed. He gave me one last menacing look (I almost asked him if this was an example of her making use of his extraordinary talents) before going into the kitchen through a narrow doorway on the far side of the apartment.

Isaacs went to a high-backed, Victorian-looking chair and perched primly on the edge, motioning for me to follow. I sank warily down onto one of the couch cushions across from her. Neither of us spoke for a long moment, just regarded each other to the sounds of Schrader clumsily making tea in the other room and uttering a curse under his breath every few seconds. I thought about running, thought about leaping across the coffee table and strangling the old hag, but decided that neither would get me very far before Schrader and his axe—or the rest of the psychotics outside—caught up to me.

"If I'm going to be tortured," I finally said, "I'd prefer to just get on with it."

"Tortured?" Isaacs asked, as if the very idea was ludicrous.

"Isn't that your new plan? Get us good and scared with pain to speed along the induction process?"

She shook her head. "No, I don't think there's any need for that. I still try to keep some measure of civility here within the bounds of my home."

"*Civility?* Jesus Christ, you're raping teenage girls and murdering cops around here. Isn't civility exactly what you people are crusading against?"

"To paraphrase the good book, everything in its place and time, Mr. Jefferson." Her already dark eyes seemed to deepen a few more shades. "Besides...I'm not convinced that torture would even work with you."

"What's that supposed to mean?"

"It means that you interest me. You're a unique case. I haven't known quite what to make of you, not from the very start. That's why I figured it was time we had a private chat, face-to-face, just you and me."

"As opposed to your midnight prank calls? Then again, with the phones out, I guess you can't dial me up to ask if my refrigerator is running anymore."

She gave me another of those lingering, reptilian stares, one that made my flippancy wilt even more than Schrader's axe. "You seemed like a good early candidate to join our ranks. A single man, living alone, barely leaving your apartment. I saw you changing, saw you succumbing to the still, small voice." She gestured toward the window, where she would've watched me as I had my explosive orgasm down in the alley, right where Javier and the others were now cavorting. "But you were able to fight. To will yourself not to heed. I soon came to understand you were polluted, in a fundamentally different way than the others."

"Yeah. Alcohol destroyed my brain long before that noise could get to it."

"Indeed." She nodded slowly, and, for some reason, a weird little ping went off in the back of my head. "That alone would've been bad enough, but you also seemed to have an uncanny knack for sticking your nose where it wasn't wanted. You continued to bring outside attention to us through your various altercations at a time when we simply weren't prepared for it. I knew when you brought the authorities here for the second time—after you and Mr. Gordon killed Joan McCaffery—that you would have to be dealt with."

"Which is when you gave me a bottle of whiskey in the hopes I would drink myself to death."

"That was one scenario, yes."

I wanted to laugh. If she'd just left me alone to stew in the Squall for one more night, I'd probably be down in the alley right now, dancing around the transformer with the others. This bitch wasn't nearly as smart as she thought she was.

"But I also forced Tony to give you back the corpse of your dog and frame young Mr. Tinsley for its death. Another fight with a neighbor would surely have landed you in jail and out of our hair. But the two of you were able to...resolve your differences."

"I'm guessing you didn't let Jacob in on your plan."

"The intent was to have you both removed from the premises. You see, for a time, I believed the boy might be a problem as well. But he has fallen into line quite nicely."

I plunged ahead with another question to keep the truth from showing on my face. "But why bother with something that elaborate at all? You had me on tape spray painting the building! Martha threatened to have me arrested that morning if I didn't behave!"

Isaacs laughed, a sound like dry hiccups. "Mr. Jefferson, we couldn't have shown that recording to the authorities! The less they knew, the better. When nothing else worked, my only option was to keep you pacified long enough for a final consolidation, to insure we had enough manpower to take the complex entirely."

"I thought there was no 'we' in this paradise," I said sullenly. "Only 'I'. When the id's in charge, shouldn't it be every man for himself? Then again, you've built yourself quite a little kingdom here, so you must be looking out for *numero uno* after all."

In lieu of an answer, a shrill whistle came from the kitchen that caused me to jump. The tea was ready. We sat in silence while glass clinked in the other room, and all the time that ping was still going in my brain, like a radar wave bouncing off an anomaly. Something was wrong here, I'd been feeling it for a while, but somehow my last words had begun to crystallize my vague unease.

Schrader came out of the kitchen, looking utterly ridiculous painted like a native war chief while carrying two steaming china teacups on saucers. He put one down in front of each of us. Isaacs picked hers up immediately and, as only the practiced tea drinker can do when they've finally burned calluses all over their mouth, she took a long swallow of the liquid.

I looked down at my own cup, almost laughed when I thought how the caffeine would keep me up all night even if the Squall didn't, and suddenly felt the light of truth come blazing into my head.

I studied the woman across from me. She didn't look or act or dress like any of the Heeders, and she had acknowledged the Squall when I mentioned it earlier, as though consciously aware of it.

And Jacob said that Isaacs had outlawed coffee and soda, just in case caffeine could break the spell, but here she sat, drinking a tea loaded with the stuff.

"You're not even one of them," I concluded in amazement.

8

Mother Isaacs smiled sweetly, then said to Schrader, "John, be a dear and bring our other guest out, would you?" He started for the back hallway. She waited until he was out of earshot before regarding me coyly. "Blood pressure medication. Had to take it for nearly fifteen years now. Unfortunately, it keeps me from reaching the level of redemption the rest of my followers enjoy."

"B-but...but how? *Why?*" I stammered. My mind couldn't wrap itself around the concept. "If you're not like them then... why the hell are you doing this?"

She replaced her steaming cup on the saucer and gestured at the pictures on the oak shelf. "My late husband was a Unitarian minister, did you know that? He had such faith in the very concept of unification, not just of the Lord, but of humankind. He believed that we could only come together in salvation if we embraced our more primitive tendencies, the only traits common to us all."

I glanced at the grim man. "And you think *this* was what he meant?"

"A means to an end," she said patiently, uncurling her spindly fingers to one side, as though flicking a bug off the arm of the chair. "I know, I know, it's not easy for everyone to grasp. There is an inherent duality in the idea that we must embrace our selfishness in order to come together, but that's why there must be a thread of balance—of order—in the chaos. Believe you me, his teachings got us cast out of several churches before he passed."

"Then you should've taken the hint!" I spat. "Those people out there are only acting like this because of that noise, but you...you're just plain ol', garden-variety, straitjacket nuts! For God's sake, you're actually advocating all this violence to—!"

"*Yes*," she interrupted sharply, losing her patience for the first time. "For God's sake, yes, I am. And don't act so surprised at the idea of violence being used to advance belief. You're a scholarly man, Mr. Jefferson, surely you realize that religion is, by its very nature, a brutal undertaking."

"That noise isn't a voice," I growled. "Certainly not God's."

But I wondered.

I wondered.

There were a hundred other questions I wanted to ask, but none of them really mattered except one. "What do you think your followers will do when I tell them you're just faking it?"

The narrow shoulders of her Puritan dress rose and fell. "As long as I'm preaching what they so badly want to hear, I don't think they'll be too concerned. Such is the way of the prophet, to lead but not partake."

I shook my head. "You can't be so deluded that you think you can get away with this forever. Even if you get the rest of us under your spell, what's your plan? We stay here at the Estates forever, fucking each other's brains out? What happens when you run out of food? What happens when someone comes looking for the people you've killed, like that poor technician from the electric company, or, hell, when the rest of the management staff comes back on Monday?"

"We have already turned away several that came seeking their friends and loved ones. When they become too persistent, they will be held here until they heed."

"Oh, really? You prepared to do that with the entire world?"

"Until we find a way to deliver our message to them," she answered, and before I could even ask what that meant, she went on. "But for now, I'm more concerned with you, Mr. Jefferson. You have become an experiment for me. The people with you are the last holdouts, the only ones who have not given themselves over, and I believe it is somehow your very presence that leads them astray. If you fall, so will they."

I barked laughter. If she only knew that my cellmates' resistance came from a big bag of hillbilly cocaine. "Then just kill me, you lunatic, because I'm gonna fight you every step of the way."

In the hallway beside her, two shadows appeared.

"I think we can do better than kill you."

Schrader stepped back into the light from the living room, leading Delbert behind him.

And he really was being lead, because both of the elderly man's eyeballs had been scooped out of his head, leaving bloody, puckered craters. What remained was a terrible, dead mask. My mouth drew open in horror. Schrader held the hand attached to Delbert's unbroken arm and guided him to the woman's side like a seeing-eye dog.

"Mr. Johnson?" she asked.

"Yes, Mother Isaacs?"

"Tell Mr. Jefferson how much happier you are now that you have heeded the still, small voice."

Delbert giggled, a horrible sound that I couldn't quite match to the uppity old fart I had known just this morning. His eye sockets were shadowy pits as he whispered, "I...I want to eat someone. I want to use my teeth and tear their flesh right off the bone while they're still alive. Can I, Mother Isaacs, *please*, you promised!"

Isaacs's eyes had never left me as her newest follower spoke. "In due time, Mr. Johnson. In fact, if Mr. Jefferson doesn't join us by tomorrow, I'll start giving you pieces of him. One at a time."

9

Schrader designated two other men in caveman garb to return me to my cell. Neither of them spoke on the trip other than an occasional grunt. The night was hot and heavy, filled with the Squall, and I felt like I'd been run over by a cement mixer. It seemed surreal to think that this time last week, I'd been in my own home, trying to grab some sleep on the couch with Mickey at my feet.

As we rounded the last corner and came within sight of our cell—which, if Isaacs was to be believed, held the last bastion of normalcy left in the Estates of North Hills—I could see the outside guards, but they stood at the bars with their backs to us, and appeared to be talking with someone on the other side. Past the threshold of the door, where the moonlight couldn't reach, it was just too dark to see for sure. When they heard us coming, both guards spun around, looking almost guilty, then set to unlocking the door so they could push me in. The stink of packed bodies walloped me before I could even pass through, especially strong after my respite of fresh night air.

Inside the apartment, waking heads popped up all over the room, like prairie dogs from their burrows. I couldn't tell who had been speaking with the guards—if, in fact, anyone had—but I soon forgot about it as Katie came running and threw her arms around me.

"Are you okay?" she asked.

"I'm fine."

Beth and the rest of the group surrounded me, all except Kirk, who hadn't heard me come in, because he would never hear anything again.

"What happened, where'd they take you?" Ron demanded.

I didn't need to see their eyes to know they were all high; I could hear the jittering energy in their voices. They continued to ask questions, but when I only continued to stare, Beth said, "Elliot? What's wrong?"

"Nothing. Where's the bag? Give it to me."

I didn't even know if my sudden desire to take Jacob's poison was bred from a renewed desire not to become one of Isaacs's zombies, or because I just wanted to lose myself and forget all my pains and despairs, to block out the sight of Delbert's missing eyeballs and Kirk standing in the stinking darkness of this apartment after puncturing his own eardrums, all to find out that it didn't make any difference, we weren't hearing the Squall but rather sensing it directly in our brains, like telepathy.

In any case, I had resolved on the way back here to swap monkeys and see where the new one took me.

Laura retrieved the bag of powdered amphetamine from the vent and brought it over. I didn't hesitate this time, just plunged two fingers in, built a tidy pile the circumference of a dime on my palm, and snorted it all up.

The rush hit me immediately. So did the relief from the Squall, just like when I'd knocked back that whiskey, the sound fading into the background. The ecstasy of that alone caused my eyes to roll back.

"It's a trip, huh?" Ron asked.

It was, an instant high the likes of which I'd never experienced. Time slowed down to a crawl, except for my heart, which picked up a marathon rhythm. My muscles turned tight and hard as a feeling like raw electricity coursed through me. I remember thinking, *Jesus, why the hell did I waste time with liquor*, before my thoughts were moving too fast to single out, a freight train of warm fuzziness.

With this stuff pounding through my veins, I didn't know how I could possibly hope to sleep, but I pushed away from the others anyway, stretched out in the floor, and closed my eyes.

Then opened them an undetermined amount of time later.

Someone hunched over me in the darkness, shaking me gently. I opened my mouth to speak and a hand slid over it. When the fog of sleep finally thinned, I recognized Beth.

She put her lips practically inside the cup of my ear and whispered so lightly it was more like wind than speech, "Come with me."

I stood up. I was groggy, but otherwise I felt great. Full of energy. I knew it was the drug, still humming in my bloodstream, and that I would feel like shit once I crashed out.

Beth took my hand and pulled me toward the front door of the apartment. Everyone else lay sprawled out on the floor in all directions, and I followed her lead, tip-toeing through the maze of bodies, careful not to step on outstretched limbs.

The living room narrowed to the short tile corridor lead-ing to the garage and front door. There was no place else to go, so I couldn't figure why she'd brought me here. But then she made a sudden turn and pulled me into the tiny coat closet set into the wall.

As soon as we were hidden away in the tight enclosure, she attacked.

Her tongue snaked into my mouth before I could react, hot and moist. I kissed her back, just as I had after the party, lost in an avalanche of sudden overwhelming sensation. Beth tore at my clothes, undoing my belt and pulling so hard at the fastenings of my filthy shorts she ripped off the button. My cock stood at stiff attention between us, so hard I could've used it to hammer nails. That was one point I had to give Jacob's concoction; I never would've been able to maintain an erection like this while drunk. She grasped it near the base and gave it a few rough squeezes that almost set me off right in her hand, like a firecracker with a short fuse.

I pushed her against the wall, smothered her with my body. The drugs lent everything a euphoric haze, made every hair on my body stand up. I hadn't felt this erotically-charged since our workout session. She sucked at my shoulder hard enough to bruise while wiggling out of shorts and panties. The heat between her legs scorched me. I grabbed her under the arms and lifted her small frame up, and she braced her knees against the narrow walls on either side, giving me all the opening I needed.

She grunted as I forced my way into her, an ugly, needful sound. This wasn't urgent and passionate like last time in her bed; this was quick and mean, more fistfight than lovemak-ing, an outlet for all our frustration. I pounded against her until my dick was raw and my hips ached and I must be close to snapping her like a twig, but then she shifted her weight, wrapping her legs around me as though encouraging, and I laid into her even harder.

We went on like that, sexual warfare waged in breathy silence, until she eventually stiffened against me, hissing between her teeth, and at that moment I let go of the dam I'd been holding back and came deep inside her.

When she was back on her own feet, I collapsed against the opposite wall, panting and sweaty, my knees like pudding, and watched while she got dressed, stepped out of the closet, and walked away into the dark without a look back.

SATURDAY MORNING AGAIN

1

A shriek woke me, followed by a squawk of pain that instantly cut short.

My head felt so heavy, it took another few seconds to even remember how to peel open my eyelids. This was worse than hangover; my brain had been replaced by a sludgy ball of pain.

But I didn't have time to nurse myself. Another screech came from somewhere close by, an animalistic sound full of rage.

I sat up, blinked the blurriness out of my vision, and saw Carolyn just a few yards away, in the middle of the living room. The middle-aged woman squatted on her haunches next to someone lying face down on the floor in front of her. The form didn't move, and its shirt was smeared with stains that looked black in the bars of morning light spearing through the barricaded window. Carolyn crouched over it, then leered around maniacally at the other people waking up all around her. The movements of another woman sitting up in the floor seemed to catch her attention. She jerked toward the motion and hissed, like a cat.

Joan, I thought.

Ron, who had been sleeping just a few feet from Carolyn, shouted, *"She's one of 'em!"* He frantically scooted away from her.

The declaration ignited panic. People screamed and ran or crawled away like a live grenade had been tossed into their midst. Those close enough to the door—Katie among them—fled into the bedroom while the rest pressed themselves against the wall. I got to my feet. Carolyn tossed her head back to issue a completely feral howl, and snatched at anyone who got too close.

Ron was still closest to her, and having trouble heaving his bulk up to escape. She launched herself at him, skittering forward on hands and feet with her bony butt pooched up in the air, moving faster than I would've thought possible in such a manner. He yelped as she fell upon him. Carolyn pummeled his chest and scratched at his face as he tried to fend her off, then, when he managed to get hold of her wrists, she dipped her head and latched onto his throat like a vampire. His cries became gurgles as her jaw worked. A river of blood flowed down the sides of his neck.

I leapt forward, seized her by the shoulders, and hauled her away from Ron, then tossed her roughly aside. She hit the carpeted floor and bounced right back up, hurtling at me in a mindless frenzy, hands out and fingers hooked into talons. Ron's blood dripped down her chin. I ducked backward, but one of her nails sliced me open across the cheekbone; an inch higher and Delbert wouldn't have been the only one missing eyeballs.

As she reared back for another try, I grabbed her short hair and slung her away from me, sent her stumbling toward another group of our cellmates. They twittered in terror and scattered, leaving Carolyn to slam into the wall. She looked back at me with an expression of dumb, frustrated rage and gnashed her bloodstained teeth.

"Carolyn, wake up, snap out of it!" I yelled. I didn't want to hurt her, not like I had Joan, but my options were limited. This was a steel cage death match. I wouldn't be able to elude her for long in the cramped apartment, but maybe I could subdue her somehow, hold her down long enough for us to get some of the drug in her.

She hunched low, preparing to spring at me again.

And then her head exploded, spraying chunks of red matter all over the bare white wall behind her.

2

One of the guards—I thought it might be one of the two who escorted me back last night—stood outside the door of our cell with a shotgun jutting through the bars, smoke drifting from the barrel. The concussion of the shot rang in my ears, muted the volume on the rest of the world, but just like Kirk said, I could still hear the Squall buzzing just as loud. Across the room, Carolyn's nearly headless corpse slid into the floor, leaving a trail of chunky slime down the wall.

"What the fuck did you do that for?" I choked out.

The guard didn't answer as he unlocked the door and came inside, followed by two other men. Now the other prisoners shied away from them. In the floor, Ron had fallen still, lying with his eyes open in a pool of blood from his savaged neck, next to the man that Carolyn had attacked before I woke up. Both of them looked dead.

The armed guard stayed at the door while the other two lumbered inside. Both wore only jeans that had been shredded so much, the remaining material looked more like denim diapers, and they twitched so much they could barely walk a straight line. They went past me, picked up Carolyn by the arms, and dragged her toward the door.

"Hey, I'm talking to you, goddamn it!" I moved toward the one at the door, my fists balled at my sides. "Why'd you kill her? She turned into one of you, heeded your fucking voice, isn't that what you wanted?"

The man at the door met my gaze. At school, I'd been called to sit in on individual lesson plan reviews for special needs students, a meeting that the state requires at least one general ed teacher attend. I had been around plenty of mentally deficient kids in those conferences, some of them on the severe end of the scale, so I recognized the dull, placid glaze in this guy's eye for what it was.

All he needed was a thick, overhanging brow to be the spitting image of every Neanderthal drawing I'd ever seen.

"Back," he grunted. His facial muscles constantly contracted and relaxed, so one side of his mouth yanked back so hard every other second I could see his gumline all the way to the molars.

"You didn't have to kill her." I would rather the poor woman have gone and joined them than be dead. At least then, she would still have a chance of being saved if this nightmare ever ended.

"No. No good." Each word seemed to be a struggle for him to get out. He leveled the shotgun at me. "Away. *Now!*"

As much as he twitched, I feared he might pull the trigger and blow me away by accident. I stood aside as they carried Carolyn out, dumped her in the grass beside the porch like a bag of lawn trimmings, then came back for the other two bodies. Ron was last. His head lolled to the side as they dragged him away, eyes open and glassy, throat chewed open to the bone. Then they shut the door again, leaving us alone with the gore that now coated the walls and carpet.

There were twelve of us left.

3

When breakfast came (nothing but stale cornflakes this time), hardly any one touched it, despite the fact that we'd all lost between five and ten pounds and were beginning to resemble starving Ethiopian children, complete with buzzing flies. Katie's cheekbones strained against her flesh as she came and sat down beside me in the bedroom, where we wouldn't have to look at the blood stains, and Beth's muscle tone was slowly melting away from her athletic body. She said nothing about last night, but then again, I didn't really expect her to. I had become her sexual punching bag, a role I wasn't entirely uncomfortable with.

Kirk looked worse than any of us, his face a gaunt and sunken mask and his stomach showing the first signs of hunger bloat beneath his shirt. He had slept throughout the entire episode with Carolyn, unable to hear the shotgun blast, and didn't speak to the rest of the group when he finally sat up, leaned against the wall, and stared at his hands in his lap.

"Get the bag," I told Laura. "Everybody needs to take another hit."

She shook her head. "I don't want any more of that stuff. I feel so sick."

I did too, sick to my stomach and confused in my thinking. The Squall still blared and all I wanted to do was lay down and go back to sleep. We were at the end of our ropes, physically and psychologically, edging toward a breaking point that would either lead us to becoming Heeders or leave us drooling, empty shells. Looking at Kirk again, he might already be beyond that. "We have to do it," I said. "And we have to do it right now. They could be coming any minute to take us away again."

Katie stiffened in alarm. "Do you really think they will?"

"Yeah. I do."

She hugged herself and began to rock back and forth. "No no no no no, not again, I can't, I can't go through that again, please don't let them take me."

I put an arm around her and looked around at the remaining prisoners. "We don't have any choice. If we want to survive until help comes, we have to be able to take whatever they throw at us."

And if Isaacs made good on her threat from last night, I was sure I would get the worst of it.

Laura brought the bag. This time, nobody turned it down, not even Kirk. I took another snort, passed it to Beth, and closed my eyes as bliss rolled over me like a fluffy cloud.

The mood lifted, but we all still sat around, waiting to find out who would be taken first.

But when the door opened again, we didn't lose anyone.

In fact, we gained another prisoner instead.

4

Katie and I leaned against one another to doze when we heard the rattle of the cell bars in the other room. The Squall had been quiet for a while now, probably saving up its energy for another assault, so the sound was startlingly loud in the still apartment. We were all up and on our feet just as Schrader came flying into the bedroom with an entire posse of mostly-naked suburban tribesmen behind him. He arrowed at me like a wrecking ball as everyone else scattered away, body-slammed me into the wall, and then grabbed me by the windpipe.

"Where?" he demanded. "*Where the fuck is it?*"

"What are you...?" was all I got out before he cut off my air supply entirely.

His teeth clenched so hard behind his spasming lips, I expected them to shatter. "I want whatever you people are using to pollute yourselves and I want it right fucking now."

He released his stranglehold just enough for me to wheeze out half-formed lies. "We don't...I don't know what..."

Schrader released me, stormed across the room to where the others huddled, grabbed Katie by the hair, and dragged her away from the group as she cried and pleaded. He shoved her into the hands of the natives gathered just inside the doorway. "Fuck this bitch with the most splintered mop handle you can find."

"No, wait, stop!" I shouted. "It's in the air vent! The air vent!"

Schrader pushed through his men, back into the living room. We all followed. He kicked at the vent until the metal grating was a bent, twisted mess, then reached in and pulled out our one and only salvation. As he led his men back toward the door of the cell, they let Katie go. She sank into the floor next to the dried puddle of Ron's blood and wept. We gathered around her, watching as the cell door began to close.

But first, someone else got shoved through.

Jacob's feet tangled and he fell on his face just a few feet away from me.

5

Katie burst into fresh tears when she saw him, then lurched forward and threw her arms around his bare shoulders. I couldn't help feeling a small pang of completely platonic jealousy.

"What happened?" Beth asked.

"You tell me," he answered over Katie's shoulder, goggling around at us. His split lower lip was the least of his injuries now; his whole face had been battered into a lumpy purple mountain range, still smeared with the faded remnants of his war paint. "An hour ago I'm asleep in one of the apartments with the rest of them when that psycho Schrader comes at me hard, askin questions he already knew the answer to, and then beat the shit outta me until I confessed. He knew everything. About the drugs, that I was fakin. Everything."

"How?" I asked.

His bloodshot eyes pierced me. "Ain't it obvious? Somebody ratted me out."

Katie finally broke her tearful embrace and turned slowly to look at me. "Mr. Jefferson...you wouldn't."

"What?" I blinked at her. My buzz was still going strong and I had a hard time stoking the fires enough to get my train of thought moving. "You don't think...why would *I* tell them he was helping us?"

"You sure seemed to have some sort of grudge against him yesterday," Laura said quietly, flicking her eyes up to my face and then back down again.

"And you really think that would've been enough for me to turn him in and ruin the only chance we have at getting out of here? Not to mention the fact that we needed that stuff!"

"I see the high-and-mighty finally came around," Jacob muttered.

"Oh, shut up," I told him sourly. "What makes you think it was one of us anyway? It could've been someone from one of the other cells. Isaacs told me they all changed, so maybe—"

"When did you see Isaacs?" Beth's question hung in the air amid a thick silence.

I saw instantly the pit of quicksand I'd stepped into and took a moment to choose my words before answering. "Last night, when they took me out, they brought me to Isaacs's apartment. She...she talked to me...told me some things..."

"So everyone else gets tortured, and you get a private meeting with their leader?"

"Yes, okay, I know how it sounds, but my point is, she said we're the last ones left. So anybody else he tried to help could've tattled on him after they changed."

"Except I never actually got to the other apartments," Jacob said. "Couldn't figure a way to get the guards to leave. If someone narced, it was someone right here."

"Yeah, but...that's...this is completely..." Even I could hear the guilt in my stuttering, and I knew for a fact I was innocent. Now everyone stared at me with open suspicion, Katie with a brow-furrowed expression of anger. I flapped a hand at Jacob on the ground, desperate to shift the blame. "I bet you're real happy with yourself. You finally got your revenge on me. I mean, this is so perfect I wouldn't be surprised if you planned it all from the beginning."

He pointed at his bruised face. "You think I went through all this just to get you back? Jesus Jefferson, the whole world revolves around you, don't it?"

"We should be questioning *you*, you little shit. You said you just blended in with them when they took over the complex, right? What exactly did that entail? What all did you have to do to get them to trust you? How many people did you rape and murder?"

At that, Jacob gently pushed Katie away from him and got to his feet. He came and stood in front of me, inches away, like he had that night in front of 3204's garage, when Tate split us up before we could come to blows. This time though, he regarded me calmly as he said, "Can I speak to you in the other room?"

He walked past me without waiting. I followed him into the bedroom, ready for round two of what we'd begun at the pool party. He shut the door, then turned and went into the bathroom. The space would be small for a fight, but I went in anyway, and watched as he closed that door also and leaned against it. It was dark in here, just enough light leaking in under the door for us to see each other and the ghostly outline of our reflections in the long mirror above the sink counters beside us.

Jacob glared at me for a few more seconds without speaking.

And then burst into tears.

All I could do is stare at him. The last time I'd seen him cry had been that day, in the back of my classroom, as he tried to convince me of his innocence.

"I'm sorry, I'm sorry," he finally choked out, swiping at his nose and mouth with the back of one hand. "I'm crashin out, man, comin down from this high, and I think it's gonna be bad."

"Okay," I ventured. "You brought me in here to tell me that?"

He shook his head. "Out there...you don't know what it's like, what they're doing. They're starvin, and they're gettin bored. There's no one else for them to take out their bloodlust on, and since Isaacs won't let them have you guys, they're torturin each other. Gettin off on it. They're...they're god-damned animals, man, and that's no exaggeration. Most of 'em can barely even talk anymore. I don't know how much longer I could've kept up the act anyway." He caught sight of himself in the mirror—a beat-up kid wearing the same frayed jeans he'd had on yesterday—and looked away again quickly. "I swear, I thought they were gonna kill me. I just...I just went along with them. Most of the time I just stood back and, like, cheered. I wanted to help those people, wanted to help Tate, but I couldn't. And then, they woulda caught me, I know it, so I had to join in, had to...to do things..."

I held up a hand. "I don't care, Jacob. I'm not your priest and I'm not your therapist. You can rationalize all you want, but it's no excuse. You don't have to be one of them to get off on hurting other people. Trust me on that."

The anger I had expected earlier finally filled his face. "Fuck you, man! What the fuck is wrong with you? Why do you have it out for me so bad?"

"Because you're a low-life addict."

"So is Katie! So are you, for fuck's sake! What makes me different from her, huh? Why did you take one look at me and assume I'm a fuckin lost cause, but you won't believe for a second that she's anything other than perfect?"

"She *tries*, Jacob! She's tries to make something of herself while people like you and her mother tear her down! What the hell did you ever do, except deal drugs and sit in the back of the class to make infantile jokes with your friends?" I clenched a fist at him. "What do you want from me anyway? To admit I lied about seeing the gun in your locker? Fine, I lied. But even if it wasn't yours, it was the right thing to do, to get you out of that school. What do you care anyway, all you got was a year in juvie. Get over it. I mean, why does my opinion of you mean so goddamn much?"

"Because you were my favorite teacher, you dick!"

I gaped at him.

Fresh tears welled up in his eyes. "I know we weren't best friends, and I didn't hang out in your class at lunch like some of those nerds, but believe me, we got along a helluva lot better than my other teachers. They looked for any excuse to write me up, give me detention, send me to the principal, whatever they had to do just to get me outta their hair, but you...I don't know, you just always seemed cool to me. Like someone that would give a guy like me a chance. But when it came down to it, you were just like those other shitheads. You didn't listen to me, didn't believe a word I said that day. And then you lied just to pound the knife in a little harder. And I realized, that's what I got for trustin anyone but me."

Words had always been my friend, my shield, and my weapon, but at that moment, I had not a single one. It all made sense suddenly, why he'd had it out for me so intently ever since that day. Because he'd considered the whole incident not just an unjust punishment, but a complete betrayal. But even it if was all true, and not just a ploy from a master manipulator, I didn't know if I could ever let go of the image of him I'd held in my head for nearly five years. Chalk it up to the fact that we humans tend to carve our prejudices in steel. "Jacob..."

More commotion came from the living room, screams of fear, audible through both doors. I pushed Jacob out of the way and rushed toward it.

Schrader was back. He held Beth in a headlock under his arm, and pointed at me when I walked into the room.

"Let's go," he commanded. "Both of you."

6

They herded Beth and me up the street at a jog, jabbing us in the back with sharp instruments and rifle barrels whenever our pace got too slow. Both of us panted and lost our breath in seconds, too weak to do more than stumble along. My vision became studded with black spots. But, while I'm sure they enjoyed every second of our misery, the treatment didn't seem borne solely from their love of cruelty; there was an urgency behind this, a franticness, an almost—dare I say it—fear. Every few seconds, Schrader would wheeze, "*Faster, keep moving*," despite the fact that even he had trouble keeping up.

We reached another apartment building and Schrader called a halt. All of us stood for a moment, bent over and gasping until we caught our breath. Then he motioned to an aluminum ladder leaned against the wall, stretching all the way up to the slanted rooftop. "Climb."

"Why? What's up there?"

He raised a hand and backhanded me across the face. The impact sounded like a whip crack. I could feel my cheek already beginning to swell. "*Climb*," he repeated.

I started up the ladder and got about ten rungs up before a wave of exertion dizziness hit me so hard I expected to faint. But, by then, Beth had been forced up right behind me, and I had no place to go but up.

The top of the roof slanted steeply for three yards before it leveled out to a flat surface. I crawled up the incline, the rough shingles scratching my knees bloody, and collapsed at the top. A few feet away, at the very edge, Mother Isaacs waited for me, wind ruffling her thin, grey hair. Miles and

Rick flanked either side of her, the last remnants of the Jock Trinity, wearing toga-style, bedsheet loincloths and carrying not guns but spears made from tree branches with knives duct taped to the end. They stood stoically, eyes straight ahead like Buckingham Palace guards, their backs slightly hunched in a way that completed the caveman look.

Isaacs beckoned me forward impatiently to the sheer drop-off at the roof's edge. "Come, Mr. Jefferson. We don't have much time. Miss Charles, you may wait there."

I didn't think I'd be able to stand again, but when Schrader reached the rooftop and started kicking me, I somehow did. I came forward hesitantly, sure I was about to be pushed off the two-story roof. Maybe with a nice, fat noose around my neck. "If this is about Jacob and the drug…"

"We will have that conversation later, Mr. Jefferson. Now, come here." She grabbed me by the wrist and pulled me across the last few feet. From here, I had a good view of the rest of the complex. Building rooftops spread out in all directions, separated by the network of streets and grass alleyways. The property wall ran just on the other side of the building to our right; I could see the open field on the other side, all the way to Midtown Road, where a single car trundled by, oblivious to our plight.

"Here." Isaacs jammed a pair of collapsible binoculars in front of my face. When I put them to my eyes, she directed me with a finger to look toward the office, easy to pinpoint because of the early morning glare coming off the pool. "Do you see it?"

It took me several long seconds to understand what she meant. And then my heart leapt into my throat.

Through the wrought iron bars of the complex gate, a cop car was visible, parked on the circular driveway in front of the office, just outside the makeshift barricade.

"This is your fault," she growled in my ear.

"How so?"

"The result of all your meddling. What you see down there is a detective who wishes to speak to you about Joan McCaffery's death."

My good friend Hammond. Had to be. Apparently he wasn't as finished with me as Tate believed. I had the sudden overwhelming urge to lay a big, wet kiss on his bulldoggish cheek.

"Don't get your hopes up, you stubborn cretin." Isaacs slapped the back of my head only slightly less hard than Schrader had my cheek, and snatched away the binoculars. Behind her, either Miles or Rick gave a hiccupping guffaw that sounded like a baboon.

"I don't have to hope," I said. "Because if that's who I think it is, he's not gonna go away until he talks to me. You see, I'm part of a murder investigation, so he's not gonna listen to whatever excuses you guys try to feed him for why he can't see me. And even if, by some miracle, you get him to believe I'm not here or that I've disappeared, I have a feeling he's gonna want to see my apartment pretty damn bad."

"Yes, yes, I'm sure that is all correct. That is why you will go down there, speak to him, give him whatever information he wants, and then send him on his way, unharmed and none the wiser."

"Yeah, sure. I'll get right on that."

Isaacs grabbed hold of my face, squeezing my jaw until my cheeks squished over to cover my mouth. "Because if you raise his suspicions...give him the slightest indication that anything is amiss...or give him any reason to attempt to remove you from the premises...then he will have to be taken into our custody as well, to be held until such time as he heeds."

I slapped her hand away from my mouth. Rick and Miles snarled in my direction, brandishing their spears. "And what happens if that takes days? People might not've started looking for Tate yet, but someone will be after this cop in a few hours if he just disappears."

"We have other methods of coercion to get him to cooperate, if it comes to that." She leaned in, pushing her stony, lined face into mine. "But you, Mr. Jefferson, should concern yourself with the more immediate consequences of what will happen if you give him reason to linger here in our kingdom."

She grabbed hold of my chin again and turned my head back to where Schrader stood at the far edge of the roof with Beth. He slung an arm around my neighbor's waist, pulled her against his hairy chest, and put a knife to her throat. Beth squeezed her eyes shut as he stuck a tongue deep inside her ear. She whimpered.

"Because if it comes to that," Isaacs told me, "Miss Charles will be the one who suffers, just before she dies."

7

They took me down to a vacant apartment, gave me a fresh pair of jeans and a polo shirt, and allowed two minutes in the bathroom for me to dress and freshen up. One look in the mirror told me this would never work; I looked like a starving crack addict, pale and clammy, hair greasy, with a three-day beard growth and eyes bloodshot to the point of hemorrhage. The scratch Carolyn gave me had crusted on my cheek. At least my last high was on the ebb, so I could function normally. I washed the grime off my face, tamed my hair with water and my fingers, and tried out a smile that just made me look worse.

Inside though, I was in an agony of indecision. This could be our last opportunity to get help; I couldn't let it slip through my fingers. But Isaacs still had complete control of the situation. If I found a way to tip off Hammond, they would easily overpower him, then just break his fingers or something until he agreed to call his station and his family and anyone else that might be looking for him with some excuse. All it would accomplish is getting him captured and turned also.

And Beth killed. I believed Isaacs would do it, if only to punish me.

But why should she? As long as she has Beth and Katie to dangle over your head, she's got you firmly by the balls.

Nevertheless, I had pretty much made up my mind to do what she asked—barring some unforeseen opportunity too good to pass up—as two Heeders rushed me up the street toward the office. They delivered me to the back door like a baby dropped off by a stork, right under the leering face I'd painted on the building during my fugue, and bade me, in growling, pidgin English, "*You not do bad.*" I took that to translate to, 'don't fuck up,' and stepped inside the office.

I heard voices around the corner. When I stepped past the pool table, into the hallway, I spotted Hammond and Martha by the front door, the latter fully dressed with impeccable hair and makeup, looking as bright and fresh as morning dew, nothing at all to indicate the extracurricular activities she'd been engaged in. She jabbered at him about some cop TV show, but the conversation stopped when they saw me.

"Jefferson," Hammond hailed me. Today the detective wore a short-sleeve pin-striped shirt and a tie much too thin for his husky frame. And a pistol in a holster around his waist. "Jesus Christ, I've never seen an apartment complex where they page the residents. Like a New York City doorman or somethin. Thought I was gonna have to get a warrant just to talk to you."

"What can I say, we love our residents!" Martha sounded like her usual chipper self, but as soon as Hammond turned his back on her, the smile fell away as she glared in my direction.

Hammond walked toward me, passing the door to Tony's putrefied critter closet. He got close enough to get a good look at me and stopped dead in his tracks. His wide brow wrinkled; not in concern, but suspicion. "You feelin all right, Jefferson?"

"Just tired." I forced a casual grin back onto my face and tried not to stare at that gun dangling from his belt. I had the insane urge to just grab it and shoot my way out of here. "Drank a little too much last night. Last weekend of spring break. You know how it is."

"Uh huh. Sure." He nodded slowly, still examining me, then motioned to the door I'd just come through. "C'mon, let's take a walk. I wanna head back down to the McCaffery's place."

"Um...uh," I stuttered, looking to Martha for help.

"Oh no, you don't have to do that," she said quickly, surging forward to squeeze her bulk between us and the door. "We'd rather not have more police tromping through the grounds, scaring the residents. You know how it is. I have a conference room right over there you can talk in."

Hammond gave her a long, hard stare, during which her facial muscles pulled in about fifteen different directions. "Ma'am, the McCaffery apartment is an active crime scene; therefore, I don't need a warrant to visit whenever I feel it's necessary. So if you don't step outta my way, I'll cuff you, throw you in the back of my car, and run you in for obstruction after I get finished with Mr. Jefferson."

Martha squirmed; I had to hold in laughter. "Well then," she finally purred, "at least let me give you a ride!"

8

The Estates's golf cart was parked in front of the building, a few spaces down from the squad car Hammond had driven here. Martha unrolled the plastic sunscreens from the roof and let them drape along the sides and back of the vehicle, claiming that her skin was extremely sensitive. Then she made Hammond sit on the rear-facing back seat, where he would be able to see nothing of the complex as we drove. The detective rolled his eyes, but submitted without comment.

I sat up front beside Martha, who loosed a steady stream of babble as we hummed down Tulip Boulevard, keeping Hammond distracted. One look around at the war-torn streets and car barricades would surely have been enough to make him ask questions.

Turn around, I mentally willed him. *Turn around and look through the goddamned windshield.*

But he just sat on the back seat right where the dead cat had been and tolerated Martha's questions.

She turned on the offshoot for my building and pulled the golf cart to the curb in front of Dan and Joan's front door, right about where Kirk and I had been interrogated. The area had to've been hurriedly scoured, because there was no sign here that anything was amiss. Buildings on either side were unmarred except for one boarded up window, the side streets swept of debris and glass, even the graffitied mat removed from the McCaffery's doorstep. I imagined the Heeders out here in their loincloths just a few minutes before we drove up, working fast and hard and then fading into the wings, like a theater crew changing out stage sets between acts. They had even torn down the scaffolding around the portion of the rock wall visible from here.

Javier and one of the other maintenance men squatted in front of the bushes along the edge of the building with their backs to us, pretending to fiddle with an A/C unit. Just like Martha, they were fully clothed once more in their tan jumpsuits. Apparently they could still act like members of modern society when they wanted to.

Hammond jumped out of the cart. Martha escorted us all the way to the door, where Hammond pulled down the police crossing tape as she undid the lock. I glanced over at Javier and found both maintenance men watching me with their teeth bared. I hoisted a middle finger at them behind the detective's back.

Martha tried to follow us into the tiny vestibule between the door and the stairs leading up to the McCaffery's unit, but Hammond blocked her path this time. "That's fine, thank you for your assistance, ma'am. I need some time alone with Mr. Jefferson so we can get this investigation finished up and turn the apartment back over to you." When she just continued to stare at him blankly, he prompted, "That is what you want, isn't it?"

"Well, uh....yes. Yes, of course!" Martha said, wringing her hands. I could see her struggling to maintain control of the situation, but she was just out of excuses to accompany us. "I'll just be right here. Waiting for you." She tittered nervously and waggled that thick finger at me. "Don't do anything I wouldn't do!"

Hammond frowned and raised an eyebrow. "Riiiight." He closed the door in her face and leaned back against it with a sigh of relief. "For cryin out loud, that woman talks more than my mother-in-law! How do you live with that?"

I had a sudden flash of the Estates office manager on her knees, sucking cock while watching a man get dismembered, like a theatergoer munching on popcorn. "It's not easy."

The detective chuckled. To be having a normal conversation again, after my three days of duress and captivity, was like stretching a muscle I hadn't worked in a while. "I felt a little bad being short with her—what with her Parkinson's and all—but c'mon…"

"Parkinson's?"

"Or MS. You know, whatever makes her twitch like that." He gave an exaggerated shiver. "Looks like there's an electrical current flowing under her skin."

I only trusted myself to nod in response. "What did you need to see me about, Detective?"

He straightened up; back to business. "I'm trying to clear up a few more items in the investigation for the DA's office."

"So are Kirk and I gonna be charged?"

"If you were, I'd already have you in handcuffs by now." He shrugged. "You wanna know the absolute truth, the DA thinks this is pretty open and shut. You probably have Officer Maxwell to thank for that. He stuck up for you and Gordon at every turn, said he'd even testify on your behalf if he had to. Has them just about convinced you two idiots were just trying to be good neighbors."

I swallowed a wad of thick spit that almost wouldn't go down. "I'll…I'll have to tell him I appreciate it next time I see him."

"Good luck with that. He hasn't answered my calls in three days. Wherever he is, he better find his way back onto the grid in time to report for duty on Monday."

I nodded again, working to keep my face neutral. "If the prosecutors think we're clear, I don't know what else I can tell you."

Hammond's jaw began to grind, jutting his crooked lower teeth out beyond his upper lip. "Just because they think you smell like a rose, doesn't mean I do. Something's off about all this. I thought so Tuesday night, and I think so now."

"Well...what you see is what you get."

"Yeah, and what I'm seeing is a guy that looks like he's had nothing to eat but booze and coke since the night he killed a woman. I have to ask myself if that's from a little PTSD, or guilt. Or maybe something else entirely." He pointed up the staircase behind me. "So what I want you to do, now that you've had some time to decompress, is walk me through the whole thing again, right here where it happened. Then maybe I'll pay a visit to Mr. Gordon, have him do the same thing. Just to see if you're still in agreement."

I sighed. I'd been through so many other horrors since the incident with Joan that reliving it was tantamount to a tax audit. "All right, Detective. Let's get this over with."

9

It took almost a half hour for me to retell the story of Dan and Joan McCaffery's last night on earth, with Hammond asking questions constantly and scribbling the answers in his notebook. Some of these seemed genuine; others obviously designed to trip me up. I tried to tell the story Kirk and I had that night, with all the embellishments, but Hammond caught me in a few minor contradictions that I just shrugged off. It's pretty easy not to get worked up about lying to the cops when going to jail sounds like paradise compared to your current predicament. In the end, I think my calmness went a long way toward persuading him.

Even with all the lights turned on, the apartment felt like an animal den. The place was exactly as I had left it that night, with the mess in the kitchen, the shattered lamp in the bedroom along with a tape outline of Dan's body, and one in the living room for Joan in the middle of a huge, dried bloodstain on the carpet, and the overturned sculpture beside it. I couldn't peel my gaze away from it as I recounted how the woman had attacked me, all the time thinking about Carolyn's transformation this morning, and how Jacob had said they were all getting worse.

"From what the coroner tells me, the injuries on the bodies support what you're claiming," Hammond admitted grudgingly.

"Did they...do an autopsy?"

My tone must not've been nonchalant enough, because Hammond looked up from where he hunkered next to the bloodstain and squinted at me. "What kinda question is that?"

"Just curious," I mumbled. I had been very careful with every word out of my mouth, just in case Isaacs was still listening in somehow. I kept imagining microphones hidden throughout the unit, or ears pressed to the other side of the walls.

He didn't answer for a moment, then sighed and nodded. "Yeah, they did. I'm still waiting on results, but there was definitely something wrong with her. Something with her brain. A tumor or something, I don't know, I didn't understand what they were talking about, but they seemed pretty excited about it."

My heart started to thud almost painfully inside my chest. They knew. Somebody, somewhere, some lab technician, understood the problem, but not what had caused it. The Squall was still silent (as if the damn thing was waiting for the detective to leave) but if I started talking right now, explained the whole situation to Hammond, he might believe me.

And then what? His cell phone wouldn't work anymore than mine had, and he didn't carry a portable radio on him like a uniformed beat cop would; he would have to make it back to his squad car before he could call for help, and there were a lot of Heeders between us and it. As Jacob had said, his gun wouldn't be enough firepower to get us out.

Then convince him that he has to leave like nothing is wrong.

It was risky—he might think I was nuts after all, or, if he did believe me, he still might do something to accidentally tip off Martha—but it was the only shot we had. I opened my mouth to speak.

But he beat me to it. "Let's get outta here." He walked out without waiting for me, heading back down the stairs. I scrambled after him.

Outside, Martha waited next to the door. She took Hammond's arm and walked him away from me, toward the golf cart. Sheer panic gripped me as I realized our chance for rescue was almost gone. But then the detective stopped on the grass and turned back to me.

"One more thing, Jefferson. What were you about to tell me that night? You said something was going on here."

I stared at him. Martha stared at me around his shoulder. Javier stopped his work on the A/C unit to wait for my response.

"N-nothing," I said. Cowardice scorched my cheeks. "I don't even remember, really. It was...a pretty stressful night."

"All right," Hammond said after a second. "Get some sleep. I'll be in touch."

He started back toward the golf cart.

And made it only a few more steps before the other maintenance man with Javier went ape shit.

10

The guy let go with a horrid, piercing scream, so unexpected it made me jump. We all turned to him.

This maintenance man was smaller than Javier, a little old Hispanic barely five feet tall with dark olive skin and silvery-gray hair combed straight down off the back of his head into a little duck's tail. He twitched fiercely now, so hard he swayed drunkenly on his feet. We watched, dumbfounded, as he reached down and tore open his tan uniform shirt like Clark Kent, but instead of revealing a Superman costume, his bare chest was covered by loops and swirls painted in what looked like lipstick. He beat upon his frail ribcage with his fists—an action far more Tarzan than Man of Steel—then threw back his head and howled mindlessly at the open sky in a lunatic rage.

"What in hell...?" Hammond wondered aloud. He didn't seem to know whether to laugh or not. I couldn't blame him. The guy looked like he weighed seventy pounds, and seeing him suddenly turn feral would've been borderline cute under other circumstances.

But I'd seen it before. Twice now. And I knew enough to be very afraid.

"No, stop!" Martha squealed. "Stop it *this instant!*"

But he didn't. He was far too gone—too *devolved*—for such rationality. The maintenance man snatched up a hammer from atop the A/C unit and charged at the detective, swinging the tool back and forth in wild arcs.

"Stay back! I'm a cop!" Hammond was no longer amused. He moved fast for his size, backing away and scrabbling for the gun at his waist.

Martha jumped between Hammond and the rampaging man. She waved her flabby arms over her head like a drowning swimmer. "*Get away! Javier, catch hiiiim!*"

Javier—who'd been standing frozen with a manic expression of glee sliding across his face as events unfolded—seemed to wake up and lurched forward. He made a grab at his fellow blue collar, but was too far away to do any good.

The maintenance man didn't slow for the fat woman in his path. The flat head of the hammer swung around and cracked against her temple just before he plowed into her. His momentum bowled her over, and, as she fell, I saw that the entire upper half of her face had caved in, one eyeball bulging from its socket. She flopped and thrashed on the ground with blood frothing in her open mouth.

By now, Hammond had freed his gun from the holster and aimed it at his attacker, who leapt over Martha's body and kept barreling at him. The detective pulled the trigger twice, not bothering with further warnings. The little Hispanic man jerked as bullets slammed into his chest, but he was too juiced up to even register his injuries. He collided with Hammond hard enough to take him down, too. When the detective hit the ground, the pistol flew out of his hand, bounced once, and skidded to a stop almost directly between my feet.

Hammond shouted and tried to defend himself as the little old maintenance man sat on his chest and began to beat him to death with the hammer. The sounds of the metal *thunk*ing on his skull were sickening.

It had all happened so fast up to this point, my weary brain couldn't even process it, let alone react. Now, as my wits finally caught up, I bent, grabbed the gun, pointed it at the maintenance man, and opened fire. As the pistol bucked in my hand, I realized the Squall had started up again with a rusty, jubilant screech.

Bleeding holes opened along the old guy's side like a zipper. He finally went down. I turned, meaning to shoot Javier too, but he was on me before I could get the gun around. He shoved me hard into the McCaffery's front door, then pried at my fingers until he could rip the gun out of them. The next thing I knew, I lay face down on the ground with his foot on my neck. From there, I could see Martha and the maintenance man, both dead, and Hammond pawing feebly at the air. His face was a bloody ruin from the hammer blows. That long, bulldog's jaw skewed to the side at a disgusting angle.

It took less than a minute for the first of the Heeders to gather in the street. Isaacs came flying around the corner of the building soon after, the back of her long dress dragging the pavement as she hurried toward us.

"What happened?" she demanded, her gravelly voice about three octaves higher as she surveyed the bodies. Hammond clutched at her leg, but she kicked him away and pointed at me. "Did he do this? *Tell me at once!*"

From above me, I heard Javier explain, in English even more broken than usual, "He change. Only heed. No man. Beast."

"*No!*" Isaacs shrieked. She stamped her tiny foot, then did an odd, frustrated shuffle, grabbed at her tight bun of gray hair, and wrenched. It was the first time I had ever seen her look anything other than calm, cool, and completely in charge. "*No, damn it all, noooo!*"

On the ground, with my face pressed into the sidewalk leading away from the McCaffery's door, I began to chuckle.

Her tantrum stopped, and those sharp-as-a-sickle eyes latched onto me. "What are you laughing at?"

"You can't control them, can you?" I asked. "They're too volatile. Too unstable. That's what all that 'beast within' and 'order in the chaos' crap was about, why Joan and Carolyn and everyone at the pool party just snapped and started acting like rabid animals. You're letting them indulge in their fantasies while trying to keep them smart and rational enough to be tame. But eventually they reach a certain point from listening to that noise and just...go berserk." I laughed again, but this time it was a harsh, vengeful bark. "Only this time, it got you into something you won't be able to hide. Not for long, anyway."

I waited for her fit to resume, but she smiled sweetly and said, "Get him up. And put the detective out of his misery."

Javier pulled me up and passed me to several of the other Heeders. A sizeable crowd had gathered by now. I watched as Javier put the gun to Hammond's forehead but turned away just before he pulled the trigger.

"Would you like to see *unstable*, Mr. Jefferson?" Isaacs asked. "Would you like to see *volatile*?"

Schrader pushed his way through the crowd with Beth still held in front of him.

"That's not fair, I did what you asked!" I yelled. "He was leaving! It's not my fault one of your guys went nuts! Don't take it out on her!"

Isaacs leaned close and hissed, "Why ever would I do that...when she's done so much to help us?"

A few feet away, Schrader released Beth. She took a few stumbling steps forward, looked up at me...and smiled.

And began to twitch.

11

"No," I whimpered.

Beth's pretty face jerked to one side and then the other, a gross parody of the woman I'd come to care for. "Woo, boy! Didn't think I'd be able to hide from you assholes much longer!"

My empty stomach pumped bile up the back of my throat. "But you can't be...I saw you take the drug..."

She raised an eyebrow. "You saw me get some. You never actually saw me take it, now did you?"

I tried to think back and just couldn't remember.

"Who do you think told us about Mr. Tinsley's deception in the first place?" Isaacs purred, taking great pleasure at rubbing my nose in the truth. "You had your little spy, and I had mine."

I recalled the guards the night before, how they'd been talking to someone standing in the shadows inside our cell. Then I remembered the rough, almost angry sex we'd had in the middle of the night.

And what about the time before, at her place, when she'd seemed confused about it the next morning? God, it had been right in front of me the whole time; she'd been slipping in and out of the trance, just as I had, before she finally turned for good at some point while we were locked up.

Beth seemed to read my thoughts as she glided toward me and ran a hand down my cheek, along my neck and chest, all the way down to my genitals, which she'd wielded with such expertise last night. "Can't thank you enough for helping me scratch that itch, baby. I pretended you were my grandfather last night while I fucked your brains out. He and I used to have a lot of fun when I was a kid." She grinned. "Maybe we can do it again once you finally stop resisting."

I shook my head adamantly. "You're pretending, aren't you? Like Jacob. To find a way to get help. I know it."

Isaacs crooned to Beth, "Let's make sure Mr. Jefferson doesn't harbor any such silly hopes about your allegiance."

From the edge of the crowd, Schrader produced an instrument I knew all too well.

"This is for Yonk," he said through his teeth, and handed the long hedge trimmers to Beth.

She approached me, opening and closing the handles so that the blades made a *shink-shink-shink* sound. I tried to fight, but the Heeders held my arms out away from my body, like they did to Avery. Others wrapped themselves around my waist and legs, until I couldn't wiggle so much as an inch.

Beth put the point of the blades against my chest and dragged them along my stomach, stopping at my groin. She closed the handles just enough to put pressure on my cock through the shorts. I gasped.

"No," she said. "Might wanna use that again later."

"The good book says, if thy hand offends thee, cut it off," Isaacs told her. "And Mr. Jefferson has done nothing but offend me."

Beth opened the trimmers wide and moved them back up, positioning my left wrist in the angle of the V. Even though the day had heated up, the blades felt cold as ice.

"Please," I begged, not talking to her, but to Mother Isaacs. I had to raise my voice to be heard; the gathered crowd murmured in anticipation. Their eyes were round excited circles as they swayed back and forth to the music of the Squall. "Please don't do this, I'll do anything!"

"Yes," she agreed. "You will."

Beth brought the handles crashing together.

The agony was bright and instantaneous, a fire that burned up the length of my arm and consumed my mind. The dog bite had been nothing compared to this, a scraped knee, a bruised shin. Through the haze, I saw the blades slice through flesh and gristle and stop just short of closing when they hit bone. Blood sprayed from the wound like an open fire hydrant, across Beth, across the Heeders, across the ground. I screamed and screamed, but, to my pain-wracked brain, it sounded like the Squall pouring out of my mouth, the Squall, the Squall, always the Squall.

Then Beth put some muscle into closing the hedge trimmers, and I felt the blades grind into my wrist, the pressure finally cracking the bones like crab claws.

The last thing I saw before I passed out was my left hand separating from the rest of my body.

SATURDAY EVENING AGAIN

1

When I try to remember the end of that day, it's nothing but a series of blurry fade ins-and-outs, quick, second-long blips of consciousness all set to the backbeat of the Squall.

Being half-carried, half-dragged back to the cell.

A few horrified screams as the others got a look at me.

Sitting propped against the wall, shuddering uncontrollably, while bodies scrambled around me.

Laura holding my mangled arm in the air, above my head, so that blood squirted out in a tight arc, like a drinking fountain.

Shouting voices, one demanding to be given medical supplies.

My arm being wrapped in a silvery bandage.

A long stretch of darkness in which a dream about Darcy surfaced, and we were signing the divorce papers all over again, upon the conclusion of which she took the pen she'd been using to scrawl her name and stabbed me through the palm with it.

Waking sometime later on the carpet—or maybe it was right after the dream—and screaming from the pain that clawed at my nerve endings.

Katie hovering over me, gently cleaning blood from my face while she wept.

Opening my eyes to discover Jacob lying beside me, rocking back and forth with his arms wrapped around his stomach as he moaned and shivered.

2

It was dark the next time I came fully awake. The sun was down, the apartment full of hazy shadows again. I found myself stretched out in the bedroom of our cell, with Jacob sleeping fitfully beside me. Beyond the window, the Squall blatted over and over again, like sharp jazz notes from a trumpet.

I shifted, but as soon as I moved my arm, the room spun. I waited till it stopped before slowly sitting up and lifting my wounded appendage to my face.

Even the sensation of moving the limb was strange. The weight distribution I'd been used to my whole life now felt wrong. Too light. A clear plastic shopping bag prevented me from seeing the actual wound, the opening duct taped around my forearm. Beneath it, I could make out a towel or cloth similarly affixed, with a bracelet of tape so thick and tight it looked like a steel manacle.

Even if my memories of the amputation weren't crystal clear, it would still be obvious from the stumpy shape that my hand was missing.

I only have one hand. I blinked in dumb fascination. The idea seemed ludicrous, something that happened to people in comic books and movies. I gently probed at the tip with my other hand, wincing more from the uncomfortable lack of sensory data than from any pain. Surprisingly, it didn't even hurt; just a low throb of uncomfortable heat and a weird tingle when I tried to move my non-existent fingers. My pain receptors had probably overloaded and shut down in the face of such trauma.

The tourniquet might've saved my life, but I didn't know how much it had done to stop the bleeding. Through the outer bag, I could see the towel over the wound was stained with damp redness. How long could I last like this without some real medical attention? My skin felt like ice, and I was thirsty enough to guzzle an entire lake's worth of water.

Well, maybe you can build a fire in the oven, in case you feel like a little self-cauterization.

Beside me, Jacob groaned in his sleep and curled up into a fetal ball. Sweat poured off him in continuous rivulets. I recognized the symptoms of full-blown withdrawal, but couldn't find the energy to sympathize. In fact, instead of water, I suddenly wanted more of that whiskey so bad I would've cut off my other hand.

I struggled to stand, swooning again from the head rush, and made it three steps before collapsing. Both hands tried to break my fall from instinct; my severed limb rammed into the carpet, sending a rush of seething pain through my body. I clenched my jaw and focused on breathing until it subsided. I'd never felt so weak in my life, as if my body had been built out of wet tissue paper. This time when I got up, I shuffled slowly and deliberately forward until I could grab hold of the doorway into the living room.

Kirk, Katie and Laura sat in here with four other people, the quiet guy named Simon and three women whose names I just couldn't recall, all of them far across the room, away from the dark patch on the carpet where Ron had bled out. None of them spoke, just sat with their heads lowered or propped up by a hands braced against their elbows, drowsing in the clamor of the Squall.

When she saw me clinging to the doorframe, Katie leapt to her feet and rushed to hug me. "I thought you were dying."

"Not...not yet."

"You shouldn't be up!"

She tried to usher me back into the bedroom, but I waved her away. "Doesn't matter." My voice sounded hoarse, barely more than a whisper. The effort just to speak exhausted me. "Could use some water, though."

"She's right," Laura added, while Katie ran to the sink. "You're probably still in shock. You lost so much blood..."

"I'll make more." I gulped from the glass Katie brought me and then indicated the rest of the room with a weak sweep of my good arm. "Where is everybody else?"

"Turned," Kirk uttered. It was the first time I'd heard him speak since he punctured his eardrums. He wore his glasses again, although they barely fit on his bruised face. I didn't know whether he'd intuited my question or read my lips. "All of them turned throughout the day. Went to join the others."

That meant there were eight of us left. Nine, including Jacob. Everyone else who lived at the Estates of North Hills had either been killed, or become a monster.

Katie bit her lower lip. "Beth...she never came back. Do you know what happened to her?"

"Well...let's see." I held up my shrink-wrapped stump. "Last I saw, she was chopping off my hand with a pair of hedge trimmers and loving every second of it."

She nodded. "I don't know which I was more scared of, that or..." Katie covered her face with her hands. Something

I would never be able to do again. I wanted to comfort her, but I was scared I would fall if I moved away from the safety of the wall.

"This is it," Kirk said after a few moments. "I don't see how we can even last through the night."

"We can and we will," I told them. "Because help is coming."

"What do you mean?" Laura asked. There wasn't even any hope in the question; they were too broken for that.

I told them the story of what had happened, ending with how Beth had been the one to sell out Jacob but sparing them the gory details of my amputation. Katie helped me across the room to them as I spoke, my shortened arm draped over her shoulder. We had to translate a few things into rudimentary sign language for Kirk, but he actually picked up the gist pretty fast.

"Poor Hammond," he murmured. "Didn't like the guy, but he didn't deserve that."

"But you see what it means, right? *They killed a cop.* An on-duty one, I mean, one that'll be missed instantly. Someone is gonna come looking for him."

Kirk shook his head. "Even if they do, Elliot, it'll be too late for us."

"How do you figure?"

"Because even if they came right now, and they saw the whole situation immediately, they wouldn't storm the place, they'd treat it as a hostage situation. Remember Waco, and those Branch Davidian loons? A siege could take days. Days we don't have." He squinted and pinched the bridge of his nose. "We've all been feeling weird. Having...not-so-pleasant thoughts. It's close. Maybe it's best if we just...don't fight anymore."

The defeatism shocked me, considering he'd been gung-ho, take-charge from the second I met him. "Damn it, we can't let them win! I told you, her control is slipping! If we can't count on help coming, then all we have to do is keep our shit together until they stop listening to her!"

"I don't see how going from a complex full of sadistic lunatics to one full of those wild creatures helps us."

"It just goes to show you that this whole thing is unraveling!" My vision wavered for a moment; I let my overtaxed heart calm before I continued. "It's just a matter of time. They're losing cohesion, they're starving, and they can't stay holed up in this apartment complex forever."

"They won't have to," a voice said behind me.

Jacob emerged from the bedroom, his face a sickly greenish-white in the last few rays of dim sunlight. He shuffled toward us with a gait just as decrepit as mine.

"They won't have to what?" I asked.

"Stay here. I was gonna tell you earlier, but then you got dragged out and I spent most of the day in extreme pain." He lowered himself to the floor on the other side of Katie, who held his hand. He leaned against her, shoulder-to-shoulder, and took a few seconds to breathe before continuing. "Everything you're sayin makes sense with what I saw. Mother Isaacs can't keep the troops happy, so they're goin AWOL, no matter how much she preaches not to listen to the *beast within*. But she knew they couldn't survive here forever. So she's been workin on a way to get them out."

"How?"

"You know my neighbor Connelly across the street? The one you were playin Peeping Tom with?"

"Yeah, I've seen his handiwork," I grumbled.

"Well, in his day job, he's some kinda engineer or somethin. Super smart. So Isaacs put him to work on a project. I never saw it, just heard some other people talkin. They call it a 'speaking totem,' but it's really a portable electric generator designed to make that sound. So they can leave and still be exposed to it. They wanna use it to get supplies first, but then…" He stopped, swallowed heavily, and shivered so violently the joints of his spine cracked. "Then they wanna build *more*. Bigger ones, that they can use to start converting other people." No one said anything, and when Jacob spoke again, his voice grew loud and shrill. "*Do you understand what I'm tellin you, for Christ's sake? That crazy bitch wants to make the whole world into those fuckers!*"

"God, she really did find a way to spread her message." Another dizzy spell, this one fear-induced. I closed my eyes. "We can't let that happen."

"Except we're still on the sidelines," Kirk said. "Not much we can do while we're locked in here."

His words were punctuated by an odd scratching, metallic sound across the room. We looked toward the A/C vent that Schrader had kicked in earlier, when he'd confiscated our drugs, the one that led to outside. We'd discounted it as an escape route before, because Beth had said none of would fit. And she'd been right, none of *us* would.

A tiny hand reached out of the dark air shaft and moved the twisted vent shield aside.

And then a face I recognized peered out at us.

Rory Bergman squirmed his way into the room.

3

The kid was even filthier than us, and severely malnourished. He must've dropped ten pounds since the time I'd seen him last, and he didn't have much to spare then. He still wore the ripped Captain America shirt, and goggled at us from behind those thick, bottle lenses.

It took only a few minutes to get an idea of what he'd been through; the rest I learned after the fact, while in the hospital. Back before all this started, he lived alone with his father, who took Phenobarbital for mild seizures. When the Squall started, Paul Bergman had, of course, been unaffected. But, being a protective father, when his son claimed to not be able to hear the noise, he took him to a specialist overnight for a battery of tests that turned up nothing, and probably saved the boy from turning into a Heeder.

They arrived back home to find that uncomfortable vibe in the air that the rest of us had been feeling. Everyone they met acted strange. Then, the next morning, two of their neighbors broke into the apartment and demanded all their medication. Paul Bergman, intuiting the situation much faster than I had, barely managed to get his son out the bathroom window with his prescription bottle, telling the boy to get help and take a pill if he felt strange. The neighborhood kids chased him down and tried to beat him to death, which is where I ran into him.

Since then, he'd been hunted by Isaacs's people, unable to escape from the Estates. He had no idea what happened to his father. The kid survived by hiding in A/C shafts and maintenance crawlspaces, coming out only to forage for food, and high on Phenobarbital most of the time. His eyes were glazed as he told us this story, drool crusted around his mouth, his demeanor completely spaced out while he explained that he'd decided to take a chance and make contact with us.

"That's good, Rory, that's really good," I told the boy, patting his shoulder. We had all crammed into the bathroom to hear him talk, in case someone came into our cell. Katie listened for the sound of the lock so we would have time to hide him. "Do you still have any of the medication?"

"I think so." Everything the kid said sounded blurry and slowed down; I wondered how much lasting damage he'd done to himself as he produced the bottle from his jeans pocket. I could hear a few last pills rattling around the bottom.

"Who cares about that?" Jacob exclaimed from where he sat on the edge of the bathtub. "He needs to get us the fuck outta here!"

"And how's he gonna do that?"

"I dunno, maybe he can find a hacksaw! Or hell, just bring us the key!"

"Is he supposed to fight both guards to do it? He's twelve, jackass."

Jacob looked stung. "Jesus, it was just an idea."

I tried not to lose my temper—every time my heart rate elevated, I felt woozy all over again—but Jacob's petulance made me furious. "You know, you weren't too keen on letting us out when it was you on the other side risking your life, but you got no problem with him doing it, huh?"

"Things have changed now, man! We gotta—!"

"There's only one guard," Rory interrupted dreamily. "He's sleeping."

"*What?*"

We all hurried to the back door, cracked it open, and looked through the outer bars. Before, the guards had been diligent about standing along the building wall, out of sight. Now one of them sprawled in the grass just beyond the concrete patio on his stomach, completely naked, moonlight shining on his bare ass as he loudly snored.

Just another sign that Mother Isaacs's kingdom was breaking down.

"I don't see the keys," Katie whispered.

Rory reached back inside the pocket he'd taken the prescription bottle from and drew out a ring with one key dangling from it.

"Cause I already got them," he said.

4

"We move fast as soon as we're out, and keep together," I said. It took less than a minute for everyone to prepare themselves to leave our prison. "There's no telling what the situation is out there, so the most important thing is not to be seen."

Murmurs of agreement came back.

"But where are we going?" Katie asked.

"To the wall. The closest route would be to cut across the complex to the south, toward our apartments—"

"You do not want to go that way," Jacob put in.

"—but that's where they seem to be congregated, so we'll go north. We make it to the wall, get over it somehow, and run for help. Once we're outside the Squall's range, they won't be able to come after us."

Kirk leaned closer and asked, "What about the guards?"

"I'm hoping they've already abandoned their posts too, but if not..." I shrugged. "We do what we have to."

A buzz of excitement went through the group. They whispered among themselves, setting up the escape order, Katie and Laura each claiming responsibility for Rory (I decided to let them keep their illusions rather than point out that the boy had survived just fine without us), but Jacob broke away from the group and beckoned me with two fingers.

"What if there's someone else pretending?" he asked when we were out of earshot. "You know, someone who's already turned into one of them, like that Beth chick? We get outside, they could start screamin their head off, bring the whole place down on us."

Shit. He was right. I scanned the group, looking for twitches. But perhaps they weren't as evident in the early stages. Beth hadn't looked any different.

No, but she'd certainly felt *different. You were just enjoying it too much to notice.*

Inspiration hit me, and I pulled out Paul Bergman's prescription bottle and shook the pills inside. "Before we go out, everybody should take a dose of this," I said aloud.

The others had piled up by the door, waiting on us. Kirk said, "For god's sake Elliot, let's just go!"

"Not yet." I went to the kitchen counter and spilled the pills out after letting Jacob open the bottle for me. There were five left. I put one back in and crushed up the other four with the palm of my hand, then divided the powder up into ten tiny piles. Jacob and I each took one, me having to wet a finger, roll it in the powder, and then lick it off. It wasn't the rush we'd gotten from the other stuff—was such a small dose that we probably wouldn't be aware of the effects at all—but hopefully it would help us keep our sanity a little longer. "Go for it, everyone. Then we leave."

The others came over and took their doses. I watched carefully to make sure they did, squinting in the darkness while trying not to be too obvious about it. Kirk hung back until only one Pheno pile remained.

"Now you," I told him.

"That's okay. I'm feeling well enough to make it out of this godforsaken place. And I think I've poisoned my body enough for a lifetime."

"I'm afraid I have to insist, Kirk."

A tired grin spread across his face. "So it's a test then?"

"Can't be too careful."

He bent his head to the counter and licked his dose off in one clean swipe. "Happy?"

Overcome with sudden relief, I put my good arm around him and pulled him to me. He stiffened at first, then hugged me back. "Very."

I went to the door. The guard continued to snore just a few yards away. I reached through the bars as quietly as possible, felt for the lock, and turned the key in it.

"Let's do this."

For the first time in three days, we stepped outside as free men and women. The next time I saw the cell where we'd been imprisoned, it was nothing but charred ashes.

5

With the moon on the wane, we had ample shadows to hide us. But as we slid onto the patio, the sleeping guard snorted and sat up. I froze, sure that our escape had ended before it began.

Kirk moved forward, sure-footed and silent even with his broken rib, and decked him hard across the face, knuckles landing squarely against the man's temple. The guard grunted and slumped back to the ground. I stared at Kirk in blunt amazement as he rubbed at his hand until Jacob elbowed me impatiently.

We ran to the corner of the building and looked out on the street. The complex was still dark, not a single electric light anywhere in sight. Somewhere to the south, I could hear voices over the Squall's unceasing whine. It sounded like that mindless hum the group outside Mother Isaacs's unit had been making.

The tribe was worshipping their pagan god again. I turned in the opposite direction and got moving.

Five minutes, I told myself. *Five minutes from now, and this is all over.*

We moved single file with me in the lead, slinking from shadow to shadow with the skill of trained ninjas. The rooftops were empty; the men who had so diligently guarded the complex were gone. Even so, I avoided the streets, sticking to the back alleys. I couldn't stop thinking about the night I'd followed Connelly from 3204, the mad scientist of the Heeder army. God, that seemed an eternity ago. This place had gone from my home to a battleground to a prison camp in the span of a few days. Once we reached civilization and brought back help, it would become a haunted graveyard. Surely no one would ever live here again. I realized I would miss it, even though I tried so hard to keep myself apart from it.

I set a pace just fast enough to make sure everyone kept up, barely above walking speed, but it was still too much for my traumatized body. Each breath became more difficult with every block we passed, as though my lungs just wouldn't fully expand. My heartbeat felt irregular, a skipping record. Black spots grew and shrank in front of me. At one point, I looked down at my mangled arm to find a steady drip of blood leaking from the end of the shopping bag.

Despite everything else we'd been through, this was the first time my own death seemed frighteningly possible.

Rounding the corner of another building, I got my first glance at the complex wall in the distance just as a wave of dizziness snatched the ground out from under me. I lurched to the side, my equilibrium gone, and collapsed on the grass.

The impact barely registered. The ground felt as soft and fluffy as a bed made of clouds.

"Mr. Jefferson!" Katie hissed. My name echoed from the end of a long tunnel. I knew she was shaking me, but I couldn't feel it. Unconsciousness fluttered my eyes.

Funny; the sensation of dying wasn't all that different from slipping into one of the Squall-induced fugues.

"Soooorry, teeeeach," Jacob said above me, sounding like he was underwater. A hand slid over my mouth.

Then he stepped on my stump.

The world snapped back into focus amid a volcanic eruption of torment. I tried to scream but his fingers were there, working into my mouth and down my throat, gagging me before I could make a sound. I vomited a milky gruel of stomach acid all over his hand and the grass.

"Get up," he whispered fiercely in my ear. "I got enough to feel guilty for when we get outta this without leavin your worthless ass behind."

He and Kirk hauled me upright. We moved on, this time with me dangling from their shoulders, trying to make my stubborn feet work. Now Katie led the way, and we hurried behind her, and the wall was ahead, right *there*, so close I could make out the junkyard scaffolding even in the dark, and there was no one there, it was a wide open shot to freedom, and—

Katie moved to cross the last grass alley between us and the wall, glanced to her right, and jerked back. She urged us all into the shadows of the building, her eyes wide with terror, and put a finger to her lips.

Jacob inched forward to the corner. Kirk tried to lower me to the ground, but I pushed away and followed, determined to see what stood in our way now.

Midway down the alley, just ten yards from us, a figure crouched on its haunches with knees bowed out, like a cat, genitals drooping low enough to brush the grass. After a moment, I was able to make out the crooked, bulbous nose.

Tony.

He stared up at the night sky as though trying to comprehend its vastness, face and neck and shoulders twitching in big, violent jerks. Beside him, the body of a young woman lay on the ground, its torso so ravaged and torn apart it looked like a bomb had gone off inside, with guts scattered in all directions.

The former leasing agent wasn't alone either. Six more naked people occupied the alley, three men and two women engaged in a vigorous orgy further down, by the alley's transformer, and another lithe woman walking on palms and toes toward the body with her bare bottom stuck in the air, just like Carolyn had after waking up as one of these strange hybrid creatures. The human body just doesn't have the structure to move in such quadrupedal fashion, but somehow, she made it look sinuous, almost graceful. When she reached Tony, she shouldered him aside so she could sniff at the dead girl. The whole scene looked like the den of some particularly vicious predator.

This was the Squall's endgame, what it would turn all of us into if given enough time. These people weren't Heeders anymore. There was nothing remotely intelligent left in them. They had regressed to some primitive, primal stage beyond mankind's earliest history, where Beth's four F's of the amygdala had become their entire world.

They had embraced the beast within, as Mother Isaacs would put it.

In the alley, the woman dipped her face into the corpse's viscera. A quick shake of her head, and a piece of meat tore loose with a wet *rip* I heard all the way around the corner. She chewed vigorously while Tony came around behind her, jammed his nose between her ass cheeks for a good whiff, and then proceeded to mount her, proving that he wasn't entirely gay.

My stomach heaved again, but there was nothing left in it to throw up. A clicking noise from deep in my throat drifted out of my open mouth before I could stop it.

The woman's head snapped up from her feeding. Her face and mouth were smeared with gore. She sniffed the air, then hissed at Tony as he pumped into her exposed backside. When he gave no sign of stopping, she kicked him away and scuttled toward us in that strange palm-and-toe gait.

No time to prepare. Jacob and I backpedaled, spun around and tried to get everyone to move around the corner, into the next alley, but it was too late. The woman rounded the corner and spotted us. She gave a surprised squeal and bounded forward.

Simon stood closest to her. At the last second, he tried to run, but she tackled his legs, knocking him hard to the ground, then squatted on his chest and clawed at his face and neck. His screams rolled across the complex as he struggled with her. Kirk leapt forward to help, but the other hybrids came tromping around the corner and cut him off. They snarled like a pack of dingoes and started to close in.

I tried to keep the rest of our group together, but they scattered in terror. Tony and one of the other females split off to give chase. The female snagged a woman from our group by her hair and yanked so hard her neck snapped audibly. Tony came at Jacob, but the kid landed a boot in his face before he could attack. The blow knocked out a handful of teeth, but slowed him down only for a moment.

They were just too damn strong. Whatever mental process the Squall used to transform them into these cannibal
nightmares had also given them uncanny agility and strength.
Laura scooped Rory up and ran with him, but I just stood in
the midst of the unfolding slaughter, swaying on my feet, and
looked for Katie.

A ululating screech drifted over the buildings, almost in
perfect harmony with the Squall.

The battle in the alley came to a crashing halt. Everyone
froze, even the bestial creatures. They tilted their heads to
the side, like dogs.

Voices echoed from the street. Heeders. A lot of them,
from the sound.

The beasts screeched furiously and bolted up the alley to
meet the newcomers head on. The rest of us remained where
we were.

"*Over here!*"

Katie stood at the next building, in front of an open
apartment door, waving to us frantically.

"Get inside," I croaked. "Hurry." If the Heeders saw us
now, this was all over.

The group ran for the door and headed inside one by one.
I waited for Kirk, who checked Simon's body for signs of life
and then shook his head. We left him and the other woman
behind.

Another war cry sounded before we could even get the
door of the apartment closed. At first, I thought the Heeders
had seen us after all, but then I heard a howl of pain and
realized they were fighting Tony and the beasts.

We stumbled through the dark unit until we reached a
window that gave a good vantage point on the alley and the
street beyond. A posse of twenty Heeders stood in the street,

battling their devolved brethren. Some of them chucked homemade spears as the creatures charged, while a few waded in with knifes and machetes when the beasts got too close. Shouts, growls and cries of pain filled the alley. Through the chaos, I spotted Schrader, shirtless and war-painted, looking like John Wayne if he'd been on the side of the Indians instead of the cowboys. As Tony ran at him, he brandished a spear made from a sharpened metal pipe and skewered the other man through the neck with it.

When it was over, and bodies littered the alley, he turned to bark at the other Heeders, "See? This is what happens when you succumb to the fuckin beast! We'll never get anything done if we all start crawlin around on all fours and eating each other! So have a good goddamned look, and remember what'll happen if any of you feel the urge to drop to all fours! Now get these bodies up!" He pointed further up the street. "And I want three men on that fuckin wall patrolling this side of the complex! You desert your post, you desert your life!" A few Heeders split off from the group to follow his orders.

All we could hear for a few minutes after that were the grunts as they picked up the bodies and carried them away. They took the dead girl the beasts had been feeding on, but never came far enough into the alley to see the ones from our group.

Then they were gone, and the night returned to silence.

6

None of us dared to speak for another ten minutes.

"I think we should stay here for a while," I whispered.

Katie nodded eagerly, along with Laura and one of the other women.

"What?" Jacob stood up and slapped Katie's hand away when she reached for him. "Why the hell should we do that? We're almost out, the wall's right there!"

"Yes, and now we know it's guarded," I told him.

"What happened to all that bullshit about *doin what we have to*?"

"I think we just proved we're in no shape to take anyone on, especially if they're armed."

"I gotta say, Elliot, I'm with the kid on this one," Kirk said, squinting back and forth between us to follow the flow of conversation. "Once they find out we've escaped, they'll scour the whole complex for us. We have to get out while we can."

"Kirk, they barely have the manpower to keep their perimeter guarded anymore, let alone search door to door." A coughing fit seized me. When it was over, I said, "Look, I'm not talking about staying long. A few hours, maybe. We can rest and hope that the guys Schrader put on the wall leave. If not, we can move on and try to find another way out."

They reluctantly agreed. We posted Rory as a lookout at the window while the rest of us checked the apartment. The previous owner's furniture and belongings were all still here, but the Heeders had ransacked the place. We did find a package of stale marshmallows and a can of corn in the pantry, which the eight of us devoured. Just having something in our bellies raised everyone's spirits.

In the bathroom, we came across a bottle of aspirin that the Heeders had missed in their medicinal purge. Everyone took three except for me; Kirk said it would thin my blood too much. He and Katie inspected my arm and wrapped an even tighter layer of tape around the wound.

"It's...it's looking a little gamey," Kirk told me quietly. "We need to get you some help."

"I'll be fine."

He shook his head, and then grinned. "Elliot...you've gotta be the toughest English teacher that ever walked the face of the earth."

"I don't think my students or my ex-wife share that sentiment."

After that, the four women retreated to the bedroom. Katie, Laura and the others sprawled on the king size bed with Rory, too exhausted for even the Squall to keep them up; their snores drifted out within minutes. We might still be trapped in the Estates, but the fact that we were out of our filthy cell relieved a lot of tension.

Kirk, Jacob and I decided to take shifts watching the window while the other two rested. They made me sleep while Kirk took the first watch. When he checked on me again, I was clammy and shivering so hard my teeth chattered. Ice water pumped through my veins.

"Rest some more, I'll keep watching," he said.

I shook my head and sat up. My stump burned and ached. "No, I n-need to be conscious. Otherwise I m-might not wake up next time."

It was two in the morning when I sat down at the window, draped in blankets. After a few minutes, my thoughts turned to Beth. I tried not to focus on the last time I'd seen her, or what atrocity she might be committing right that second, but rather how she'd looked that first day, when we met. I made a vow to save her, no matter what. The distraction helped; I had actually stopped shivering when Jacob came in an hour later.

"Still my turn," I told him.

"I know," he grumbled. "Couldn't sleep." He squatted in the floor beside me and rested his head against the sill. I noticed his hands shook, too.

"Withdrawals?" I asked.

He nodded. "I puked up the medley of corn and marsh-mallow. Don't know how I got it down to begin with. The stomach cramps are fuckin killin me."

"They'll pass."

Jacob watched me, his eyes too shadowed to see. "You went through this too, huh?"

"A version of it. Vomited my guts out for a week, felt like dried-up shit for another month. But then I got better."

He didn't respond. It was even stranger to have a normal conversation with him than it had been to pretend every-thing was peachy keen with Hammond.

"Thank you," I said abruptly. "For what you did. You saved my life. Actually, you probably saved all our lives."

"Yeah, well. I still think you're an asshole."

I laughed. It sounded old and creaky.

Outside, I caught a flicker of movement on the small sec-tion of scaffolding we could see from the window. Schrader's men were still out there, and we needed a way past them.

Jacob followed my gaze and asked, "So how are we get-tin outta here, man?"

"When it's time, I'll know," I said.

I just hoped it was true.

SUNDAY MORNING AGAIN

1

Kirk awoke first, but his voice brought the women out of the bedroom right behind him.

"We have to move. They're gonna realize we're gone, if they haven't already. The more time we give them to prepare, the less chance we have at escaping."

"I agree." I reached out and patted Jacob's cheek where he'd fallen asleep, sitting against the wall next to me. He flailed before seeing it was me.

Kirk's hands clenched at his sides. "Then what do we do?"

The sun had just breached the horizon outside, and orange fingers of dawn crept between the buildings. Before I answered Kirk, I looked out the window. Not at the wall and the scaffolding, where patrolling Heeders still walked by every few minutes, but at what I'd noticed in the building across from us sometime during my watch. Now that I had light, I wanted to confirm it was really there.

"I'll tell you what we're gonna do." I stayed at the window, bracing for the response I knew I would get. "I'm going out there to create a diversion and bring the guards on the wall after me, while the rest of you find a way to escape."

The room erupted in denials and arguments, Katie's voice rising above them all. The only one who didn't speak was Jacob.

"That is not gonna happen," Kirk told me firmly, after the others got him to understand what I'd said. "We've come this far together and we're not leaving you now."

"You were always gonna have to leave me." I turned away from the window, took them all in, and held up my handless arm. "I'm on my last leg here. Figuratively speaking. I can barely walk, let alone climb over that wall. Even if I could, I'd only be a burden. But at least I can give the rest of you a chance."

"I have a pretty good idea what you're saying, and you're not convincing me, Elliot."

I looked at him directly, knowing he couldn't hear my words but hoping he would be able to read my face. "There's more at stake than one man now, Kirk. Any one of us is expendable. I can accept that; why can't you?"

"Oh, you son of a bitch. That woman might be a religious zealot, but you're the one with the Jesus complex." Kirk crossed his arms and turned away from me. I gave him time to do the math himself. When he faced me again, he asked, "How're you gonna create this diversion, go streaking down the middle of the street?"

"Nope. I'll just do what I should've in the first place." I nodded at the window, at the building across from us. Over there, the door to the small maintenance closet that every building had hung wide open on one set of busted hinges.

Mounted on the interior wall was a fire axe just like the one Schrader favored. Chips of sunlight danced on the blade tip.

"I'm gonna hit 'em where it hurts. Take out as many of those damned transformers as I can."

Kirk didn't speak for so long, I thought he hadn't under-stood, but then a smile worked its way across his puffy face. "God, yes."

"I'll help," Jacob said softly.

I shook my head. "No thanks."

His expression told me he hadn't expected the response. "Why not?"

"For starters, you're sick as a dog."

"And you're not?"

"Jacob, I don't need your help."

"I don't give a fuck." He grabbed hold of my shoulders and forced me to look at him. "Those shitheads put me through hell. If there's a chance to get some revenge, I want it." His hands fell away from me. I could see the pain in him, burning like a forest fire just below the surface. "Please. I *need* this."

"I tell you this for your own good, Jacob: you're the last person I would ever want on my team. Now get the hell outta here, and don't look back."

That old anger spread across his face, but he said noth-ing.

I turned and left the apartment.

2

Inside the maintenance closet, some basic first aid and fire fighting equipment sat on metal shelves, along with vari-ous tools and the master fuse box for the building. Nothing else looked useful. I started to reach for the axe with my left hand, realized my mistake, and used the right instead. My new handicap just kept surprising me all over again. I could foresee this happening a lot in my future.

If I had one.

The axe felt good. Something solid to cling to. I gave it an experimental swing. With only one hand, I could either grip the bottom of the handle and have power, or choke up and have control. I opted for the power; I would need every ounce of strength to penetrate the metal shell over the transformers.

When I turned back around, the others had come out of the apartment and gathered around me. Kirk stepped forward.

"Take them that way," I said, sweeping the axe further up the alley. "Look for a place where you can get over the wall fast, and then wait for me to draw them off. I'll give you three minutes before I start. Once you're over, keep running and don't stop."

Kirk nodded. "We'll bring back help as soon as we can."

We faced one another in silence for another moment before I said, "I hope you get your family back."

"Thank you for this, Elliot." He held out his hand.

I hefted the axe. "Have to take a rain check. Don't have any appendages to spare at the moment."

He laughed, as he had that first day, and clapped me on the shoulder before moving aside.

The others filed by, saying quiet goodbyes, Laura and Rory and the others I barely knew. Jacob walked past me without a word. Katie was last, and she threw her arms around me once more.

"Please don't do this," she whispered.

"I have to, Katie. But I need you to make me another promise. One you can't break this time."

She looked up at me.

"When this is all over...and you're far away from here... try to forget. Just be happy, and don't let anybody live your life for you. Not Jacob, not your mother, not anybody."

She studied me, the tears frozen in her eyes, and then nod-ded. She went to join the others. I watched as they moved up the alley, peering cautiously around the corner of each building before they finally disappeared around one.

And then I was alone.

3

I hurried the opposite direction, past the bodies of Simon and the other woman, through the alley where the den of hybrids had been feeding, all the way to the other end. From there, the alley opened onto a short, perpendicular side street bounded by parked cars at one end and the complex wall on the other, a few yards away to the left. The transformer sat just beyond the mouth, anchored to the ground beside the curb, its caterwaul at this range almost deafening. When I stepped out to get to it, I would be totally exposed.

I peeked around the corner far enough to see the scaf-folding, then ducked back as one of the loinclothed guards, hunched and armed with a spear, walked past the other side of the building and out of sight. There had to be more around somewhere. They would hear the noise and come running, which meant I would have only seconds.

Would they kill me on sight, or take me prisoner again?

Do you really care anymore?

No. I found I didn't.

A few feet away, the transformer continued to screech. But there seemed to be a panicked edge to that racket now, like the distressed bleating of a sheep. I saw now that some-one had painted Reverend Isaacs's face on the lid in bright red that looked like blood. That noise might've been coming from his mouth.

"Scream all you want," I told him, and then stepped out of the alley.

My dream came back to me, that first one, where a sense of impending doom had all but suffocated me as I went to touch one of the steel boxes. For the first time, I suspected the Squall had implanted that subconscious fear in my head, just like it had given me those other sadistic thoughts. A defense mechanism, to keep us away. It might not be a gift from God, as Mother Isaacs believed, but I had just about convinced myself that it was sentient. Now, as I approached this transformer, the Squall buffeted me like a stiff wind. My eardrums throbbed. I wanted to cover them, but it wouldn't do any good. The only thing that would help is silencing that terrible noise once and for all.

I kept moving forward until I stood right in front of the squat little box. The noise was unbearable. Something wet trickled down my left earlobe. And now I could hear that voice just beneath, purring at me, seducing me, promising my every fantasy and desire if I would just submit, submit and heed its call.

My head began to swim. I could feel my control slipping away. I lifted the axe all the way over my head, bending my elbow, and let the handle rest along my spine, so I would have maximum swing range.

"Heed this, you fucker." With a grim smile, I swung the axe in a whistling, overhead arc.

If I'd had both hands, I would've aimed for the padlock on the side, down near the base, but I had nowhere near that kind of precision. Instead, I brought the blade down right in the middle of that green cover and the brooding countenance of Reverend Isaacs, intending to cleave the metal to get to the vital organs beneath.

The axe head struck the box, producing a loud *CLANG!* that I felt up my arm and into my ribcage. It caromed away with enough force to almost make me lose my grip. I looked down at my handiwork and felt the smile fade from my lips.

The single blow had been enough to leave me breathless and dizzy. Some of the green paint had flaked away, but otherwise, the metal wasn't so much as dented. Paul Bunyan, I was not.

But it was enough to do the job of distracting, at least. From the wall came an alarmed shout, and then the sound of multiple running footsteps heading in my direction.

I raised the axe again. The muscles in my arm quivered from the effort. I couldn't do this. I would only be able to get another one or two weak strikes in before the guards were on me, and I might become one of them by the time they got here.

The Squall gave a triumphant surge that clawed at my brain.

Then the axe was snatched from my hands. Someone shouldered me aside.

I looked over to find Jacob standing next to me.

I can't remember ever having been so happy to see another human being.

"Amateur," he said, and began chopping at the lock on the transformer's casing like a crazed lumberjack. Each of his blows bit deep into the metal. It took only a few swings for him to tear enough away for me to reach down and pull the lid up, revealing a complicated array of wires and lights beneath. From somewhere inside that mess of electrical engineering, the Squall cried out in abject terror.

Two guards charged around the corner. When they saw us, they bellowed and jabbered in a language so base I could barely understand it, then lifted their spears menacingly and eased closer.

Jacob and I looked at each other. I nodded.

He brought the axe up again and sent it smashing down into the guts of the transformer.

Parts were crushed, wires severed. The pitch of the Squall changed, dropping to a deep, irregular hum. The Heeders cried out and dropped their spears to clutch the sides of their heads. After a few seconds, the noise returned to its normal level, but the Heeders dropped to all fours, regressing right in front of us. They snarled and gnashed their teeth as bloody foam leaked from the sides of their mouths.

"*Hit it again!*" I yelled.

Jacob gave the transformer one last titanic chop. Something inside exploded in a spray of sparks. Every hair on my body stood up in rigid quills as electricity prickled across us. The lights blinking deep inside blew out, and, a second later, the Squall gave a final plaintive wail and ground to a rusty halt.

A few feet away, the guards twitched like electrocution victims, then collapsed. Their chests moved as they breathed, but they didn't get back up.

I was perfectly aware that, elsewhere in the Estates, the Squall was still going, but in the tiny little corner that had been serviced by this transformer, it sounded distant and unimportant. We stood in the near-silence, drinking it in, the relief like those first seconds after a cramped muscle eases up.

Jacob grinned wickedly. "Let's do another one."

4

Our giddy destruction spree began across the street, at the very next transformer we saw. This time, Jacob got the casing open even faster, but I stopped him and held out my hand once he'd exposed the insides.

"Gimme that. I wanna do this one myself."

Even with my weak, one-handed swings, it took only three hits to destroy the delicate innards. The sound of the Squall winding down like a lawnmower engine was beautiful beyond words.

We continued on, going from transformer to transformer, Jacob's blows falling into a rhythm as we reclaimed the complex section-by-section. More unconscious Heeders lay everywhere in the areas we liberated. Our shirts dripped with sweat in minutes, but the work was so satisfying, neither of us noticed. I remembered a carnival Darcy and I had gone to on our third date, where I'd wasted a hundred bucks playing skee ball and ring toss and, more importantly, the game where you bash the giant mallet down on the pad to try to hit the bell. That had been a good time, one of my favorite memories from my marriage, but, Jesus, the raw thrill of destroying those hateful green boxes left it in the dust. We hooted and laughed every time one of the things winked out, releasing that last burst of electricity, like a dying man's final breath. The Squall lessened with each transformer we wrecked, but there was always another one and another.

It was only when we got to the sixth or seventh that we began to hear the screams drifting up from the opposite side of the complex every time we silenced a transformer.

They were distant and ethereal in the still air, anguished, pain-wracked cries that all blended together above the sound of the remaining Squall. We stopped and looked toward them.

"Yeah, they're feelin it now, aren't they?" Jacob hoisted a middle finger high in the air. "*Fuck you, you old bitch!*"

"Enough," I said. "Let's just take down as many of these things as possible."

"What's the rush? You think the others made it out?"

"Yeah, I do. But maybe we can end this ourselves right now."

We moved on, working block by block, no longer in such high spirits. Those screams were terrible, even if they did herald the end of Mother Isaacs's reign. For all I knew, we were killing the very people we wanted to save.

Including Beth.

We stopped at a new transformer. Jacob had just taken his first swing when my name cracked down from the heavens, coming from everywhere at once.

"*Mr. Jefferson.*"

I jumped, thinking that maybe God Himself actually had gotten involved in this terrible business, until I realized the amplified voice sounded like a raspy old woman.

"*Mr. Jefferson, I know it's you.*" With the air so still, the megaphone broadcast Mother Isaacs's unusually loud voice over the whole complex, the Squall seeming to boost the words even further. "*Stop what you're doing at once. If you do not surrender, I will make you very, very sorry.*"

"Don't listen to her." Jacob wiped sweat from his forehead. "She's scared. We got 'em on the run."

"Hold on." I had learned not to underestimate the architect of my misery.

There was a click over the speaker, and a new, frightened voice came on.

"Elliot? Elliot, for God's sake, help me, these people are—!"

Jacob glanced at me after the plea cut off. "You know who that is?"

"Yes. My ex-wife."

5

They had snatched her sometime during the night, the first field test for 3204's new portable Squall generator. Which worked like a horrible charm, I might add. I don't believe Darcy was kidnapped specifically with the intent to draw me out; there's no way Isaacs could've known about our escape by then. She was just looking for another way to break me, and reached out to the closest relative I had. The Heeders showed up at her place, murdered her new boyfriend, and dragged her back to the Estates.

I knew none of that then, of course. All I could think about—the only image my brain could conjure—was Darcy in the clutches of those monsters.

"You have five minutes, Mr. Jefferson," Isaacs resumed speaking. *"If you do not halt your destruction and show your face in front of my building, we will kill her. Painfully. I won't blame you if you can't convince the rest of your little group to accompany you. We'll take care of them in time. For now...it's only you I want. Five minutes. Not a second more."*

The speaker clicked off. I stood in the new silence and flexed my only hand at my side so hard the muscles ached.

"Don't you even think about it," Jacob said.

"I'm going."

"The fuck you are."

I raised my arm and stared at the bag over the end of it. "They've already taken so much from me. I can't let them hurt her."

"And what do you think surrendering is gonna do, man? Notice how that bitch never said anything about letting her go if you did! You go back, she'll just kill both of you!"

"Maybe."

I tried to leave, but he grabbed my upper arm. "Jesus, man, we've done all we can! This is almost over, just ride it the fuck out!"

I swallowed. Or tried. Sandpaper lined my throat, my arm throbbed with a feverish heat, and my eyelids felt like they weighed a ton each. But I said, "That's all I've ever done, is ride it out. For once in my life, I need to do the right thing, instead of the easy thing." I brushed his hand away and stepped off the curb beside the transformer. "Go, Jacob. Catch up with the others. Keep them safe."

"Mr. Jefferson?"

The two words were so small and unexpected, I stopped dead. The kid had never called me that, not even in my class. I faced him one last time, waited for him to convince me, but that seemed to be the last of his ammo. Everything he wanted to say was there, plainly stamped on his face, but he would never be able to get the words past his stubborn lips.

I knew the feeling.

"I'm sorry for what I did," I told him. "You're not...what I thought. And even if you were, it was still wrong. If I could take one thing in my life back, it wouldn't be the drinking. It would be lying about you and that gun."

I saw his mouth fall open, his chin quiver. But before I could see more, I turned away and started down the street as fast as I could.

6

That walk took a quick eternity. If you've ever been sent to the principal's office in school, you know what I mean. I navigated the deserted streets, and the Squall grew in intensity as I reached the areas Jacob and I hadn't touched yet. That was the only time I almost turned back, upon realizing I would have to plunge back into that fucking noise. Only the knowledge that I wouldn't have to suffer for long kept me going. When I hit Tulip Boulevard, I didn't bother to hide or recon the situation; I just strode out to the middle of the lane like a gunslinger. The sun, still hugging the horizon, threw my shadow out long in front of me.

The last of the Heeders stood in front of Isaacs's building, barely two blocks away. Their numbers had dwindled to around eighty or ninety filthy individuals dressed in primitive garb, but that was still far more manpower than I would've figured. They blocked the road entirely, clustered in tight formation as they awaited me. And there were still so many familiar faces in that twitching crowd of men, women, and children. Javier. Rick. Miles. Samantha Adler and Teresa Gordon, both women with their breasts exposed and wearing tribal skirts patched together from torn fabric. I prayed that Kirk's kids were in there somewhere.

Mother Isaacs stood at the head of her army in another of those prim, gothic dresses. Schrader flanked her on one side, axe in hand, and Beth on the other, with an arm around Darcy's waist and a knife to her throat. My heart plummeted at the sight of her, but conversely, relief swept over my ex's face when she saw me.

"I don't know what you thought you were accomplishing

with this stunt!" Isaacs yelled. She needed no megaphone now; her gravelly voice carried up the street just fine. "It changes *nothing!* Did you really think that *you* could silence the voice that the Lord Himself has chosen to speak through? You are nothing but a grain of sand caught in a hurricane of His will!"

"It doesn't matter!" I called back, not bothering to point out that Jacob and I had been fairly successful in silencing her damned voice thus far. "This is over! The others already made it out! By now they will've called the police and told them everything!"

"You let me worry about that!" She held out one of her shriveled hands. "Come to me, Mr. Jefferson!"

I shook my head in denial. She didn't need me to come any closer. I couldn't escape now; her minions would be on me in seconds if I tried to run. This was all just for show, part of her domineering power trip, a symbolic victory over me, but it was the only leverage I had. "Let her go and I'll do whatever you want!"

Her outstretched hand balled into a fist. "This is NOT a negotiation! Come now, or she dies!"

Once again, I was at her mercy. Whatever hopes I'd had for this situation withered away.

I walked down the street toward them slowly, warily, like a dog approaching an angry master. I expected the Heeders to rush me, but none of them moved from their positions as I drew closer. The Squall pounded at my skull with every step, prying at whatever was left of my defenses.

Darcy stood rigid in Beth's arms, the knife at her throat. She wore a pair of flannel cow pajamas I remembered well. She looked vulnerable, helpless...and beautiful. Even more so than she had at the lawyer's office. Any lingering bitterness or resentment toward her that I'd harbored evaporated in that moment, and my love for her—the love I'd had way back at the beginning, when the torch between us burned as bright as an acetylene flame—hit me hard, all at once, an emotional wallop that made my knees buckle.

Oh god, Darcy. I'm sorry, baby.

"So this is the cunt that got away, eh Jefferson?" Beth taunted over Darcy's shoulder. Her free hand slid upward and squeezed one of my ex-wife's ample breasts through the pajama top. "Body's not bad, but I bet she ain't half as wild in the sack as me."

"Elliot, what is going on? Who are these people?" Darcy asked, a high thread of fear in her voice that I had never heard before. Beth pressed the knife deeper into her flesh, drawing a gasp.

"It's okay," I lied. "I'll get you out of this, just hang on."

From Isaac's other side, Schrader snorted laughter. I saw—with absolute, gut-twisting horror—that my severed hand hung around his neck on a leather strap, the decaying fingers that had once worn my wedding ring entwined in his chest hair.

"Enough of this," Isaacs barked. Her hand still floated in the air between us, palm up, like a lord offering a dance at a cotillion. She fixed me with her coal black eyes as the Squall continued to blare. "The time has come for you to make a choice, Mr. Jefferson, and I don't rightly care which it is anymore. Heed...or die."

"Release her," I said, "and I will do whatever you want. Anything. I swear."

Isaacs looked over at Beth. "You heard him. Release her."

Beth's grin revealed more teeth than should've been humanly possible.

She ripped the knife across Darcy's throat.

"*Stop!*" I pleaded, as if that would somehow undo the act. Beth shoved Darcy toward me. I caught her as she fell, and was rewarded with a splash of blood across my chest from her gushing jugular.

I sank to the ground with her in my arms, landing on the warm pavement in front of my apartment building, unconscious denials streaming from my mouth. Darcy looked up at me in confusion as blood gurgled from the hole in her neck. She grabbed my hand. I cradled her head in my lap until the life faded from her eyes.

"Let that be a lesson." Isaacs's shadow fell across me. "You do not make demands here. Your role is but to serve in paradise, or be destroyed."

I brushed a few strands of bloody hair from Darcy's face. "Then by all means, destroy. I have a feeling we're all heading to the same place, and it sure ain't paradise. I'll just get there a little sooner." I bared my teeth up at her savagely. "But not by much."

She stepped back again, making room for Schrader, who stood over me and raised the axe as Beth hopped from foot to foot in excitement.

With a roar like Judgment Day, my building exploded.

7

It wasn't actually the whole building, just the first floor, but the concussion blew out the windows of my apartment and knocked the wave of Heeders closest to the curb off their feet. A split second later, when Beth's unit went up, most of the others hit the ground on their own. Schrader fell to the street beside me, a sliver of glass jutting from his forearm.

"*What is this?*" Isaacs demanded, using that same shrill tone as when Hammond died. She was one of the few still standing, holding her arms up to the heavens just before she whirled on me. "*What have you done?*"

A chuckle built in my throat and escaped before I could stop it.

Because Tate had been right: Jacob *was* burning the place down.

8

When I took the axe, there had been one other item in the maintenance closet that I hadn't noticed: a three gallon jug of highly flammable liquid weed killer. But Jacob had seen it, and as soon I hobbled away to rescue Darcy, he went back to retrieve the canister, along with a few more from the maintenance rooms of other buildings.

With all the Heeders focused on me, it was easy for him to sneak past, into my apartment, then into Beth's. He doused both units in the weed killer, soaking carpets and furniture, then threw one entire bottle in her oven, one in mine, and set the temperature to broil. And, just to make sure the resulting explosions achieved maximum destruction, he closed all the air vents, so the expanding hot gases would have no place to go.

I never said the kid was stupid.

9

The fire ate up the buildings with frightening speed. Tongues of flame shot from the windows of the apartment where I had spent the last year of my life and licked at the wooden siding. Within seconds, the roof eaves blazed, and the air filled with embers that drifted toward the surrounding buildings. The heat was so intense, even the grass began to catch.

"*Nooo!*" Isaacs shrieked, her booming voice barely audible over the competing cacophony of the Squall and the swelling crackle and grind of the fire. She held her arms up again, as though she believed God would reach down and put out the flames. The thought made me laugh even harder. When she heard me, one arm extended a fist in my direction.

"*KILL HIM!*"

Most of the Heeders still lay in the street, a few of them moaning from injuries. I squirmed out from under Darcy, sliding through the puddle of her blood, and then Schrader's hand closed around my ankle.

He crawled toward me, murder in his eyes. I kicked out with my free leg, trying to catch him in the face, and grazed my toe off his scalp. Schrader slithered over me, reaching for my throat. My own severed appendage dangled from his neck, right in front of my face. With only one hand, I had no hope of fighting him.

Another explosion boomed between the burning buildings, this one smaller and accompanied by a burst of white light that imprinted its image on the retinas. The fire had reached our transformer, the one that started this whole nightmare. The electrical buzz of the Squall lifted even higher, into something that sounded like a cat yowling. There was pain and fear in that sound, I'm almost sure of it. I put my hands to my head as Schrader rolled away from me, convulsing. The others writhed in agony along with him, until the whole street resembled a carpet of overgrown worms. Foam filled their open mouths.

"*What's the matter with you?*" Isaacs shouted. She swung a tiny leg back and kicked Schrader in the stomach. "*Get up!*"

Schrader's eyes snapped open and fixed upon Isaacs. He snarled so ferociously, spittle sprayed from his lips.

By now, mine and Beth's buildings were a blazing inferno. At least three other nearby structures had started to burn. A thin pall of black smoke hung across the street. Jacob materialized out of it, still carrying the axe, and pulled desperately at me.

"*C'mon, run!*"

I let him manhandle me to a standing position, but I couldn't look away from what was happening in front of us. The Heeders sat up dazedly, like bears waking from hibernation, then got to all fours. Isaacs still stood in their midst, but, judging by the alarm on her face, she had awoken to the danger.

Schrader and Beth circled her, clawing and snapping at the air just like Yonkers. They jerked and spasmed so much now, they seemed to have trouble controlling their limbs. The old woman gave a startled cry and backed away, but ran into another of the beasts. This one latched on to her calf with its mouth, and tore out a hunk of flesh.

"*Whatta you want, a front row seat?*" Jacob shouted in my ear, the only way I could hear him over the fire whistle of the Squall. "*They'll come for us next! Let's go!*"

I tore myself away and started up the street with him, but couldn't help looking back once more. Darcy lay on the ground where I'd left her, eyes open and staring skyward.

The last I saw of Mother Isaacs, the beasts were closing in on all sides while she commanded them to stay back.

10

We ran, exhausted and limping, in the general direction of the front gate. The smoke had gotten so thick and black, visibility narrowed to a few yards. Catching a breath in the greasy stuff became steadily harder. The fire seemed to race us up the street, jumping from building to building with impossible speed. It didn't lend much confidence to the quality of the construction material.

And the Squall continued to increase in volume or pitch or radiation level or whatever the hell the transformers produced. I could *feel* it inside my skull now, like sinus pressure, threatening to burst my head open from the inside. It had accelerated the Heeders' transformation into the hybrids and agitated them into a frenzy, perhaps as another defense mechanism.

No sooner had this thought presented itself than gleeful squeals began to echo out of the gloom around us, like the excited yips of a wolf pack on the prowl. We were being hunted. I jerked my head toward each sound, but didn't dare slow down.

Without warning, Javier loped out of the haze alongside us, scampering naked on all fours, penis flopping freely between his legs. He went for Jacob, and the kid swung the axe in a wild arc. The blade buried itself in the man's ribcage. Javier yelped and tumbled away, pulling the weapon from Jacob's hand. He stopped to retrieve it.

"*Hurry up!*" I veered over to help, coughing uncontrollably. Javier pawed at us as I wrenched the axe out of him. But when we started to run again, I wasn't sure which direction to go. The fire seemed to be all around us, glowing red in the haze, the heat suffocating. More of those awful howls joined the chorus. Scampering figures flashed in the smoke, there and gone. For just a moment, Samantha Adler appeared, no more than three yards away, her thick, nude body hunched low to the ground like some obscene sow. She hissed at me before fading away again.

Jacob coughed until he pulled his shirt up over his mouth and nose, then pointed. "*There!*"

A building loomed on our left, ghostly orange sparks already dancing atop its roof. Jacob sprinted ahead of me and threw open the first door he saw, leading to a second floor apartment. I could hear the creatures right at my heels as I plunged inside and sprawled across the stairs with the axe, banging the ragged end of my arm in the process. Before I could even get to my knees, Jacob screamed for me to help him.

He held the door with both hands, leaned against it, but several arms stuck through the gap, clawing at him. Furious snarls came from the other side. I got up and put my back against it and braced my feet against the stairs, holding the door shut against the press of bodies. The wood around the hinges had already started to crack from the frantic pounding.

"*What do we do?*"

"*Go on, up the stairs!*" I gasped. Oily smoke coated my throat and lungs every time I tried to breathe. I didn't know if I was more worried about that, or the painful pressure still building in my head. "*We gotta get out before the whole place burns!*"

He went without argument, charging up the stairwell, where the first tendrils of smoke drifted down from the fire on the roof. I gave him as much of a head start as I dared and then jumped away from the door.

A flood of ravening maniacs boiled through the entrance. I charged up the staircase with them right behind me, biting and shoving and crawling over one another in the narrow space to get at me.

Near the top, my toe caught on a riser. I went down.

Hands grabbed at my ankles. I flipped over and scrambled up the stairs on my back as best I could with only one arm. To my surprise, Schrader led the pack, bloody foam leaking from both sides of his mouth as he kicked at the others to keep them back. My severed hand still dangled around his neck.

In his eyes, there was nothing, no humanity, just mindless fury.

I brought the axe whistling down on top of his head. The blade cleaved through his forehead, splitting his skull like a coconut. Grayish brains sloshed onto the carpet. He went limp.

Schrader's body provided just enough of an obstruction for the others to give me time to get on my feet and run up the last of the stairs, leaving the axe behind this time.

The upper floor of the building blazed. Fire moved across the walls in undulating curtains, devouring everything it touched. The smoke was so thick, I was sure I would suffocate. As I moved blindly across the open space of the living room, something in the building's structure snapped, and the whole room canted to the side, leaving the floor at a nearly 45 degree angle.

"*Jefferson!*" Jacob's voice, almost lost in the thunder of the fire. I climbed up the slanted surface toward it until I reached a hallway where the floor was even again. A square of daylight floated in the gloom ahead. The kid stood at a broken window in the apartment's bedroom, waving both arms at me.

From up here, above the smoke, we had a much better view of the complex. Fires burned everywhere. A few of the buildings had already collapsed into smoldering ruins, as I was sure this one would any minute. We could see the front gate too, just fifty yards away.

"Jump," I told him.

He leapt first, back into the roiling cauldron of smoke below, and I went right afterward. My legs took the impact like a champ, but when I fell forward onto my only good hand, my right wrist snapped. Jacob pulled me up, and we ran.

Rubble littered the street from a building whose front had sheared away, some of it still burning. We picked our way through, the gate now visible ahead as the smoke finally started to thin. Fire had beaten us there, torching the grass and blackening the wall and even climbing up that first wooden utility pole just beyond. The gate had come off the sliding track and hung open, as inviting as a desert oasis.

We didn't stop when we reached it. For the first time since Wednesday morning, I stepped outside the Estates. I expected the Squall to recede once we were beyond the property border but I could still feel that horrible pressure in my head. That last boost from the transformers must've extended its range. We kept running, down the driveway toward the street, but our pace was little more than a stumbling walk now.

At the opposite end, a string of police cars turned in from the main street, lights and sirens blazing. They seemed to move in blurry slow motion as they squealed to a stop just yards in front of us. Officers spilled out with guns already drawn and pointed in our direction. I could only imagine how we looked, covered in ash and blood and me missing a hand. They ran to meet us, screaming for us to get down on the ground.

We dropped. I couldn't have gone another step anyway. Jacob and I lay facing one another, and just about the time I caught my breath, one of the cops dropped a knee on my back, heavy enough to force the air from my lungs. The world started to go dark. Jacob shouted something, but I couldn't make out the words.

Then the cop on top of me froze in the act of wrenching my arms back to cuff me. Even through the mental fog, I heard him say, with complete awe, "My god."

I twisted around beneath him, turning my head to look back at the Estates. Fire still blazed across the entire complex, the flames stretching nearly fifty feet in the air, but the hellish inferno wasn't what amazed him.

People scrambled over the wall in droves, like rats from a sinking ship. They squirmed and fell and leapt from the top, all naked, some of them on fire, and when they hit the ground, those that saw us got to all fours and charged without a moment's hesitation. Within seconds, there were at least thirty monsters streaking toward us, the last of the bestial creatures that had once been my neighbors. They looked like a herd of angry chimpanzees, screeching and snapping at the air.

Beth was among them, most of her blond hair charred away. Her eyes zeroed in on me.

The police forgot about Jacob and me in a hurry. The pressure disappeared from my back. One of the cops shouted, "*Stand down! Stand down, or we will open fire!*"

"Don't shoot!" I pleaded. I sat up and clutched at the officer closest to me, who shoved me away with his knee. All of the cops had their guns pointed at the approaching horde. "They're just people, don't shoot them!"

But they would. They would have to. In seconds, the beasts would be on us, and they would tear us to shreds.

An eruption of sparks rained down on us. We all covered our heads. Above us, the fire had finally climbed the utility poles and reached the hanging power lines that fed the Estates of North Hills its electricity. They melted through, cords swinging free, trailing arcs of blue lightning.

And, just as quickly as it started, the high-pitched drone of the Squall faded away.

The pressure in my head vanished, and, for the first time in days, the world fell silent. Only the crackling roar of the fire remained, but that seemed like a blessing in comparison.

The mob lost interest in us. Most of them collapsed midgallop, their bodies unable to sustain the awkward running stance. They crashed to a painful halt and lay panting on the pavement. A few of them sat up and blinked around in confusion.

Beth fell a few yards away from me and curled into a shuddering ball. I saw her eyes clear, like clouds after a rain storm, just as Joan's had.

As the police swarmed over them, unconsciousness tried to take me again.

This time, I let it.

LATER

1

I spent a month in the hospital.

Besides the trauma of my missing hand, I also received treatment for one broken wrist, severe malnourishment, dehydration, smoke inhalation and blood loss, and my raw stump had developed a massive gangrene infection that, I was told, would've killed me in another few hours.

And, if that wasn't enough, I was also kept isolated and handcuffed to the bed for most of my stay, while the authorities attempted to sort out what the hell happened at the Estates of North Hills.

All I could do is tell the same story I've now told you, over and over, to the endless parade of cops, detectives, and—eventually—FBI agents that came to see me. Which no one believed. My recent involvement in Joan McCaffery's death and the fact that Hammond had been on his way to see me about it just before he disappeared ensured that I shot instantly to the top of the suspect list, no matter how many logical problems it presented.

Of course, it probably didn't help my case when I tested positive for extreme alcohol and amphetamine use, with trace amounts of phenobarbital thrown in for good measure.

The interrogations continued non-stop for the first week. I'd have new faces waking me up at three in the morning to drill me about some new topic, looking for ways to poke holes in my story, forcing me to talk until my voice went scratchy and the doctors chased them out. The initial prevailing theory seemed to be that a meth lab had exploded.

The FBI agent that advanced this idea to me didn't seem to appreciate it when I laughed in his face for nearly five minutes. Then the Q and A sessions got downright mean.

But when the brains scans began to come back, they listened. Oh yes; I had their undivided attention then, especially once they compared them to the results from Joan McCaffery's autopsy. That was when my inquisitors stopped wearing blue uniforms, and started wearing white lab coats. Doctors that treated me less like a patient and more like fuzzy mold in the bottom of a Petri dish. They put me through a battery of invasive medical and psychological tests than would've made an astronaut blush.

I shit you not, at one point, they asked if I would be okay with them cutting open my head to take brain tissue samples.

After that, I stopped cooperating as much.

Then there were the government-types who visited me one afternoon and wanted to know about the transformers, and the Squall itself. Men who gave me a last name only; no title or agency affiliation. One of them—a mean-eyed SOB with a slightly crazy grin and a question mark snarl of scar tissue around his jaw—seemed particularly interested in the idea of 3204's portable noise generator. Thank god the prototype had been destroyed in the fire, or I'm sure it would've been mass-produced in some lab somewhere, probably for use on foreign soil. Based on some of their questions, I'm almost sure they hooked the power back up at the Estates, and found the transformers too melted to dissect.

Meanwhile, the round-the-clock media coverage held the entire nation in thrall. Of the 568 souls that called the Estates home, only 73 survived. Since the authorities wouldn't let a camera or microphone anywhere near us until after the investigation, the news outlets were left to their own speculation. They aired a two-hour prime time special when the Heeder's torture chair got pulled from the wreckage. And, since only another thirty or so bodies were found in the charred remains, hundreds of residents were still listed as missing. Every channel set about finding the dumbest yokel on the street to interview, who then put forth conjectures ranging from terrorist kidnapping to alien abduction.

The discovery of a mass grave in the hayfield beside the complex soon put those to rest.

I watched the footage on the television in my hospital room, as they pulled out body after body, women and men and children, all the people killed during the Heeder occupation and the ones that had finally gone feral and had to be put down. A few of the corpses were partially consumed. Somewhere in there, I knew, would be Tate and Ron and Carolyn. It would be another eight months before all the dead could be identified and laid to rest, but the ones from the fire were so burned, even dental records wouldn't help. Jacob's little bonfire got so hot, it melted the concrete of the streets.

Which meant they would never be able to determine which one had been Mother Isaacs, so I could piss on her grave.

The public demanded retribution for this atrocity. The President himself went on TV, calling for the FBI to bring the responsible parties to justice.

They quickly came to realize just how hard that would be.

At a press conference, some scientist-type—the same one that asked for permission to slice up my brain—jabbered through an explanation about electromagnetic fields and their effect on the human body, dissociative fugues, and how the people that committed these terrible deeds couldn't be held responsible, because they were under an outside influence.

It proved too complicated for most people to grasp.

I understood. My students never really liked the books with the philosophical brand of antagonist either. Most people need a villain they can hold on to, and the Squall just didn't cut it.

In the end, the authorities pacified the public with a simplified story about a murderous cult that had brainwashed its members, but they had all been killed in the fire they started to worship their pagan god. Everyone still alive was a victim, nothing more. No charges would be pressed, no arrests made.

That was why, nearly three weeks after leaving the Estates, I woke from a morphine-induced slumber to find Beth Charles standing in the door of my hospital room.

2

Silent tears coursed down both cheeks in the florescent glare. When she realized I was awake, she turned to leave. "I'm sorry, I...I shouldn't have come..."

"Wait." The word came out a puff of dry air. I tried to sit up on the hospital bed and fell right back onto the pillows. Not because of the handcuff—that had been taken off a few days ago, after the FBI officially cleared me of any wrongdoing—but because I still had about as much strength as a wet dishrag.

She paused in the doorway. I waited, afraid to say more lest it frighten her off for good. Through the room's window, I could see two uniformed cops watching us from the nurse's station. Finally, she came all the way into the room and approached me with tiny, hesitant steps.

Her face was a little banged up, bruised and scratched, and her hair had been trimmed almost to the scalp to get rid of what had been burned. She'd lost twenty or thirty pounds too, so much that her cheekbones and clavicle tried to poke through the skin.

But damned if she wasn't still gorgeous.

Then I got a flash of what she'd looked like as one of *them*. Face twitching. Her awful grin when she'd cut off my hand. That terrible laugh when she'd slit Darcy's throat.

It must've shown in my eyes. She froze at the foot of the bed, and searched my face.

I wanted to slap myself. Throughout my time in the hospital, I'd begged to see Katie and Jacob and Kirk and Beth, but the only update I could get is that they were fine. I'd waited for this moment, fantasized about what I would say to her, and here I was, fucking it up.

"Are they here with you?" I nodded at the cops still observing us from the hall. "I thought there weren't gonna be any charges."

"There's not, but they wouldn't let me in here without supervision. In case I...had a relapse or something." She wiped tears from her nose. "They had us at some mental hospital upstate. All of us that...you know. Kept us locked in padded cells until they could determine that we were not *a danger to ourselves or others*. And the way that they figure that out, apparently, is by playing Rorschach bingo with you five times a day and jamming every electrode they can find up your ass."

"Yeah, I can sympathize." I watched her breathe for a moment before asking, "When did you get out?"

"They finally started letting some of us go about two days ago. The ones who weren't curled up in a corner bawling all day. I caught a bus into the city. Been staying at a motel across the street, trying to work up the nerve to come see you."

"I'm glad you did." I tried out a smile. "Have you seen any of the others? Katie? Kirk?"

"No. And I don't really want to."

She came a few steps further, up the left side of the bed. Her fingertips gently brushed the severed end of my arm, but I couldn't feel them through the wad of bandages. It would be another three months before I'd be fitted for the prosthetic I would wear for the rest of my life.

"They told you, didn't they?" I brought my other fist up and slammed it into the bedrail. She flinched from the crash. "Damn it, I told them not to! There's no need for you to know every grisly detail about what happened!"

Beth shook her head. "I appreciate the effort Jefferson, but they didn't have to tell me anything. I remember almost all of it. Right up until the very end."

The words hit me like a slap across the face. My mouth fell open. "No. No, that can't be right. They said it was a fugue state. No recall at all. It had to be."

"That was just more BS they fed the public, so we don't have lynch mobs after us. They actually think it's a matter of intelligence." Her eyes followed the sweep of my heart monitor beside the bed as she said this. "I got to be friends with a few of the guys studying us at the loony bin. Believe it or not, they offered me a research job if I wanted to stay and offer my *unique perspective*." She made a sound halfway between a sigh and a laugh. "A month ago, I'd've jumped at a shot to be involved in something like this. Instead I ran the first chance I got, and didn't let the door hit me in the *unique perspective* on the way out."

"Beth, hold on. What are you talking about? *What's* a matter of intelligence?"

"Animals," she answered after a moment. "That's what the Squall was turning us into. Knocking us down one peg after another on the evolutionary ladder, by stealing our fear, just like we said. One guy called it, 'breaking our social contract.' Those...those *monsters* crawling around on all fours? They were the end result. A creature living entirely in the moment, only able to see as far as satisfying their next urge. An animal with that level of intelligence can't hold on to memories. So after the fire started, and the Squall went into overdrive, my memory is wiped clean. But everything leading up to that..." She tapped her temple.

"No," I said again. An oozing horror dribbled down the back of my neck. To wake up and be told what you'd done was one thing, but to actually *remember* it first hand, torturing your loved ones and engaging in acts of such depravity? It was too much like Kirk's story about Charles Whitman. "When I...when I changed, I wasn't as bad off as those things, but I still didn't—"

"*Well, good for fucking you, Jefferson!*" she screamed abruptly. The cops in the hallway started toward us, but I waved them back. "*Who knows, maybe your fucked-up, alcohol-damaged brain protected you! I don't have all the answers, and neither do the geniuses the government has working on this! I'm sure they'd love to cut you into bite-size pieces and study you for years if you'd let them! But consider yourself goddamn lucky to be blissfully ignorant of what it was like, because the rest of us have to live with what we... what we did...!"*

She covered her face and sobbed miserably. I struggled up from the pillows this time, put my arms around her and pulled her to me. She fell halfway on the bed.

"Oh god, I'm so sorry, Elliot, I can never say it enough," she cried against my shoulder. *"Your hand...your ex...I'm a fucking murderer..."*

"You have nothing to be sorry for," I told her. Hot tears pricked my eyes. "You didn't do those things, not a single one. Don't you see, whether you can remember it or not, *that wasn't you.*"

"But it was. That's the whole point." The tears stopped, and she broke away so she could look me in the eye, still lying across my chest with our arms intertwined. "The Squall just brought out the worst in us. Everything I did, I wanted to do, somewhere deep down inside. I can still remember how much I wanted to hurt you. How good it felt to just surrender to every desire. Jesus, the things I did with them..."

"It'll get better with time."

"Maybe. For now though, I have to leave."

I stared at her. "Where?"

"Home, for now. Back to my parents' place. The reporters are getting pretty thick around here, and I just can't deal with them."

"Are you coming back?"

She sniffled and grinned. "I gave the snake orgy a shot, but I don't think it's quite for me."

"But what about us? What about...?" I trailed, realizing how ridiculous I sounded. I had known this woman for a week, and for most of that time, she had been brainwashed. The times we'd had sex were tantamount to rape.

Beth could've said any of this to me, and I wouldn't have blamed her. But she only placed a hand on my cheek and said, "Do you really think we could ever be normal? That we could keep looking each other in the eye after the shock wears off? If you honestly think so, just say 'yes,' and...I'll stay."

It was a sentiment I would hear repeated over and over again in the coming months. There was so much grief and mourning for the slain residents of the Estates in the aftermath of the tragedy, and even the families that survived intact were never the same. I later heard through the grapevine that Kirk—who I never saw or spoke to again—was reunited with his entire family two months after our escape, only to divorce Teresa nearly a year later.

And two years after that, on the kid's thirteenth birthday, Kirk's son committed suicide.

But that would all come later. As for me, in that moment, lying in my hospital bed, I asked myself if I would ever be able to not blame this woman for everything she'd done to me, if I was capable of forgetting the twitching ghoul that had occupied her body. I found that my heart knew the answer immediately.

So I looked at Beth.

And said nothing.

She nodded and climbed down off the bed. Without another word, she gave my shoulder a squeeze and started back across the room.

"Beth," I called, just before she reached the door.

"Yeah?" she asked over her shoulder without looking back.

"Do they...for God's sake, do they know what caused it? Do they have any idea how the transformers were able to make that noise?"

"Between you and me, I don't think they have a fucking clue. Just some random electrical interference in our brains."

"But what about that voice? I heard it. I know I did."

"That was just your subconscious, giving you permission to go nuts." Beth gave me one last look, her eyes dark and haunted. "Trust me...it was all in your head."

3

Katie and Jacob came to see me the day before my release. Both of them looked healthy, the latter clean and past withdrawal. He'd granted a brief, thirty-second interview to CNN, for which he'd been paid a sum of almost two-hundred thousand dollars. The media touted him as the hero of the whole affair, a title I was more than happy to let him have. When they came to see me, Jacob had just purchased a brand new, fully-loaded Winnebago, and was bound for Alaska.

"Why Alaska?" I asked.

"Because there's nobody else there," Jacob answered, as if this should be obvious. "I'm done with other people for the rest of my life, man."

Again, I never said the kid was stupid.

They hadn't had any contact with Kirk either, but they did tell me that Rory's father was still unaccounted for, presumed to be one of the bodies in the mass grave. The boy had no other family, so Laura had been granted temporary custody. The two of them had already left the state to live with relatives of hers.

When the topic had been avoided long enough, I finally asked Katie, "What about you? Have you seen your mother?"

A shadow passed over the girl's face. "She's still in the hospital. The doctor told me she's not making a lot of progress."

I couldn't even begin to guess what that meant. "I'm sorry."

"I'm not. I don't really know if I want to see her."

"So what will you do then?"

She shrugged, and I suddenly knew, beyond a doubt, that whatever else got thrown at this young woman, she would survive. "Stay with my grandparents, finish school...and live my life."

They each said goodbye, Katie with a hug, Jacob with a handshake. I wanted them to stay, wanted to keep them in my life somehow, but knew that was no more realistic than keeping Beth in it.

Just before they walked out, Jacob turned to me with a smirk tugging at the corners of his mouth.

"If you ever get as far north as Alaska...look me up, teach."

I smiled, and watched them leave.

4

The day I checked out, I wanted booze. I intended for my first stop to be the closest AA meeting, and from there...I had no idea. My job waited for me if I wanted it, but I felt an itch to hit the open road and shed the trappings of my life like a snakeskin. Everything I owned had gone up in the fire, so I was well on the way.

Also, my nightmares had gotten bad in the last week. Dreams of Darcy and Mother Isaacs and the drone of the Squall.

Beth wasn't the only one who would never be able to forget.

I signed some paperwork at the front desk, then waited while they found a wheelchair to roll me literally about twenty feet to the door. I told them I was missing a hand not a foot, but they insisted it was hospital policy.

While I stood at the desk, glancing around the crowded waiting room, I caught the eye of a young guy with short black hair sitting on a bench a few rows away, near the exit door. Or rather, *he* caught *my* eye. He sat bolt upright in his chair, a kid around Jacob's age, his head cocked directly at me. I might've glanced right past him, but was stopped by the utter lack of expression on his face.

A gloss of blankness coated his features, as though his mind were somewhere far away, but his eyes never left me. Headphone buds were jammed deep in both ears, the cords trailing down to an MP3 player in his lap. And he didn't politely look away when I met his gaze, just continued to sit and stare. The intensity unnerved me.

The wheelchair arrived, and I settled into the plastic seat. The orderly steered me toward the exit, on a path that would take us directly past my admirer. His head swiveled to follow me.

We passed well within range to pick up the residual music leaking past his headphones and out of his ears. I expected to hear the tinny thumps and creaks of a punk band or metal group turned to full volume.

The waiting room was noisy, but even so…I could swear I heard nothing but a loud, buzzing whine coming from the plastic shoved in his ears.

Just before we rolled through the exit, I looked back at him.

His blank mask broke. A vacant grin spread across his face. One side of it jerked upward before settling back into place.

Like this novel?

YOUR REVIEWS HELP!

In the modern world, customer reviews are essential for any product. The artists who create the work you enjoy need your help growing their audience. Please visit Goodreads or the website of the company that sold you this novel to leave a review, or even just a star rating. Posting about the book on social media is also appreciated.

About the Author

Russell C. Connor has been writing horror since the age of five, and is the author of two short story collections, five eNovellas, and ten novels. His books have won two Independent Publisher Awards and a Readers' Favorite Award. He has been a member of the DFW Writers' Workshop since 2006, and served as president for two years. He lives in Fort Worth, Texas with his rabid dog, demented film collection, mistress of the dark, and demonspawn daughter.

His next novel—*The Halls of Moambati*, Volume III of *The Dark Filament Ephemeris*—will be available in 2020.